PASSION'S TOUCH

For a long moment their gazes held. Joanna caught her breath. She could feel Giles's need now and it was answered by her own. Slowly, without conscious thought, she stepped toward him. "Hold me again. The way you did the other day," she whispered.

His arms came about her, his hands stroking her back. She could feel his face buried in her hair. She burned up and down the length of her body with the heat of him pressed against her.

"You are so beautiful," he whispered, pulling back to look at her. "I haven't thought of anything but you since the moment I first laid eyes on you."

Other *Leisure Books* by Corey McFadden:
DECEPTION AT MIDNIGHT

Dark Moon

Corey McFadden

LEISURE BOOKS   NEW YORK CITY

A LEISURE BOOK®

December 1995

Published by

Dorchester Publishing Co., Inc.
276 Fifth Avenue
New York, NY 10001

Printed in the United States of America.

Dark Moon

Chapter One

Shropshire, England
February 1770

Squire had died at last. Papa had crawled from his own sick bed to tend his dying friend, even though his daughter, Joanna, had begged him not to go. This was a foul winter; it had rained nasty, icy sleet until the roads were slick with it and horses and people slid in the miserable muck. But he had looked at his pretty daughter gently and said in his kindly but firm way that Squire needed him now and he would go. Joanna knew better than to argue, but she'd made him bundle up, and carefully tucked his scarf into his coat, hoping it would keep the worst of the sleet from his throat. She'd heard his racking cough as he set out in Squire's cart. Squire must be ill indeed, she'd thought, to have sent the open cart for Papa in this weather instead of his carriage.

Papa had not come back for two days, and when he walked in she was shocked at the sight of him, pale and drawn, as if someone had taken a paint brush and washed him over in grays and whites. She had risen in alarm, but he gave her a tired smile as he removed his wet coat and scarf.

"He's dead, then, Papa? In town, they said it was just a matter of hours." Her voice held no grief. Squire had always been kind to her, but he had been dying and in pain for months and his release was merciful.

"Aye, my dear, and a peaceful end it was." Her father shook out his coat and hung it on the back of a chair near the fire. He carefully draped the scarf over it. He was a tidy man, never any bother to anyone. But there was a shadow about his eyes that did not come from illness, and that worried Joanna because he was not one to fret about things.

He drew up another chair near the fire and sat down, coughing his throaty cough and leaning in close, stretching his chilled hands to the warm glow. Joanna could see how they shook in the fire-light and she knelt before him, taking his hands in hers and chafing them. Father and daughter were silent for a moment. Squire and he had been boys together; they had tumbled like puppies all through childhood, and while schools and tutors had parted them, as had the later demands of their respective stations, nothing had dimmed their fast friendship. It was natural, thought Joanna, that Papa would be troubled, that he would grieve. There were so few of his contemporaries left;

Mama had died long ago, and one by one the others had dropped away.

"Papa," she began tentatively, knowing she intruded on sorrow, however well he hid it. "Perhaps we should go away for a while, just a change of scenery. It's been so cold and wet—I suppose it's cold and wet everywhere, but wouldn't it be nice? Maybe we could go to the shore; I've never seen the shore . . ." She trailed off, aware that a stricken look had come into her father's eyes.

"What is it, Papa?" she said in alarm. "Why do you look at me that way?"

He reached a cold, trembling hand to her dark hair, where errant curls escaped their pins. He hesitated a moment, then spoke so low she could barely hear him. "I'm afraid I've been remiss, my dear. I'm afraid I haven't given enough thought to your future."

"My future?" she said, surprised. "Whyever shall we worry about that? I'll just stay here and take care of you as I've always done, Papa." There was a hint of bravado in her smiling words. She knew in her mind that he would die someday, but in her heart it was not to be thought of.

"But that's just it, my dear," he said sadly. "It won't be like it's always been, not anymore."

"What do you mean, Papa?" she said, putting a lightheartedness she did not feel into her words. "Nothing's changed. Squire has been ill for a long time. You must have known this would happen. You're just tired and cold, and missing your friend." She smiled at him and, standing up, tugged on his hands. "Come, I'll fix you a nice warm cup of broth and put you to bed. Things will seem better in the morning." Odd, she was talking to him the way he had always talked to her.

But it didn't work. William Carpenter just sighed and patted her shoulder. "No, my dear, it must be faced," he said sadly. "I've spent all my life scorning material goods, and now see what I've done to you. Better I had taken the trouble to store up a few treasures on earth."

Joanna was horrified. It was as close to blasphemy as she had ever heard him speak, and to hear her unworldly father lament his lack of material possessions was something she never thought to hear. She knelt back down and gazed earnestly at his dear face. "Papa, one of the best things about being your daughter is that I've learned how unimportant worldly wealth is." She smiled again, hoping to dislodge whatever black demons gripped his soul.

"Yes, my dear, but only to a point," he said sadly. "We must have bread on the table, and shelter. And now I'm afraid we will lose even that."

"I don't understand, Papa."

"Well, I might as well tell you the truth, Joanna, and maybe you can help me see a way out of this dilemma. I've just come from meeting young Ambrose. He's Squire now, of course . . ." He could feel Joanna stiffen beside him. "Well, for these last three hours, anyway. It seems he has a friend he's planning to give the living to. He wants us gone in a few weeks, by early spring, no later . . ." William trailed off, his voice breaking, unable to continue.

There was a moment's silence while Joanna gathered her stunned wits. She'd been born in this cozy little thatched cottage, the vicarage that was part of the small living afforded by Little Haver. Squire had promised, hadn't he? She'd expected to die here, and happily, at that. She managed a great smile.

"Why, that's splendid, Papa! Think how nice it will be! Why, we can go to London, or to the shore, or . . . or, just anywhere at all. We can retire on your pension and see the world. Let's go to Spain and have the sun bake out that nasty cough you've had all winter." She finished triumphantly and patted him on the knee. It had been an effort, thinking up all that nonsense to say. She was a homebody, through and through, and all the traveling she cared to do was done by reading books. Still, if they were to be heaved from the vicarage by that odious Ambrose, she had better start now to develop an enthusiasm for change. Her smile faded as she gazed at her father's stricken face. His eyes, rimmed with tears, spilled over. "What is it, Papa?" she asked gently, as if she were talking to a child. "Surely we can manage. Anywhere we go will seem like home if we're together."

"There's no pension, Joanna. Ambrose says there's not enough money to give me one." His words fell flat, almost bitter, a tone she had never heard from him before.

"No pension? But what about Squire's promise? He always said you'd be well looked after. It's in his will, Papa, he told me so. You must demand to see his will!" Papa was too accepting, he could believe ill of no one, but if Joanna knew anything, she knew Squire would not have left her father penniless, not after all his years of selfless devotion.

"There is no will, Joanna. Ambrose made that clear. He is the only heir at law. He inherits everything, and there are no provisions for us at all."

"But that's impossible, Papa!" she cried. "I know there is a will. Squire told me so just a few weeks ago when I went to see him."

"Did you ever see it?" There was almost a little hope in his eyes.

"N-no," she said slowly. Comprehension was beginning to dawn on her. "I never saw it." She paused a moment, thinking. "But can't you see? There must have been one. Ambrose is lying, Papa! Squire told me there was a will!"

He sighed heavily, his eyes going dim again. "Joanna, we can prove nothing. Squire was old and ill, he rambled in his mind. If there was a will, Ambrose has destroyed it. He's not going to help us. He's made that quite clear. Why, I was reduced to begging him, and he turned me down. There's nothing to be done."

If there had been nothing else to hate him for, she would hate Ambrose for this, the loss of Papa's faith in mankind. He recognized Ambrose as a liar and a cheat. William Carpenter had gone through his life seeing the good in all men, and until now, no one had had the heart to disillusion him. Joanna had always fancied that Papa made bad men into good just by believing in them when no one else could. But now he had recognized the bad in Ambrose and bowed his head in defeat.

"There is a small pension from the church, isn't there, Papa?" she asked hopefully.

"Very small, my dear, and it stops upon my death." He began to cough heavily. His cough was worse than it had been when he left, Joanna noted.

"Well, we don't need much to live on. And I've a few jewels from Mama, don't forget," she went on. "They'll fetch something, I'm sure. Why, everyone's always admired the garnets."

"You'll not sell your mother's jewels, Joanna. They were her mother's before her, and she loved them. Not for their value but because they were so pretty. She used to say God made pretty things too, that we couldn't always wallow in deprivation. Your mother was always wiser than I," he said, his tone fond but rueful.

"Mama would have sold them in an instant to put food on the table, Papa. She was no more attached to worldly goods than we are." She stressed the *we* for his benefit but felt a pang nonetheless at the thought of parting with her pretty mother's pretty jewels. She could remember playing with them in a patch of sunlight on the floor when she was a toddler, and Mama laughing at her cooing delight over the shifting sparkles.

"There is a little money, Papa," she went on brightly. "Squire gave me ten guineas on my twentieth birthday. Why, we could dine on that for a long time." She smiled up at him, hoping to coax a smile in return.

"Bless your optimism, my dear," he said, giving back her smile. "When you talk, I can almost believe it will be a great adventure being homeless and destitute." The smile wavered. The little joke had a dark echo.

"But it will, Papa," Joanna said, laughing. "Why, we'll present ourselves to the bishop himself and tell him how badly you've been treated. Heavens, Papa, the church will look after you. They must!"

He smiled at her faith, knowing he could expect little from that direction. The living at Little Haver had been created for him at Squire's insistence, against the wishes of the bishop at the time who had wanted several villages clumped together. Squire had shouldered all the burden of the living with little enthusiasm or aid from the church.

"We'll go to London, Papa," she went on, caught

up in her own enthusiasm. "We'll take lodgings, something modest, of course, and we'll . . . we'll do what?" she paused for a moment, searching. Her face lit up. "We'll teach, that's what we'll do! You can teach theology, no one knows the Bible better than you, and I can get a position as . . . oh, something or other, surely I can do something!" She finished with a flourish as if it were all settled, and right nicely too.

He gave a warm chuckle which turned into a racking cough.

"Come to bed, Papa." She pulled at him insistently. "I'll just bet you've had no sleep at all since you left here, have you?" He shook his head. "Well, that's it, then. No wonder you feel so discouraged. You've lost your best friend and you're bone weary to boot." He rose and she shepherded him toward the stairs. "You get into bed and I'll bring you some broth. And remember to wrap up your neck with flannel. I don't like the sound of your cough."

He started up the stairs, then paused and turned back to her. She caught the firelight dancing in his eyes, now clear and bright. Her heart gave a little leap. "I believe you are right, after all, my dear," he said with some of the old strength back in his voice. "Everything will be fine. I lost my faith for a little while, didn't I? What an awful feeling. No wonder those who are estranged from the church are so lost. I shall ask forgiveness for doubting, and give thanks for the blessing I have in my wonderful daughter. Everything will be fine in the morning, my dear. I don't want you worrying at all."

He gave her a radiant smile and turned with a light tread to climb the stairs. There was a light from a lamp at the top of the stairs, and as her vision blurred through her tears it looked as though William Carpenter had a halo.

But everything was not fine in the morning. He had a fever and the cough was worse, deeper and more racking. Joanna ran up and down stairs with tea, with broth, and with warm cloths for his feet, which were like ice in spite of the fever. He shook with chill and was vague, almost unconscious, all day. At midday she sent for the doctor, who came and was kind. But she could see in his eyes that he was troubled by William's condition and there was nothing more he could prescribe than bed rest, tea, and warm cloths.

The hours stretched into days. Joanna heard nothing from the Manor House, but had no time to give it a thought. Old Mistress Gertie came by in a cart driven by her half-witted son, Tom. She brought a large pot of rich soup which smelled delicious and tasted even better. Joanna had had no time to cook for herself and had made nothing but tea and broth since Papa had taken ill. But Mistress Gertie, too, looked troubled when she took her leave, and she patted Joanna's hand as if there were more she would say if she had the words.

Then one morning there was a change. Joanna awoke with a feeling of urgency. Without waiting to don her dressing gown she fairly flew into her father's room, propelled by some nameless fear that clutched at her heart. She stopped short and smiled in relief to see him sitting up, awake and alert for the first time in a fortnight. He patted the bed, and she rushed over to sit beside him, taking his hand in hers. She was shocked at the heat of it. Somehow she had thought the fever was gone, that he would be well now and they could go on.

He looked into her eyes as if he understood her confusion, and smiled at her. "Everything will be fine, my dear," he rasped out. "I've been puzzling it out and I'm quite sure of it." His eyes were too bright, as if his soul burned within, or perhaps it was just the fever. "But you must promise me you will never lose your faith, not even for a moment. Promise me."

Joanna nodded, unable to speak, tears spilling from her eyes. He was better. He was sitting up. Things would be fine now. William watched her nod and squeezed her hand. He smiled and closed his eyes. She could feel a certain tension leave him, as if he had willed himself to find the strength to sit up and speak to her and now he needed it no more. He slept.

Joanna held his hand for a long time, noting that his breathing was troubled and shallow. The room was freezing. Gently she pulled her hand from his light grasp and stood up to tend the fire. She slipped into her dressing gown and went downstairs to put water on to boil on the kitchen fire. When the water was hot, she made two cups of tea and brought them up. He was sleeping still, so she put his cup down by the fire and took his hand again in hers. She sat that way for several hours until his breathing slowed, then stilled altogether. She sat quietly and held his hand, noting how it cooled in hers. There would be time later to tend to things. For now she would sit with Papa.

The large, wet clods of black dirt hammered on the lid of the coffin, each thud like a blow to her heart. She stood in the icy, gray drizzle, alone except for the young curate from the next village who fumbled with a wet prayer book and stumbled miserably over the words, and two grave diggers, respectful enough but distant in their grim task. Joanna thought with bitter sorrow that someone, some one of the many to whom her father had ministered over the years, should have braved the cold, wet day to pay tribute to the passing of this good man, William Carpenter, vicar of Little Haver these thirty years.

But there was no one much left, really. Little Haver was a dying village without the old-world charm that kept some villages alive, or the burgeoning trade and industry that rescued others. It was off the beaten path and had nothing more to recommend it than decent grazing and rocky farmland. The inhabitants had grown old. The smarter of the young ones had looked around and seen nothing much to hold them there. London was close enough to lure away those who, mistaken or not, felt that the city offered dreams for the asking. Papa had always asked the old ones for news of these young folk, but more and more of late the response had been tight-lipped and laconic until finally he had asked no more.

And he had buried the old ones, with this same prayer book in hand. Only he had not needed to read the words printed there. The holy words were written in his soul, and he had no need of a book to help him talk to God. But the young folk did not come back for the funerals of their elders, and the graves sank low and untended and there was no one to mourn. Except Papa.

And now there was no one to mourn Papa except his daughter, Joanna.

Now at the gravesite, chilled to the bone and alone, Joanna could barely hear the words of faith, sputtered out as they were over the sounds of the rain and the heavy mud hitting the coffin. She held fast to the image of her father, alive with his grace and goodness, smiling and whole, not the poor, pale shell she had finally surrendered to the undertaker. Bitterly did she refuse to think of the future, as much as the fear tried to encroach on her consciousness. This was her last tribute to her wonderful father, and she would not allow her doubts, her dwindling faith, to mock the man going now into his grave.

". . . then shall be brought to pass the saying that is written, Death is swallowed up in victory. Death, where is thy sting? Hell, where is thy victory? . . ."

The sound of hoofbeats startled Joanna. The young curate, Mr. Conway, faltered as they both looked up to see a horse, coming too fast, nearly upon them. With mud flying and splashing on Joanna's black dress, the horse was reined in. A figure on its back was heavily cloaked against the icy rain, but Joanna knew who it was. The horse came to a stop inches from her. Stifling her rage, Joanna turned back to the curate, signaling him to resume. Behind her, she could hear the sounds of the man dismounting, then she felt his presence close to her.

"My condolences, Joanna," the voice seemed to hiss in her ear as she felt a hand on her arm. Resisting the urge to shake him off, she made no acknowledgment. The young curate had returned to his scriptures, but his nervous eyes darted again and again to the figure behind her and the words became more and more muddled. Joanna seethed inwardly that this venomous man had dared to intrude upon her father's burial.

"I know you are upset just now, but I would like

to talk to you," the voice continued low in her ear. There was a slight pressure as he squeezed her arm. She stood immobile. Faltering to the last, the young curate stumbled to a halt and closed his soggy book. He stood in the rain and looked up miserably at Joanna as if he were uncertain what he ought to do next. Behind him the relentless thuds continued as the heavy, wet dirt, shovelful after shovelful, sealed William Carpenter from the light of day.

Joanna gave the young curate a small smile. He had been kind, and now he was cold and wet, after all. Pulling her arm away from the intruder, she walked toward the young man. In her hand were several shillings for his trouble. Papa would have wanted her to make some small emolument, she told herself, no matter that these shillings would be sorely missed and soon. As she handed him the small gift, he gave her a grateful look.

"May I do anything else for you, Miss Joanna?" he asked gently. William Carpenter had been widely known in these parts as a generous, godly man, of the rarer sort who came to the church by way of real calling instead of family expediency. The young man had been awed to find himself called upon to conduct this service, then shocked to find that this good man would go to his grave alone, but for his lovely daughter. Well, his own vicar was in bed with a bad cold, after all, and the other neighboring villages were too far away for a cold, wet journey. Still, he felt rather sad at this bleak, lonely farewell, and found himself wondering in a rather maudlin way who would be on hand at his own funeral.

"Thank you, no, Mr. Conway," Joanna said warmly. "But I am very grateful to you for coming all this way in the rain. You had to walk, didn't you? Why not come back with me for some tea before you start back home?" A flicker in his eyes as he looked past her warned her of the approach of the intruder.

"I'll not hear of him walking in this weather, Joanna," the voice behind her said, too loudly. "And as for tea, since I must speak with you anyway, you will both return with me to the manor. Then I can send the curate home in my coach."

Joanna stiffened, aware that she had received not an invitation, but a summons. As his tenant at sufferance, she had no choice but to obey his order, nor did she wish to cause any kind of scene.

"Squire, I should be most grateful for a little tea, but I wouldn't dream of inconveniencing you over a coach," began Mr. Conway diffidently, stumbling over his words in the presence of real gentry. "And may I offer you condolences on the recent death of your father."

"Nonsense, man. It's no inconvenience at all, and everyone is wet enough as is." He took Joanna's arm again and held fast. "Would you care to ride, Joanna, while I lead the horse?" he said as he propelled her toward the beast.

"No, Squire, I am not a good rider. I would prefer to walk." Joanna spoke in tones as chilly as she could manage without giving overt offense.

"As you wish, my dear," he answered, swinging his leg up over the horse's back as he mounted with ease. "Come along now, no point in any of us getting any colder." As the horse moved off, Mr. Conway fell in quickly, eager, understandably, for a nice cup of tea. Joanna stood for a moment, closing her eyes, fighting her grief.

Oh, Papa! she thought, willing the tears not to

fall, I will miss you so much, but I will not lose my faith, I will not, no matter what!

The grave diggers had stopped throwing dirt and were tidying up the gravesite. She stood and looked at the mound, aware that the horse continued its slow pace away from her. The sleet continued to fall. "Bless you, Papa," she said gently, then turned away to follow the horse.

She noted that Ambrose had not stopped to see whether she would follow, assuming in his arrogance that she would not dare refuse his kind "offer." Well, he was right, she thought ruefully to herself, making her way behind the horse. She had best find out how much time she had before she would have to vacate the vicarage. She hurried her steps, as anxious to get it over with as to avoid irritating him. She caught up quickly and fell in with them just behind Ambrose's line of vision. He and Mr. Conway were engaged in a chummy sort of a chat. She could imagine that were it not so cold, Mr. Conway would be blushing to the roots over the condescension and kindness being shown him. Joanna herself was at a loss to explain it. She had never known Ambrose to exert himself in the least degree except for his own pleasure.

It did not take them long to reach the manor since the cemetery was adjacent to the grounds. The rambling old house looked gray and forbidding, its stones streaked and darkened with constant rain, and what vegetation had bloomed with abandon last summer was twisted and black in the winter wind. Still, she had loved this house, she thought to herself, looking up at its forbidding facade. It had been the site of many a happy evening spent with Papa and Squire, the old Squire, of course. Ambrose had been sent off to school when

Joanna was a toddler and had been home infrequently since then, so the house held no dark memories of him for her.

Handing off the horse to a stableboy, Ambrose strode quickly up the stone steps of the front entrance, leaving Mr. Conway and Joanna to make their way behind him. The door was opened by Benson, an elderly man, old Squire's retainer who had been there nearly all his life. He'd always had a smile and a nod for Miss Joanna, but today, though he gave her a look of sympathy, his eyes shifted quickly and nervously back to his new master. Joanna noted that his hands trembled and that his steps were uncertain. Poor man, she thought. He is old and Squire is gone. Things will be different under Ambrose and he knows it.

They followed Ambrose into the drawing room, Ambrose calling out over his shoulder, "Tea, man, and quickly! We're all freezing and wet. And have the gig brought round to take the curate home." Benson hurried away, too fast, thought Joanna, for his elderly legs. Gig, indeed! It had no cover on it and would offer no protection from the weather. But it could be drawn by one horse and thus would inconvenience Ambrose less. Well, at least Mr. Conway would not have to walk.

Ambrose stood with his back to the fire, warming himself, and, indeed, taking up all the heat. He was a large man, imposing in bearing, with a face that would have been considered handsome were it not for the petulant mouth and the perpetually sardonic expression about the eyes, as if he found the world amusing at everyone else's expense. His black hair was tied in the back in a greasy queue, since he had not seen fit to wear his powdered tye wig in the rain. His frock coat was up-to-the-minute in fashion, a pastel brocade nipped at the waist and falling to the knee where his breeches met his white silk stockings. He cut a formidable figure and he never failed to use it to his advantage, imposing and intimidating where he wished.

Joanna, having divested herself of her wet cloak in the hallway, willed herself not to shiver, noting that Mr. Conway gave the occasional involuntary shake. She put her hands behind her back and chafed them to warm herself. Neither had been asked to sit, an oversight, no doubt, but one that could not be remedied by merely taking it upon oneself to sit down. Ambrose, never at a disadvantage because of his height, beamed down on Mr. Conway.

"Well, I suppose you've already heard—I know what a gossipy community you clerics have—that I'm bringing in a friend of mine to take over the Little Haver living," Ambrose said, smiling broadly at Mr. Conway. Beside him, Joanna stiffened but allowed her face to register nothing. How dare the man be so unfeeling as to bring up the subject of her father's replacement in such an insensitive way, not even speaking directly to her! Mr Conway had obviously heard nothing of the sort and was sensitive enough to feel the slight to Joanna. He reddened as he stumbled through a polite denial.

"Well, you disappoint me, man. I had thought there was great commerce between our little villages. Indeed, I was counting on it."

"Well, you see, sir, with my vicar doing so poorly this winter, and Mr. Carpenter being so ill, there hasn't been . . ." The curate broke off, confused at the drift of the conversation.

"Exactly! Well, time for a change, eh, Conway? Life goes on and all that." Ambrose paused as the door opened and the tea cart was wheeled in. Mr. Conway glanced gratefully over to the tray with its silver pots and delicate little cups.

"Well, sit down, sit down," Ambrose gestured magnanimously at the two and took a seat himself on the small loveseat. Mr. Conway sat on a chair next to it. "Joanna, will you do the honors? Dainty little fingers and all that," Ambrose said, smiling at her.

Joanna turned toward the tea cart, glad to have her back to the Squire for a moment. Honors, indeed! He couldn't exert himself to pour. He'd have asked a servant to do it if he hadn't had her there. Deliberately keeping her back to Ambrose, she poured the tea, waiting for him to return to the subject at hand. She was not disappointed.

"My friend Cornelius Almquist will be here in a few weeks. I'd hoped you could take over the pastoral duties of the area, such as they are, until he arrives. Not much to do really, it's more of a sinecure actually, has been since Father insisted on creating it," Ambrose said. Joanna clutched at the teacup so tightly it could have snapped in her hand. She knew Ambrose well enough to know he was not merely too dense to recognize that he had just grossly insulted her father. No, it was deliberate cruelty that motivated this venomous man. Willing herself to be calm, she turned and offered the cup to Ambrose, who took it, giving her a merry smile. She handed Mr. Conway a cup, then took her own and sat down. There was room for her on the divan next to Ambrose, but she deliberately selected a small, carved, and highly uncomfortable chair, made for decoration no doubt, as it had no relationship to the contours of the human derriere. Better to be uncomfortable than sit down next to an adder, she thought to herself.

Mr. Conway kept his eyes on his teacup and looked as if he might go through the floor. He was a kindly young man with a real religious calling, and would have been angry on Joanna's behalf had he not been so unnerved.

"Well, that's settled, then," Ambrose said broadly, draining his cup and setting it down on the small table next to him. He stood. Mr. Conway, too, scrambled to his feet, aware that the tête-à-tête was at an end, and set down his nearly full teacup with a wistful look at the steam rising invitingly from it. "If any matters arise that need some sort of spirit intervention, I'll send them to you, and anyone who feels the need of attending a service can get himself to your village until Cornelius can get settled." The squire smiled again at Mr. Conway, as if pleased that everything had been so simply arranged. Joanna noted through her rage that Ambrose had said absolutely nothing about recompense. Nor would he, she was sure. She stood herself, intending to get away. Now she knew what the beast's plans were and she had no need to hear any more.

"No, you stay, Joanna," Ambrose commanded over his shoulder as he walked Mr. Conway firmly to the door. "We have to talk about your future." He handed the curate out to Benson as if the young man were a handful of dirty wash, forgotten within seconds. Joanna felt a fury rise again within her. Her future was none of his business if he had chosen to cut off her father's pension and throw her out of the vicarage. She'd starve in a ditch before she discussed her private business

25

with this crass man! She continued to stand. He turned back to face her. Was it her fancy or did his eyes glitter at her?

"Ah, my dear Joanna, I'm sure you are quite devastated by your father's untimely demise." He crossed the room in two long strides, his arms extended as if he meant to embrace her. With a quick step she moved behind the tea cart and set down her cup.

He stopped short of the cart and smiled warmly at her. She was looking particularly lovely on this dreary morning in her shabby black dress, her dark hair in damp disarray, and two high spots of angry color on her cheeks. Ambrose had long been aware of the delectable bit of stuff living right down the lane in the vicarage, but it hadn't been worth the battle he knew he'd have with the two old men to take what he knew was waiting for him. She was ripe for a man, he calculated, must be 22 or thereabouts, if he himself was 27. He seemed to recall there were some five years between them, even if he hadn't taken much notice of the chit until recent years. And now the two old sods were dead and she was alone and penniless; he'd seen to that. . . .

"Thank you for your concern, Squire," she said as coolly as she dared.

"I wouldn't want any hard feelings between us about the living, Joanna, but of course I must give it to someone with your father gone now."

"Of course," she answered simply, not choosing to remind him that he had taken the living away from her father before he died.

Ambrose sat himself rather elaborately on the small loveseat, flinging the tails of his brocaded frock coat up behind him. "Come and sit, my dear," he said companionably, patting the small space beside him on the loveseat. Ignoring the gesture, Joanna sat again on the awkward chair near the tea cart. She fancied she saw the briefest flare of amusement in his eyes, as if he thought they were playing some game for his entertainment.

"Have you given any thought to what you will do now, Joanna?" he asked casually, sliding over toward her and reaching to pour himself another cup.

She felt a helpless anger flood through her. Throughout the burial preparations she had flatly refused to let thoughts of her grim future surface. It was an issue that would have to be faced, but not until she had laid her precious father to rest. And now Ambrose, the cause of all her trouble, was lightly asking what she would do with no money and nowhere to live for the rest of her life. And her father not half an hour in the ground!

"I am making plans, Squire," she said tightly. "May I ask how soon I must vacate the vicarage?" Again there was that glitter in his eyes, as if he were enjoying himself immensely.

"Well, I'm not sure that will be entirely necessary, my dear. You must leave the vicarage, to be sure—I doubt whether you'd appreciate sharing quarters with Conny, he's a bit of a pig, do you know." Ambrose smirked suggestively. "But there might be a pleasant alternative for you . . ." He paused, letting it sink in. He was aware from his last conversation with that maudlin old man, her father, that she would now be penniless and at his mercy. Just where he wanted her. She was obviously enraged. So much the better. She must recognize the helplessness of her position. Her large

27

brown eyes snapped at him in impotent rage and her pretty, smooth cheeks were flushed with fury. She was a lovely little thing, not too tall, with a well-ripened figure and luxurious dark hair that spilled willy-nilly from her pins. Oh, yes, he had lusted after her these last few years, but she had been out of his reach while his prudish father and hers were around to protect her. But now she was all his.

Joanna said nothing. She was angry and uncomfortable. The sooner she could be away from this malicious man, the better. There was something about his manner that was setting her teeth on edge, and she'd be damned if she would play into his hands. No proposal he could make to her could be of any interest whatsoever, unless it involved never laying eyes on him again for the rest of her life.

"You see, I know that your circumstances are dire, Joanna." His tone would have been kindly had there not been that glint in his eye, as if he were the cat and she the mouse. "Your poor father explained your financial difficulties to me the last time I saw him. I was much affected, I can assure you." He glanced down, as if momentarily overcome with the poignant memory. Joanna would have broken the Wedgwood teapot over his head if she hadn't thought he would retaliate.

Suddenly he reached for her, seizing her hand in both of his before she could pull away. With a gasp, she tried to pull free, but he only laughed and squeezed her hand more tightly. "Please relax, my dear," he said smoothly, his fingers caressing hers. "You are so tense. I am sure you are most distraught at your situation and I simply wish to assure you that you have no reason for concern at all. Your future is secure here with me."

"What?" she fairly shrieked, at the same time wrenching her hand away from his. She stared at him, aghast. What on earth did this mean?

"You will stay here, of course, Joanna. At the manor. With me." Now his eyes glittered like an adder's. The trap was sprung.

"You . . . you want me to marry you?" Joanna could barely croak out a whisper. This was some sort of a nightmare. Surely she would awaken soon.

"Marry?" Ambrose gave a great guffaw. "Good heavens, girl, when I am forced to marry I shall have to do it for money, nothing else. No, my dear." He stood, then leaned forward, his bulk looming over her, and smiled deliberately, showing bad teeth. "I have in mind an arrangement much more pleasant than marriage, Joanna, comfortable for both of us, shall we say?"

Joanna was rigid with shock. There was no doubt in her mind now what he was driving at. He wanted her to live here as his mistress. She stared at him for a moment. Oh, he was enjoying himself, indeed! He was grinning hugely, his face too close to hers, his eyes gleaming. Abruptly, she pushed back her chair and stood, moving quickly behind the chair.

"I don't believe there is anything further for us to discuss, Squire. I shall vacate the vicarage as soon as I can get a wagon for my things."

Like lightning he stepped around the small cart and, reaching out, grabbed her by the shoulders. "Oh, the little parson's daughter is offended, is she? Such high-and-mighty sentiments are all well and good for those who can afford them, aren't they, my sweet? But you, on the other hand . . ." Swiftly he bent his face down to hers, his large, fleshy lips approaching her own.

The pointed toe of a short leather boot landed with great force on his white-stockinged shin. With a howl, he leaped back, releasing her from his grasp. Free, she ran to the door and opened it, then turned back to look at him. He was glaring daggers at her and rubbing his leg.

"Where is your father's will, Squire?" she asked, her tone deliberate and cool. She could see Benson hovering with her cloak to the side of her vision a few feet away. Not even Ambrose would dare to pursue an attack on her in front of his retainer.

"There is no will, you silly bitch," he snarled. "I told your old man that the last time I saw him."

"But you are mistaken, Squire. I saw the will myself, and my father and I were mentioned in it." It was a lie and a shot in the dark, but it was worth it to give him a bad turn. There was no mistaking that her shot went home. For the briefest instant he looked shaken.

"Well, you are wrong in what you think you saw. We turned the place upside down and we found no will. And that is that." He smiled with triumph.

"There was a will and you and I both know it." She was enraged beyond caution now. "You destroyed it," she went on relentlessly. "You burned it here in this house while your father lay dead or dying, didn't you?"

She watched as his face drained of color. He stared at her, mouth agape, and in that moment she knew to a certainty she was looking at a thief. A thief who would never be brought to justice.

"You can't prove anything," he managed to croak. "There is no will and you can't prove otherwise." With a visible effort he drew himself up. His face hardened. "And I'd be very careful how you throw around baseless accusations, my girl," he said, his voice strengthening. "I could have you brought up on slander charges, you know."

Joanna laughed outright. "I don't think I have anything to fear on that score, Squire," she said smoothly. "In addition to being a thief, sir, you are a coward and a fool." And having delivered her last riposte, she turned on her heel and marched into the hallway, leaving him sputtering impotently behind. She snatched her cloak from a trembling Benson and hissed at the old man to get himself into the kitchen and out of sight immediately. No point in leaving him to catch the brunt of Squire's wrath. With a slam of the massive door she was gone. And if she had a cold, wet walk home, her rage kept her from noticing.

Chapter Two

At Queen's Hall, a large, dark manorhouse atop a rise overlooking Solway Firth in Cumberland, the sound of the furious sea breaking on the rocky beach matched the angry words that flew in Lady Eleanor's bedchamber. It was just past dawn and the window draperies had been flung open by Sir Giles just after he had stormed into his stepsister's room. He doubted the windows had been uncovered in years. It was unnatural how the woman craved the dark. All the better to make the caked, leaded cosmetics look smooth and flawless, he thought to himself in disgust. Now she sat up, sputtering, clutching the bedclothes to her chest, demanding in outraged tones to know the meaning of this intrusion. It was a fair enough question, after all. He doubted whether he'd been in this chamber even once in the last ten years. He'd had to use an old key borrowed from the housekeeper to unlock the door.

It was odd, looking at her in the morning light. He had been a mere seventeen, a green boy, when Henry Chapman, his father, had married the haughty Lady Margaret Holcombe, widow of an earl. Lady Margaret had one child of her own, Eleanor, an exotic, sophisticated 21-year-old beauty. Giles had been besotted by Eleanor's much-touted loveliness, bewitched by those dark, slanting eyes and that white-skinned perfection. She had been much amused by his calf-eyed adoration, teasing him with a flash of leg from her night rail, a peek at a pink-tipped breast from a careless little gap in her dressing gown, a suggestive, scandalous remark. At seventeen, he had burned with helpless passion for her and with humiliation at her mocking laughter.

Now, as he gazed on Eleanor in the unforgiving light of morning, he could find little trace of the proud beauty that had haunted his adolescence. Her hair still fell in dark waves around her heart-shaped face, but now it hung lank and oily since she inevitably wore it pinned unseen and unwashed into an elaborate powdered wig. And the perfect white skin, still stretched taut over fine bones, looked pasty and unnatural, mocked by the light of the sun. No doubt she had not even bothered to scrub the leaded paint from her face before tumbling half drunk into bed a scant few hours ago. The deep, black paint smudges around her eyes had run onto the white satin pillowcase, and she reeked, even half the room away, of a cloying, stale perfume, mixed with brandy fumes. This afternoon, again, she would appear as a goddess, pale and perfect in the dim rooms where she and her chic houseguests would entertain each other with foul gossip and high-stakes card games.

None would see beneath the paint and powder to the souls rotting within.

"I am here at this ungodly—as you put it, madame—hour because I am leaving in a few minutes for Dufton. You were in no condition for me to speak with you last night, so I had no choice but to awaken you this morning."

"There's nothing you have to say to me that couldn't be communicated through Hawton," Lady Eleanor snapped back. "You're only here because you take pleasure in disturbing my rest."

"On the contrary, madame, I take no pleasure in the sight of you at all, resting or awake. And I wish to speak with you about this matter directly because I want to be absolutely certain you understand my instructions."

"Say what you have to say and get out," she spat. Despise him she might, but he held the purse strings in this family and she had no wish to see her entertainments curtailed, as he had threatened to do on occasion.

"I have written to London for a new governess for the children—"

"You have the nerve to barge in here unannounced and wake me up to talk about that half-witted, drooling boy and his mealy-mouthed sister?" she interrupted with a shriek. "I have told you they have nothing to do with me and I meant it! They are your brother's brats, not mine. It's embarrassing enough that you insisted on bringing them here." She flounced herself back down to her pillow, pulling the covers over her head.

With a snarl, he crossed the room in two long strides and ripped the covers away from her head, careful to pull them no lower than her neck. If she slept naked he had no wish to see it.

"You will listen and you will obey me in this, madame. I have sent to London for another governess. I have hopes one will arrive within the fortnight. When she does, I expect her to be treated with appropriate courtesy. So help me God, Eleanor, if you drive away one more governess you shall have the post yourself!" he finished in a near shout. The woman had the power to infuriate him beyond reason.

There was a slow, malicious smile from her, a bad sign.

"And what if I refuse, dear brother?" she purred. "I don't believe even you can make me nursemaid those brats. Anyway, I don't think you'd like what I would teach them." She stretched languidly, sensuously, under the satin sheet, aware she was uncovered underneath and that he was discomfited when she teased him with her sensuality.

"Actually, no, I don't want you anywhere near the children, but I can cut off your considerable expenses. I do not think your fast set would enjoy your company for long if they were to discover that you had no money with which to wager or to feed them."

Recognizing that she was on boggy ground, Eleanor sat back and contemplated a change in tactic, surveying him through half-lidded, puffy eyes. It always came down to money. She, daughter of an earl, long in lineage and short of scratch, was forced to beg for her very bread from this pompous, over-principled stick, this bumpkin, his knighthood conferred recently by the king for technical improvements in canal design or some such trivial, merchant-class detail. Giles's father had been a wealthy merchant, nothing more, and her mother had stooped to wed him on the strength of his bank accounts, when her husband, the noble but near penniless Robert Holcombe, Earl of Bickham, had had the ill grace to die and leave them much in debt.

She sighed. If only Giles would give up and simply let her seduce him. Then, perhaps, he would cease to be so niggardly with his money. He was handsome still, she thought to herself, as she gazed at him, gauging just how far she could push him this morning. His hair was dark brown, thick and pulled back in a queue. He disdained the short, powdered tye wig, so popular now, saying he couldn't gallop a horse and worry about his hair flying off. At 30 years of age, he was lean and well-formed, his broad shoulders and torso tapering to a hard, flat belly and well-muscled thighs. He had large dark eyes that had once been warm with a puppy-like passion for her, and a generous mouth. But an ugly scar ran from the corner of his lip down his cheek, and when he smiled it pulled his mouth into a cruel twist. That was perhaps her one regret with regard to their relationship, that in a fit of temper she had slashed his face with her riding crop when he had sought to curb what he called her unsavory pastimes. She had not been able to bring herself to apologize, and it did seem, in retrospect, that that incident, more than any other, had marked the beginning of their descent into the mutual dislike that ate into the very soul of this house. It was perhaps an unfortunate facet in her personality that she couldn't let well enough alone, that she felt obliged to go on with the small needles and torments, long after it had really ceased to matter. But it was so much fun to see him squirm in his prudishness, to know that by the terms of his father's will he was required to take care of her until she married or died. And it still rankled so much, after all these years, that old Henry, Giles's father, had left nothing outright to Eleanor, going so far as to mention in his will that he considered her a profligate, not to be trusted with money. That nasty little phrase had made her embezzlements over the years all the sweeter.

"I don't understand what you are going on about, Giles," she stated coolly, determined to defuse his temper. If he was going away this morning she wanted plenty of cash available in the accounts for her pleasure. "I've no intention of driving away the governess. If the others left, it was because they could not bear looking at the drooling half-wit, not because of anything I've done."

"You managed to get rid of each one of them, Eleanor, and don't tell me the boy drove them away. Only the first one had difficulty with the boy, and that was because she was an ignorant country girl with irrational, fanciful ideas in her head about his sort of affliction. The other two got along fine with him—I made sure of that before I went away each time. Then when I returned they were gone, with no explanation. No, madame, you may not blame little Tom for this. And let me assure you that if we cannot find a governess to suit, I shall cease traveling and stay here. I am sure neither of us wants that."

Eleanor froze at his words. As much fun as it was to annoy him, it was no pleasure at all to have him around for long periods. He was so stifling and disapproving, with such conventional tastes. As long as he busied himself in Dufton looking after his lead-mining operations she was free to come and go as she pleased here.

"I will give you my word, darling, the new governess will be treated like royalty. She'll have absolutely nothing to complain of in me. Now, whether she can tolerate the brats is something else." She smiled sweetly at him.

"They are my brother's children, Eleanor. They have been orphaned. They deserve some kindness in their lives. All I ask is that you stay out of the way so that they can get it."

"Nothing pleases me more, dear boy. I won't bother them and they won't bother me." She smiled up at him again and turned her back to him with a much affected, weary sigh. She was through teasing him this morning.

"Then I'll bid you good morning, Eleanor. I shall not return for the better part of a month. If you have need of anything, ask Hawton or write me."

"Good-bye, Giles," she said languidly, eyeing him from the rear as he left. The man still had a remarkable derriere, tight and well-formed. But then so did Hawton, and the steward had fewer inhibitions. She smiled to herself when she thought of how the last governess had bolted in the middle of the night when she had finally figured out what they were getting at. She had been a lovely little thing, and Hawton had been, as ever, eager to oblige. But the girl had been such a prude, not wanting Eleanor to participate. Pity. And the one before that had been so horse-faced and fat they had run her off in no time. Now it seemed she and Hawton must stay their games, at least for now, until they could see which way the wind blew. It would not do for Giles to decide he must spend more time at home. No, it would not do at all.

* * *

Joanna emerged from the tiny, airless office of the employment agent and took a deep breath, only to be sorry. Pah, how this city air stank! She turned to the left, as Mrs. Sneed had suggested, and began the two-block walk to the Hart's Leap, which the woman had assured her was a respectable inn, at least by London standards.

Joanna had secured a position as a governess. After all the uncertainty and the nameless fears, Mrs. Sneed, the agent to whom the bishop had recommended Joanna, had offered her a post, in spite of what the woman had termed Joanna's overly academic, woefully insufficient womanly skills. Womanly skills, indeed. It hadn't seemed to matter at all that Joanna could read and write in both Greek and Latin, and that her mathematics could have qualified her for university study. No, all Mrs. Sneed had cared about was that Joanna could not play the stupid pianoforte, could not sing a note, and, when pressed, had had to admit that her needlework was nothing better than utilitarian.

Mrs. Sneed had made it clear that with no prior experience and such an odd assortment of skills, the only position Joanna could aspire to would be one in a remote location or where the children were perhaps on the difficult side. And Joanna was willing to accept this. But Cumberland! Up north on the west coast, right up next to the Scots border. The very end of the universe!

Mrs. Sneed had obviously expected Joanna to balk, but not because of the location. There were two children at Queen's Hall, a very bright ten-year-old girl and a younger boy. Mrs. Sneed had described him as a half-wit, an idiot, but it was clear to Joanna that the child suffered from the same affliction as Mistress Gertie's overgrown bear of a boy, Tom, with his lumbering, heavy body and his great moon face, marked by oddly rounded and creased eyes. But Tom was a warm, benign presence in Mistress Gertie's old age, and Joanna, taught by her father that God prized all of his creatures, had found nothing to fear in Tom, and much to love.

So she had swallowed her fear of the unknown and accepted Mrs. Sneed's offer. Not that she had had any choice. Mrs. Sneed had been tight-lipped and stern and had made it clear that it was this post or none at all, bishop's reference or no.

So Cumberland it would be.

Joanna sighed as she thought of climbing back into a fetid, badly-sprung public coach tomorrow. It had taken two full days to get to London from Little Haver and now it would be four more days to Queen's Hall.

Well, at least tonight she could have a nice wash and something decent to eat. And, she fervently hoped, no lice to share her bed.

Chapter Three

Joanna nodded fitfully, grateful to be alone at last. The Chapman carriage was well-sprung and well-padded and smelled of oiled leather instead of unwashed bodies, a welcome change.

She was exhausted. For the last four days she had burned with fever, sleeping in snatches to the rhythm of the horses and the sway of the public coach, only to be jolted awake every few minutes by a rut or rock in the road. Awake, she was in pain, tormented as much by her fears as by the fever. Sleep offered little better—nightmares of strange landscape and malevolent figures. There was no love or kindness for her now, awake or asleep.

Last night, in Barnard, she finally had been able to rouse herself to think clearly. She had asked the innkeeper for a private room, pleading a fever and the danger of contagion. She was

41

cheated on the price nonetheless, but paid without protest, thankful for a clean, quiet bed, a warm fire, and a great deal of hot tea.

She remembered little of the travel as far as York, where she had changed to a local coach night before last. Perhaps that was merciful since what little she did remember involved having a constant, vicious headache, and being horribly cramped in a fetid coach with the same sort of anonymous, noisome fellow travelers as had accompanied her on the trip from Little Haver to London. In her fevered brain, she rather wondered if they weren't actually the same people, doomed to travel the length and breadth of England forever in public coaches, bathless and friendless, for eternity.

It was early evening by now and the light slanting through the chinks in the window flaps was fading. She sat up with a stretch, trying to still the fears of her heart. The Chapman coachman had met her in Penrith. He was pleasant-faced but seemed shy and awkward, offering only that it would be about three hours to Queen's Hall and asking in a red-faced stammer if she'd care to use the inn convenience before they got started. She would indeed. She'd had about enough of being at the mercy of the public coach company's schedule for comfort stops. The coachman had introduced himself as Charles and helped her with her meager belongings, closing her firmly but alone inside the coach. She knew as little now as she had learned sitting before Mrs. Sneed's austere countenance.

For the hundredth time Joanna berated herself for failing to get even the most basic of information from Mrs. Sneed about this post. She knew nothing more than that Queen's Hall was the home of Sir Giles Chapman and his stepsister, Lady Eleanor, and that there were two children. She had no idea how much she would be paid, and no experience whatsoever in asking about her duties or her days off. And what she had been told only served to feed her fears. Mrs. Sneed had almost casually let drop that she had placed two young women in this same position, each of whom had lasted only a matter of days before bolting mysteriously. Then the woman had asked Joanna to please let her know if there were anything unsavory or untoward about this post! Perhaps Joanna should have thought to ask whether anyone had actually laid eyes on either of these two women since they allegedly left. Perhaps she'd be murdered in her bed and buried in an unmarked grave on a rocky beach in Cumberland!

Well, like it or not, she was here, a million miles from anyone she knew or who cared about her. Not that there were so many left who did. She thought with a pang of Mistress Gertie and Tom. She had promised to write the woman and had, indeed, sent her a hastily penned note from the inn last night, the first night she had felt well enough to put pen to paper. Mistress Gertie had been kind enough to give Joanna a place to stay for a few days while she awaited a reply to the rather desperate letter she had sent to the bishop. It had been obvious she could not stay in the vicarage—not after the words she had exchanged with the odious Ambrose. And Tom, with his great strength and good nature, had moved Joanna's few belongings from the vicarage, treating her watercolors with an awed reverence. There had not been much, really. The furniture itself belonged to the vicarage. Papa's belongings and her own amounted to no more than a few bags. And now it was all reduced to these two bags at her feet, and one well-wrapped parcel—her water-color of the vicarage in late spring, rife with the flowers Joanna's mother had adored and Joanna herself had so lovingly tended. She wondered what Conny Almquist would do with her mother's flowers, being "a bit of a pig," as Ambrose had de-scribed him.

Biting back her anxiety, she reached out and pulled open the shutter of the window, just a bit. An icy blast hit her full in the face, but it smelled clean and fresh and she inhaled in great gulps. She let out her breath with a gasp as her eyes met an incredible landscape. Stretched out before her as far as she could see was the most magnificent countryside she had ever seen. An endless, rolling valley of green and brown met softly sloping peaks in the distance, and she could see the brilliant blue shimmer of a large lake not far away. She pushed her head as far out of the window as it would fit and breathed in the glorious air and the majestic sights. She felt clean for the first time in days.

Drinking in the sights that met her eyes along with the invigorating air, she smiled as she thought of her watercolors. She itched to do jus-tice to the gray mist that spilled over the moun-tains. Even now, in late winter, the subtle colors blended the light and the shadow so delicately, washing the hills and valleys with the spectacle of a muted sunset. Contemplating the splendor of the canvas before her, she eventually drifted into a pleasant nap, rocked by the gentle sway of the well-sprung carriage.

* * *

"And you are not to trouble Lady Eleanor about the children for any reason whatsoever, Miss Carpenter, is that understood?" Mr. Hawton, the steward, was just finishing his precise explanation of Joanna's duties. He sat in his small, cluttered office in the back of the house, sprawled in his chair, his heavy, booted feet propped casually on the corner of the desk. Joanna stood, not having been invited to sit down. It was not so much that she minded being put in her place—she must get used to that sort of thing, after all— it was more his manner of looking at her that had her nerves on edge. He was a handsome man, no doubt about that, and there was no doubt either that he was well aware of that fact. One could see it in the cut of his breeches—too tight they were for decency—and in his white cambric shirt, casually open at the neck so that a tuft of black hair showed rather aggressively from beneath. But it was his eyes that held Joanna's attention; blue and heavy-lidded, they surveyed her with an unnerving arrogance, almost a possessiveness, that suggested he thought she was his for the taking, at his pleasure. His mouth had a cruel twist to it, almost a mocking expression, as if she had just said something unbearably stupid. Not for the first time this week did Joanna regret that Little Haver had been such a small village. She felt quite at a loss in the world of men, and a sense of vast discomfort.

"I do understand, Mr. Hawton. But in case of an emergency, an illness, for instance—"

"Even then, Miss Carpenter," he interrupted, a trace of impatience in his voice. "I have explained to you that the children are Sir Giles's niece and nephew, children of his dead older brother. Sir

Giles is away most of the time. He looks after the family's lead-mining interests in Dufton. The children are nothing to her ladyship, and she does not wish to be bothered under any circumstances. In case of dire emergency you may consult me or any of the upper staff. Now, have I made myself clear?"

For a brief moment Joanna stared back at him, a slight tendency to mutiny at war with her good sense, then she nodded slowly. It was fast becoming clear to her what was really wrong with this post. This family was as cold as ice. It had not escaped her attention that at no time during this brief discussion had Mr. Hawton even mentioned Sir Giles's attitude toward the children. If he was even worse than his indifferent stepsister, God help these poor orphans.

It had been rather late when she had arrived last night. Stepping out of the carriage into a rainy darkness, she had been confronted by an imposing facade of dark gray, rain-streaked blocks, looming dark and unwelcoming, shadowing her insignificance. Inside, the house was as dark and forbidding as the outside. There seemed to be no light anywhere she looked. The young maidservant who led her through the silent house held a long taper, shielding the flame with the palm of her hand. It cast a small pool of light around them, but did little to illuminate the hallway through which they moved as silently as possible. Joanna had had the feeling she was in a cave, spacious enough, she could tell from the echo of her footsteps and the cold drafts around her feet, but gloomy and forbidding all the same. There had been candles standing unlit in brackets in the hallways. Joanna rather feared this would prove to be

a painfully frugal household. Papa had always remarked that God had said, "Let there be light," so
he had never bothered to stint on oil lamps or tapers. Joanna was used to a cozy brightness, not a
brooding, cavernous dark, and her spirits, already
low, had sunk further with every step.

At least her room seemed well-appointed,
though it, too, was dark when the girl had gone,
leaving only one lamp lit in the room. Joanna had
blessed Mistress Gertie as she dug from her bag
the candles that the good woman had insisted she
take along with her, lest the rooms at the inns
prove too dark.

The extra light revealed a large, comfortable-
looking bed covered with a beautiful quilt whose
bright colors, if faded, were nevertheless a cheer-
ful sight in the gloom. There was a small table next
to the bed, a dresser which held a washbasin and
pitcher, and a dressing table with a small mirror.
A large overstuffed wing chair was set to face the
window. Although the heavy draperies were
drawn tightly closed, Joanna rather hoped that a
chair positioned to look outward augured well for
a lovely view.

And there had been a cold supper waiting for
her, mercifully delicious, and warmish water for
a much-needed wash.

She had been aroused this morning from a
heavy but troubled slumber at an early hour by a
tap on the door and a tray of tea with toasted
bread and butter. She supposed this sufficed for
breakfast as she had been offered nothing further
this morning. Now, at half past eight in the morning, having received some twenty minutes of in-
struction from Mr. Hawton, she had yet to meet
the children and had heard nothing of them, not

the sound of laughter, not even small footsteps. The house was cold and dark, even in daylight, and her spirits were much oppressed.

"I should like to meet the children as soon as possible, Mr. Hawton. I am prepared to begin with them right away," she said, trying to keep her voice steady. The man continued to stare at her the way she'd seen a cat watch a mousehole, and it was doing nothing for her composure.

"Indeed you will, Miss Carpenter. I shall take you to the schoolroom now where I trust the children are waiting for you. And may I remind you that they are to be seen and not heard, most especially when her ladyship is in residence. She is not expected to return until next week, but it's best that you get in the habit of keeping the children out of the way and quiet at all costs."

"I see," Joanna replied in a tight voice. Already her heart went out to these poor orphans. No one had seen fit to mention to her until this morning, as if it were an afterthought, that these were not the children of Sir Giles, but rather the children of an older brother and sister-in-law who had died in a carriage accident a few months ago. And there was no love for these babies in this house from Sir Giles or his stepsister. Of that much she was now certain.

She trailed behind Mr. Hawton, trying unobtrusively to take in the house around her as she passed through it. From the rear office off the kitchen they came into the main hall, a vast, almost cavernous space with a number of closed doors leading from it. Although there were candles in sconces arranged along the walls, none were lit. From what furniture and appointments she had glimpsed so far, it did not seem that money was a problem, but for the life of her she could imagine no other reason for the deliberate gloom.

On the third floor, down the hall and across from her own bedroom, they stopped before a closed door. Mr. Hawton opened it without a knock and stepped in, Joanna behind him. The first impression to assail her was that it, like everywhere else in the house, was dark, dark and so quiet that she assumed no one else was there. There was a large window facing west, but despite the hour no one had thought to open the heavy draperies that covered every inch of it. No lamp or taper burned. But Joanna forgot the dark directly, as she spied the two small figures seated silently in the gloom, at desks several feet apart in the center of the room. Two pairs of young eyes looked back at hers. Expressionless.

Joanna started to smile at them when she was interrupted by Mr. Hawton's voice. "Annie, you may go now," he said, no warmth in his tone. "You may collect the children for the noon meal as usual, then arrange with Miss Carpenter as to what time she wishes to finish for the day." He waited while a youngish girl detached herself from the shadows in the corner of the room and, bobbing a curtsey, made a quick exit.

"I trust that is all you will need from me, Miss Carpenter," he went on coolly. "The housekeeper, Mrs. Davies, will give you further instructions about the household arrangements. If there are any difficulties with the children, you will bring them directly to me as we discussed." His eyes strayed to the boy and a look of disgust crossed his face, his lip curling. "Understood?" he finished, with a look at Joanna. There was a faint smile about his mouth, but it was not pleasant. Again there was that look in his eyes that held the suggestion of something Joanna did not want to even think about. She nodded to him, trying to meet his unnerving gaze, and was relieved when he turned and left the room, shutting the door firmly behind him. She no longer wondered why the other governesses had left so soon. Rather, she wondered why they had stayed so long.

Resisting the impulse to stick her tongue out at the door, she took a deep breath and turned to face the children once again. There were the two little pairs of eyes on her. As far as she could tell, neither child seemed to have moved a muscle since she had entered the room. She put what she hoped was a merry smile on her face. It was a real effort. There was no answering smile from either child. She started to say hello, then realized with a start that no one had ever told her what their names were. Orphaned, nameless, motionless, seated silent in the gloom.

Suppressing a snarl, she strode over to the window and pulled back the draperies. Instantly the room was flooded with light. Was it her imagination or did she hear a small gasp of surprise behind her? Before she turned from the window, she caught a glimpse of a rather magnificent sight, a glittering stretch of blue water, sparkling in the morning sun. Resolutely she put it from her mind. There would be time enough for scenery later. Right now these two benighted children needed all her attention.

Still wearing her happiest smile, she crossed back to the children, pulling with her a small child's chair that had been sitting by the window. She planted the little chair between the two desks and sat herself down on it. She was now at their eye level. There was still not so much as a flicker of expression from either child. They could have been statues from all she could tell so far.

"My name is Miss Carpenter and I have come from Little Haver in Shropshire to be your new governess," she began pleasantly. There was no response. "Now tell me," Joanna said to the girl, trying to keep her voice bright, "what is your name? No one has told me what your names are."

There was a moment's hesitation in the girl who stared back at Joanna, eyes large. Then in a very small voice the girl said, "Emma, Miss Carpenter." That was all. Joanna smiled at Emma and turned to the boy. As her gaze fell on him in the light, her breath caught in her throat. He looked so much like Mistress Gertie's Tom, moon-faced, with wide eyes, a slight fold across the lid giving them the unusual look. But where Tom's eyes were always dancing with laughter and love, these eyes were dark and mistrustful, as if in looking upon Joanna he knew he looked upon an enemy.

"What is your name, lad?" she asked gently. Tom could have answered such a question, but he was much older and Mistress Gertie had worked hard to teach him some of the simpler things. This boy simply looked back at her, saying nothing.

"His name's Tom, miss," came the small voice at her elbow.

"Tom?" Joanna answered. "What an odd coincidence. I have a very dear young friend back home in Little Haver. He is very much like you, Tom, and his name is Tom also." She smiled at him but got no smile in return. Nothing except that dark suspicion in his eyes.

Not taking her eyes from his, Joanna asked,

"Emma, can Tom speak for himself?"

Again there was a long pause, then the girl's small voice answered only, "He talks to me."

"My friend at home is very like your brother, Emma," Joanna said gently. "He doesn't talk much but he understands much of what is said to him. Does your brother understand us when we speak to him?"

Now the silence was long enough that Joanna turned back to face Emma. The girl looked uncertain and somewhat mutinous as if she couldn't decide how to answer this question.

"Emma, I think you are used to people not being very nice to Tom. That happens to my Tom, too. When people don't understand things they can be ignorant and cruel. But I promise you, I will be nice to him." She waited. It would be very hard to build any trust with this unloved, ignored little girl.

Finally, Emma seemed to make up her mind. She squared her little shoulders and in a louder voice than Joanna had heard her use thus far she said, "My brother understands a great deal of what is said to him. He is *not* an idiot, I don't care what they say. And he can talk if he wants to. He just doesn't bother, because no one here will take the trouble to listen."

Joanna stared back at the grim little face. The girl's chin was lifted in defiance as if she dared Joanna to laugh at her and tell her that indeed, the boy was a fool.

"Well, I am glad you told me the truth, Emma," Joanna said gently. Her heart was twisting. How long had these children been in this stark, cold environment? How long had it been since anyone had taken the trouble to listen to either of them?

She realized that apart from knowing that they had been orphaned, she knew absolutely nothing about these poor waifs, and she made up her mind to approach Mrs. Davies for more information as soon as possible.

She patted Emma on the hand, noting that the girl's hand was ice cold and that she suffered it to lie beneath Joanna's like a dead fish.

"Well," Joanna said brightly, looking around her for the first time. "Tell me what you have been studying so far." She noted with relief that the room seemed well equipped for scholarly pursuits. There was a large, well-stocked bookshelf along one wall, and an enormous standing globe took up an entire corner. A large desk at the end of the room must be meant for the governess, Joanna thought, making a mental note to move the children's desks closer to her own. The room was clean, not a speck of dust anywhere, and it was warm enough from a fire which burned briskly in the fireplace along the far wall. She realized that Emma had not answered her and turned back to the child questioningly.

"We haven't been studying anything, miss. You're our fourth governess since we've come here and no one stays long. I just read books to Tom. That's all we do."

Fourth? Joanna had been told two governesses had preceded her. Well, perhaps Mrs. Sneed had not placed the other one. It barely mattered now. Not only did she have nowhere else to go but she would not abandon these children now, not if the hounds of hell made their home here.

Further questioning revealed that at least the child's reading selections were sound, if a bit adult for them both. Joanna was pleased to find that the schoolroom library was large and varied. One or two gently-phrased questions produced the information that the books and other schoolroom furnishings had come from their parents' house in Yorkshire, now closed up and sold.

Joanna decided to devote the morning to geography, the very size and bright colors of the globe enticing her. She was pleased to note that Emma was quick and attentive, though the girl was so quiet it was difficult to gauge her actual enthusiasm. Tom said nothing, sitting silently, rarely even changing position, an unusual thing for a seven-year-old. Joanna could see that he was watchful, though, and when she referred to a spot on the globe his eyes followed her hands. It was impossible to know how much, if anything, he understood, but his eyes were not vacant; if anything, they still held their expression of dark mistrust.

Finally, there was a timid tap on the door and Annie came into the room. Emma and Tom both stood without being prompted. "May we be excused, Miss Carpenter?" the girl asked in her small voice.

"Of course, Emma, and I will see you both here after your dinner," Joanna replied.

"If you please, Miss Carpenter," came Annie's voice, if anything even tinier than Emma's, "Mrs. Davies wishes to know if you'd care to have your dinner sent to your room or to the governess's parlor?"

Actually, Joanna would have preferred to eat in the kitchen with no bother about formality. It had been a long time since her tea and toast and she found herself ravenous. She hoped this household was not going to prove as stingy on food as it appeared to be on candles.

"I think the parlor will be fine for today, Annie. And would you ask Mrs. Davies if she has the time to dine with me? Tell her I should be glad of her company." Propriety be damned, she didn't wish to eat like a hermit in some dark little room tucked away somewhere in this sepulchral house. Besides, she needed information immediately.

"And, by the way, Annie, could someone fetch me from my room when dinner is served? I've no idea where you keep the governess's parlor." Joanna smiled warmly at the girl and was rewarded with a broad grin in return. Annie turned to go and the children followed, quiet and orderly at her heels. It was unnerving to watch them. In three hours' time she had not heard a raised voice or even so much as a giggle from either of them. Emma had given her a tight, tentative sort of smile once or twice, and Joanna supposed she ought to count that as enough of a victory for the first morning, although a grin from Tom would have been worth far more.

Now that she was alone she walked over to the window. Her glance had strayed to it once or twice during the morning, and the dancing brightness had held such promise. A truly glorious sight met her eyes. The house sat high on a bluff that overlooked the sea. In the distance, as far as her eyes could see, stretched the blue water, with the sun, which must be overhead now, glinting fiercely off the waves. Although she could see nothing of the beach below, she knew what she would see when she could get free of this house—miles and miles of sandy, rocky coast, with inlets and coves, all for glorious exploring and painting.

With a sigh she turned away from the gladsome sight, telling herself that surely she would be able to leave the confines of the house soon. Feeling like a prisoner with one small window onto the outside world, she left the room, stepping again into the gloomy dark of the hallway.

"He was married for a time, you see. But it—well, it seemed—that is, Mrs. Chapman died in childbed. I suppose it's been about five years now . . ." Mrs. Davies broke off and turned her attention to her boiled potatoes.

"Oh, how dreadful for the poor man," Joanna sighed, her own potatoes forgotten.

"Er, yes, of course it was." Mrs. Davies looked a bit peculiar.

"I should think he'd have wanted to remarry. At least, he's young and he would want children . . ." Joanna stopped, coloring, aware her comment might suggest that she herself was on the lookout for a rich widower.

"Oh, I don't think he'd want to remarry, dear," Mrs. Davies replied, now decidedly uncomfortable.

They ate in awkward silence for a moment. Joanna was anxious to hear more of this odd household, but reluctant to appear a gossip.

Finally, the woman sat back and gave Joanna a long perusal. Then with a small shrug she went on. "I suppose if you are to stay here you should understand things a bit. It might make it easier to accept the—situation as it is. Sir Giles—he was Mr. Chapman then—and his wife did not get on well together. Violet Chapman and Lady Eleanor were inseparable, like peas in a pod they were. They had been friends for years. Indeed, Lady Eleanor introduced them to one another. Mrs. Chapman was a bit older than he was, and Sir

Giles was—odd man out. There was no love lost, you see."

"No, I do not see," said Joanna, sitting back as well. The food was sticking in her throat. This was a strange bunch of cold-hearted people! "Why would he care that his wife was good friends with his stepsister? Not that it's any of my business, I suppose."

"It was not just that they were friends, dear. Lady Eleanor is—rather abandoned in her pursuit of pleasure, and Mrs. Chapman and she . . . well, I suppose I should just say that Mrs. Chapman chafed at the confines of marriage and Lady Eleanor rather egged her on . . ." Mrs. Davies trailed off. She sat forward again, rather red in the face, and made for the potatoes.

Joanna just stared at her. She was aware of the implications of this rather elliptical conversation. And while she certainly would never consider herself a prude, it seemed the drift was unsavory to say the least.

The potatoes exhausted, Mrs. Davies looked up. She patted her mouth daintily with a napkin. "I tell you this, Miss Carpenter, not because I approve of household gossip, which I do not, but because I have hopes that you will stay with us. You don't seem frightened or disgusted by the boy, and I actually heard little Emma tell Annie that you were very nice. So you see, I am encouraged." Mrs. Davies gave Joanna a warm smile. "But I think you will find this a cold household, and you must accept that if you stay. Sir Giles and his sister, when they are here together, which is not often, are not on good terms."

"How long have you been here, Mrs. Davies?" asked Joanna.

"I've been with the Chapman family for many years, since before Henry Chapman—that was Sir Giles's father—married Lady Eleanor's mother." The woman's lips tightened. "I've been here long enough to see him turn from a happy, handsome lad into an embittered, cold man, so I would beg your tolerance of us, Miss Carpenter. There is much to be forgiven here, but there are reasons to forgive." She eyed Joanna speculatively, as if weighing her reaction.

"Why did the other governesses leave, Mrs. Davies?" asked Joanna, unwilling as yet to offer to forgive anything about this family.

The woman looked at her in surprise. "Why, they could not tolerate the boy's idiocy, Miss Carpenter. Although I must say he's no real trouble and none of them gave him a chance."

Joanna said nothing, wiping her mouth on her napkin. She couldn't for the life of her see what there was to run away from in little Tom. He was, if anything, quieter and more mannerly than boys his age of normal wits.

"Well, my dear, I hope I haven't frightened you off," said Mrs. Davies, patting her hand. "I'll be off now, for I need to talk with Cook about supper. Please don't brood on anything I've said. I simply want you to understand things so you won't find it too odd."

Odd? Any odder and it would be the demented section of Old Bailey!

"I am really not too concerned with the master and mistress, Mrs. Davies," Joanna said with a touch of asperity. "I assume I'll be seeing little enough of either of them, and as you say, if I keep the children quiet when they are here, I suppose we'll get along tolerably well. I am, however, terribly concerned about these poor children. I imagine the catacombs in Rome are cheerier than this house. Why on earth is there so little light?"

"Oh, yes, it is gloomy, isn't it? I've lived here so long I don't think I notice anymore. It did not used to be this way, but Lady Eleanor despises bright light and the smell of burning wax and oil. She likes us to keep the draperies closed so as not to fade the carpets and upholstery. Still, I could give you another lamp and some extra tapers for your room, if you like."

"Yes, thank you. I would be most grateful. And for the schoolroom, too, please. I cannot imagine that Lady Eleanor will be visiting us there."

Mrs. Davies laughed as they walked toward the door. "I imagine she'll stay as far away as she can from your schoolroom, Miss Carpenter. Say what you will about this household, at least no one will be peering over your shoulder, telling you how to do your job." She and Joanna stepped out into the somber dark of the hallway.

That evening Joanna prepared for bed, grateful for the extra oil-burning lamp that Mrs. Davies had sent up to the room earlier. It had been a tolerable day after all. Emma had actually giggled at something Joanna had said, and the boy had let her take him on her lap for a story before supper.

And the bath had been sublime. There was an entire room set aside on each upper floor for bathing, small to be sure, but free of drafts. An ingenious system of pulleys and a platform raised the buckets of hot water from the kitchen to each level, designed, Mrs. Davies had been proud to point out, by Sir Giles himself. Joanna had lolled about in the warm water feeling like Cleopatra on her barge, the steam rising around her, her fears dissipating in the warm, fragrant, candle-lit mist.

She knelt now on the cold floor by her bed, pleased that there was a worn but still serviceable carpet to keep the chill away. She prayed as she always did before retiring, but more and more these nights it seemed her thoughts jumbled God and Papa together and she hoped she wasn't committing blasphemy by praying to them both. Tired and frayed, she asked for patience and guidance and blessings for Tom and Emma.

Far below her she heard the heavy slam of the door, but as it had nothing to do with her, she trimmed the lamp and slipped, exhausted, into bed.

Chapter Four

Mr. Hawton stood before Sir Giles's desk and attempted to conceal his lack of ease behind a respectful demeanor. Sir Giles had no right to come home unexpectedly, injured arm or no. This would put a crimp into Hawton's plans and he would have to scramble to set things right. If only Eleanor weren't off at one of her infernal house-parties. It irritated him no end that although he acted as her business partner and her stud, performing prodigious feats for her rapacious pleasure, he was still just the steward and was entitled to no crossover privileges in regard to her glittering social life.

"And I take it you have seen to her comfort, Hawton," the master continued. "Please understand me. I expect this governess to stay, unless she is entirely unsuitable with respect to the children. If she leaves like the others, flying in the dead of night with no explanation, I shall hold you accountable." That he had told his stepsister the same thing gave Sir Giles no qualms. It would not hurt to have everyone on their best behavior.

"I can assure you, sir," replied Hawton, "that everything has been done to see to Miss Carpenter's comfort, and she seemed content enough last night after her first day here, according to Mrs. Davies."

"Very well," Sir Giles said dismissively. "And bring me the estate books to look at. As long as I am holed up here, I might as well occupy my time usefully."

With effort, Hawton kept his expression neutral and suppressed a slight trembling in his hands as he nodded and left the room. On his way back to his small office he made a rapid review of the situation. The records were in some disarray. He was not much of a paper-keeper, and Sir Giles had shown absolutely no interest in the books in the past eighteen months of his stewardship. Fortunately, Hawton was guilty of only small embezzlements himself, since he was a cautious man by nature and unwilling to run serious risk. Still, Eleanor was constantly pressuring him for funds, skimmed from this or that account, to cover her occasional steep gaming losses. While Sir Giles, as a wealthy, indifferent stepbrother, could be expected to turn a blind eye to the casual bad run of cards, Eleanor's proclivities had led her into deep water recently and she was anxious that the extent of her difficulties not be exposed. Her embezzlements were more substantial than Hawton's own and much harder to hide from serious scrutiny.

He quietly closed the door to his office behind him, then slammed his fist into his palm. Damn the man for interfering! Now he was glad that he had had the foresight to send for Eleanor this morning, uncertain of what Sir Giles's unexpected visit heralded. He would have to do some fancy scrambling in the next short while to come up with plausible entries to cover Eleanor's petty thefts. The bitch had better show him the proper gratitude.

Giles sat at his desk and stared out at the sea from the large window in his office. He had chosen the room for its vista, and it was the one room in the house where the draperies were never closed. His arm pained him a great deal and he cursed his foul luck. He had known the lead mines were dangerous, but he would have no worker face any danger he himself would not face. Thus when the recent rains had caused a mud slide, he had insisted on being first to go down into the pit, to ascertain the safety for his crew. It had been sheer bad fortune that the ground above had chosen that moment to shift again, sending a loaded cart down on top of him. He supposed he was lucky he had seen it in time to throw up an arm to ward off the worst of the impact. Had it struck his head, he would have been killed. As it was, his arm had borne the brunt, sustaining a severe gash which ripped through coat, shirt, and flesh to expose the bone below. He had been cleaned up and bandaged on the spot, but there had been no physician on site and the foreman had begged him to consider that such a deep wound would surely fester if not properly treated. Hence Giles had headed for Penrith, where the local surgeon had clucked and tsked and generally allowed as how

Giles would die or lose the arm if he weren't very careful.

Giles had refused the laudanum offered, preferring pain to a sleepy, stupid feeling. But the constant severe pain racked him now, and he had slept very little last night, making his temper short. Thank God Eleanor was off at one of her debaucheries. At least he could be spared dueling with her during what he hoped would be an extremely short convalescence.

He was bored and restless with his enforced inactivity. He spent as little time as possible in this house. It was a cold, uninviting place, purchased at the behest of Lady Eleanor when he had accepted this meaningless title, so that they could live "as befitted their proper station." Proper station, indeed! He had more respect for his foreman and the men who worked under him than he did for any of the useless peacocks and popinjays who paraded around here whenever Eleanor was "in residence."

He turned to the diagram on his desk and tried to concentrate on the intricacies of the effect of gravity on water flow and the various measurements and engineering tactics he'd need to improve the transportation system from Dufton. Usually he could lose himself in the purity of numbers. Mathematics and physics, he thought to himself, not for the first time, were so incorruptible, so predictable. But today the pain gnawed at him, ate into his disciplined concentration. He swung around in his chair, gritting his teeth against the hot stab of agony that tore through his shoulder at the sudden movement. He stared with dull eyes at the sea. It should be such a beautiful sight, with the afternoon sun and the brilliant blue of the sky reflecting off the calm water. But no matter where he tried to find beauty or tranquility in this cursed house, he felt the taint of darkness and disquiet.

Behind him, through the closed door, came a sound so unusual he strained to place it. Yes, there it was again, unmistakably the sound of a child's giggle, followed by the shuffle of little footsteps and a rich, melodic laugh he had not heard before. As he turned toward the sound, another stab of pain shot through his shoulder. With a grimace, he rose from his desk. Might as well see the woman now and make sure she had a decent attitude toward the children. He had nothing to do while he waited for Hawton anyway.

Striding to the door, he flung it open, surprising the three figures who stopped in a frozen tableau at the sight of him. The hallway was dark except for the light of a lone candle, but the sun from the window behind him spilled its bright light across the woman and her two small charges. Giles had time to note the look of apprehension in her eyes before she bent her head down, pulling both children to her, her arms clasped tightly around them.

"Good afternoon," he said. "You must be Miss— I'm sorry, I cannot remember . . ." He trailed off, waiting for her to supply her name.

Joanna struggled to hold her knees steady. The man had appeared from nowhere, from the dark of the rear hall. Now he stood, his face in shadow, towering over her and the children, who gave not a sign of welcome. She released her hold on the children just long enough to make a small curtsey, then, drawing in a deep breath, she said, "Carpenter. I am Miss Carpenter, the new governess, sir," She was annoyed to hear that her voice held a hint of a tremble. This dratted house had her nerves on edge.

"I am Sir Giles Chapman, Miss Carpenter. I am the children's uncle."

Sir Giles! He was supposed to be away. Always! And now he had caught them traipsing rather loudly through the hall. Of all the rotten luck!

Joanna dropped into a real curtsey and stood. "How do you do, sir?" she greeted him, as evenly as she could manage, aware that her face had suffused red. "Children, say 'how do you do' to your uncle." She pushed them each forward a trifle and held her breath. She heard the faintest of greetings from Emma and nothing at all from Tom, but she was relieved to see that Emma dropped a proper curtsey.

Sir Giles lounged against the door frame, perusing the young woman as she stood, her face now in the sunlight. His breath caught in his throat. Damnation! Dark hair, warm brown eyes, a prettily shaped, soft, pink mouth. She was the very image of his wife, the lovely Violet, fair of face and foul of heart, kindred spirit to her best friend, Eleanor. Dead these last five years. Even that look of trembling innocence was the same.

"You are young," he said coldly. He had been expecting someone a bit older, more seasoned, considering the blistering letter he had sent to Mrs. Sneed regarding the unsuitability and flightiness of the two young women she had sent previously. This one was young by the looks of her, too young, perhaps, to bring discipline and order to small children.

"I—I am twenty-two, Sir Giles," Joanna managed to stammer.

"You don't look that old," was his clipped reply.

Joanna said nothing, aware that he had not meant this as a compliment. Annoyance rose in her. This was the brute of a man who had allowed these children to languish in the dark these last few months. He had not so much as glanced at them! She looked up just as he gave an inclination of his head toward his niece. The faint light of the candle in the hall fell across his face, and she had to stifle a small gasp. She had time to take in the twist to his mouth where an ugly scar slashed across it, and the large white sling that held his left arm immobile. Neither peculiarity soothed her nerves. There was no smile on his face, nor any in his dark eyes.

Just then, the baize-covered door to the back quarters opened and Annie stepped into the hall, stopping suddenly and blinking in confusion as her eyes went to Sir Giles, then back to Joanna in frantic questioning.

"It's all right, Annie," Joanna said softly. Then, turning back to the large man towering over her and willing herself to meet his eye, she said, "Sir Giles, if you will excuse us, the children usually have their baths and supper at this time."

"Certainly, Miss Carpenter," he said smoothly. He was aware that he had frightened the girl. Although she was making every effort to master her fear, her hands betrayed her as she clutched the children still in her trembling, white-knuckled grasp. It would not bode well for her tenure here if she were frightened of her own shadow. It wasn't her fault that she looked like the faithless Violet, he thought. Still, he knew what sort of scheming lay behind soft brown eyes. He'd been taken in once before and never again. He turned to the young maid. "Annie, is it?" he asked. "You may take the children, and keep to your normal schedule."

Emma had not looked at him since her curtsey, nor uttered another word. Tom just watched him, his bland face expressionless. Annie bobbed a little curtsey and collected the children, ushering them through the door, which shut with a whisk behind them.

Joanna stood and watched them go, confused and embarrassed. Was she dismissed as well? He hadn't said so exactly, but then she did not really remember what he had said. Perhaps she could just excuse herself and make for the sanctuary of her room. She was aware that his eyes were on her, and she made herself turn to meet his gaze. His face was impassive. There was nothing warm about his eyes, and if the twist to his mouth was his attempt at a smile, it was a dismal failure.

"Perhaps you could join me for a glass of sherry before your own supper, Miss Carpenter?" he asked. He might as well get to her bona fides at once. If she were to prove unsuitable, it would be best to find it out sooner rather than later.

"Why, of course, sir," she answered, trying very hard to keep a blank, neutral expression and an even tone. Sherry? With him? What could he possibly want of her? She had been given to understand in no uncertain terms by both Mr. Hawton and Mrs. Davies that neither Sir Giles nor Lady Eleanor wanted anything to do with her or the children.

"You may join me in the drawing room in an hour, Miss Carpenter," he said. He tried to give her a smile, but broke it off as he felt his mouth twist down into a grimace. Damn, he was so long between smiles that sometimes he forgot what

Eleanor had done to his face. Maybe that's what had so frightened this girl. Maybe she thought he looked like an ogre.

Joanna watched him in confusion. For a moment he had looked as if he might smile, then his eyes had gone cold again.

With a curt bow, he turned and strode away from her, leaving Joanna staring nonplused at his back. She drew in a deep, shaky breath, aware that her heart was pounding. Then when his footsteps had receded down the hallway, she ventured for the stairs and ran for her own room, shutting the door behind her.

Drat! Drat! Drat! She sank into her one comfortable chair and stared with desultory eyes out the window. Throwing open the draperies yesterday morning, she had been pleased to discover that her room, facing east, looked out over a rolling green landscape with hills a hazy purple in the distance. Though her heart delighted in the crashing, mad sea to the west, she was glad of a retreat to the serenity of the fells, where she could sit behind a closed door, in a bright, pleasant room, and shut out the nameless fears that assailed her in this dark house. She drew a deep breath and let it out with a great sigh.

There was nothing to be afraid of! She'd had a lovely day with the children today and yesterday. They had thawed visibly, to the point where she had actually gotten spontaneous laughter from both of them, and then that man had appeared from nowhere and frozen them up again. And now she had to deal with the ogre of a master. At least, she reasoned to herself, he cannot be planning to give me the sack. He wouldn't do that over a glass of sherry, would he? Unless he was the kind of man who enjoyed that sort of thing, a slow, painful, sociable torture. This house was making her fanciful to the point of absurdity! She giggled to herself and sprang from her chair. There was nothing wrong with this post that a few lamps and candles wouldn't fix.

Opening her armoire, she surveyed her meager attire. There wasn't actually much point in staring, since she knew she had only one dress presentable enough to wear. At least she would not be dining with him. She pulled out the one good gown and frowned over it. It was a dark green silk which she'd worn to one of Squire's very rare soirees. How long ago had that been? At least four years, she figured, recalling having to argue with Papa that, at eighteen, she was old enough to attend an evening with the adults. She smiled to herself, remembering what a crashing bore it had proved to be, with not a soul there under forty, if that young. She gave the dress a shake. It was probably hopelessly out of style, but as she had never cared much about the latest mode, she couldn't worry now about offending the fashion sense of Sir Giles Chapman. She laid the dress out on the bed and was relieved to see that the wrinkles from her long journey had smoothed out. She had almost an hour to kill before she had to join Sir Giles. Too bad, because she was already starving and her supper would be rock hard and cold by the time she got to it. Well, she could have a nice rest and maybe send off a note to Mistress Gertie, then gird herself for the glass of sherry with the dark and brooding master.

An hour later, hair patted into place and cheeks glowing pink from an icy cold rinse, a seemingly calm and collected Joanna presented herself to an unoccupied drawing room. With a start she realized that the room was bright with light. All the candles in the sconces around the walls were lit, and a candelabrum glowed with all its many candles blazing away. Let there be light, indeed! It was amazing the fears that could be banished by the letting in of a little light.

Looking about her, she was surprised at the glittering beauty of the room. It was sumptuous both in size and decor. It was filled with furniture, scattered about in cozy groupings. An enormous, thick carpet, woven in many muted colors and intricate patterns, covered much of the floor. Everywhere were signs of opulence and great wealth. There were a number of tables, small and large, each elaborately carved and polished to a mirror finish. There were chairs, a good many, and several divans and small settees, all upholstered in rich, colorful satins and brocades. Each grouping seemed to carry its own pattern and color scheme, but the effect, far from being discordant, blended harmoniously, the color groupings flowing from one to another in a pleasing concordance. And while Joanna couldn't tell rococo from baroque, her artist's eye registered the quality and the punctilious attention to detail.

She heard the door open softly and turned quickly, tension seizing her again. Sir Giles stood in the doorway staring at her. She moved forward hastily, unnerved by his scrutiny. He looked as though he might be smiling, but his mouth twisted down into a sardonic grimace. Taking some courage from the fact that his eyes were not cold, Joanna gave him a small curtsey and stood waiting, a bit uncomfortable as to what she should do next.

Giles moved into the room, aware that the girl was still unnerved by his presence. "Good evening, Miss Carpenter," he said. "Please have a seat and I'll pour you a taste of sherry."

She chose a plush, elaborately upholstered settee, and fussed unnecessarily with the folds of her dress while he poured her a sherry from a crystal decanter, and for himself a brandy.

Turning her head to face Sir Giles, she practically bumped her nose on the painstakingly sculpted manhood of a rather large, terribly well-endowed statue of Apollo that stood on the small table next to her settee. Drawing back in alarm, she stole a quick glance at Sir Giles to see if he had noticed. Behind him, his back to her, she caught sight of the enormous painting that dominated the wall between two long windows. She fought to strangle the gasp that rose in her throat.

With a delicate crystal glass of sherry and a large snifter of brandy in his hands, Giles turned to Joanna and stopped in his tracks at the open-mouthed look on her face. His eyes following hers, he turned and beheld the sight that had her so startled. He moaned. He had long ago stopped noticing Eleanor's bizarre, overripe artwork, sensual to the point of near obscenity. Above them both, larger than life, hung a voluptuous odalisque reclining in opulence, attended by a variety of over-dressed blackamoors. The lady, painted in meticulous detail, was utterly sans attire. And judging from the expression on her pink, plump face, she was delighted about it.

"I—I'm sorry," he began in confusion. Joanna's expression was almost comical on her beet-red face, and he found himself fighting the urge to laugh. "It's my stepsister's, really. I had absolutely nothing to do with the decorating of the place . . ." He trailed off lamely as she turned her head to him. With a start, he realized that it wasn't horror he was seeing in her eyes; it was merriment.

"Sir Giles, that painting is absolutely . . . edifying. I can safely say I've never seen anything like it in my life." She sat rather primly, hands folded neatly in her lap. She was as unlike the odalisque as anyone could be, and all the more appealing for it. In spite of himself he gave her a lopsided grin, and she grinned back.

"Here," he said, holding out a small glass filled with a glowing amber liquid. "Perhaps this will help restore your equilibrium." He sat himself in a large overstuffed wing chair next to her. As he turned to face her, he was smartly confronted by the gloriously sculpted buttocks of the Apollo.

Joanna, in the act of swallowing her first sip of sherry, caught his eye over the Apollo. He had a very peculiar expression on his face, and she choked, trying hard to get the sherry down her throat instead of her windpipe.

Giles watched her sputter and choke, willing himself not to laugh. He could just imagine what the business end of this little "artwork" must look like on her side, if the arse was this well defined. He finally handed her a handkerchief to wipe her streaming eyes, allowing himself a smile.

"Your stepsister's taste in art is certainly—unrestrained, Sir Giles," she finally ventured. She was quite sure she had gotten sherry up her nose.

"Perhaps we ought to cover it, Miss Carpenter," he offered. "I'm not at all sure it's appropriate for us to converse under these circumstances."

"Well, I am a vicar's daughter, sir, and we do have certain standards . . ." The laughter in her eyes belied the severity of her sentiments. She handed him back his large square of white silk and he wrapped it deftly around the Apollo.

"Is that better, Miss Carpenter? I wouldn't wish to offend your delicate sensibilities."

"Yes, that will do nicely, sir." Joanna smiled at him. The sherry she had managed to get down her throat was warming her and it felt good.

"Tell me about your credentials. Mrs. Sneed's letter was rather brief," he said smoothly, taking a sip from his glass.

Her credentials! What credentials? She had come prepared to talk about the children, not about her credentials.

"You say you are a vicar's daughter?" Giles prompted, aware that his question had unsettled the girl. Perhaps her credentials were slim, though he was damned if he could see that he had much choice at the moment. It did not seem, after all, to be a much-sought-after post.

"My father died a few weeks ago, sir. But, yes, he was a vicar."

"I see. I'm sorry to have distressed you by mentioning it."

There was an awkward pause as each sipped at the spirits. Joanna, fighting a sinking feeling, decided she had better address his question about credentials, uninspiring though they may be.

"Actually, Sir Giles, my father's being a vicar has a great deal to do with the nature of my accomplishments. You see, he was quite a learned man and he did not much approve of denying girls the same academic opportunities as boys . . ." She paused and took another sip, venturing a peep at

Sir Giles, who, she decided, looked vaguely uncomfortable.

"So you see," she continued, "I have a rather extensive background in several academic areas. I know Latin and Greek, for instance, and I am rather good at mathematics and geography . . ." She trailed off again, seeking some sort of response. The man positively looked like a stuffed frog at the moment.

Giles sat back and took a deep gulp of his brandy. A bloody bluestocking! Of all the pointless. . . . Here he was saddled with a boy who couldn't speak English, much less Greek, and a girl who needed to be taught how to embroider and play the pianoforte, and this governess was a mathematician!

"And have you any of the more usual feminine skills, Miss Carpenter? Stitchery, music, painting—you know the sort of thing I mean," he asked, trying to keep a note of exasperation out of his voice.

Joanna could feel her face flaming, as much from anger as discomfort. Feminine, indeed! Mindless ninny work, he meant! She swallowed her anger, nevertheless, hoping to keep a roof over her head a while longer. "I am told I am quite a good watercolorist, Sir Giles," she said after taking a deep breath, "and naturally I am versed in oils as well. But I must admit, I have little skill in music and my needlework is utilitarian, nothing more." There. He knew the worst. He could pack her off to Mrs. Sneed tonight or he could make the best of it. She waited.

"I see," was his only response.

There was a long, sherry-sipping pause. Joanna was mentally reviewing how much money she had left and how much she could expect to be paid for a few days' work. If he were fair-minded, he might even offer her a small severance allowance. It was four days back to London, after all.

"Actually, I am something of a mathematician as well," came his startling response.

"Are you?" she managed to stammer back.

"Well, not exactly a mathematician, precisely," he answered. "Actually, I use mathematics in my work. I design things, you see. My family has been involved in mining for some years, and I took an interest in how to improve the mining itself and our transportation systems." He stopped, painfully aware that, bluestocking or no, she was not likely to be fascinated by the subject of the action of water flow against a wheel. He was making a perfect ass of himself.

"Oh, but that's splendid, Sir Giles," she said with real enthusiasm. "You see, I always complained to my teachers that pure mathematics was absurd if one had nothing to which to apply the principles. I mean, theorems and arcane equations are rather pointless standing alone . . ." She hesitated. Why on earth would Sir Giles, a self-described mathematician, be the least bit interested in her rather pedestrian opinion of mathematical theory? She was making a perfect ass of herself.

"Precisely, Miss Carpenter. I carried on the same arguments with my tutors, who despaired of teaching me anything at all unless they could show me the point of it."

There was another silence. Joanna was in danger of finishing her glass of sherry and then how would she fill the awkward pauses? She felt she had gained an unexpected reprieve. "About the children, Sir Giles . . ." she began tentatively, unwilling to allow the silence to continue.

He gave her a questioning glance. She drew in a deep breath and continued.

"I haven't really been with them long enough to form a particularly accurate assessment of their relative abilities. I just met them yesterday. But I do feel that Tom has some aptitude that he is hiding at the moment—I am not sure why. And both children seem—forgive me for saying this—extraordinarily depressed. Not that it isn't natural under the circumstances. It's just that . . ." She trailed off, aware that he was looking at her. She flushed, fearing she had offended him by criticizing his household's care of the children.

"They're not getting much love here, isn't that what you mean, Miss Carpenter?" Giles raised his glass to his lips and Joanna could not see his eyes.

"I—I," she began, then stopped. That's exactly what she meant but she couldn't very well say it. Perhaps he was already angry with her. She couldn't tell from his voice.

"It's all right," he said, not looking at her. He rose and walked over to the brandy decanter.

"It happens I agree wholeheartedly with you," he went on, filling his snifter again. "And I would like to ask your help in remedying the situation." He walked to the window where the draperies were pulled back, revealing the dark of the night beyond. At a distance Joanna could hear the crashing of the sea. The wind must have come up, she reflected irrelevantly. The sea had been calm this afternoon.

"I suppose you already know that the other governesses we've engaged did not stay long," he said flatly, looking out into the dark.

"Yes, sir. I was so informed. But no one seems

to know why they left, sir." She stopped, then plunged on to the question that had plagued her. "Why did they leave, sir?"

"I regret to say that I never took the time to talk with the other governesses, Miss Carpenter. You may have surmised that I am not often in residence. They had each left before I had the chance to question them."

There was a long pause. Joanna could not think of anything to say. And she still had no answer to her question. She took a sip of sherry.

"I am not going to ask you to stay against your will, Miss Carpenter. I couldn't if I wanted to. But I would like to request that if you should ever feel it necessary to resign your post, please write to me, even if after the fact, and let me know what your reasons were." He stopped. He wasn't even sure what he wanted from her, but more and more this evening he had found himself hoping that this one would stay, would care for the children and create some semblance of normalcy for the blighted little things.

Joanna felt a sudden chill, reminded of Mrs. Sneed's parting remarks. The woman had asked almost the same thing of Joanna and there had been the suggestion of something unknown, something almost unsavory about the post.

"I would never just run off, Sir Giles. And besides, I have seen nothing yet that would lead me to wish to resign. Indeed, I find myself rather drawn to the children. When I make them laugh it all seems worthwhile, somehow." She took the last sip of her sherry. How could she explain to this stranger that she needed the children right now as much as they needed her? They were all she had in the world to love at the moment, and she hoped she could bring them to love her. She needed it so badly. She felt her eyes filling with tears and looked away, missing the thoughtful look he bestowed on her from the window.

The massive carved doors to the hallway opened suddenly, startling them both into turning around. A woman stood in the doorway. Joanna had time to note that she was tall and rail thin. She wore a powdered wig, high and elaborate, with several ornaments intertwined into the false, whitened hair. Her dress was a dark rose, with a deeply plunging décolletage. Her face, neck, and arms were white with a thick powder. Her eyes were sharp and mocking, and a tight, sardonic smile twisted her features.

"Cozy, darling. Very cozy," the woman purred. "I seem to have arrived in the nick of time." Her voice was deep and husky. Joanna had the sudden thought that this would be the voice of the painted odalisque, could she talk. Joanna glanced at Sir Giles uncertainly, and was startled by the change in his face. Had she not just shared a pleasant half hour with him, she would have been frightened to death of this man, now a stranger, who stood facing this woman with a look of pure loathing.

There was a moment of charged silence, then he spoke. His voice was cold and deliberate. "What brings you home, Eleanor? I had understood you to be off at one of your floating parties."

Not for her life would Eleanor tell him that a hasty summons from Hawton had arrived early this afternoon. Hawton's note had been cryptic and unenlightening, but urgent in its message: "Come home at once." No signature. She had assumed he feared some sort of discovery. Now, looking at this pretty little morsel, tête-à-tête with her handsome, if ice cold, stepbrother, she wondered what the summons was all about. Hawton was not in the house—she had ascertained as much after arriving a few minutes ago—but he would surely be available later to explain the urgency. And he'd better have a good explanation. She'd left a particularly nice party. There was a new young pup up from London and she'd been having much amusement with a slow seduction.

"Why, I understood that our little governess had arrived, darling, and you did tell me, didn't you, to make sure that she got a warm welcome? Although it seems I am too late. You've already given her a warm welcome. Hasn't he, dear?" Eleanor turned her smiling gaze on Joanna, who had scrambled to her feet and now dropped a curtsey.

"Yes, my lady, thank you. I've been welcomed very nicely," Joanna stammered. Mrs. Sneed's written instructions had been very specific about the titles and forms of address in this household. Lady Eleanor, as the daughter of an earl, was entitled to the honorific in her own right, and it was grander than that of a simple knight. Joanna hoped she'd got it right, disconcerted as she was.

"Splendid, my dear." Eleanor turned her languid gaze on her brother. Joanna noted that he still stood by the window. His face was a mask, but his eyes were cold and his lips were thinned and tight. "How about fixing me a little brandy, darling?" Eleanor purred. "I had a long, cold ride this evening."

Without saying a word, Giles moved over to the decanter and poured her a large snifter full. Eleanor crossed the room with slithering grace and took the glass from his hand. Joanna stood silent, uncomfortable and confused as to what she

should do now. Was it late enough to plead suppertime? She cast a furtive look at the clock on
the mantel and nearly rolled her eyes. The clock
face was all but obscured by carved, naked cherubs, painted in gilt, bottoms dimpled and shining
in the candlelight. At least the clock showed the
hour to be late enough to pass for a governess's
suppertime. She watched as Lady Eleanor lifted
her glass and drained a great deal of it one gulp.
Licking her red lips, the woman smiled at Joanna,
but the smile did not reach her eyes.

"Delicious. Very warming. Your glass is nearly
empty, my dear. Would you care for another jot
to jolly you up a bit? This is such a gloomy house
when we're all alone, isn't it, brother dear?"
Eleanor turned back to Giles, who made no answer. He watched his stepsister the way a mon-
goose might watch a snake, thought Joanna.
There was something decidedly wrong between
brother and sister, and it was definitely time for
the governess to disappear.

"Thank you, my lady, no. I must be up early to
teach the children, so I should have a quick supper
and retire shortly."

"Nonsense, dear, you will sup with us. I am just
agog to hear all the latest educational theories.
Won't that just be fascinating, Giles?" she trilled
in his direction, not bothering to pause for his answer. She moved over to the wall and gave a tug
to the elaborate bell pull. "And besides, dear, Giles
and I are bored to death with each other. We'd
much rather have you to talk to, wouldn't we,
Giles?" Now she paused and gave him a brilliant,
hard-eyed smile, holding out her glass for a refill.

"I would much rather sup alone in my office,
Eleanor," he answered, taking the glass from her.

"As you can see, I am handicapped by my accident and eating will be difficult enough as is."

"Oh, yes, your poor arm, darling. Pity the cart didn't come crashing down on your head. Then we'd have been quit of one another." She laughed merrily and accepted the full snifter he proffered. "Nevertheless, you must join us, brother. I'll cut your meat for you, like the good sister that I am. And anyway, if you're not there we'll have nothing to talk about except you, will we, Miss . . . ?" she turned to Joanna with her brittle smile. "Let's see, it's sort of a workman's name isn't it? You know, a Middle Ages sort of name when all the working people were called for their skills. . . . "

"Carpenter, Eleanor. Her name is Miss Carpenter," Giles snapped. "And perhaps she, too, would prefer eating alone to your company."

"Silly boy. She'd love to eat with us, wouldn't you, Miss Carpenter?" There was just enough of an emphasis on her last name to let Joanna know her family background had been thoroughly examined and discarded as socially worthless.

Swallowing her anger, Joanna put what she hoped was a pleasant look on her face. No, she damn well didn't want to eat with either of them, but she also knew she was trapped.

"I shall be delighted, Lady Eleanor," she said, horrified to hear herself give a slight emphasis to the "lady." She looked up as Giles approached her and was surprised to see a look of amusement flare in his eyes at her words. They were brown eyes, she noticed, and rather nice when not icy with anger. Silently, he took her glass.

"Oh, thank you, Sir Giles, but I think I've had enough sherry. I'm not really used to drinking spirits."

"How quaint, dear," Eleanor said, draining her glass. "What on earth do you do for entertainment?"

There was a light tap at the door and Mrs. Davies entered. A hint of confusion showed in the woman's face as she surveyed the group, but she quickly schooled her expression into a bland calm.

"You wished to see me, Lady Eleanor?" the housekeeper asked.

"Indeed, Mrs. Davies. Please set an extra place at the table this evening. Miss Carpenter will be supping with us. Cook can manage to give us a decent meal, I suppose?"

"I am sure we will be able to serve something satisfactory, Lady Eleanor. I shall go and see to it at once. If that will be all?" she said uncertainly then turned away when Eleanor, wandering back to the decanter, gave her an absent nod.

Joanna, standing near the door, caught a brief look from Mrs. Davies. Was it fear or sympathy? Or both?

"Would you care to change into something more suitable for supper, Miss Carpenter? I'm sure we have half an hour or so before it is served," Eleanor said casually, pouring herself a liberal portion.

Joanna could feel her face flaming. Surely the woman must know that a governess did not arrive with a wardrobe suitable for a London season.

"She looks fine as she is, Eleanor," snarled Giles. "In fact, why don't you change? You look absurd in that fancy getup."

"Oh, don't you just loathe the country, dear?" Eleanor tossed the question to Joanna. "Here we are in the middle of nowhere, and it's not even considered fashionable to dress. Of course, we also keep to the most ridiculous of country schedules. Why, in town we would just be finishing our dinner by now and supper wouldn't be for many hours yet." Eleanor stood beneath the odalisque, and Joanna had the oddest feeling that of the two, the woman on canvas was the more respectable.

"I prefer this schedule, Lady Eleanor." Joanna found herself inclined to contradict the woman and be damned to the consequences. "It's more suitable for the children."

"Ah, yes, the children," purred Eleanor. "I don't know how you can stand being around children all day long. I would go mad if I were forced to work as a governess. You will keep them quiet, won't you, dear? I can't bear their noise." Her lips were smiling but her eyes were icy. There was a cruel nonchalance about her that cut deeper than her words. No wonder the children were so frightened and silent in this house.

Joanna looked away to hide the anger she knew must show in her eyes, and encountered the amused, approving gaze of Sir Giles. His mouth quirked up on one side in the barest hint of a smile. She found herself thinking that he was rather handsome, in spite of the gash along his mouth, and she allowed just a ghost of an answering smile. It was good to feel that she had one ally, however tenuous, in this room.

"Well, I believe I will freshen up," Eleanor said, placing her glass down on a table. "Coming, Miss Carpenter?" It seemed more a command than a request. Joanna dropped a curtsey to Sir Giles and followed Lady Eleanor from the room.

Outside in the gloom of the hallway, it was as if the curtain had fallen and they were now off stage.

Eleanor said not one word to Joanna, nor, in fact, did the woman so much as glance over her shoulder to note that Joanna was behind her. Eleanor moved into the hallway on the second landing, and Joanna made her way up to the third floor, wondering what she would do with herself in the half hour before supper. She certainly had nothing better to change into, and she had done all the freshening up she cared to do before coming down! Well, perhaps she had time to make a quick sketch of Lady Eleanor from memory. There was that something about the woman's face, something sharp and a bit cruel, and the artist in Joanna just itched to see if it could be captured.

Chapter Five

Three-quarters of an hour later, after a timid tap on her door from Annie, Joanna entered the dining room and found herself alone in the grand chamber. She glanced about her and was once again overwhelmed by the sheer elegance of her surroundings. It was not as brightly lit as the drawing room had been, but she was relieved that she could see by the light of the candles in the sconces on the walls and a rather elaborate candelabrum. The room was spacious, in spite of the long, polished mahogany table that dominated the center. The table was surrounded by such a number of chairs that Joanna knew she'd have to make a surreptitious count just to satisfy her curiosity. Not even Squire's table could seat so many, not by half at least! Around the walls of the room were set several elaborate sideboards, each one exquisitely carved in dark, rich mahogany. The walls were painted in a creamy beige, broken by panels of molding in a darker color. There were several large paintings of rolling pastoral landscapes—local, perhaps, Joanna couldn't tell—and a life-sized painting of a rather scantily draped, voluptuous Venus, attended by a number of pink-bottomed cherubs, that brought a blush to Joanna's cheeks. In the corner by the door to the hallway, a tall, carved stand held a delicate, ever-so-naked winged cupid, poised on one foot as if about to lift off in flight. This recurring motif was an odd theme, she thought, for such a loveless, cold house.

Joanna moved over to stand by the sideboard where several silver chafing dishes steamed invitingly. A corner of the long dining table was set for three, she noticed.

"This is a rather grandiose room for only three of us to have our supper in, wouldn't you say, Miss Carpenter?" said a voice behind her.

Joanna turned and found Sir Giles standing in the doorway. Again, he seemed distant, staring down at her with eyes that were unreadable, and Joanna felt her heart sink. This would be a long meal, indeed, if she had two enemies to contend with. She offered him a pleasant smile and a good evening.

Giles stood quietly, reluctant to enter. He had spent the last three-quarters of an hour berating himself for giving into Eleanor's petty demand that he sup with her and the governess. He still did not know what had possessed him to agree—years ago he had learned how to sidestep his stepsister's manipulations—yet the thought of allowing young Miss Carpenter to sup alone with his harpy of a sister had made him ill at ease, enough that he had found himself accepting the loathsome invitation in spite of himself.

Now he was here with the girl. She was smiling up at him with that winsome, innocent expression he had loved so dearly in his faithless wife. He found it hard not to stare. In the last half hour he had told himself that she indeed looked nothing like Violet, that it was a mere trick of the light and the similarity in their coloring. Indeed, he had convinced himself that she had been a rather plain-looking thing, that her comely appearance had been rather a question of favorable comparison with Eleanor. But here, with no Eleanor to enrage him, and in the gentle light of the many candles, he could see that hers was a real beauty, a gift of nature and good health; it was a matter of soap and water and fresh air. Candlelight danced in her brown hair, clean and unpowdered, which she wore caught up in the back, curls escaping their pins. It framed a very nice face that showed not a trace of paint or artifice. She had a tip-tilted nose and a generous mouth, a natural, healthy shade of pink. He already knew it was a very pretty mouth when she smiled. Her eyes were large and a rich brown, but at the moment shadowed with deep apprehension. She smelled of a lightly scented soap and clean, pressed cotton, utterly fresh. And her plain dark green silk dress was simple and becomingly modest. It had been a long time since he had seen a female who looked like this. Indeed, the resemblance to Violet was a passing thing, already fading in his mind as Joanna's face replaced the one dark in his memory.

"It is a very beautiful room, Sir Giles. I am not used to such large rooms. Our vicarage was quite tiny compared to this house."

Vicarage? Oh, yes, she had said her father was a vicar. He tried to collect his thoughts.

"It's too big. Eleanor insisted that we buy the house because Mary, Queen of Scots, is supposed to have stayed here at some time during her reign. Hence, the appellation. Although, if Mary, Queen of Scots, slept everywhere she is alleged to have slept, she must not have ever slept at home. It is absurd for the two of us to live in a house this large. Although," he added, "I suppose it's really four of us now, with the children."

The doors were flung open and in sailed Lady Eleanor. If Joanna had expected the woman to tone down her attire for a simple country supper, she was much mistaken. Instead, Lady Eleanor was, if anything, even more elaborately done up than she had been earlier. She appeared to be wearing a different wig; this one had jewelry twined through it. And her bright yellow silk dress was remarkable. Joanna found her eyes traveling down a long expanse of heavily whitened chest, and she was quite sure, before she lifted her gaze in alarm, that the tops of Eleanor's nipples were peeking from the edge of the décolletage.

Joanna felt just a light touch on her arm as Giles led her to the table and pulled out her chair for her. Eleanor seated herself as he walked over to the bell pull and gave it a quick tug, then he sat himself at the head of the table.

"Pour us all some wine, brother, dear. We can't all sit around like ninnies waiting for the servants to do it. Would you care for some wine, Miss Carpenter? A little wine with meals is considered civilized behavior in higher circles."

"Yes, thank you, Lady Eleanor," Joanna answered evenly, refusing to allow the woman to bait her.

As Giles poured the chilled white wine into the heavy cut crystal glasses, the side door opened and three servants paraded in, bearing trays. Joanna was startled to see that the men wore livery. She hadn't seen anyone in livery until now and had assumed that this far out in the country things were somewhat more relaxed. Even Squire's staff only bothered with livery when there were fancy guests about.

"You know, Giles, the girl has a startling resemblance to Violet, don't you think? I think it's that pretty, pouty little mouth. And all those masses of dark hair. Tell me, dear, haven't you a decent wig to your name? Absolutely no one goes about in her own hair these days. It simply isn't done. And I must say, Violet wouldn't have been caught dead in that terribly sweet little dress. It positively screams 'governess,' dear, and its fashionable days are ancient history. What do you think, Giles? Have we another Violet on our hands? What fun that would be around this dreary old house!"

"Leave off, Eleanor," growled Giles. "Miss Carpenter is nothing at all like my late wife. And, by the way, Miss Carpenter," he said, turning toward her, his face a mask, "your attire and style are entirely suitable."

Joanna supposed he meant it kindly. Suitable for her station in life. Then why did his remark make her feel as if she were a stout forty-year-old wearing something too dowdy for words?

The only noise in the room came now from the discreet rattling of china and muffled clangs of the steaming silver serving dishes. Joanna concentrated on serving herself from the various dishes that were presented to her. Although she had met and exchanged pleasantries with all three of the servants in the room, there was not so much as a flicker of recognition from any of them as they served her. They were stiff with duty, and Joanna could hardly believe that young Bessie and Mick, whom she'd seen saucing each other so merrily in the kitchen at noon, were the same two standing at rigid attention beside the table now.

She helped herself from the new dish put in front of her. It appeared to be some sort of pureed, puffed-up green stuff. Papa's taste and their budget had inclined them toward simple fare, and she did not consider herself particularly adventurous where food was concerned. At least the poached fish looked innocuous, although it swam in some sort of questionable cream sauce, and if those were potatoes, one couldn't tell it by the looks of them.

"You'll have to forgive my stepbrother, Miss Carpenter. He has been an absolute beast since Violet died. Cannot bear to have her name mentioned. I am sure he blames himself for her death—"

"Eleanor, that will do!" Giles slammed his stemmed wineglass down so hard Joanna was surprised it did not break.

"See how sensitive he is about it, dear? We'll have to have a little heart-to-heart talk about it when he's not around to be beastly to us." Without waiting for the servants to finish serving Giles, Eleanor cut into her fish.

While Sir Giles was serving himself the fish, Joanna had a moment of near panic as she worried whether she should insult Sir Giles by not waiting for him or insult Lady Eleanor by refusing to follow her lead. It was useless. She could not remember ever having been taught such a tedious social detail. Wonderful! The governess, who was supposed to teach the children everything there was to know about manners, was about to commit an atrocious dining faux pas, within the first two minutes of sitting down to table! Maybe she should just resign the post now and save herself having to eat the green stuff.

With a start, she realized that Sir Giles had already picked up his fork and was cutting into his fish. Relieved, she, too, started on the fish. It was sublime. The dubious cream sauce was lightly flavored with tarragon, that much she could recognize, and the fish itself was fresh and moist.

The silence was broken only by the little clicks and clanks of the forks hitting the plates, but at least they were busy eating. Joanna was starving and concentrated on trying to stifle the impulse to shovel it in as fast as she could.

"How does it come that a delectable little morsel like you isn't married, Miss Carpenter?" Lady Eleanor asked, her mouth full.

Joanna sighed inwardly. She had been asked more personal questions in this last week than she had ever been asked in her whole life! At least, everyone in Little Haver had known everyone else's business, so questions had been unnecessary.

"I come from a very small town, Lady Eleanor. There really weren't any eligible young men there, and I guess I just did not think much on the subject." Joanna took a bite of the potatoes, hoping the subject was closed.

"Oh, surely there must have been some young swain straining to get at you, dear? No town is too small for that."

Lady Eleanor was toying with her. The image of Ambrose arose in her mind, and Joanna gave a slight shudder. "It was a rather poor village, Lady Eleanor. And the only eligible swain, as you put it, was Squire's son, and he was too old for me." And too stupid. And too disgusting. Joanna took another bite of the potatoes and chewed with a vengeance.

"Ah, Giles. There, you see, we have uncovered the mystery. Search out this Squire's son and I believe we will find a broken heart somewhere in the picture. Hers or his? Which will you wager on, dear brother?"

"Allow Miss Carpenter to eat unmolested, Eleanor, for God's sake. It's her business, not yours," Giles said coldly. He looked up at Joanna as he spoke and gave her a slight smile.

"Watch out, Miss Carpenter. If you let Giles select the topic of conversation, we'll be hearing about the Duke of Somebody or Other's new plans for a canal to nowhere. Fascinating conversationalist, my brother."

"Bridgewater," said Joanna, wiping her mouth with the large linen square.

"I beg your pardon?" Eleanor looked confused.

"Bridgewater, Lady Eleanor," Joanna continued, her voice mild. "The Duke of Bridgewater is building a canal from his coal pits in Worsley to Manchester. It took two acts of Parliament to authorize the work, and it's considered very innovative. Quite revolutionary, in fact. If the canal is a success, it could quite change the costs and methods of transportation. It's a very modern concept and very exciting. There's been a good bit about it in the papers." Joanna finished and looked back down at her plate, a flush creeping up her neck. She had not meant to go on like that, but the woman had annoyed her so about Ambrose and she seemed so ignorant about things that really mattered in the world. Joanna stole a glance at Sir Giles and was startled to find him smiling broadly at her.

"How utterly . . . stupefying, Miss Carpenter," said Lady Eleanor, her voice brittle. "I see I am to be surrounded by the studious types. You and Giles may get along well together after all, if you enjoy his scientific pursuits. Why, his precious knighthood was conferred for just that sort of tedious detail, improving the drainage. The king thought he'd helped to eliminate typhus because of it. But for the life of me, I cannot see what is so wonderful about that. Poor people need to die of something, and the sooner the better, as far as I'm concerned."

"Why, that's wonderful, Sir Giles," Joanna said, deliberately ignoring Lady Eleanor's ignoble sentiment. "I see you have actually found a way to put your mathematics to practical use."

"The drainage improvements were only a small part of it, Miss Carpenter," Giles replied. "A number of people were responsible for the improvements, paving and lighting, that sort of thing. But all these things together have improved overall health in cities and larger towns."

"Well, you can bore each other to death if you want to," said Eleanor, throwing down her napkin, "but I've had all I can bear to eat of this swill, so if you'll excuse me, I'll go roust out Hawton for a game of cards. Giles, I'll leave you to the little bluestocking and you can talk about sewer drainage to your heart's content." Without so much as a nod in Joanna's direction, Eleanor drained her glass and swept out of the room.

"Well done, Miss Carpenter," said Giles as the door closed behind Eleanor. "I don't know when I have so enjoyed my stepsister's company. I would apologize for her rudeness, but I've the distinct impression that you can hold your own with her."

"I am sure she is just tired from her traveling, Sir Giles," Joanna remarked blandly. She couldn't very well say that Lady Eleanor was without a doubt the nastiest woman she had ever met in her life! "And I'm sure our paths will scarcely cross," she added. She looked back down at her plate. It was odd. She had been relieved when Lady Eleanor had left the room, but now she felt awkward. She took another bite of the fish, willing herself to think of something intelligent to say.

Giles, too, cast about for some pleasant topic, aware that the girl would not feel comfortable initiating a conversation. Drat it, anyway. It had been a long time since he'd had a sociable meal with a lady. God only knew when he had last shared a table with Eleanor or any of her guests. His meals at Dufton were almost all taken at local pubs and inns with his foreman and crew, and polite conversation was never a problem.

"You have a good appetite, Miss Carpenter," he finally ventured, then cursed himself as an expression of consternation crossed her face. "No, no, please," he continued as she put down her fork. "I think it's healthy to have a good appetite. Most of the ladies I know never eat anything . . ." he trailed off miserably. What on earth had possessed him to inflict himself on this nice young woman? He bent his head back to the fish. His shoulder hurt like the devil, and he wished he were back in Dufton on his third pint of ale with his foreman.

Joanna picked up her fork again, feeling like a perfect fool. Her voracious appetite had always made her father and Squire laugh about her "unladylike ways." Anyway, by what rules of etiquette she could scare up out of her brain, it was her turn to say something now, embarrassed or not.

"I'm afraid I've never been very ladylike in my portions, Sir Giles. Papa always said I'd wind up as big as a house . . ." She bit her lip in confusion. What a stupid thing to say! Oh, how she wished she were eating alone in the governess's parlor.

"Well, I don't know where it goes then, Miss Carpenter, because there is certainly not an ounce of fat on you . . ." He stopped suddenly. That did it. Now she'd think he was ogling her. He couldn't remember when he'd last felt so awkward and uncomfortable. He eyed the green dish with trepidation, wondering what on earth it was. It was the last thing left on his plate except for a bit of fish, although of course he could ring for the servants to offer them second helpings. What a lot of stupid bother this business of formal dining was, anyway. The servants were running about looking like little tin soldiers, even though he hadn't ordered them to put on that ridiculous braided and bedecked livery that Eleanor set such store by. In fact, this whole meal was absurd, so stiff and fancy he could hardly enjoy the food. He made a mental note to himself to tell Mrs. Davies to dispense with these idiotic formalities whenever he was here, then reminded himself that he was rarely here at all. While he was at it, he'd consult with her on the menu as well. Oh, for a bowl of pub stew right now, he thought to himself morosely, as he stabbed his fork into the green pile on his plate.

"I think it's because I walk a great deal, Sir Giles," Joanna said gamely, her fork, poised over the green stuff. This conversation was a nightmare, and it was all her fault. All well-bred young ladies were expected to know how to lead a lively repartee around pleasant topics. How much she ate and how fat she got did not pass for tasteful table talk. Perhaps she should just move right on to the topic of her digestion and be done with it. She took a tentative bite of the green stuff.

"What is this stuff anyway?" Sir Giles exploded, setting down his fork and grabbing his wineglass, taking in the expensive wine in great gulps. Venturing a look at her over his glass, he noticed she was chewing with a rather desperate look in her eye. A big grin, one-sided to be sure, spread slowly over his face as he watched her efforts, then he started to laugh. Joanna grabbed her napkin and clapped it over her mouth.

"Don't make me laugh, sir. I've got an absolute mouthful of the stuff," she begged, her eyes watering over the tip of the napkin.

He went on laughing, a rich bellow that seemed to fill the room. "You should see your face right now, Miss Carpenter. Are you going to swallow it or not?"

In response, Joanna took a deep breath, then like a child with a mouth full of cod liver oil she gulped. "There," she said primly, patting her mouth, then, meeting his eyes again, she burst out laughing. "I don't know what it is," she said, gasping. "I've never had anything like it in my life."

He picked up his fork and poked at the malevolent mass on his plate. "It looks like a vegetable, I suppose. All mushed up," he said, his tone dubious.

"And baked. I think it's a soufflé. But I don't know what kind," she responded, poking at her own dish thoughtfully. "It's got too much of something, or maybe not enough of something else. I don't really know much about cooking," she finished lamely. She looked up at him and caught the laughter still in his eyes. Odd, up close and when he wasn't scowling at her, he was rather handsome, with his dark hair and dark brown eyes. And the scar didn't seem so noticeable when his generous mouth was quirked in amusement as it was now.

"Perhaps some more fish will sate your prodigious appetite, Miss Carpenter. Shall we?" he asked, standing and taking his plate to the sideboard.

Joanna stood, relieved that he had not rung for the parade of tin soldiers. She helped herself to what she hoped were modest portions of the fish and potatoes.

"I am impressed with your knowledge about Bridgewater's canal, Miss Carpenter," Giles remarked, seating her again. "Not too many people have followed the matter this far north."

Joanna colored at the unexpected praise. "In Little Haver, there is not so much to do, Sir Giles," she replied. "One must read the papers for sheer entertainment."

They ate in companionable silence. Joanna longed to help herself to a third helping but did not dare.

"May I tempt you with a sweet for dessert, Miss

Carpenter?" Giles asked, setting down his fork. "That is, if we can be certain it's edible," he finished, frowning again at the unappetizing green mound congealed on his plate. "I don't really know this cook and I wouldn't want to hurt her feelings, but I don't care to see this dish on my table ever again." He picked up the wine bottle and poured more wine into each glass, then rang the small silver bell by his plate.

Immediately the door swung open and in marched the liveried small army. Both Joanna and Giles waved away the offer of third helpings, and couldn't help stealing a glance at each other as Mick cleared the offending dish from the sideboard. Bessie wheeled in a small cart which contained a teapot, a coffee pot, and several rather spectacular-looking pastries. Smiling happily at the cart, Joanna was unaware that she had sighed in relief until she heard what sounded like a stifled snort from Sir Giles. Meeting his eyes again was a mistake. She had to grab her napkin and clap it over her mouth as if smothering a cough, while he stared at her, eyes dancing with mischief, willing her to laugh out loud.

"How could you?" she protested as soon as the door closed behind the servants. "A governess should maintain some semblance of dignity before the staff."

"Sorry," he replied smoothly. "But you were looking at the pastries with such adoration in your eyes. Now," he said, turning his eye on the cart, "coffee or tea? You'll have to pour, I'm afraid, because I'll make a mess of it one-handed." He realized with a start that he had barely thought about his shoulder since entering the room, nor had he felt more than a twinge. "I'll take coffee, thank you," he said as Joanna reached toward the pots and gave him a questioning glance. "And help yourself to three or four tarts. You can tuck one up in your napkin for later if you like."

"Just one tart will do, thank you," she answered, pouring them each a cup of the rich, steaming black coffee. "Anyway, I can come down and steal one if I get hungry in the middle of the night."

"So much for the security of my larder," he remarked, taking a sip. "I shall have to check with Mrs. Davies and see whether our food expenses go up measurably during your tenure with us."

Joanna served them each a tart and they settled down to the comforting business of dessert. The sweet was absolutely delicious, she was relieved to find, with no unpleasant surprises.

"This makes up for the green thing, doesn't it?" he asked between bites, and Joanna murmured her assent with mouth full.

"If you like walking, I should think you'd enjoy the countryside around here. It's really quite beautiful," he ventured, unwilling to let the camaraderie disappear with the soufflé.

"Indeed, yes. What little I've seen is just spectacular. I do hope to do a great deal of walking, and some painting as well."

"Ah, yes, you paint," he answered. "What sort of painting?"

"Watercolor, mostly. I enjoy doing landscapes. And whatever direction I look here, I see something beautiful that I want to paint."

The light from many candles sparkled deep in her brown eyes. There was such a freshness, an innocence to her that it almost took his breath away. There was no hint of Violet anywhere about her face. How could he have thought there was?

Eleanor and her lady friends were so jaded, so stale and brittle, he had almost forgotten that there were guileless, unspoiled creatures among the fairer sex.

"I would like to see your paintings. Did you bring any with you?"

"Just one that I did of the vicarage. I had to leave the others behind." The sparkling light in her eyes dimmed a bit.

"Are you missing your home?" he asked gently, aware that he must tread lightly.

Joanna didn't answer at once. A large lump had risen in her throat at the thought of Papa and the vicarage. Home. It wasn't home anymore, yet it would never stop being the only home she really knew. Ahead of her, for the rest of her life, lay a series of posts, children to care for, but no home of her own. She reached for her coffee to cover the surge of sorrow that threatened her composure. She supposed it was the wine and the fact that he was being kind that made her feel so suddenly weepy. She took a deep breath, determined not to disgrace herself just as they had managed to get off to a good start.

"Never mind. I'm sorry," Giles interposed quickly, seeing the little twist to her mouth and the shadow in her eyes as she fought for composure. I am such a lumbering ox, he thought to himself. Things were going so well and now I've made her sad.

"I will be here for a few days of forced convalescence, Miss Carpenter. Perhaps we could talk further after you've had more of a chance to observe the children." He finished the last of his coffee, feeling awkward.

He wanted to talk about the children? She

101

looked up and gave him a shy smile. Maybe she could interest him in their welfare. He no longer seemed like the cruel, cold man she had built up in her mind. Perhaps he could care enough to help her create an atmosphere of love and trust so that the little ones could grow and prosper. If she could do nothing else in this post, perhaps she could engender a little love between uncle and niece and nephew.

"That would be wonderful, Sir Giles. I'm sure I'll be able to give you a good report in a few days. They are lovely children. They just need . . ." She trailed off, aware that she was once again about to insult his guardianship.

"Please give them whatever they need, Miss Carpenter," he said, smiling. He rose and offered her his good arm and they made their way from the room. In the dark of the hallway they stood for the space of an awkward heartbeat.

"Well, good night, Sir Giles. Thank you for a pleasant evening," Joanna murmured.

"Parts of it, anyway," he answered with a smile.

With a slight curtsey, she turned and made her way up the stairs.

Gaining the sanctuary of her room, she sank again into the comfortable wing chair and stared at the quick sketch she had made of Lady Eleanor before going down to supper. The sketch was quite unlike her usual style. Indeed, had she not just done it herself, she would not have taken it for her own work. It was dark and cold, with a great deal of cruelty shadowed in the face.

Lady Eleanor was a monster, there was no doubt of it. There was just that something in the woman's tone and in her look, something suggestive and malevolent, something that made Joanna uneasy and uncertain. But with luck she and the children could stay out of the woman's way. Sir Giles, however . . . she found herself thinking of his brown eyes, the warm ones, not the icy ones. For some inexplicable reason she wanted to cry, but she fought down the urge. She was tired, after all, and it had been a difficult few weeks, to say the least. Surely things would seem better in the morning.

Shivering, she roused herself and made for the bowl of warmish water that sat on the washstand. At least she had the children to look forward to tomorrow. Although, if Lady Eleanor was planning to remain at home, it had better be a nice enough day to spend outside, away from the house. As Joanna raised a soaped cloth to her face, she began to plan a lovely day out of doors. They could study nature and they could do some drawing, and the sort of messy, splashy painting that children so love. Perhaps it would be wise to take a picnic and stay out all day. Finished with her ablutions, Joanna pulled the soft, well-worn nightgown over her head. She sank to her knees for her nightly chat with God . . . or was it Papa?

Chapter Six

Giles strode into his office in a foul temper. His shoulder was paining him to madness. He had slept little, finding no position even remotely comfortable, and no respite from the steady, throbbing pain. Last evening with Eleanor had not helped matters. He had retired to the library to read after supper and she had found him there. Her needling and carping about money he had long since learned to ignore, giving her extra allowance just to shut her up. But last night she had switched topics and hit a raw nerve. Didn't Miss Carpenter have a naughty look in her eye, just like Violet? And that sweet little face. Just like Violet. Why, Eleanor wouldn't be at all surprised if Giles fell madly in love with the charming little governess. Just like Violet . . .

She had jabbed and taunted and told ribald stories about the antics of her debauched crowd. She did it deliberately, knowing he disapproved of her friends, knowing that he was embarrassed by her excesses and her proclivities. Finally, he'd slammed his book shut in disgust and bid her a curt good night, leaving her laughing a little too loudly, yet another brandy in her hand. Sometimes he wondered if she were quite sane.

This morning the room was dark with the gloom pervasive and peculiar to this blighted home. With a snarl he pulled back the draperies, wincing at the pain that ripped through his arm at the sudden movement. He shut his eyes against the brilliant light glinting off the sea, then opened them to take in the magnificent view. Gulls wheeled overhead and he could hear their insistent, piercing cries faintly through the heavy leaded-glass panes. He spotted a figure, wavering in the glass, standing on the bluff that overlooked the small beach below. Surprised, he opened the casement and leaned out.

It was the pretty little governess, Miss Carpenter, standing at an easel working at what appeared to be a painting. The wind seemed to be playing havoc with her bonnet. As he watched, he heard a shriek of laughter, then a head of blond curls appeared over the rise, followed by another child at top speed.

"Miss Carpenter! Tom's got something nasty. Do take it from him!" came the girl's voice, carrying in the breeze.

Indeed, the boy held out in front of him something clawed and wiggly as he chased his sister, gaining with every step.

"Oh, no you don't, my little man," Giles heard Joanna say as she halted Tom's progress. Rather gingerly she pried the offensive object from the boy's hand and with a wry face bent down and turned it loose.

"Let's send him home to his children, Tom. He'll be much happier down on the beach, don't you think?" She held Tom's hand while they watched the thing scuttle away. Emma seemed to make sure it was well gone before she returned to the fold.

"Race me back down to the beach, Tom," Emma shouted, then took off as fast as her little legs could take her. Giles watched as the boy scurried after her, noting with surprise that the boy seemed to understand what had been said to him. Perhaps there was some hope, after all. Perhaps he should give some attention to the boy. It was not unheard of, after all, for these poor idiots to have more sense than the world gave them credit for. He closed the window and turned away. Suddenly the room seemed cramped and airless. . . .

Outside, Joanna watched fondly as the children tore down the path that led to the beach. They had no shoes on, and although she had insisted that they wear their least fancy outfits, they were much too well-dressed for beachcombing. If she was allowed to stay in this post, she would insist on having some real playclothes made. It was preposterous to dress up children like tiny adults all the time.

The gentle waves rolled to shore. The sound was soothing and the smell of the sea spray was exhilarating. She would never stop missing Little Haver, but there was something wonderful about the magnificent sea, a sight she had never thought to see in her life. She looked up from her easel and feasted her eyes on the rolling surf that pounded against the rocky sand of the little beach below her, bright in the late winter sun. It was a mild day. The breeze was brisk but not chill, and it held the luring promise of spring soon to come. She heard the children squeal again with laughter. They must have found another poor, helpless beach creature, scrambling and stranded and at their mercy.

Joanna looked back at her canvas and grinned in satisfaction. Perhaps it was the glory of the seascape spread out before her, or perhaps it was the lovely innocence of two small children frolicking on the sand, but whatever it was, she was rather certain she had never painted anything better. The colors were right, soft but sure, reflecting the muted blue of the water and the brilliance of the sky. And the two little sketched-in figures, bent over with heads close together, spoke of such joy it was hard to believe they were the same two sad little ones she had just met a few days ago.

"You didn't tell me you were such a fine painter, Miss Carpenter," said a low voice behind her.

Whirling, she found herself staring into the brown eyes of Sir Giles.

"Oh, you startled me, sir. I had thought we were quite alone." Joanna flushed, then looked quickly up at him. "Did we disturb you and Lady Eleanor, sir? We came out here this morning so that we wouldn't make a racket, but I suppose the sound could carry up from the beach." She stopped in confusion, realizing that there was no sign of annoyance in his eyes.

"Actually, you did disturb me, Miss Carpenter. I kept looking out of my window and seeing you all having such fun, and it was such a startling sight that I thought I had better investigate." He smiled at her. Her hair was windblown, escaping naughtily from the adorable, almost girlish bonnet, utterly unstylish and all the more fetching for it. Her cheeks were a bright pink—from the wind, not from a rouge pot, he would bet his life on it. Her lovely brown eyes sparkled in the noonday sun. And intermingled with the mist of the salt spray he could catch a hint of a clean, fresh scent, a bit of lilac perhaps.

"I must apologize again for my stepsister's—demeanor last night, Miss Carpenter. She is—rather unrestrained. I am sure that, as a vicar's daughter, you are not used to this sort of thing." He looked uncomfortable. Joanna took pity on him.

"Oh, to the contrary, Sir Giles. Little Haver, village that it is, has a rich variety of inhabitants. I hope you won't judge me too provincial." She had to stop short of adding the required observation that Lady Eleanor had been utterly charming last night. Social convention be hanged, the man was not a perfect idiot.

"Provincial? Now that you mention it, Miss Carpenter, I am hardly in a position to judge you provincial. Not when you consider how remote we are here." His eyes found the sea, and Joanna could see a certain pleasure in their depths at the sight.

"I think this area is one of the most beautiful I have ever seen, Sir Giles. Well, that is"—she halted in some confusion, then plunged on—"of course, I've been nowhere else in my life, unless you count those dreadful coach rides to and from London. But you can't really, because I was pressed in between so many people and the windows were mostly shuttered, so I could see nothing at all." Oh, Lord, she was nattering on at him like a fool. So much for convincing him she was not a provincial ninny.

Giles watched as the flush spread across her cheeks. Now he could see that she wasn't merely pretty. She was quite obviously beautiful. And there was no artifice about her—no white lead, no kohl, no rouge—not even any of the brittle, brilliant chatter that passed for conversation among his stepsister's jaded set. He felt a certain stirring of warmth within him, pleasurable, but disconcerting too.

"I am glad you find it beautiful, Miss Carpenter. I may be prejudiced but I have seen a great deal of England and I still think we are quite exquisite here." He paused, then added, almost as an afterthought, "Do the children nap in midafternoon? Would you like to ride out into the fells? I have several horses that might suit you."

"Well," she hesitated. She wasn't much of a horsewoman, to be sure; indeed, she had never met a horse that showed her anything but contempt, but the chance of getting out into the countryside was not to be missed. It seemed she had been cooped up, one way or another, since she had first stepped into the coach for London. "I would really like that, Sir Giles, but I must confess I am not a good rider. Papa did not keep stables, you see, and so my experience is limited," she finished, hoping he would accept her limitations and not withdraw the invitation.

"I have one particular horse that will suit you, I think. And she could use some exercise. She's a fat, lazy thing and wouldn't bolt on you even if she stepped on a hive of bees."

"But can you ride with your shoulder all bandaged up? I imagine you cannot use that arm terribly well."

Giles was bemused. He hadn't given his shoul-

109

der a thought since he came outside. Now that she mentioned it, it did still hurt, but it was a distant, bearable pain, something he could ignore if he was otherwise occupied. "I can ride my horse with one arm," he said. "But you must promise not to take off at a dead run and make me chase you."

"You wouldn't have far to chase, sir, because I would fall right off," she said, smiling. She turned back to her painting and began to pack up her supplies.

"I see you have had a picnic," he said, eyeing the basket. "Dare I ask if the cook packed any of that—ah, interesting dish we were served last night?"

Joanna laughed. "I was afraid she might have, so I asked Mrs. Davies about it this morning. Apparently there was a serious revolt at the servants' table last night over that dish. It seems that Cook is of the 'waste not, want not' discipline, and when we wouldn't eat it, she served it to the staff. There was quite a scene. She's new, by the way, and Mrs. Davies allowed as how she had come from a rather frugal establishment. It seems the dish was made from the tops of all sorts of vegetables, cut up together, the kinds of greens one normally associates with fodder. Anyway, Cook went off to bed in a sniff and the green dish went out in the back for the dogs, and, according to Mick, the dogs have been trying to scratch dirt over it ever since."

Giles let out a great guffaw at her speech, and she laughed with him, glad that the companionability of the night before had not been her imagination.

"I must compliment you again on your work, Miss Carpenter. That is an extraordinarily fine painting. Please feel free to have Hawton order whatever supplies you need from Penrith."

"Thank you, Sir Giles. Actually, there are a few things I would like to order for the children, paint and sketch paper and some books, if it is permissible?" She looked up at him with a smile, eyes crinkling against the sun.

"Anything at all. I will leave word with Hawton. You won't find Penrith terribly well stocked—it's a small town, after all, but I'm sure we can acquire what you need."

Joanna went on with her packing up. She was oddly pleased that he had praised her artwork. And with the prospect of a ride with Sir Giles out into the fells before her, she found her heart tripping rather oddly. Too much of being cooped up and brooding in that dark house, she thought, giving herself a mental shake.

"What time do the children nap?" he asked.

"In just a few minutes, sir. Shall I come to the stables when I get them settled?"

"Yes, and bring a cloak. The wind can be fierce in the fells even on a mild day."

There was a shriek from Emma and another chase was on. This time it was Giles who caught the boy in mid-stride and pried the offending beastie from his hands. Their laughter echoed in the wind.

Eleanor stood in the long window of her sitting room, holding back the heavy brocade drapery. The bright sun struck at her face like slivers of flying glass. Her mouth was a thin vermilion slit and her darkened eyes glittered with anger as they swept the seascape that lay before her. There they were. Just like last night. He was obviously sniffing around the simpering little bitch, and Eleanor was surprised how much it vexed her. She'd never given a damn whom Giles took to his bed. Once or twice she'd even obliquely tried to forward a dalliance between Giles and one of her smitten friends, but he'd brushed off all such suggestions and innuendos with scorn and anger, and she'd given up caring where or if he sought his pleasure.

But this girl . . . there was something unsettling about this idyllic picture . . . something about the girl herself that made Eleanor feel uneasy.

The light was hurting her eyes. She let the drapery fall back into place, and the room darkened to its usual state. Anger stabbed again through her. That was what was bothering her—the light. Last night she had come home to find the house blazing away like a royal ballroom, with her stepbrother and that little porcelain doll, pretty as a picture, dimpling and smiling at him. And now today, outside in the bright of the sun, there she was again, smiling up at him with her young, perfect face.

In the light.

Eleanor hadn't let anyone but her maid see her in the light of day for years, or without her face paint, for that matter. But she would lay any odds that little Miss Carpenter wore no face paint and had no reason to hide from the light.

Years ago Eleanor had had a face like that. She had taken London by storm during her Season, had any number of young men swarming around her. But her antics had gotten her quickly into trouble; she had been indiscreet. And the faster the tongues wagged, the fewer grew the number of marriage prospects, until finally there had been no offer at all and Eleanor had finished the Season in disgrace, her mother angry and waspish, her father, as usual, too lost in his drink and cards to care. Then, three years later, came the final insult with her newly widowed mother's rather desperate remarriage, and Eleanor had been packed away to this godforsaken country to molder ever since. And Giles would not even keep a London townhouse. He had no use for London, so he said, but Eleanor rather thought it was just to spite her.

Thank God she'd found a number of London acquaintances who were willing to forgo town from time to time for long jaunts in the country. She did not delude herself as to why, either. It had not escaped her notice that her crowd belonged to the fringe of the ton. Oh, they had credentials of sorts, distant, tenuous, vague connections, but few of them had any real money; enough to gamble for a living, perhaps, but not enough to keep up their own toney households. On the social fringe, they drifted from houseparty to houseparty, their malicious wits and gaming purses enough to give them continuing entree to the lesser houses. And Eleanor, trapped here beyond nowhere, was the glittering jewel in the diadem, the honest-to-God earl's daughter, with a fancy house and a great deal more money than most could ever hope to see. They cut a swath throughout England, this crowd, traveling in one big party from house to house, from card game to card game, from bed to bed. It was all very amusing.

And she'd give it all to have a face like that again.

There was a soft knock at the door, then it opened and shut again quickly with a quiet whisk.

"You wished to see me, my lady?" Hawton asked in stilted tones. It galled him that in spite of their intimacies she insisted upon the haughty formalities of title and distance even when they were alone. She could grind over him like a two-shilling whore at night, then demand all the "my lady's" due her the next morning. And he had learned immediately never to initiate intimacy with her, nor even voice an endearment, outside of the crudities he was free to utter in bed. He was her stud and nothing more, and whatever pleasure he had once taken in futtering the high-and-mighty Sir Giles Chapman's stepsister right under his roof, had long since faded under the man's obvious indifference.

"I wished to see you last night, Hawton. You gave me a peremptory summons, as if I were your chambermaid, then you were nowhere to be found." Eleanor's tone was icy and her eyes were no warmer. She was not in good form this afternoon, he noted. She had barely repaired last night's makeup; it was still somewhat smudged from her pillow, and she had not yet bothered to don her wig. Her hair hung lank and greasy, pinned in a desultory fashion upon her head. There were dark circles under her eyes and tight lines around her too red mouth. She was angry, and he'd have to soothe her. But he'd known this would happen when he'd panicked and sent for her yesterday, and he was ready with a truthful answer.

"I was in my cottage last night, my lady. When Sir Giles arrived unexpectedly, he was in a beast of a temper and he demanded to see the books. Fortunately, he got sidetracked and I had all evening to fix them up." He finished, expecting to hear her relief that he had saved her petty thievery from discovery. He was wrong.

"What do you mean, sidetracked?" she asked sharply.

"I beg your pardon, Lady Eleanor?" Hawton asked, confused.

"You just said Giles got sidetracked, man," she snapped. "What do you mean?"

Clearly at a loss as to why they were off on this tangent when discovery threatened, Hawton took a deep breath and willed himself not to snap back. "I meant that he visited with the new governess, madame, and I've seen nothing of him since."

Eleanor muttered an unladylike curse and threw herself into the large upholstered chair a few steps away.

"Tell me about this governess you've hired, Hawton. I've met her, and I'm not at all sure she will do." She glared up at him, an imperious, cold look on her tight face.

Now Hawton was truly at sea. Since when did this woman give a damn who or what the governess was? He stood, still at ramrod attention, trying to figure out what to say.

"I met her the first morning, my lady, and again at the end of that day. She is quiet, unprepossessing. Rather timid, actually. I don't think she'll give any trouble. Wasn't horrified about the boy, apparently . . ." He trailed off, watching the scowl deepen on her face. He could see the cracks in the paint even in this dim light.

"Look out the window there, Hawton, and tell me what you see." Eleanor gestured peremptorily toward the draperies. Not for the world would she stand up and walk over to the light with him. She slouched down in the chair, facing away from the window.

Hawton walked to the window in some alarm.

115

He had no idea what was going on inside the woman's head. Clearly she was agitated and angry, but he could not fathom why. He pulled back one of the draperies and peered out into the brightness. It took some time for his eyes to adjust. At first he could make out what seemed to be black specks against the light, then these resolved themselves into figures. His vision at a distance was not terribly good, but he was too vain to get spectacles, so he squinted as tightly as he could to get a clearer picture. Yes, now he could see, and he drew in an audible breath. The sight was rather remarkable, given the climate in this house since he'd lived here. There were Sir Giles and Miss Carpenter standing rather cozily together while the children danced around them. They were all laughing. As he watched, Miss Carpenter's bonnet, dislodged apparently by a sudden gust, blew off her head. Sir Giles made a lunge and retrieved it. There was something in the way he looked at her as he handed it back, something that spoke of joy.

Quickly, Hawton lowered the curtain and turned back to Lady Eleanor. The contrast struck him now in full force, and he wondered that he had not seen it before. In all his months here he had never seen Sir Giles and Lady Eleanor exchange a pleasantry, not even a meaningless good morning. The atmosphere in this house when the two of them were here together was thick enough to cut with a knife. After a while he had ceased to notice it, since the master and mistress's disaffection with each other suited his needs just fine. But here was the man cavorting like a schoolboy with the fresh-faced and innocent Miss Carpenter while his aging jade of a stepsister

116

snarled and spat within her darkened chamber, ignored and alone.

"Well?" she snapped at him, breaking into his thoughts.

"It would appear Sir Giles has developed some sort of affection for the children, my lady," he ventured, deliberately misstating his actual conclusions. Odd, how old she looked this afternoon. Eleanor was a handsome woman, no doubt, but now he was more conscious that hers was the memory of beauty, rather than the beauty itself. No wonder she was feeling so threatened. And well she should. Miss Carpenter was as delectable a virgin morsel as he had come upon in some time, and he had rather hoped to be the first one across that threshold. Now he wondered whether the stuffy, over-principled Sir Giles had stolen a march on him.

"You know perfectly well it has nothing to do with those sniveling brats. It's that girl. What do you know of her?" There was something in Eleanor's voice that he had not heard before from her. Her tone was usually so haughty, so self-assured, so dominant. Now there was an edge of desperation. He could see it in her eyes—the fear that she was losing a war.

Suddenly he felt more buoyant than he had felt in a long time. Perhaps here was the opportunity he had despaired of—the chance to make Lady Eleanor dependent on him. Never before, in all his dealings with women, had he been forced to adopt the subservient role he was forced to play with Eleanor. It did not sit well with him. His women had always been his to control. He enjoyed his dominant role, and it had chafed beyond measure to have this sneering woman take her pleasure from him, then dismiss him as the servant he was. Now, perhaps . . .

"If you think there is something between Sir Giles and that whey-faced chit, Lady Eleanor, I can only assume you are mistaken, or that the man has lost his mind." The smell of control made him daring. Never before had he spoken with such familiarity to her, outside of the mutterings in bed. He waited and watched her. He was rewarded with the slight look of confusion that crossed her face. Now, if she lashed out at him for daring to contradict her, he had misread the situation, but if she . . .

"What do you mean, whey-faced?" Eleanor asked uncertainly. "I thought she was rather pretty last night."

You are mine now, you bitch! he crowed to himself. Allowing his eyes to linger warmly on her form, he hesitated a moment, as if mustering the audacity to speak.

"My lady, the girl is drab and plain. She is a parson's daughter. She reads Latin. She stammers when she is uncertain of herself. I checked my office floor for a puddle after she left, she was so nervous." It was working. Eleanor curled her feet up cozily in the chair and gave a little giggle at his words.

"And although I overstep myself, Lady Eleanor, I must tell you that you would be more beautiful than she if you went out and covered yourself in mud." He paused. So far, so good. She was smiling up at him. Now for the kill. He put out his hand, slowly, as if hesitant. Gently he traced a line down her whitened cheek. He could feel the coarseness of the dried and cracked paint.

"And more desirable," he whispered softly. He let his eyes smolder at her. "If Sir Giles is poking around at that pale, puny puss, it's because he's frightened of a real woman . . . like you." His hand tightened around her chin. Sharply, he twisted her face up to his. He licked his lips slowly. Her eyes were hot now and half-lidded, riveted on his. She raised her arms and locked them around his neck, pulling him down. Their lips touched and he plunged his tongue deep into her mouth, probing hot and hard. She moaned as he slid his hand into her dressing gown and fondled her breast. He wrenched his mouth from hers and slid his lips down her throat. The powder tasted awful, flaking into his mouth, and he resisted the urge to pull away and spit.

"Hard, you're so hard, Hawton," she moaned, fumbling at his crotch. Indeed, he was. Like a rock. It felt good, having this arrogant bitch at his mercy. Now she needed him, and he would see to it that she continued to need him.

She was twisting at the fastenings on his breeches and as she pulled them open, his swollen shaft thrust out. She grabbed him in her hand and began to rub him up and down, fast and hard. Feeling his control slipping away, he pulled her dressing gown apart at her waist and slid his hand between her legs, probing her sheath with his fingers. She was slick and ready for him. Pushing her legs apart, he mounted her swiftly, jabbing deep and hard.

She moaned deep in her throat and began to match his rhythm, slowly at first, then faster and faster as he thrust at her again and again.

The feeling of power was exhilarating. She was putty in his hands. He would make her grovel, as she had made him crawl all these months. With a cry, he slumped forward, shooting his seed hard into her, not noticing that she cried out herself and shuddered against him.

All was silence for a moment except for their panting, jagged breathing. Hawton didn't move, afraid to say anything, afraid to break the spell and find himself the servant once more. At last he felt her shift beneath him and he pulled away. He looked at her, reading her eyes. Yes, it was still there, the raw need, not physical—no, it was more subtle than that and more basic. He smiled slowly into her eyes and she smiled back, but now her smile was hesitant, uncertain; there was none of the hauteur about her that had characterized all of their previous couplings, when he had performed for her like a trained horse. This time she had serviced him, and from now on it would stay that way.

Lazily, he got to his feet and cleaned himself with his handkerchief. Eleanor was rearranging her dressing gown, covering herself.

"I've managed to cover over the tracks of our little financial indiscretions with some interesting bookkeeping techniques," he said, deliberately leaving out the "my lady." "I don't think Sir Giles will be any the wiser, unless he wishes to probe much more deeply into the household purchasing accounts." As he spoke he was refastening his breeches. It was gratifying to see that she had not taken her eyes off his crotch while he had worked at it. "But I think we'll need to figure out something safer for the future. It was unwise to trust to Sir Giles's utter disinterest in the household." He had brought up the subject of Giles's unexplained renewed concern on purpose, to put her insecurities back into her thoughts. It worked. Eleanor looked up at him, alarm in her eyes.

"What shall we do, Hawton? I lost again this week, rather heavily, I'm afraid. I'd counted on getting enough from you to cover my losses." She was breathless, afraid, and she needed him to solve the problem for her. This was a new Lady Eleanor, all right, and he was enjoying it.

"Well, don't worry your beautiful head about it, my dear," he said softly, tracing a finger down her cheek." They had graduated from "my lady" to "my dear," and he didn't think she'd even noticed his temerity. "I will solve the problem. Leave everything to me. And as far as our little governess is concerned, she cannot hold a candle to you, so put her out of your thoughts entirely." He gave her a chuck on the chin, then turned abruptly and strode from the room. Once outside in the hallway, he allowed a huge grin to spread across his face, but it wasn't until he was sure he was out of earshot that he started laughing out loud.

Giles stood in the entrance to the stables and watched the young woman hurrying toward him. He could see that she seemed a bit anxious.

"I am so sorry, Sir Giles," she exclaimed breathlessly, stopping before him. "I know I have kept you waiting but I wanted to make sure the children were properly settled before I left."

"Indeed, you have not kept me waiting. The horses are only being saddled now, Miss Carpenter." He eyed her dress with some misgiving, noting that it was a modest, serviceable cotton gown.

"I should have realized you would have no riding habit, Miss Carpenter, since you rarely ride. I'd hate for you to spoil your gown." She flushed at his words and he cursed himself. He should have stopped to think it would embarrass her for him to comment on her meager wardrobe. Indeed, looking at her, he noted that the dark blue gown, though simple, was clean, well pressed, and closed tightly at the throat with a white, pretty lace collar. It was so different from anything he had ever seen on Eleanor or Violet.

"Never mind," he said quickly to cover her discomfort. "It won't be a hard ride, and Angel hasn't worked herself into a lather since she was a filly." He took her arm and gently led her into the stable. If she was nervous about the horse, it would do well to show her what a docile mount she would be riding. Angel was worse than docile. Most of her unfortunate riders swore that she snoozed while she walked.

Joanna's arm felt warm beneath his fingers, and he thought he detected a hint of a tremble. Was it the horse she was afraid of or himself? They stopped before a small, wide mare who was being saddled by Jims, the ancient stablemaster.

"There, Miss Carpenter. Behold your steed."

The horse turned a baleful eye in their direction. One could almost see the indignation in the brown depths. Angel loved nothing so much as to get her nose into her feedbag, and nothing so little as whatever exercise was forced upon her.

Joanna returned the glare. Ever since she had agreed to go on this excursion, she had been growing more and more apprehensive about it. It had been so long since she'd been on a horse, she'd forgotten how little she cared for it. Big, smelly things who didn't care a whit for what she wanted them to do. Never mind all that nonsense about a firm grip on the reins and an infinitesimal tug this way or that to communicate one's innermost wishes to one's valiant steed. Hah! Every horse she'd ever ridden had been quick to establish control over her. The last time she'd ventured forth on one of Squire's allegedly "docile" creatures, the dratted thing had nearly knocked her head off on a branch going at a dead run back to the stables, in spite of the fact that the rest of the party was nowhere near completing the outing. This Angel had that same look in her eye. Angel didn't like her. Angel was not going to cooperate. Angel was going to make her look like an idiot, and it wasn't going to be too hard to do, at that. Oh, why hadn't she pleaded other duties and spared herself this humiliation?

"There, see, Miss Carpenter? She likes you. Don't you, girl?" murmured Giles fondly, slipping the horse a bit of sugar.

Joanna could not bring herself to make a lighthearted reply. The horse had a very smug look about her. Oh, they were enemies all right and they were going to war.

"Are we ready, Jims?" Giles asked the wizened old man standing at his elbow.

"Aye, sir. I'll take Angel to the mountin' block and help Miss Carpenter to mount. Your Red Devil is all ready for you, snortin' and stampin,' he is."

Giles walked away, leaving Joanna staring morosely as Jims led Angel to the block. What on earth had possessed her to agree to this awful outing? She could have taken a nice walk, for heaven's sake. There was no reason whatsoever to get up on this infernal horse. Still, she would look like a fool if she turned tail now, so with a sigh she made herself walk over to the wicked beast. Angel turned to regard her as she approached. The large brown eyes gleamed with absolute malevolence;

there was no doubt about it.

"Here you are, miss. Angel is as sweet as her name. You'll have no trouble with her, not a bit," said Jims.

Were they all blind? The horse was the devil on all fours! Joanna stepped up onto the block, refusing to meet the horse's maleficent eye. With a discreet boost from Jims, she found herself astride. She tugged at her skirt on either side, but she was aware that her ankles were showing over the tops of her low boots. Well, modesty was going to be the least of her problems for now.

"There now, miss. Ain't Angel a grand lady? Just the slightest tug on the reins and she'll go just where you want her to go," Jims said, stepping back and touching his cap to her.

Joanna rolled her eyes. The horse beneath her was trembling slightly. Laughing, no doubt. Drat! Drat! Drat!

Giles, mounted on a beautiful sorrel, drew alongside Joanna. He hid his smile as he noted the expression of terrified determination on her face. Perhaps he should offer to cancel this outing and get the poor girl back on the ground where she so obviously wished to be.

"You know, it might rain, at that, Miss Carpenter," he said, feigning a frown at the cloudless blue sky. "Perhaps we would do well to make this jaunt some other day."

"Oh, no, Sir Giles," replied Joanna through clenched teeth. "I'm sure it will be a lovely day for a ride." She'd made it this far and she would be damned if she'd let the beast have the satisfaction.

Good. The girl had some pluck. Well, Angel would give her no trouble. Giles touched his knee to his mount and started forward.

Joanna gently dug her heels into Angel's sides and waited expectantly. Nothing happened. Naturally.

"There now, pretty girl, you go on with Red Devil and have yourselves a nice ride." Jims gave Angel a pat on her rear and she ambled off.

Giles slowed Red Devil and turned to wait for Angel and Joanna. The expression on the girl's face was comical, but he knew better than to laugh. At last, Angel managed to catch up and he started forward again. Angel was following obediently.

"I would suggest we ride down into Caldbeck Fells a bit, Miss Carpenter. It's still somewhat barren at this time of year, but then when you see it in a few weeks' time, it will be all the more beautiful." He kept their pace to a slow walk. The trails were rocky and some were steep, and although Red Devil could howl through the fells like the wind, Giles was quite sure neither Angel nor Miss Carpenter was up to a wild ride.

They rode for some time in companionable silence. Giles and Red Devil led, picking the easier trails along the stony incline. Joanna was feeling better as they proceeded. Angel was being nice, just moving along, not making any trouble. Joanna felt a little of the tension leave her, and she began noticing her surroundings. Away to the east stretched miles of rolling hills, wild and solitary moorlands, stark in barren winter beauty.

They reached a level spot in the trail, wide enough for both horses to stand. Giles stopped. "We are nearly surrounded by mountains here, Miss Carpenter," he said, breaking into her thoughts. "To the east are the Pennines, to the north are the Cheviot Hills, and south of us are the Cumbrian Mountains. That's why our weather is so unpredictable. With an ocean to the west we can never be sure what sort of day it will be."

"It's splendid, sir," Joanna said. "I don't know that I've ever seen anything quite so beautiful."

Joanna was alongside him now as they started down, and he could see the appreciation in her eyes. The wind had put color in her cheeks and she was smiling ear to ear. Her hands had relaxed on the reins, too, he noted, and she had so forgotten her fear that she leaned forward in excitement on the horse, almost straining to go faster. Unbidden, the thought of his first ride out with Violet came to mind. He had been so proud of his homeland, eager to show off its wild beauty to his beautiful bride. Violet had managed about twenty minutes on the horse, complaining all the while about how she disliked the country and wished desperately to return to the pleasures of London. There had been nothing in her eyes then but contempt for what she called a bare, godforsaken hole in the earth.

"There are some rather pleasant lakes, too, Miss Carpenter, to the south of us," he ventured again. Of course, it was always possible that she was just being polite. Most of the women with whom he came into contact these days—Eleanor's friends, when he hadn't managed to avoid them—hung thus on his every word. But there was always something else in their eyes, something that had nothing to do with the topic of conversation, and nothing to do with being polite either.

"I am just longing for my watercolors, Sir Giles. See, there is just a hint of green budding." She gestured with her right hand, forgetting that the rein was tangled rather tightly in her fingers.

With a snort of annoyance, Angel skittered, then lost her footing on a rock which slipped beneath her hoof. Losing her purchase, the horse began to slide down the trail, a hail of stones flying beneath her hooves.

Joanna gave a shriek, then, abandoning the reins altogether, threw her arms about the horse's neck, holding on as tightly as she could, eyes squeezed shut. Beneath her she could feel the horse bucking and straining wildly to regain its footing on the precarious scree.

Suddenly Joanna felt the horse's neck jerk beneath her head. The horse quieted immediately as its hooves found purchase. Slowly she raised her head and met the anxious eyes of Sir Giles. His hand held Angel's reins short and tight, and his face was inches from hers as he half lay over Angel, stretched as far as he could from his seat on Red Devil.

"Are you all right?" he asked.

"I—I am fine. I'm so sorry, I should never . . ."

"Let me get you down before she slips again," he said quickly, his voice tense. "She is favoring her hoof and I need to see if she is hurt." He slid with fluid grace from the back of Red Devil, never releasing his tight grip on Angel's reins. He reached up and put his one good arm around Joanna's waist.

"You'll have to let go, you know, if you want to get off," he said, a hint of amusement in his voice.

With chagrin, Joanna realized her arms were still tightly clenched around the horse's neck. She forced herself to loosen her grip, surprised at how her muscles screamed with the strain.

"It's a wonder you didn't strangle that horse, Miss Carpenter," came his voice, close to her ear as he lifted her down.

Red with humiliation, Joanna stood quietly

while he bent down to examine Angel. She was keenly aware that she stood between the two large beasts, on a narrow incline with precarious footing. Well, if one slipped and swept her down the steep, rocky trail, at least she wouldn't have to look Sir Giles Chapman in the eye again.

"Well, she's lamed, but I don't think it's broken," said Giles, kneeling by the horse's foreleg. "I'd hate to have to shoot her, and I didn't bring my pistol out with me in any case."

"Shoot her?" asked Joanna, shocked. "Why on earth would you shoot her?"

"Well, if the leg is broken, she'll have to be put down," he said calmly, standing and wiping his dusty hands on his pants legs. "Horses can't stay off their legs long enough to heal a break. Just can't be done."

He looked up at the sound of a strangled sob and saw her face crumpling.

"What on earth? What's wrong?" he asked in alarm, reaching out and taking her arm. "Oh, I am sorry. I should have realized you've had a frightening time of it. Do you want to sit down for a minute?"

"It's not that," she sobbed. "I am so sorry. I was so anxious to get out. It's all my fault. I can't ride at all. Horses and I hate each other, but that's no reason for her to be shot. I made her fall with my stupid ill-handling. Oh, please don't shoot her," Joanna ended up on hiccup.

Two tears, one on either side of her nose, made their way down her cheeks. More than anything else in the world, he wanted to reach over and wipe them away with his big, clumsy thumb. The thought unnerved him with its sudden, unexpected intrusion. Taking a deep breath, he pulled from his waistcoat pocket a large white silk square.

"It's not your fault," he said gently, unable to stop himself from dabbing her cheeks with it. Such a clean, white cheek. Red now with distress, but not the sort of red that would have to be laundered later out of the cloth.

"Oh, but it is, Sir Giles. I am such an idiot. I knew I couldn't ride well enough but I came out anyway. It was thoughtless and selfish of me, and now you may shoot Angel because of me."

It was all he could do not to take her in his arms. The thought quickened something inside him, and he suppressed it immediately, shocked by its intensity.

"But I won't have to shoot her, not unless her leg is broken, and I don't think it is. Please don't cry, Miss—whatever is your first name, Miss Carpenter?"

"Joanna," she said with another hiccup.

"Joanna, then. Look, see, Angel is in no distress. It cannot be broken or she'd be wild with pain. She's just lamed. She'll be just fine after Jims fusses over her awhile."

Joanna did look at Angel. Indeed, the horse was holding her hoof up, but she was calm. If the horse's large brown eyes held reproach, at least there was no malice and no pain. Joanna took a deep breath and hiccupped again.

"And actually, I think I should apologize to you, Joanna. I could see that you were not comfortable on horseback but I insisted on riding out anyway. I am sorry I put you through all that." He took one last swipe at her cheeks and gave her a twisted grin. "Anyway, are the fells at least scenic enough to make up for my bad judgment?"

"It's just beautiful, Sir Giles. Little Haver is in

rather flat countryside. Of course, Little Haver is beautiful, too, but the fells are simply breathtaking," she finished, her eyes on the distant hills.

Good. Perhaps he could get her mind off the awful mishap. She must have no idea how close she came to death or grotesque maiming. He had damned near dislocated his one good shoulder grabbing and holding Angel until the horse could find her footing. Had she slipped any further, she would have fallen on the treacherous, rocky incline. Joanna would have fallen with her, rolling under the heavy horse, perhaps.

Amazing how the girl could feel so badly about the horse. It had been so clear that she and the horse had wanted nothing to do with one another. Eleanor would have held the pistol herself and laughed about it, while this girl cried at the very possibility. Angel was too old to withstand a serious injury to her leg. But he'd make sure Joanna never learned of the outcome, should the worst transpire.

He took Joanna's arm and moved further down the trail away from the horses. Angel would need a few moments to rest, and Red Devil would have to do double duty on the way back. The girl trembled a bit under his grasp, and again he fought the urge to put his arm around her.

"How are you getting on with the children?" he asked, casting about for something to talk about besides horses. "You seemed to be having fun at the beach this afternoon."

"I think we're doing rather well so far, sir. They seem to be opening up. I've gotten them both to laughing a bit, and they are attentive to their studies. Emma is quite bright, I think, and Tom has some intelligence in those sweet brown eyes."

"They seem happier, I think. Less melancholy," he observed. He always had a stab of guilt when he thought of the children. He certainly had done nothing to ease their sense of loss, or to make them feel welcome in the few months they had been here.

"I think they will grow and prosper, Sir Giles. They are carrying around a great deal of grief on such little shoulders. It just takes time."

"And love, I think," he said sadly. "I've neglected them rather badly, I'm sorry to say. I was not close to my older brother. We were a good number of years apart and we did not share the same mother. He was nearly grown and gone when I was born, so I barely knew him. When the accident happened, and there was no one else to take the children, I agreed to do so, but Eleanor . . ." He trailed off, uncomfortable. It was clear this young woman was a godsend to his blighted household, but there were some things he could not tell her.

A crack of thunder startled them both. Looking up, Giles noticed for the first time that the sky had grown dark and ominous.

"There, you see, you made it rain," Joanna said with a laugh beside him. "There wasn't a cloud in the sky until you made that transparent attempt to get me off the horse back at the stables. But oh, I wish I hadn't been so stubborn," she finished sadly.

"Come on," he said, laughing and taking her arm again. "We'll have to both ride Red Devil and lead Angel behind us."

"But can Red Devil carry all that weight?" asked Joanna, somewhat aghast at the thought of getting up on that huge beast. "I can walk alongside. I like walking, honestly," she added rather lamely.

He laughed and pulled her along. Great big raindrops were just beginning to fall. "Now, don't turn into a coward on me, Joanna," he said. "I was proud of you when you refused to get off the horse. Besides, I'll be right behind you."

They had reached the spot where the two horses stood together. Giles had not bothered to tie either of them. Angel couldn't wander off, and Red Devil wouldn't. Giles tied Angel's reins to the back of Red Devil's saddle. If Angel couldn't manage the slow walk back, he'd have to leave her behind, and just not tell Joanna how she would probably be dealt with.

"All right," he said, straightening up. "I'll have to get you into the saddle one-armed. Let's see if we can manage it." He grabbed her around the waist with his good arm and lifted her effortlessly. She kicked her leg up over Red Devil's back and astonished herself by gaining a seat on the tall horse. For a brief moment she teetered up there alone, then with an easy leap, Giles was behind her and she was safe.

The rain had begun falling in earnest. The wind had picked up, and Joanna shivered. "Here's your cloak, Joanna," Giles said behind her. "I took it from Angel's pack." He unfurled the cloak in front of her and covered her with it, settling her back against him. His own cloak surrounded him and overlapped hers, its great hood sheltering them both.

"I know you don't much like this, Joanna," he said close to her ear, "but I promise I'll keep you safe."

To the contrary, she liked it very much indeed. The warmth from his body at her back soothed her chill, and his arm tight around her waist made her feel secure on the great beast. Beneath the shelter of his large cloak, she watched the cold rain fall and touch them not. Even when he gave Red Devil a nudge and they started on their slow trudge home, the rhythmic sway held no terror for her.

Giles, however, felt no such ease. He did not fear the treacherous path. Red Devil had a sense of balance that defied physics. But the slow gait of the horse and the contour of the saddle brought Joanna tight up against him. He could feel her round derriere pushing close with every step of the horse, and the feeling was pure torture. His cloak hood covering them both, he inhaled the sweet fragrance of her clean hair, along with the fresh, wild scent of the spring rain. He must have been mad to bring this young woman out onto the fells. He had forgotten his sleeping hunger. . . .

Joanna blinked her eyes, confused by the light of the stables. Has she actually slept on that great beast, on a steep, wet trail where one misstep could have brought death to them all?

"Down you come, Miss Carpenter," came Jims's flat accent. She felt hands reaching toward her and pulling her away from the comfortable warmth of her dream. Her feet touched the earth just about when she cleared her muddled, sleepy head. She looked up, smiling at Sir Giles.

"I am so sorry, sir. I must have slept. I hope I was not a great dead weight for you and Red Devil to manage." Her smile died on her lips. The man was rigid, his eyes not meeting hers.

"I—I am glad to see Angel made it back with us," Joanna ventured again, confused, hoping for some flicker of his earlier warmth.

"Oh, she'll be just fine, miss, no need to worry

about Angel," she heard Jims say heartily. "Tough as nails, she is."

Giles gave her a curt nod and rode Red Devil back into the depth of the stables. Joanna watched his retreating back with sinking heart. What had she done wrong? What had she said to turn his face cold and his eyes so hard? With a small, tight smile for Jims, she turned and made her way back to the rear entrance of the house, gathering her cloak around her, some remnant of his clean scent lingering. . . .

Inside the stables, Giles swung down from Red Devil, furious with himself. He had not dared dismount in front of the girl. In fact, he'd like to get away from the stables before anyone noticed. Perhaps he'd go down to the beach. Perhaps a dip in the pounding, icy surf would take away the hard, insistent swelling, the pain, the madness of desire. Never again would he succumb to a pretty smile. Once before, he had surrendered his soul, only to have it trampled beneath Violet's dainty, treacherous feet. Never again . . .

In the back of the house, in the steward's small office, Hawton let the drapery drop back into place, a self-satisfied smile curving his lips. So the master and little puss were out riding today, were they? And come back seated all cozied up on one horse. He'd have to find a way to drop this little tidbit into his next conversation with the high-and-mighty Lady Eleanor. She would not like it one bit.

Chapter Seven

Emma's little voice droned on with her reading lesson. Joanna was finding it difficult to keep her mind on the child's work. She had already been surprised once or twice out of her morose reverie by a question from the girl. The draperies in the schoolroom were pulled open, but she almost wished they were not. Outside was as gray and rainy a day as she had seen in her fortnight here. The rain blew in sheets against the glass, obscuring all view of the sea. Just as well. Considering the wind howling around the great house, the sea was probably not a comforting sight just now.

With a sigh, Joanna turned her attention away from the gray of the window and tried to give Emma a bright smile. "Your reading is improving every day, my dear," she said, putting some enthusiasm into her voice. The girl gave her a shy smile in return.

Each day had been better than the last with these dear children. Emma had opened up like a flower parched for water, suddenly given a long drink, and while Tom still did not talk, it was clear that he understood a great deal of what was said to him and could follow simple directions. More importantly, the boy's eyes were bright and merry, and the room would ring with his joyous laughter.

And his laughter was part of what was bothering Joanna, she reflected grimly. Lady Eleanor had returned home last night with a large party of her friends. Joanna hadn't yet seen any of them, but she had heard the raucous arrival long after the household was in bed. And this morning Mrs. Davies had put her head in at breakfast and reminded Joanna that the children must be kept quiet at all costs. There had been a tightening about the housekeeper's lips and a terseness to her remarks. Already, Joanna could feel the tension in the house, as if the stones themselves reflected the strain.

And Sir Giles was nowhere to be seen, gone as if he had never been there at all. He had simply disappeared the day after their ill-fated ride. She had asked after him in the kitchen—for the children's sake, of course. But she had received little more than a shrug from Mrs. Davies, who explained that Sir Giles never stayed longer than a few days and that his arm had healed enough for him to go back to the mines. Joanna had felt such a stab of disappointment. He hadn't even said good-bye, not to her, of course—why should he?—but to the children. It had been small comfort that Lady Eleanor had disappeared as well—Joanna hadn't asked about her—but now the woman was back and there would be the devil to pay if the children inconvenienced her or her guests.

As she had done repeatedly during the morning, Joanna sighed and turned her thoughts again to the children who were waiting quietly and expectantly at their desks.

"It's rather a dreary day, isn't it? Perhaps we could work on geography. Then we can imagine all sorts of different weather. For instance, I'll bet it's not raining right this minute in the Sahara Desert, is it?" Joanna said brightly. Emma giggled and Tom grinned. "Let's look at the globe, shall we, and imagine ourselves somewhere where the sun is sure to be shining." They moved toward the brightly colored globe, and Joanna cast another mournful glance at the rain. It would have been so lovely to take the children to the beach, away from the sleeping, fashionable guests. But instead she had the rest of this long, slow, rainy afternoon to keep them very quiet. What a dreadful day. . . .

Giles arrived about half past four in the afternoon, riding into the stables to the rear of the house in a streaming downpour. He noted the array of carriages standing outside. Thank God he had arranged with Mrs. Davies before he left to notify him at once if Eleanor returned to the house.

He had been uneasy since he'd left. His life at the Dufton mines was usually stimulating and pleasantly absorbing, but these last ten days he had found himself at odds over everything, arguing over the least significant points, sometimes just for the sake of argument.

He told himself it was the children that were bothering him. His half brother had married young, and for love, and Giles had been pleased in a vague sort of way to hear that he had a niece, and disappointed a few years later to hear the sad news about the boy. But by the time the children had arrived on his doorstep a few months ago, all he wanted to do was find them a governess and retreat again to Dufton, away from this hell house.

But it had been such an eye-opener, that short time he had spent at the beach playing with them, chasing first one, then the other, and digging for shells.

He had supposed he didn't particularly care for children. There had been that one brief flash of joy when Violet had told him she was with child. He had been so happy, until she had laughed at him and called him a fool to think she'd swell up her belly and risk her life for a mewling, stinking baby. No, she would have the baby aborted. She'd invited him to puff up a chambermaid if he felt the need of an heir. Then had come the final blow, when she had mentioned, almost in passing, that the baby was likely not his, so he shouldn't mind if she got rid of it. Before that, there had been some hope left in him that she was just high-spirited, that she really loved him and that her flirtations with other men were just that and nothing more. He had been a fool to go on believing in her, to let the love he bore override all intelligence.

She had died of the abortion. Even then, he had held her in his arms, having found her soaked in blood, wandering the fell. At the end she was raving, and it was another man's name that she called out. And when love was gone, there was nothing left. Nothing except a hole, dark, fathomless, and empty. He would take no other wife, of that he was certain. And so the thought of children had been buried in that dark hole, where thoughts too painful to bear the light of day were put, the issue completely out of his mind.

He turned his mount over to the stableboy and made for the house through the back. He was drenched and cursed himself for not taking one of the coaches, but it had not been raining in Dufton and he could make much better time by horse. He had felt such an urgency about his return, and even now he could not explain it to himself, other than that he did not want Eleanor alone in the house with the children. Or with the governess.

And there was the problem, run from it as he would. At first it had just been the dreams, aching and adolescent, excruciatingly embarrassing in the light of day. But more lately the dreams had not faded with the morning light. He found himself assaulted again and again, no matter how hard he tried to concentrate on his work. There was the flash of her smile and the image of the silky dark depths of her shining hair, and sometimes, in the midst of the dirt and stench of the pit, would come the memory of her scent, clean and light and lilac.

Who was this Joanna Carpenter that she could invade his peace, so quickly tear away the years and layers of indifference he had so carefully erected to make his existence bearable? He had thought himself satisfied with the tacit bargain he had made with life, that he would take his contentment from his work, from the sheer talent and energy he could summon up when faced with an engineering puzzle. But one afternoon had ripped away his complacency; had shown him what a fool he had been and how empty his life really was. He swore to himself as his booted feet slid in the mud at the stairs. There was no excuse for such poor drainage this close to the house. Damn, how he had neglected this godforsaken home!

He let himself in the rear lower hallway, divesting himself of his streaming greatcoat and hanging it on a peg next to the servants' cloaks. Running his boots against the boot scrape, he thought he had gotten the worst of the mud off. Well, someone would see to it later. He was not a man given to fastidious attention to his attire. He kept no valet, much to Eleanor's derision. Not that any self-respecting valet would be caught dead with him in Dufton.

All was silent in the hall. Well, it was early yet for Eleanor's glittering crowd. Like a pack of vampires, they were, abed during daylight and venturing abroad only toward evening. Giles made for his office and shut the door behind him. With a little luck he could avoid her set altogether. Perhaps he'd have an early supper with the children. Perhaps he could prevail upon Miss Carpenter to join them.

Joanna heard the tiny tap on the schoolroom door and heaved a sigh of relief. The children's day was drawing to a close, and so far she had heard nothing of Lady Eleanor or her guests. Annie entered, bobbing her quick curtsey.

"If you please, Miss Carpenter, the children's supper be ready. Mrs. Davies asks that you bring them down with me, real quiet-like, so we don't disturb Lady Eleanor and her party."

Joanna suppressed a slight shudder. If they took the back stairs they had only to traverse a small section of the hall to get to the little breakfast parlor that the children used for their meals. Then, of course, they needed to eat rather quietly, then go to bed rather quietly, then sleep rather quietly. . . . Joanna gave herself a shake and stood, holding out her hands with a bright smile. "Let us go downstairs, my darlings. But let's make a game of it, shall we? Your aunt has guests and we need to be very, very quiet so as not to disturb them. So let's have a contest and see who can be the quietest, and the winner will have a treat before bedtime! Shhhh! What do you say to that?" she finished in a whisper, and the children, giggling, stifled their laughter with hands held over their mouths, eyes wide with delight.

Joanna took a small hand in each of hers and they proceeded from the room. "Where is Lady Eleanor, Annie?" she whispered over her shoulder.

"They all be in the drawing room, miss, but they're makin' enough noise themselves that I don't think they'll be 'earin' us," the girl said, whispering in return.

The little party made their silent way down the back stairs, the children exchanging grins, certain they were having a wonderful game. At the foot of the stairs Joanna opened the baize-covered door that led into the main hallway. So far so good! The hallway was empty, and although she could hear the murmur of faint voices, the drawing-room doors were obviously closed. She stepped into the hall, drawing the children with her, Annie following closely behind. Oh, this was such a large house! Whyever did anyone need all these rooms? she thought to herself, looking down the long hallway. Well, just a few more doors to go to safety.

Without warning, the door to the drawing room was flung open. Before Joanna could react, Lady

Eleanor swept into the hall, arm in arm with a tall woman, their backs to Joanna and the children. Joanna had time to note that Eleanor's friend wore a vibrant, shimmering green silk dress, and had blond curls pinned to the top of her head. Emma gave a gasp beside her, and as Joanna turned to the girl, Tom, with a wordless cry, launched himself forward at the woman and buried himself in the folds of her voluminous dress.

The woman gave a scream and jumped away, but Tom clung tightly around her legs.

"What is the meaning of this outrage, Miss Carpenter?" Eleanor cried. "Get him off! Get him off of her at once, do you hear me?" She drew back, as if unwilling to be near the boy. Her friend, who had caught sight of the boy's face, stood squealing and pushing at him.

"Eleanor, he's an idiot! Look at his face. He's drooling on my new gown," the woman wailed, tearing her skirts from Tom's hands. At the sound of her voice the boy looked up, an expression of confusion, then horror, crossing his face. Suddenly he set up a wail, an almost inhuman noise of fear and pain, as he let go of her and stumbled back.

"He thought she was Mama. Her dress is just like one of Mama's favorites, all shiny green, and her hair is like Mama's, too," cried Emma, pulling on Joanna's arm.

"Shut up! Shut up, you disgusting half-wit!" shrieked Eleanor. Drawing back her hand, she landed a vicious blow across Tom's face. The boy staggered back into Joanna, who had recovered enough from her shock to rush forward. She dropped to her knees behind him, pulling him toward her.

"Hush, darling, please hush!" Joanna pleaded in his ear, but the child was nearly mad with betrayal and continued his piercing wail.

Eleanor was wild with anger, her face contorted, her too-red mouth twisted with rage. From behind her, Joanna could see heads popping out from the drawing-room door, curious, painted, almost grotesque faces and tittering laughs. The woman in green continued to moan, dabbing at her dress with her handkerchief.

"Silence that idiot, Miss Carpenter, or I shall do it for you. I will not bear his noise!" Eleanor stepped forward, arm raised as if she would strike him again.

"We'll take him upstairs, Lady Eleanor," Joanna cried over the boy's screams as she shielded his face. She tried to scramble up from her knees but her dress was caught under her.

Suddenly Joanna felt a hand on her shoulder and instinctively drew back toward whatever haven was offered behind her.

"That's enough, Eleanor," growled a voice at Joanna's back.

Eleanor looked up, startled. "Giles!" she said brightly, stepping back away from Joanna and the boy. "I did not know you had returned."

At the sound of the man's voice, Tom looked up over Joanna's shoulder. Giles put his hand on the boy's head, and the child quieted immediately.

For a moment there was dead silence in the hall. Joanna, still holding tightly to Tom, felt a nudge at her side and turned to find Emma pressing against her. The girl was crying silently, her face contorted in anguish and fear. Joanna caught the child to her and buried her face in her braided hair. She desperately wanted to cry herself, but knew she must hold steady in front of the children.

"Mrs. Davies, can you help us here?" Sir Giles said, barely controlling his anger. Joanna looked up to see the housekeeper hurry forward. Giles now had both his hands on Tom's shoulders. The boy was quiet, pressed back against Giles's legs, his face lost in a distant, unreachable sorrow as he stared with deep accusation at the green lady who had so betrayed him.

Joanna held tightly to Emma, aware only now that her own legs were shaking so badly she was not sure she could stand.

Giles bent down and faced Tom so that their heads were on a level. "Tom, my lad, can you go in with Emma and Mrs. Davies for supper now? I want to speak with your aunt and Miss Carpenter for a moment, and then I will come in and have supper with you." Giles spoke carefully and softly to the boy, stroking the child's hair gently. With a barely perceptible nod the boy stepped forward to Mrs. Davies, who, with a firm hand on each little shoulder, shepherded the children toward the breakfast parlor. Joanna stood shakily, willing her legs to hold her up. She was fighting the great lump in her throat and felt as if her heart might burst with suppressed tears.

"Giles, this is intolerable," came Eleanor's voice, shrill with fury. "That little monster has terrorized Philippa and ruined my party! He has no business being anywhere near where we can see him. You can see for yourself how uncontrollable he is. He ought to be in an asylum for idiots, and you know it."

An asylum! Locked away from the light of day, never the sight of a face with any love or kindness reflected in it. Beatings and cruelty too evil to contemplate.

Choking back a sob, Joanna turned quickly and fled up the steps.

"Why don't you and your friends return to your party, Eleanor?" Giles said in a tightly controlled voice. "Madame," he said, turning to her friend, "if your dress is damaged, be sure to send me the bill."

The woman dimpled prettily at him. "I'm sure it will be fine, Sir Giles," she simpered. She gave him a naughty little smile, then turned to take Eleanor's arm. "But Eleanor, darling," she purred as they moved toward the drawing room, "if you must have something that slobbers and jumps all over you, why don't you get a dog? They're much smarter and a great deal more adorable." They tittered brightly at each other and disappeared into the drawing room.

Giles stood for a moment staring, waiting for the door to shut behind them. Their cloying scents hung in the air behind them, fighting each other in the stale air. At last he turned and made for the stairs, hearing behind him a burst of raucous laughter from the drawing room.

On the third floor he paused before the door he knew was Joanna's. He could hear nothing from inside. He knocked but heard no response. He pushed the door softly open and stepped in, quietly shutting the door behind him.

Joanna stood with her back to him, head bowed against the window, hands clutching at the glass as if she were a bird trapped and in pain. Her shoulders shook, and he could hear her sobs coming in ragged gasps.

Giles crossed the length of the room in a few

long strides, then stopped in front of her. Gently he reached for her and turned her to face him.

"I don't know what to say, Joanna. I am at a loss," he said softly. His hands burned where he touched her shoulders and he wanted nothing more than to pull her close and hold her.

"She struck him," Joanna sobbed furiously. "I wouldn't beat a dog like that. And she wants to send him to an asylum. Please don't let her send him away. He'll die in a place like that, all alone."

"I'll never send him away, Joanna. I promise you," Giles said, his heart twisting at her pain. Not knowing what else to do, he took out his handkerchief and pressed it lightly to her cheeks.

Joanna took a deep, shuddering breath, then went on, "I—Emma explained to me what happened. The lady wore a dress like one of Tom's mother's, and her hair was similar, apparently. He saw her from the rear and he thought . . ." Her voice broke with a sob and she looked down quickly as the tears came again. Never would she forget the betrayal and anguish in the child's face, and his cries would echo in her heart forever. He had thought his mama had come back to him, only to find a painted, screaming harpy instead.

"Please don't cry, Joanna," Giles said softly, taking her hand in his, feeling ineffectual. Of course she had to cry. It was hideous what had happened to the boy, and it was part of what was so important about Joanna that she would care, would feel the child's pain as her own. Over her shoulder, he caught sight of the sketch she had done of Eleanor which stood on a small easel. He was startled by the likeness, and by the malevolence reflected in the face. It was a powerful, even shocking, sketch.

"I'm sorry," Joanna said with a small sob. "We

were trying so hard to be quiet, and now Lady Eleanor is so angry." She pulled away and looked at him, wiping her eyes with the large square. "It wasn't Tom's fault. But please, can't you ask her not to hit him again? It only makes things worse. It frightens him and he doesn't understand what he's done wrong. I know it is not my place to criticize, but it was horrible that she would strike him like that. Tell her if she must hit someone to hit me instead. At least we're the same size." Joanna finished with another rush of tears and buried her face in the handkerchief.

It was unbearable watching her cry, knowing there was nothing he could say that would justify what Eleanor had done. Yielding to the insistent impulse, he put his arms around her and pulled her head to his shoulder, her small sobs tearing at him.

"It is your place to criticize, Joanna," he said softly into her hair. She smelled so freshly washed, so clean, with a light, clear scent. Lilac again, he thought. "Anything involving the welfare of the children is within your concern. I want you to care about them. They need someone to love them." His arms tightened around her as he spoke. She was quiet now, breathing in shaking gasps in his arms. She felt so good there. Unbidden came the distant thought that he needed someone to love him, too, but he pushed it away. There was no point in such thoughts.

Joanna's senses swam with confusion. He had his arms around her and she could hear his steady heartbeat in his wide, strong chest. She could smell the clean-linen smell of him, and feel the pressure of his hands on her back as he rubbed her gently. She could feel the heat of him stretched the length of her, driving all thoughts of the children from her head. The children!

"You could love them, Sir Giles," she said in a small voice at his chest, chastising herself, not even certain what for.

She could feel him tense. She made herself pull away and looked up at him. "They are missing their parents, Sir Giles. They need a papa, not a governess. You could love them," she repeated with a hopeful glance at him.

There was a stricken expression about his eyes, almost hunted, and she looked away again. She had pushed too far, presumed too much. Now he would be angry, too. Why couldn't she have minded her place?

"I don't know how, Joanna," came his answer.

"You don't know how to love them?" was her astonished reply.

Now he looked away. Feeling suddenly awkward, he pulled away from her and turned toward the window. What she was asking was impossible. He had closed off those avenues many years ago and didn't want them reopened. People disappointed him, or died. Love hurt. Better to stay away from it. He could work with his numbers and measurements. Numbers couldn't hurt him.

"I just don't think I can love anyone now," he said, his voice cold and flat. "It's been too long. All that is dead inside me."

Joanna stared at his stiff back, uncertain of what to say. He was wrong about being dead inside. She knew that for certain. She could tell from the way the children had opened up to him that day on the beach. Children were not wrong about these things; they knew who would love them and who would not. But he would need time, and perhaps he would need to learn it for himself.

He turned back to her, his face calm, devoid of emotion. "I do not wish to distress you with my peculiarities, Joanna. I know that you mean well, and believe me when I tell you the children's welfare is important to me. I will do my best to curb the evil temper of my stepsister." He paused, and Joanna could hear the tension in his voice. "I cannot promise you much on that score, however. As you must have guessed by now, Eleanor and I barely tolerate the sight of one another and she despises the children, all children, I think. I apologize for airing the family linen in front of you, but I feel you are entitled to understand what sort of broth you have landed yourself in. The artist in you has recognized much of it already," he said with a nod at the dark sketch.

His facade of calm was cracking now. Joanna could hear the pain behind his words and see it in his face. She longed to reach up and touch his cheek, to soothe away the pain, but she did not dare.

"So you can see that the only hope Emma and Tom have of normalcy is you," he went on. "You are a godsend to my blighted household, and I beg you to stay with us and love them as we cannot." There was a hopelessness to his tone that made Joanna shiver. This was how Papa had sounded in those few moments when his faith had deserted him.

She faced him. "I will never leave here, Sir Giles. Not unless you give me the sack and have me hauled off the premises," she quipped, and was rewarded with the ghost of a smile from him. "You must remember that I am alone. I need someone to love me, too." She smiled up at him reassuringly.

She needed someone to love her, too. He stared into the soft brown depths of her beautiful eyes, mesmerized by the lights that danced within.

"Do I look like an absolute fright?" Joanna asked, turning to the mirror, confused by the haunted look in his eyes. "I don't want to scare the children. Let me fix my hair," she said, walking to her dressing table. Sitting, she pulled out a few pins and tried to capture escaped tresses with them. She made quick work with her brush, twisting the errant locks back into their proper coils, pushing pins in expertly, until all was secure. As she lowered her arms, she caught sight of his face in the mirror and caught her breath. Hunger, raw need, twisted his features. He was in pain. She turned quickly and looked at him, her breath catching in her throat.

"You look—fine," he said, trying to keep his voice steady. "Will you take supper with me and the children? I think we should join them if you feel up to it." He desperately needed to get out of this room. She was so lovely in the fading light, her face flushed and her brown eyes full of emotion. He felt like a starving man staring in at a banquet through locked windows, hopeless and maddened with need.

"Let's go," he said simply, holding out his hand to her. She was so utterly beautiful, so natural. There was not a pot or paintbrush on her table, nothing but a hairbrush, comb, and pin box. He ached with the intimacy of watching her brush her hair, an intimacy he dared not pursue further, not unless he wished to mock and twist the one decent thing in his life now.

Joanna stood and walked to him, giving him a shy smile. It was so improper, having him here in her room. No decent woman would be caught dead in such a compromising position. But she didn't care about that. Not now. All she cared about was the press of his warm fingers as they closed now on hers, and the confusing but exhilarating feeling that coursed through her veins at his touch. With no more words possible between them, they made their way into the hall.

It was near dawn and Eleanor's head was pounding. More and more lately she had the headache and she couldn't understand why. She sat at her dressing table and stared at herself in the light of the single candle burning next to her. The paint was holding well enough, but she could use a touch-up here and there. She picked up her brush and opened her pot, dabbing a bit of the thick white paste onto a few spots on her face. She rarely washed it all off these days. Her face looked worse and worse without the paint. She had been blessed with beautiful, flawless skin as a young woman, but now it seemed to be dark-spotted and lined, and the paint needed to be applied ever more thickly. She left her wig on as well. Her hair underneath was in no better form than her complexion, coming out in clumps when she washed it, rare as that was. Lord Howard said it was the arsenic and lead in the paints, but he was a malicious soul and would take great delight in telling her the one thing she could not bear to hear. Besides, it was absurd. People had been using lead paint since the time of the Tudors and it caused no one any harm. Anyway, everyone died of something, didn't they?

She applied a slash of crimson to her lips and sat back to view the results. Passable. In a dim light. God, how she hated getting old. Why was 34 so old? She still had her courses; she could still have a baby. Not that she would, of course, she thought, shuddering. Children were a nasty horror. She would never forget the sight of that drooling idiot clinging to Philippa's dress and wailing on and on. She had never been so humiliated in her life, particularly as all of her bright and brittle set had needled her about it mercilessly all evening, calling her "Mama" and suggesting she go see if the children's bottoms needed wiping. Disgusting. And, of course, Philippa had not failed to notice how possessively Giles's hand had grasped that little hussy's shoulder. Oh, there was something going on there, all right, all that virginal act notwithstanding. Well, she had plans for the little tart. No doubt Giles was much taken with that phony innocence the girl seemed to wrap around her like a cloak. Well, Giles would be surprised when he realized the little whore was no better than any of the rest of them. Thought to catch herself a knight, did she? Not for long.

Eleanor stood with a snarl and walked to the door. Hawton was late. If he delayed much longer, the servants would be about, and she preferred to keep up the pretense of a business relationship with him, at least with the household. It wouldn't do for him to be seen emerging from her room at dawn, particularly if the word filtered back to Giles. They had been lucky so far in Giles's indifference, but it wouldn't do for him to become suspicious of Hawton.

Anyway, she wasn't sure she wanted Hawton's prodigious talents tonight. She had something even more exciting on her mind, something that might make her free of the fetters of her poverty, her dependence on her stepbrother, and this rotting hole of a prison in the north of nowhere. Yes, if she could take advantage of Lord Beeson's proposition she would have her own money to play with—a great deal of it, apparently. Oh, she'd have to cut Hawton in on it—it was unfortunate, but there would be no way to run this scheme without his aid, particularly after she moved to London. If she had her own money, Giles would have no hold over her. She could get herself a townhouse in London and stay there forever and let the dark stones of this hell house fall around his head.

She'd have to concoct some sort of legal scheme—a trust of some kind, left her by a distant uncle or cousin. In France, perhaps. Giles knew she had distant relations in France but he knew nothing more than that. Nor, in fact, did she, the connections were so attenuated. It would be important that the funds remain outside of the control of her stepbrother, but that could be accomplished with the right turn of a legal phrase or two, and she'd have enough cash to hire a sharp London solicitor to see to the phony documents.

Where the devil was Hawton? She'd sent word to him hours ago to meet her when the party broke up, and he was certainly able to see from his cottage down the hill that the lower-floor lamps had been extinguished. She hadn't seen him since she'd fled the house some ten days ago. There had been something so different about him that last night, almost frightening in a way. He hadn't seemed at all like a steward, more like the lord of the manor. But it hadn't been entirely unpleasant. No, there was something decidedly delicious about the way he had taken her in the chair, without so much as a by-your-leave-milady. Indeed, it had been her own twisted feelings that had driven her away the next morning, because she had felt so dependent, so uncertain of herself, and she did not like that one bit.

But now she was back in control, although that bitch of a governess was proving a thorn in her flesh.

There was a barely perceptible knock on the door. At last. She crossed to the door and opened it with a practiced, silent ease; she had seen to it that the hinges were well oiled. It was easier to have him come to her than for her to traipse down the hill to his cottage in the middle of the night.

He came in quickly and she shut the door quietly before either of them spoke.

"You're late," she said in clipped tones.

"There was a light still on in the downstairs library. I waited awhile to see if it would go out, then I decided it must have been left burning by accident. I stopped in to check, and there was no one there." Hawton deliberately left off the "my lady" and let his eyes slide possessively along her body. It had bothered him that she had run off without a word after their last encounter. He desperately needed to reestablish control over her. He could not go back to being the steward servicing her ladyship.

She gave him a long, seductive smile. She liked it when he looked at her like that. She felt a tingling between her legs. Yes, maybe she would let him take her tonight. But not until after they talked.

"Come and sit down away from the door. I need to talk with you," she said quietly, walking ahead of him. He followed, surprised. Eleanor rarely had anything to talk about.

She seated herself on her chaise and patted a place beside her. He sat, not knowing what her game was, but looking for the first opportunity to put her off stride, to get the upper hand.

"I have had a proposition put to me, Hawton. I—perhaps we—stand to make money, a great deal of money from it, but it will have to be handled with the utmost discretion." She paused, wanting to tantalize him.

"My lady?" It slipped out before he could stop himself. She had his attention.

"One of my friends has—connections—with a certain establishment in London. It's a new enterprise but should prove very popular if handled properly. He has a need for help in his—shipment route. The merchandise will be coming from Ireland to London, but, you understand, it must all be sub rosa."

"Are you talking about smuggling?" Hawton tried not to let his disappointment show. Smuggling could be lucrative but it carried great risks when the revenue agents turned their attention on the suspects, and Hawton did not consider himself a man inclined to endanger his life or liberty.

Eleanor gave a brittle little laugh. "How unimaginative of you, Hawton. I am talking about something much more interesting than that." She stopped. She was enjoying this. She was hot with the thought of the money to come—and Hawton. "I refer to a new 'virgin house,' Hawton. Do you know what that is?"

Hawton tried to keep his mouth from sagging open. A whorehouse that specialized in virgins, often real virgins, children, really. There was nothing lower on the face of this earth. He drew a deep breath before speaking.

"I do know what that is, my lady, but I wonder if you have considered the risks involved. The social opprobrium alone—"

"There is no risk to us Hawton, if that's what you mean," she snapped. Lord, she hadn't expected the man to be a prude. "My friend is well insulated in London. Those who actually run the place don't even know his name. And all we need to do is intercept the shipment of girls every few weeks. They'll be sent down here to our coast from Ireland, and we are to hold them for a few hours, a day at most, until the coaches are ready to take them away. It's just a matter of timing, and, after all, there is no one here for miles to note what we do."

"There is the household staff, Lady Eleanor. How do we get a group of young girls up the beach and into hiding without being seen?" Hawton was feeling nearly ill at the thought. He liked a good lay as much as the next man, even a virgin when he could get one, but the thought of wholesale kidnapping or buying children for the purpose was unnerving, to say the least.

"Well, perhaps we'll just forget this conversation, Hawton, since you are so faint of heart. I could arrange everything myself and keep all the money. I was going to share it with you but . . ." She waited. She was bluffing. She'd never be able to run this operation without his aid, and besides, now that she had told him about it, it was too late to keep him out of it.

"How much money are we talking about?" he heard himself asking.

"One hundred guineas per shipment, never

more than five or six girls in any load, a shipment every few weeks."

It was a staggering sum. In a matter of a few years he could be wealthy enough to buy his own home, a small manor perhaps. He could be his own steward, own the land he tended, take orders from no one, bow to no man . . . or woman.

"I suppose we could insist that no ship arrive during daylight hours," he said musingly. "If we were certain of the hour, say by flare or signal, we could be on the beach to meet the small boats."

He would do it! This was exactly what she needed to hear, some sort of planning that would take this scheme from idea to reality. Oh, she wanted this so badly. She could be in London within the year! She slid her hand to his thigh and began a languid stroking up the inside.

"There's a bluff between the beach and the house, my dear, and one cannot see the beach directly from the house," she purred near his ear. She was moving closer.

He had time to note the endearment, the first she had ever used to him. The thought of all that money and the insistent rubbing against his thigh were making him grow hard.

"My cottage, yes," he said, eyes heavy-lidded. Almost absently he reached over and grasped a breast, spilling it out from her low décolletage. He kneaded her softly. "We could take them behind the rise and bring them up the small path from the beach to my cottage. It would not be seen from the house."

"I know," she murmured huskily, her tongue seeking his ear. "Remember? We did it there once, on the beach."

In answer he groaned and stretched himself

over her. He lowered his mouth to hers and plundered her with his tongue.

"But, Hawton," she whispered breathlessly as she broke her mouth from his, fumbling with his breeches. "Remember, no touching the merchandise. They have to be virgins."

He laughed deep in his throat as he tongued her nipple. "I've told you, my dear. I have no need for virgins when I can have you." He lied, but it was the right remark. She moaned and pressed herself against him.

Rich. He would be rich. Then he'd get himself a young one and tell Lady Eleanor to go to hell.

Chapter Eight

Joanna stood before Lady Eleanor's desk, her heart hammering in her chest. It had been three days since the unfortunate incident with Tom, and although she and the children had seen nothing of the woman during that time, Joanna had lived in dread of their next meeting.

"You wished to see me, Lady Eleanor?" she asked softly, hoping her voice would hold steady.

"I do, Miss Carpenter," replied Lady Eleanor absently, penning something at her small, ornate escritoire. "Wait a moment and I'll attend you." She did not ask Joanna to sit.

Joanna stood, willing herself not to fidget, glancing around with veiled interest. Although the day was bright, the heavy draperies were all drawn and there was only the light from one candle burning at the desk. Joanna could see well enough to note, however, that the woman's sitting room was elaborately decorated. Everywhere Joanna looked were squiggles and swirls, brocades, silks, and complicated drapings. There was a great deal too much furniture, mixed in period, but of very fine quality.

But it was not the furnishings that seized Joanna's attention. Compared to the artwork in this room, the odalisque in the drawing room was fit to hang in a cloister of nuns. There were three large paintings in which none of the many figures was wearing a stitch. One of the paintings depicted a man and a woman in the throes of passion with stark realism. Joanna tore her eyes away from the remarkable sight and made sure they did not stray that way again. She was reminded all too acutely of her strange and decidedly unmaidenly reaction to Sir Giles's simple touch. And last night she had had such a dream! It made her blush just to think of it, wondering guiltily how she could have known enough about that sort of thing to have such a dream! She fought to block the thoughts that rushed unbidden through her mind, as she had fought in vain these last three days.

Sir Giles had left the day after the unfortunate incident—there had been an emergency at the mine—but this time he had sought Joanna out to tell her he was leaving. He had seemed to find it difficult to meet her eye, and she had stammered and blushed and felt like a fool, wondering whether he knew about the devils that had beset her all night long and was fleeing her shameless wantonness. But he had taken his leave without so much as touching her hand, bidding her to stay clear of Eleanor and her guests, and leaving a great, turbulent emptiness behind.

She was aware that she was blushing, which

made it all the harder to keep her composure, feeling guilty and miserable, standing before a woman who would have laughed at her missish thoughts.

Oh, please don't try to fire me, she thought desperately. Sir Giles had left strict instructions with her that his stepsister had no right to interfere with the terms of her employment and that if she tried to do so, Joanna was to ignore her and send word to him at once. But the awkwardness would be unbearable and it would likely reduce her already strained relationship with Lady Eleanor to one of open warfare.

At last Lady Eleanor raised her head from her paper and gave Joanna a slow perusal.

"You are aware that I am having a little fancy-dress soiree this evening, are you not, Miss Carpenter?" she asked. Her tone, while not icy, was condescending and perhaps a little smug.

"Indeed, I am, Lady Eleanor," was all Joanna cared to venture.

"I am including not only my out-of-town guests but a number of our neighbors as well. We are quite isolated here, as you may have noticed, but we do have neighbors at a distance and it has been a long time since I entertained," Eleanor went on. "The guests will not arrive until after nine o'clock. I assume the children will be asleep by then?"

"Yes, my lady, they will have been abed a good while by nine."

"Good. I would suggest that one of the servants be placed in each of their rooms to sit up all night in case one of them awakens. I want no repetition of what happened the other day, Miss Carpenter."

Joanna could feel her face flaming. "I shall sit up with them myself, Lady Eleanor," she began, hiding her hands in the folds of her skirt so that the woman would not see how they shook. "They have a connecting door and I can watch both rooms at once. Not that either of them ever awakens in the night. I am told they are both sound sleepers, and neither one has ever disturbed me," Joanna finished, having fought to keep her tone neutral. It was hard not to resent the inference that the children needed gaolers, or that they would cause a disruption to Eleanor's blasted party.

"You? Certainly not, Miss Carpenter," Eleanor replied, eyes alight with amusement. "You will be attending my soiree."

"I—I am to attend . . . ?" Joanna broke off, stunned. The last thing she wanted to do in this whole world was go to a party with all those horrible people.

"Of course, my dear. Isn't that what your sort is always looking for? I am sorry you've been saddled with a post in such a terrible location. Husband-hunting is scarce this far north into nowhere, but I thought the least I could do for you is introduce you to some handsome bachelors. Who knows, we may even turn up one or two who might be looking for a well-educated little wife." Eleanor laughed her brittle laugh.

"I am not . . ." Joanna began, shocked and annoyed by what she was hearing.

"Nonsense. Of course you are. And if you aren't, then you should be. Alternatively, you can stay here until you grow old and die, alone, wiping that half-witted boy's snot for the rest of his miserable life."

Joanna took a deep breath, clenching her hands to her sides. This woman was vicious, twisted, and

162

mean. She saw everything through her own perverted thinking. "Lady Eleanor," she answered, willing herself to sound calm, "you mistake my goals. I have no wish to marry, and I certainly have no such designs concerning my position here. And as far the children are concerned, I am content to stay in this post as long as I am needed. Then, naturally, I shall try to secure another post. In any event, I do not feel it would be appropriate for me to attend a social function of this magnitude. I am, after all, only the governess." There. She had set the woman straight and appealed to her sense of snobbery as well. Surely the woman would understand that the governess had no business hobnobbing with the swells at her fancy-dress affair. If Lady Eleanor understood nothing else, she understood class distinctions.

"Miss Carpenter, it is you who are mistaken," Eleanor began, her tone purring but her eyes malicious. "I must insist that you attend. I have several of my young bucks all agog at the prospect of fresh blood, if you will. I even have a costume all picked out for you. I assume you did not come with anything in your battered little valises that would be suitable for a fancy-dress ball?"

Joanna stared at her, feeling outsmarted. She had been just about to demur on the grounds of having nothing to wear. "My lady, it is most thoughtful of you, but—"

"No buts, Miss Carpenter! I have said you will attend, and so you shall. Sir Giles wishes it. He is terribly concerned about your welfare, you know. He asked me especially to make sure that you were not bored to absolute suicide here. He said to tell you he is sorry he cannot be here himself this evening, but I am to be certain that you enjoy yourself. Do you understand?" Eleanor's eyes were gleaming.

"I—I do not know what to say," stammered Joanna, truly at a loss and coloring at the very mention of his name. If Sir Giles really did wish it, then, of course, she should attend. It was just that it seemed so unlike him somehow. But perhaps he really did think she might be pining for more gaiety. Certainly he had remarked upon the gloom of the house often enough. And if the neighbors were coming, then perhaps . . .

"Say nothing. Just make yourself very fetching this evening. I shall send up the costume and one of the maids to dress you shortly before nine. Remember to stay masked. That's part of the fun, isn't it?" Eleanor smiled a smile that came nowhere near her eyes.

"Yes, my lady. I shall be ready," Joanna managed to croak. "Will that be all for now?" She needed badly to get upstairs to her room. The children were having their supper and would be put to bed shortly. She could have a few hours to herself. Perhaps she could plead a headache later . . .

"Yes, but see to it that those brats are in bed as soon as possible. And put the fear of God into them about venturing from their rooms this evening. I will not be embarrassed by them again. Do I make myself clear?"

"Of course, Lady Eleanor. They will not disturb anyone, I assure you," Joanna replied, trying to keep her voice mild. Papa would surely have found something to love in this woman, but even he'd have had to work particularly hard at it, she thought grimly. She dropped a small curtsey and left the room, making quickly for the stairs.

Once in her room, she fell into her big, comfortable chair and stared out at the beautiful purple fells that stretched as far as the eye could see to the east. If Sir Giles wanted her to go, she would go, naturally. It seemed odd that he would tell Lady Eleanor to look out for her, but it was kind of him to care, even though he had got it all wrong. She supposed it was a normal assumption that young women loved balls and parties, and he certainly didn't know her well enough to know that she was the exception to the rule. A nice quiet evening with a bath and a good book would have been much more to her liking. Well, she could still have the bath.

In front of her cluttered dressing table, Eleanor sat, snarling at her maid. "Damn you, girl! If this wig topples off into my soup, I'll have the skin off you!" Eleanor's hands reached up to grab the monstrous thing which was now tilted to the left at a precarious angle. Lily bit back a sigh and tried again. The contraption was at least a foot tall, an edifice of wire, wound about with long strands of false hair, greased and heavily powdered. Hanging from it at strategic points were a dozen little ornaments, miniature musical instruments, made of wood and gilded brightly.

Lady Eleanor was to be dressed as a notorious Italian diva, noted for wearing a half mask down the left side of her face and for her legendary number of lovers. Eleanor's dress was a riotous magenta, with very little bodice to hide her bosom. She glanced down at her chest while Lily continued to try to pin the absurd structure securely to her ladyship's scalp. Eleanor was painted all the way down to her nipples, and on her arms too. The white paint, freshly applied, was smooth and flawless, and the effect, with dress and wig, was striking, to say the least. Too bad that all the skimping on meals so that she would not grow fat had left her with such a meager bosom. Philippa was very well endowed and would no doubt appear this evening, spilling her tits all over anyone who cared to look. Still, Eleanor had managed to pad her lower bosom with cotton, thrusting her small breasts up and high into the décolletage of the gown, and, over all, she was pleased with the effect.

"Hurry up, girl, I need to be downstairs this instant. I have heard several carriages arrive already."

"I think it's done, my lady. Would you move your head a bit and let me see if there is any slipping?" The maid spoke tentatively. She had been struck before and did not relish the thought of being struck again.

Eleanor gave a great toss to her head, and the girl winced. But the wig stayed tight.

"It will do. Now fetch me my slippers and go upstairs to the little governess and get her presentable. Make her look like a woman and not like a church mouse. Here," Eleanor said, handing Lily one of her pots, "take her some rouge and see that she applies it liberally."

Lily bobbed a curtsey and took the pot, quite sure that the lovely Miss Carpenter would have none of it. She left the room quickly, glad to have been dismissed from the lioness's den without a mauling this evening. Not that the evening was over. Lily would have to sit up all night, waiting for Lady Eleanor to run in and have her makeup or costume refreshed from time to time. Occasionally the woman would need the basin quickly, to vomit the brandy she swilled down too liberally. Then Lily would be left to clean up the mess. No, the evening was far from over.

Upstairs, Joanna stared aghast at the sight that met her eyes. The costume was a nightmare of immodesty, with a décolletage past any hope of decency. It was ostensibly a shepherdess's dress, although Joanna was quite certain no shepherdess in all the history of England had ever possessed such attire. The gown was made of yards and yards of sprigged muslin, accented fetchingly with bits of delicate white lace peeping from hem and sleeves. If only there were some lace at the bosom! A great deal of it! There was a crook for her to carry, a white domino mask with lace all around it, an elaborate, musty-smelling powdered wig, and a rather lovely wide-brimmed laced and flowered bonnet. But the neckline was out of the question.

Joanna was giving it one last hopeless tug, to no avail, when she heard a light tap on the door. "Come in!" she called, desperation in her voice, shielding her chest ineffectively with her hands.

"Oh, Lily, thank heavens you've come!" Joanna wailed. "You've got to get me out of this dress. I can't possibly wear it outside of this room!"

"But why on earth not, Miss Carpenter? It's a beautiful dress!" said Lily, walking toward her, smiling. Indeed, the pretty young governess was lovely, with her clear, unpainted skin and her freshly washed scent. Even her hair was shining clean, Lily noted appreciatively. Such a contrast to her ladyship below who just continued to apply goose grease to her hair day after day, then powdered it or covered it with a wig.

"Just look at this bosom, Lily!" wailed Joanna. "I shall be embarrassed to death if I let anyone see me like this." Joanna kept tugging, but there was nothing much to tug.

Lily gave a hoot of laughter. "You won't be showing anything that most of the other woman at the party aren't showing, Miss Carpenter. And a sight prettier your bosom is, too, compared to most of those over-painted old harridans."

"Oh, hush, Lily. Someone might hear you," Joanna said, giggling nonetheless.

"You're right, though," said Lily, holding Joanna at arm's length and perusing her thoughtfully. "It really doesn't look like you. I know!" she said, her eyes lighting up. "Don't you have a pretty lacy handkerchief? I've seen you with one peeking out of your sleeve haven't I?"

"Yes, I do," replied Joanna, comprehension dawning. "It's here in my drawer." She fetched the pretty little piece, a gift from Squire on her sixteenth birthday, and held it out for inspection.

"Perfect! I was afraid it might be too small, but this will do nicely for a fichu." Lily took the lacy square and with a few deft folds tucked it neatly into the offending décolletage.

"There!" she said, stepping back to view her handiwork. "It hides a pair of sins, Miss Carpenter. Now just stand still while I pin it."

Joanna surveyed herself in the mirror while Lily worked. Yes, the handkerchief worked wonders. She breathed a sigh of relief.

"Now why don't you sit down and let me do up your hair, Miss Carpenter?" said Lily. "Are you planning to wear that—hairpiece?" Lily tried to hold her tone neutral, but Joanna could hear the disapproval.

"It is hideous, isn't it?" she replied with a grin. "Do you think I can get away with just the hat over my own hair? I suppose all the ladies will be in wigs, but I've never worn one and I must say I find them rather silly-looking. No one but Squire wore one in Little Haver, and he only wore an old tye wig when he wanted to dress up for some reason."

"I think your hair is beautiful just the way it is, miss. See how it shines?" Lily gently brushed Joanna's dark tresses. "I don't think it will matter if you don't wear the wig, particularly since the hat is so large." With a deft twist, Lily caught up Joanna's hair and began pinning with nimble fingers. Joanna was surprised to see her hair seem to spring to do Lily's bidding. Curling tendrils framed her face, and her usual tight bun in the back gave way to a cascade of curls which fell to her neck.

"You make it look so effortless, Lily," said Joanna appreciatively. "I could never get it to look like this."

"You have wonderful thick hair, miss, with lots of natural curl to it. You can make this head of hair do anything you want. And it looks so much nicer than those smelly old wigs!"

"Oh, you are very kind, Lily, but don't go to much trouble. I intend to make a brief appearance and then disappear back upstairs. I'm hoping there will be such a crush that I won't be missed."

"Just don't run afoul of Lady Eleanor, miss," Lily said, her eyes troubled. "For some reason she seems to be setting great store on your attending this evening. Look, she even sent one of her rouge pots for you. I don't suppose . . . ?" Lily trailed off questioningly, holding up the pot, a hint of a smile on her face.

"Not even if she ordered me to wear it, Lily," Joanna answered, laughing. "Besides, I'll have the domino on over my eyes, and the big hat shading my face. She won't notice if I'm wearing paint or not. And why on earth would she care? I realize that I am not up to the latest mode, but if I'm that much of a social embarrassment, why inflict me on her guests at all?" Joanna gave a nervous little tug to her makeshift fichu and noted with approval that it stayed tight.

"Oh, miss, you'll be just fine. Mrs. Davies said that some of the old-timers are invited—people from the neighborhood. They're quiet and respectable-like and you'll like them. There!" Lily stepped back and proudly surveyed her work.

"You look beautiful, miss. I shouldn't wonder if you weren't the most beautiful woman at the whole party!"

Indeed, as Joanna gave herself a once-over in her mirror, she was startled at the transformation. The hat was tied aslant, creating a shadowing that emphasized her cheekbones, and her dark curls framed her long neck.

"Well, if I had you to dress me more often, I should grow quite vain, Lily," said Joanna, laughing. But she was secretly pleased and a bit wondering at this unfamiliar image in the mirror.

Lily fastened the domino across Joanna's eyes, then handed her the long crook. "You'll put them all to shame, miss," said the maid, grinning broadly.

"I hope not, Lily," answered Joanna with a sigh, gathering her dress about her and proceeding to the door. "I don't need any more angry ladies in my life." Squaring her shoulders, she left the room.

*   *   *

Eleanor glanced with bitterness across the room to where the little hussy held all the young men in thrall. Not only were Dalton and Hayhurst sniffing after her as they had been bidden to do, but three or four other young bucks were clustered around, including the maddeningly handsome Count Damelio, of dubious Italian nobility but obvious personal talent. Eleanor's eyes strayed to the count's vaguely Elizabethan costume, with puffy, overdone sleeves, velvet tunic, glittering paste jewels, stockings, cross-garters— an elegant, studied effect. But the clear focus of the outfit was the codpiece, large beyond proportion, meant to amuse, no doubt, but to entice as well. And Eleanor was enticed. Damelio had been dancing attendance on Eleanor early in the evening, capering about, showing off, making veiled little suggestions and innuendos, undressing her with his rich, dark eyes, and brushing his hands against her at the slightest provocation.

And now he was off doing the same tricks for that little bitch. Eleanor could blame herself for it—after all, it was she who had insisted the chit appear this evening. And that costume she had supplied had been one of her own most fetching, although she was amused to note that the prim and proper Miss Carpenter had pinned lace onto the bosom. Still, it would be worth it in the end if Giles managed to show up and Dalton and Hayhurst were up to the task set for them. They certainly seemed enthusiastic enough.

"My lady," came a hiss in her ear. She turned to see Hawton next to her, attired as one of a number of harlequins in attendance.

"Yes?" she answered, smiling up at him and

linking her arm through his. Perhaps if Damelio noticed that she had other possibilities . . .

"Sir Giles has just ridden into the stables. He told me to tell you that he would change and join you shortly."

"Thank you, Hawton. Be a dear and fetch me some punch. I swear, I am dry as a bone with greeting everyone." She gave him a come-hither smile. If she lost Damelio to other pursuits this evening, she'd need alternative arrangements. She watched as Hawton threaded his way through the large crowd, disappearing into a sea of swirling colors. Wonderful! Everything was set in motion, and with a little luck she could expect the noose to tighten around the neck of little Miss Carpenter within the hour. Now if she could get that gaggle of fools away from the girl and let Dalton and Hayhurst play out the scenario . . .

Joanna felt positively stifled. Since the moment she had walked in the door she had been surrounded by a group of very attentive young men. They were all in costume, each one more outlandish than the next. One, Count Somebody or Other, was flaunting a most amazing contraption on his privates. Joanna was trying to look everywhere but there. She had tried valiantly to keep up with the repartee, and while she had never considered herself a prude—small towns, after all, provided a wealth of opportunities for learning about life— she was rather shocked at the sheer license of the conversation. It would seem, to hear them talk, that nearly everyone in the room, at least among Eleanor's set, was sleeping with someone other than his or her spouse. Joanna felt that none of it was any of her business, but she had been met with amused stares when she had tried to turn the discussion to more neutral topics, such as the lovely local landscape, or even politics.

Most of the names of the attentive young gentlemen had escaped her, but Mr. Dalton and Mr. Hayhurst she remembered, because they were the two to whom Lady Eleanor had introduced her when she had first entered. Neither had left her side for the last hour, and she now despaired of sneaking away early as she had planned.

With apprehension, she saw that Lady Eleanor was making her way toward their little group. Joanna tried again, this time successfully, to disengage her hand from the count's, only to find it seized immediately by one of the other men.

"I see you have made quite a hit with my young gentlemen, Miss Carpenter." Lady Eleanor's voice was purring, but her eyes held a glittering malice. "You all must know that our little Miss Carpenter is our governess—she takes care of Giles's niece and idiot nephew. Isn't that a dreary way to spend one's days? No wonder she's making the most of her night off!" Eleanor tittered loudly, joined by the gentlemen. Joanna could feel her face flaming. Why hadn't she just refused to come down to this infernal party?

"But I must borrow a few of you. We're going to have a rather naughty little contest and I need some particularly licentious judges to help me. Dalton and Hayhurst, you stay and keep our little man-hunter happy, and the rest of you can have your turns with her later." Eleanor linked her arm through Count Damelio's, her eyes meeting those of Dalton and Hayhurst behind him. If the count was annoyed at the interruption, he gave no sign,

173

and they walked off, trailing several other gentlemen in their wake.

"Let's step out on the terrace, Miss Carpenter,
shall we?" said Dalton or Hayhurst—Joanna
wasn't quite sure by now which was which.

"Yes, it's so stuffy in here, isn't it?" chimed in
the other.

Before Joanna could answer, they had each
taken one of her arms and made for the doors
which opened onto the terrace. Well, that was all
right with her. It was stuffy inside, with all those
elaborate costumes and stale scents, and she was
red-faced and fuming over the "man-hunter" remark. Perhaps she could contrive some way to get
away from them, now that she wasn't surrounded.

Inside, Eleanor noted with a smile that Dalton
and Hayhurst had managed to get the girl onto
the terrace, and not a moment too soon, for she
spied Giles coming down the stairs just then. Typ-
ical of him to shun fancy dress, even though she'd
left a perfectly fine costume for him on the bed,
that of a bejeweled and beturbaned pasha. Still,
he looked handsome in his formal black frock coat
and snowy white linen. It was a shame he favored
such dark colors, shunning the brocades and pas-
tels so popular now among men of the ton.
Eleanor noted with a practiced, approving eye
how his breeches molded his muscled thighs.
Well, perhaps he'd find someone among her set to
bury his sorrows in tonight. Philippa had made
several remarks about him, and if Eleanor knew
anything about Philippa, Giles would have his
hands full, literally and figuratively. Now, if she
could just keep Giles busy for five minutes, to give
Dalton and Hayhurst time to get little Joanna into
a thoroughly compromising position . . .

*   *   *

The air outside was fresh and cool on Joanna's face and she drank it in gratefully. There was the tang of the sea in each breath, and she longed to be on the beach, alone and barefoot. She felt confused and unsettled. She had never before attended anything remotely resembling this soiree. Squire's rare entertainments had been smallish country affairs, populated with familiar faces, aged and dear. The talk had run to farming and politics, and although there was the occasional naughtiness in the village, Papa was always quick to put such things right with a wedding, and not another word was ever spoken about it. Indeed, Joanna had not been brought up to consider such goings-on particularly interesting, or food for conversation, but rather the inevitable consequence of youth and high spirits, neither remarkable nor fascinating. But to hear Lady Eleanor's friends talk, there was nothing else in the world so captivating as discussing who was sleeping with whom.

The trio wandered for a moment in the dark, away from the door and the long windows which cast squares of yellow light on the gray stones of the terrace. Joanna was lost in her thoughts, feeling very much like a fish out of water.

"Let's go sit down on that bench," said one of her attentive duo amiably, gesturing to a bench near the edge of the terrace, bordered by several box yews, a good distance from the door. Their eyes met in amusement over her head. She was steered rather than led to the bench, but as she thought it might be nice to sit for a while she did not object.

Seated, however, she was discomfited to find

that neither gentleman had released her arms and each was sitting much too close, hemming her in on both sides, thighs pushing against her. There was nowhere to move except forward, but as she tried to extricate herself she found that they held her wedged in.

"I would prefer to stand, actually, Mr. Dalton," she said to neither in particular.

"And we would prefer to sit, my beauty," whispered the one on her left into her ear.

"Please let go, sir," she began, alarmed at his tone and the strength of his grip on her arm. "I do not find this sort of thing amusing at all." Although she struggled, they both held fast. The one on her right, Hayhurst, she presumed, snaked his arm about her waist after capturing her hand in his other hand.

"It can be very amusing, my dear Joanna, quite diverting if you relax and enjoy it. Eleanor thinks you're a virgin. Can that possibly be true? It's just too, too droll." The whisper came hot and moist into her other ear, and she felt lips tracing a path down her cheek.

"Stop it! How dare you!" she gasped, only to find her cry cut off as the lips suddenly covered her own. She found herself powerless, gripped tightly by the two large men, the one thrusting his tongue into her mouth, the other ripping hungrily at her décolletage. . . .

"Giles, I do think you ought to step outside and see what's become of your little governess friend," Eleanor leaned over and whispered into Giles's ear, interrupting his conversation with one of the old goats who lived in the area.

Giles excused himself from the old gentleman

and turned with a glare on his stepsister. "I had not realized Miss Carpenter was in attendance," he said with an edge to his voice. "What seems to be the problem, Eleanor?" He had scoured the room for Joanna when he had first come down and had been relieved not to find her. He had fervently hoped, when he received word that his stepsister was throwing this damned party, that Joanna would heed his warning and stay away. Most of the guests were friends of Eleanor's, an unsavory lot who had no morals about them, not at all fit companions for an unworldly parson's daughter. Now he could feel his stomach churn at her words. Why was Joanna outside?

"Oh, she insisted on being here, darling," Eleanor purred, amused at the tightening of his lips. "I don't think she's at all the little virgin she pretends to be. I saw her take Dalton and Hayhurst in tow out to the terrace a few minutes ago, and I must say she had quite a lascivious look about her. I swear, she was positively fondling them both. They're all alike, you know, these little penniless governess types, tarts on the make."

He turned away with a snarl, leaving Eleanor staring at his back, a slow smile spreading across her face. Perfect. No doubt one of those randy boys would be buried up to the hilt by now, a pretty sight for the morally upright Sir Giles Chapman. She turned and bestowed a meaningful look upon Count Damelio, who was all hers once more, now that she had removed the governess from the scene. Well, with a little luck, Giles would send the wretched girl packing tonight. Hawton could drive her to the nearest inn. Then he could take a poke at the used baggage, too. It was just too divine. . . .

Giles stepped onto the terrace, his eyes taking a moment to adjust to the dark after the brightness of the drawing room. He could make out nothing in the gloom, but he thought he heard muffled sounds from the shadows to the rear. He moved forward, uneasy in his heart. Obviously, Eleanor was lying about Joanna. But what devilment was afoot, and what was Joanna doing out in the dark with two of Eleanor's reprobates?

He stopped dead, deep in the shadows, shocked at the sight that met his eyes. It had to be Joanna. In the dim light he could just make out the tumble of her dark hair. But what cruel twist of fate could take the one bright, pure thing in his life and expose it for a foul, corrupt delusion? He felt his very soul drain away as he took in the scene. Not one, but two men. One of them was kissing her, devouring her lips, while the other, unspeakably, had pulled up her skirts and was pawing between her legs. He could not see her hands and wondered if she fumbled madly at one or both of the men's crotches. Even as he watched, she bucked wildly, clearly in the throes of passion. He had heard of women like this, who would take on two men at once, but never in his life had he expected to see such a thing, and never again would he allow himself to believe in another living soul.

As he started to turn away, he heard a strangled cry, then watched in astonishment as the man kissing her reared up, his face contorted, his body convulsed. As the one man fell back, the other cried out and twisted away. It was then that Giles could see that each of them held one of Joanna's arms, pinning her to the bench. Now she was bucking furiously, pulling away, whimpering in short, terrified gasps. The first man fell to the ground, letting go of her arm and grabbing at his crotch. He moaned piteously and writhed about on the stone floor. Joanna leaped forward, trying to stand, but the other man lunged for her and pulled her back down, drawing back his arm to strike her face.

In a heartbeat, Giles was there, grabbing the man's arm and pulling him off of Joanna. He could hear the sound of tearing cartilage as his fist connected with the man's nose, sending him bleeding to the pavement. Giles grabbed Joanna and thrust her behind him, watching his two opponents, both of whom writhed now on the ground, moaning. There was blood all over the face of the one he had struck.

"Force a woman on my property again and I'll kill you. Do I make myself clear?" The one with the bloody face glared up at him and received a kick in the gut in response. "Clean yourselves up and get out. Do not go back inside and do not speak to Eleanor. If I see either of you again I'll horsewhip you off my land. Now do you understand?" Giles's tone was murderous, his words bitten off. Behind him his hands clutched around Joanna, who seemed to be barely standing.

At the barest of nods from both young men, Giles turned, picked Joanna up into his arms, and walked away, not toward the house but down the stairs into the garden.

He could feel Joanna sag against him, sobbing convulsively.

With long strides he made his way through the garden, coming at last to the little garden door set in the wall. Turning the handle, he was relieved to find it unlocked. It was black as pitch in the lower hallway, but he made his way surely to the rear stairs, mounting them swiftly to the third floor. Fortunately, they met no one on the way, and he turned the handle to her door and stepped inside, closing and locking the door behind them, no one the wiser.

He set her gently on the bed, then turned up the wick of the lamp Joanna had left burning low on her dresser. He sat down beside her, and very carefully removed her mask.

He sat back in shock as he looked at her face. One eye was completely puffed shut and the mask edge had cut into her face, leaving a bloody line where it had been. Her lips were purple and bleeding. Her breathing came in great gasps, her eyes were wild and vacant, and he was not sure she was fully conscious.

Moving to the washstand, he quickly poured water into the bowl, then brought it, with a towel, over to her nightstand. Very gently, he pressed the wet cloth to her cheek, trying to wipe away the blood without pulling at the cut. Rinsing out the cloth, he held it to her eye.

Joanna drew a deep, shuddering breath and began to moan. As the light returned to her eyes, she suddenly tried to rise and struggle against him, her moan turning into a scream.

"Hush, hush, you're safe now!" he whispered urgently, moving his hand gently across her mouth. The last thing he wanted was curious servants responding to screams from the governess's room. She quieted, her eyes finding his. He moved his hand to her cheek and caressed her softly. She nuzzled against his hand and shut her pain-filled eyes, tears slipping from beneath her lowered eyelids.

Feeling large and clumsy, he brushed her tears

away with his thumb, his touch gentle. His heart twisted at the sight of her eye, swollen and purpling now. He should have killed the bastards while he had the chance.

He felt Joanna's hand touch his chest and, seizing it, he brought it to his lips.

"Thank you," she whispered. "I couldn't have fought them off much longer."

He closed his eyes against the image that arose in his mind, and the thought of what might have happened had he not been there.

"Well, you managed to take care of one of them pretty well," he murmured. He could still see the look of contorted pain on the man's face. She must have given him one hell of a kick where it counted.

Joanna flushed, then asked, "Why are you here? Lady Eleanor told me you were not coming."

"Did she, now?" he said, thoughtfully. "That is very interesting, since she herself sent for me, yesterday. I came because she expressed concern about you, and even though I had warned you to avoid her and her crowd, I was afraid you'd be tempted to attend such a large soiree."

"She told me you had specifically requested that I attend. It's the only reason I agreed to go."

He was silent for a moment, his jaw tight. "I know you don't want to talk about it," he finally said, "but how did . . . what happened tonight?" He held her hand with one of his. With the other he traced through her long dark hair spread out against her pillow.

"When I came downstairs this evening, Lady Eleanor pulled me over and introduced me to those two . . . men. They were Mr. Dalton and Mr. Hayhurst—I was never quite sure which was which. But after that, they never left my side, even when others joined our group. I seemed to be the center of attention, but their conversation was so—well, they seemed to go on a great deal about—things that are none of my business, certainly—and I was uncomfortable. They really weren't interested in anything I had to say, so I was hoping just to slip away. Then Lady Eleanor came and pulled away all the others—an Italian count and a few other young men. She told Mr. Dalton and Mr. Hayhurst to stay and keep me company, then she went off, with the others following behind. I thought I might be able to slip away then, but they insisted we step out for some air, and it was so stuffy, so I . . ." She broke off, her voice trembling.

"Shhh," he said softly, bending down to put his cheek next to hers, the one that was not swollen and torn. "I know what happened next. Don't say any more."

But Joanna needed to talk, needed to tell him, to banish the demons. "They were like animals," she whispered, turning her face to his. "No, not like animals. No animal would be so deliberately cruel. I couldn't even scream and they were pawing at me, holding me down . . ."

He gathered her tightly in his arms, only to release her quickly as she gasped with pain.

"What is it? Have I hurt you?" he asked, fear in his eyes.

"It's—my side," she gasped out. "One of them hit me there."

Growling with anger, he ripped at the buttons that held her bodice closed, scattering them across the bedcovers. He pulled the dress material away from her, then tugged at the chemise, pulling it down to her waist.

"Turn over on your side, Joanna," he said softly, willing himself to ignore the lovely, creamy breasts which gleamed in the lamplight.

Joanna complied, not meeting his eye. She heard him swear and looked up at him questioningly.

"You are very badly bruised, Joanna, here, along this rib. Does this hurt?" With exceeding caution he pressed lightly, withdrawing the instant he saw her wince with pain. "I think you may have a broken rib," he said in a tight voice. "I am now so sorry I did not kill them when I had the opportunity. Perhaps I will anyway."

"No, don't!" she cried, turning back to face him, eyes fearful. "I'm sure they won't bother me again, and I can't have murder on your soul just because I was a fool enough to go out onto the terrace with those jackals."

He smiled grimly at her. "Don't even think of blaming yourself for any of this, Joanna. These people are monsters." He did not add that it was obvious to him that she had been set up by Eleanor. She would figure it out soon enough.

"I'm going to go downstairs and get some fresh water and some bandages to wrap your ribs. Can you get up and lock the door behind me? I don't think anyone will bother you, but I want to be certain you are absolutely safe."

Fear shadowed her eyes, but she nodded gamely.

"Good girl." He smiled at her and gently pulled up her chemise, careful not to press on her side. Without realizing it, he breathed a sigh of relief. It had been such a strain to avoid looking at her lovely breasts. He helped her up carefully and swung her legs over the side, supporting her as

183

they walked slowly to the door.

"I will knock four times when I come back. Do not open the door until you are certain it is I. Promise me?" he asked, unlocking the door.

"I promise," she replied, and with a pat on her good cheek he was gone. Joanna closed the door swiftly behind him and locked it securely. She walked to her dressing table, wincing with each step. She hurt all over, far more than she had let on. He was angry enough already. She could feel that there was a deep scratch on the inside of her thigh—no doubt one of the beasts had been wearing a ring. She gasped when she caught sight of her face in the mirror. Lifting her fingers, she gingerly touched her eye, then traced down the angry red line where the mask edge had torn her cheek. With a sigh, she pulled up her skirt and examined her thigh. As she had suspected, a long cut ran from near the top of her thigh to her knee. She hobbled over to the washwater on the bedstand and laved herself. Better to do this herself than ask Sir Giles, she thought ruefully. Not that he hasn't already seen. . . . She found herself blushing and finished quickly, determined to change into something more suitable before he returned.

As carefully as she could manage, she pulled off the skirt and petticoats, then divested herself of the bodice. Standing in only her chemise, she pulled a clean cotton nightgown from a drawer. She pulled the chemise over her head and inspected the dark, purpling splotch across her ribs. It looks as bad as it feels, she thought to herself, wondering how long it would be before she felt whole again.

There were four quick taps on the door. Grabbing up the nightgown, she pulled it quickly over her head, flinching at the shooting pain in her side from the movement. Moving as fast as she could to the door, she paused before it uncertainly. Surely it must be he!

"Who is it?" she called softly, hoping her voice would carry through the thick paneling.

"Giles." His voice was so low that she could barely hear him.

Relieved, she pulled back the lock and opened the door, closing and locking it as soon as he entered.

His eyes swept over her, and for an instant she thought she saw that haunted, hungry look he had worn a few days ago. Saying nothing, he took her hand and led her to the bed. He had an armload of bandages and a dark colored glass bottle.

"I had to fob off Mrs. Davies with a tale of a drunken gentleman who has taken a fall," he said, a glint of amusement in his eyes. "She was all set to come running until I explained the gentleman was mortified and didn't wish anyone to know." He paused a moment and looked at her in confusion. "Actually, I didn't stop to think that you might prefer Mrs. Davies to me," he said.

"Oh no, I don't want anyone else to know about this, and you've already . . . I mean . . ." She broke off, flushing to the roots. "Oh, Sir Giles, there is so much more to the world than I ever knew, and I feel like such a fool!" she cried.

He turned to her, his brown eyes warm in the lamplight. "Stay in your world, Joanna," he said softly. "Don't let the scoundrels and knaves spoil it for you."

He rinsed out the cloth he had used earlier in fresh water. "Now, my nursing skills are slim, nonexistent to be precise, but I believe we have to get you cleaned up and bandaged and hope that there is no festering," he said, applying the warm cloth to the scratch on her cheek. "Are there any other injuries you know of?"

"Well, there's one on my thigh—a long scratch that's bleeding. I think one of them was wearing a ring. But I've already washed it," she said, reddening.

Giles said nothing, but Joanna could see the tightening around his mouth. He finished washing the scratch on her face and turned to pour something out of the bottle onto a fresh cloth.

"This will sting a bit, but my doctor gave it to me to clean my cuts when the cart fell on me, and since I am still alive, I figure it won't kill you," he said genially, just before he clapped a noxious cloth across her cheek.

"Ouch!" she cried. "That burns!"

"That proves it's good for you," he said, smiling, then pulled the cloth away. "Let me look at your thigh," he said softly, kneeling down in front of her. "I'm sorry. I know you are embarrassed, but it will be much worse if it is not kept clean."

Joanna sighed and raised her nightgown enough to let him see the scratch, which stretched nearly to the top of her thigh. She bit her lip in embarrassment, refusing to look, as he carefully washed the scratch and applied the offending medicine. She looked up as he pulled the cotton nightgown down over her legs. His head was bent down and she could not see his face.

"I'd like to bandage your ribs, if you'll let me, Joanna," he said, standing, still not meeting her eyes. "I've broken a rib myself, so I think I can manage—at least until we can get the doctor here tomorrow to see it done properly."

"I don't want the doctor—" she began.

"I know, but you'll have him nonetheless. I must be sure you are well, and I don't trust my own medical skills. Besides, the local doctor is a good man, and he will keep our confidence."

They stared at each other for a moment, then Joanna slowly pulled open the front of her nightgown. Shrugging her shoulders out of it with a wince of pain, she let it fall to her waist.

She heard his soft intake of breath and closed her eyes. She could feel the bandage slipping around her, his gentle fingers wrapping it tightly under her breasts. She knew she should be perishing of mortification, yet she felt that odd feeling again, the way she had felt when he had held her a few days ago, as if she needed something badly, but what? His hands were hot against her flesh, and the heat lingered after his hands moved on.

His breathing was ragged when he finished. Abruptly he turned away. Joanna buttoned her nightgown slowly, the memory of his hands on her, burning, burning . . . what was the matter with her?

"Are you hurt anywhere else?" he asked, his voice harsh.

Her eyes flew open. "What's wrong?" she asked in alarm. He was angry with her. What had she done? But his face, when he turned back to her, held that ravaged look, a look of hunger and pain.

For a long moment their gazes held. Joanna caught her breath. She could feel his need now, and it was answered by her own.

Slowly, without conscious thought, she stepped toward him. "Hold me again. The way you did the other day," she whispered.

His arms came about her gently, his hands

stroking her back. She could feel his face buried in her hair. She burned up and down the length of her body with the heat of him pressed against her.

"You are so beautiful," he whispered, pulling back to look at her. "I haven't thought of anything but you since the moment I first laid eyes on you." He stared into the soft brown depths of her beautiful eyes, mesmerized by the lights that danced within. Almost as if of its own volition, his hand reached up to her face. Fascinated, he watched his fingers trace a gentle line down her soft cheek, then cup her chin. He drew his face down, down to hers, then lightly touched his lips to hers. For the briefest instant they held suspended, then with a moan he deepened the kiss, his arms going about her again, but gently, as if he thought she might break at his touch. Then his lips found her cheek, burning hot along her neck, her throat.

"I can't touch you anywhere without hurting you, my love," he whispered into her hair. "I can't kiss you . . . I can't hold you," he broke off. His hands moved up and down her back. He reached down with one arm and placed it under her knees, swinging her carefully up onto the bed and sitting down next to her.

Joanna's senses swam. Her skin was on fire beneath his touch, and she felt as if she could not remember how to breathe. She was spinning, spinning down, pulled by some unknown feeling, some urgent need she could not name.

Without warning his lips moved against hers, as his mouth found hers in searing possession.

Shock chased through her but she could not pull away. His lips were hot and hard against her own, stoking the fire that burned inside her. With an answering moan, her lips parted under his as he pulled her against him, very gently. He raised his hands to her neck, tangling them in her hair, pulling her closer as his tongue found the inside of her mouth, plundering, seeking.

Joanna gasped with the shock of the intrusion and the hot pleasure that flooded through her at the intimacy of his touch. Almost without knowing what she did, her hands slid along his back against the hard length of him, feeling under her fingers his muscular strength.

Giles felt her press against him, and groaned as the heat of her flooded his loins. Oh God, it had been so long! She tasted so sweet; her lips were full and ripe and made to be kissed. His hand slid down her back, coming to rest on the swell of her buttocks. He felt like an adolescent with his first woman. He was in danger of losing all control. His other hand slid under her arm around to the small, soft mound of her breast. He felt her gasp beneath his lips, then she pulled away, her heavy-lidded brown eyes shot through with confusion and uncertainty.

For a moment they stared at one another, breathing raggedly, the heat a tangible thing between them. Then, abruptly, he thrust her away from him, holding her at arm's length in a grip tight enough to bruise, his face tortured, his eyes dark with passion and pain.

"Ahh, Joanna, please forgive me, I had no right," he rasped. He could see in the lamplight that her lips were swollen and purpled from his assault. With a clumsy finger he traced the swelling as if he could soothe it away. "I feel like an animal," he said softly, his hand lingering against her cheek. "But I cannot keep my hands off of you."

"I'm afraid I must beg your pardon, Sir Giles," she whispered shakily. "I am so confused. I have never felt such things before. I've never behaved . . . never in my life . . . you must think I'm . . ."

"Hush, don't even think such a thing," he said, smiling at her, his eyes warm. "You are a perfect lady and I am a cad to take such advantage of you. And, by the way, you must not call me sir. It's just Giles."

Joanna gave him a tentative smile and drew a deep breath. She was confused and ashamed, yet oddly exhilarated. What she had done was mad, dreadful, yet she knew without doubt that if he reached for her again she would melt into his arms and feel joy in his touch. Was this what she was at heart? No better than the tart Ambrose had suggested she had become?

He sat back, his hands gentle now on her arms. "I promise I will behave myself, but I will not leave you here alone tonight. There is some devilment afoot and I trust no one. Tomorrow I'll see to getting you a better lock for your door—the one you have could be pushed open by a child. I'll sit in your chair while you sleep, if you won't be too uncomfortable with me here."

"Yes, please, Giles, stay with me," she answered softly, her hand finding his. "But don't sleep in the chair. That's silly with this big bed here, and you'll be awake all night. You can stretch out here on the bed, if you can trust me to behave myself." She hoped she sounded as if she were joking. In truth, she was not at all sure that she could lie next to him without seeking again the heat of his kiss.

He laughed softly and slowly stretched himself the length of the bed, lying carefully on top of the bedclothes. He turned his body in toward hers and put an arm protectively over her, below her ribs, his face against her neck, his other hand lacing through her hair. She could feel her heart pounding against him and knew he could feel it too. She was a whirlwind of emotions inside, exhilarated, frightened, confused—she did not know how she felt. Safe. She felt safe. Perhaps it was a false sense of security. Perhaps the light of day would bring new fears. Perhaps she was already lost, already too many steps down the road of ruin to turn back. But for now she would sleep in the protective circle of his arms, warm and safe.

Chapter Nine

"Giles, you are simply making too much of this. It has nothing to do with me if the silly boys misinterpreted her friendliness as an invitation. She certainly looked willing enough to me, what little I could see of her, surrounded as she was by admiring men all evening. She's quite an accomplished flirt, Giles. You are much mistaken if you continue believing her to be all innocence. In fact, I am quite certain you've got it all backwards. Have you stopped to consider that she was a willing partner until she saw you? I swear, Giles, you are making a perfect fool of yourself over that cheap bit of muslin."

Eleanor was trying to sound nonchalant and exasperated but she was growing more unnerved by the minute. She had never seen Giles so angry. Not even over some of her escapades with Violet. He had been lying in wait for her when she had finally crawled from her bed this afternoon, and he had damn near dragged her into the library, slamming the massive door shut behind them. There would be bruises on her wrist from the way he had pulled her in here.

She had thought it odd when Dalton and Hayhurst had not reported back to her last night. She had looked forward to enjoying the blow-by-blow account of their success. She'd seen nothing further of Giles or Miss Carpenter, either, but then she had not really expected to. It was a great disappointment, adding to the thudding of her head and the roiling of her queasy stomach, to learn now from Giles that her carefully laid plans had somehow gone awry. Apparently the stupid boys had not managed to compromise the chit after all, and had only succeeded in getting themselves run off the property.

And how was Giles managing to link her with the scheme? Her head pounded so badly she could barely think. Waking to find that she and her naughty count had drunk up all the brandy in her bedroom last night, she had crept downstairs for a splash of it to take the pain away. Now Giles stood between her and the crystal decanter which she eyed with longing, wondering if she dared brush past him to get to it.

She stole a look at his face. It was black as a thundercloud. His hands were clenched tightly as if he were contemplating pounding her with his fists. He stood with a tension that made him seem like a tiger about to spring. Well, he would strike her or not but she must have some brandy.

With a nonchalance she did not feel, she crossed the room, coming as near to him as she had to, and poured herself a liberal tot. "Join me, darling?" she found herself taunting. It was so hard to break old habits, and, after all, he had never struck her yet.

"You are a common drunk, Eleanor. If I took the brandy away from you, you'd have the shakes and hallucinations. Look at yourself. I've seen tavern sluts who were more fastidious about themselves."

She wore her dressing gown tied loosely about her slender form. She hadn't bothered to look at herself in the mirror before leaving her room—which she rarely did until she had a chance to fix herself up. She was aware that her hair was lank and her makeup from last night was no doubt blotched and smeared. Damn him! What did the little tart of a governess look like in the morning? Lovely? Fresh?

"You wound me, brother dear," Eleanor replied, keeping the rising bitterness out of her voice. At least this was more like it, back to the usual harmless bickering. She could handle this. "You know perfectly well I am impeccable in my appearance whenever I am entertaining. I am simply tired this morning. It was a late night, after all." Indeed, Count Damelio had been all she could have asked for. And more. His outrageous codpiece had not exaggerated by much. She had made him slip away to his own room at dawn. She had told him she was tired, but it had more to do with waking up together, a face next to hers on a pillow, up close, in the light of day . . .

"Sit down, Eleanor. There will be changes here and they will affect you directly."

She took her time in seating herself gracefully on a small upholstered divan in the center of the room. She hoped he wasn't going to go on and on.

He could be such a bore when he got preachy. Perhaps he would cut her allowance. She allowed herself a small smile. Wouldn't he be surprised when she made no protest. Let him do what he liked. Lord Beeson, Hawton, and she had talked last night, and their plans to bring in the Irish girls were all set. She took a long sip of brandy, welcoming the fire in her throat, and looked up at Giles a little provocatively. She was feeling more sure of herself, the brandy and the thoughts of her own money reviving her spirits.

"I am planning to ask Miss Carpenter to marry me, Eleanor, and if she will have me, we will marry as soon as the banns can be posted," he stated flatly.

"What?" She fairly flew out of her seat, the brandy sloshing over the rim of the glass. She stood swaying almost drunkenly, doubting that she could possibly have heard him say this thing.

"I believe it takes a few weeks to post the banns," he went on coolly. "I'm sure Joanna will know. Her father was a vicar." For just a moment the sun broke through the thunder in his face, but when he turned to look at her again the darkness was back in his eyes.

"I will give you a month, Eleanor. I'm sure you will agree that you and Joanna will not be happy together under the same roof. And frankly, I am sick to death of the sight and sound of you, what little I subject myself to. I am sure it will be in agreement with the request in my father's will for me to find you a house somewhere to rent. Far enough away from us that your poison will no longer spill into our lives, but close enough so that I can keep an eye on your expenses. Don't think I don't know about your gambling debts. I have turned a blind eye because I'd rather pay than listen to your whining. But if I must go to the expense of setting you up in a separate household, you will find there are limits to my generosity. I will provide you with an adequate budget, and you will learn to live within it. Do I make myself clear?"

She had sat down again with a heavy thud, unaware that she had done so. Even the brandy was forgotten in her hand. He meant to marry that conniving little witch. The little whore with the oh, so pretty young face and the simpering innocent smile. He would dare do this to her, daughter of an earl. Foist her off into some godforsaken little cottage somewhere and dole out pennies to her like a poor relation.

"You can't be serious," was her measured reply. She had recovered enough to swill down the last of her brandy.

"I really don't expect your approval or good wishes, Eleanor," he said coldly. "I simply wish to know that you understand me. I should hate to think that you are already drunk at this time of day."

With the shriek of a madwoman she hurled the cut glass at him. He dodged it with little effort and did not bother to watch it shatter against the wall behind him.

"I will not have it, do you hear me?" she screamed. "I won't be shunted off into some hole, just so you can bed down that tuppenny tart who calls herself a governess. She may be good enough for your family—God knows your father was nothing but a merchant when Mother stooped to marry him—but she's not good enough for me. I will not have you tying yourself to that slut." She ran her hands through her hair, eyes wild. "For pity's sake, if you want to take her, just do it, Giles," she went on, her tone that of furious exasperation. "Don't be a fool! You don't need to marry the chit!"

With a snarl, she crossed to the cart for another brandy, only to be stopped short when he seized her arm in a painful grip.

"Never let me hear you speak that way again of Miss Carpenter, Eleanor," he spat out. His face was inches from hers, and she could see the veins standing out on his neck. His fingers bit so hard into her arm she thought she would scream, but she wouldn't give him the satisfaction. "I will marry the girl, and let me point out that she is too good for the likes of you, not vice versa. But I wouldn't expect you to know anything about goodness." He released her arm, pushing her away from him. She stumbled and caught herself. Drawing herself up, she gave him a haughty look, its effect marred when her eyes slid to the decanter behind him.

"Go ahead and have your drink, Eleanor. Drink straight out of the decanter if you like. I wouldn't want you to start seeing rats and snakes crawling around on the floor."

The brandy won. Her hands were shaking as she poured herself another liberal dose, sloshing it over the top of the glass. She took a long sip before she turned back to him.

"I want a house in London," she announced, willing her voice to be steady.

Giles gave a bark of laughter. "London? Not on your life, Eleanor," he replied coldly. "I cannot even imagine the outrageous expense and mischief you would get up to in London. It's like trying to contemplate the number of stars in the sky. My mind simply cannot comprehend the possibilities."

"You bastard!" she screeched. "I tell you I will not allow this thing. I will write to my father's old solicitor in London. I am sure your father's will does not permit you to throw me out of this house. I'll drag your name through the courts."

"You know nothing of it, Eleanor. My father's will simply requests that I take care of you. It's not even required. In fact, I could throw you out in your dressing gown right now if I wished to, and you would have no legal recourse. I don't give a damn what anyone in London thinks of us, but please be advised that if you do run up any solicitor bills, you will pay them out of your allowance. Now, if you'll excuse me, I wish to speak with Miss Carpenter. And in case you are thinking of deviling her, think again. I will not be returning to Dufton until you are out of this house. You are not to go near her, nor will any of your friends. Do I make myself clear?"

She would not deign to answer, staring at him with all the hatred she had nurtured all these years spilling from her eyes.

He turned to go, taking the room in long strides. At the door he paused and looked at her, his eyes thoughtful. In a surprisingly gentle voice he said, "I know we have been at each other's throats for too long for there to be any kindly feelings between us, Eleanor. But please believe me when I say I do not wish you ill. I do wonder sometimes if you are not quite well. Too much brandy, perhaps. Too little sleep, too little food, too much . . . well, too much of your sort of pleasures. It cannot be good for you to abuse your body this way, day after day. You were always high-spirited, but in the last few years, it's been almost frightening to watch you slip lower and lower. Perhaps—"

"Get out! Get out, you miserable son of a bitch! I don't need to hear any of your pompous moralizing. I live the way I wish to live, and it is none of your damned business what I do!" She ended on a scream and turned away from him, missing the look of sadness in his eyes. She heard the door close, then there was silence, broken only by the ticking of a clock on the mantel.

Mechanically she rose and made for the decanter. This time she did take it with her, back to the little table next to the divan onto which she dropped heavily. He would marry the girl. Her gut twisted at the thought. Why did it hurt so much, the thought of them together? God only knew, she could have had him years ago if she'd wanted him. In fact, she had introduced him to the impecunious Violet, hoping that he would shift his puppy love from herself to her friend. And indeed, he had. Why had it not hurt like this when he had fallen so hard for Violet? Why did it hurt so much now? She drained yet another glass. Her head still hurt but her stomach was quiet now.

Thank God for Lord Beeson. His proposal now seemed a miracle of timing. She would have her first payoff before Giles threw her out, and before long . . . with a jolt, she sat upright. Oh, God, no! Giles would pack her off somewhere and she wouldn't be able to run her end of the kidnapping operation. Even if Hawton were willing to run it without her, would they still cut her in for a share? How would she ever know how many shipments there actually were? And if they refused to pay her, what could she do about it?

Her head dropped in her hands and she massaged her scalp. The hair falling in her face reeked of rancid goose grease, and her stomach suddenly rebelled. She leaned over and spewed up all the brandy she had drunk onto the carpet. God, she was ill all the time now. She never felt well anymore. And now Giles and his little tart would be happy and she would be nothing, nowhere.... Wiping a shaking hand across her mouth, she stood, pale and trembling, and made for the door. She would clean herself up. She would find Hawton. He would fix it for her. He would have to. Yes, she needed Hawton.

Chapter Ten

Joanna lay still, in a haze of pain and confusion. She ached all over. Very carefully she stretched herself. The worst pain was in her side, but then Giles had said a broken rib would hurt a great deal. Giles. She felt herself blushing all over as thoughts she did not know enough to think yesterday came tumbling through her head. What on earth had she done? She had let him kiss her— no, she had kissed him in a way no decent spinster should ever allow herself. And he had slept in her bed—at her insistence. What had she become? And while she was unnerved and anxious, why was she so happy as well?

He had stayed with her all night, cradling her, his warmth and nearness banishing her pain and the loneliness that had been with her so long. Just after dawn, he had crept from her bed, kissing her gently and telling her to stay in bed. She had fallen back asleep, waking much later to the timid sound of a tap on her door.

"Come in," she called, slipping down into the bedcovers, hoping whoever it was could not see her face. But then, it would take weeks for her face to heal, so she had better come up with some kind of story.

In came Annie, tiptoeing, carrying a tray. Something on it steamed, and Joanna hoped it was tea.

"Good afternoon, miss. We're all so sorry about the nasty fall you took last night. Them steps can be beastly when they get wet with a spill like that. I 'ope you're feelin' better."

Bless the man! A fall! Joanna sat up very gingerly and gave the girl a smile. "Thank you, Annie. I'm sure I'll be fine in a few days. It was quite a tumble I took." She took the tray carefully onto her lap. She didn't dare embroider on the story until she had a chance to check with Giles and see what sort of tale he had told. She wasn't even sure which set of steps she had fallen on!

"Mrs. Davies says you're to rest and not worry about the children all day, but Miss Emma's been askin' for you, and I was wondrin' if they might come and say 'ello after their dinner. They seem anxious-like." It was a long speech for Annie, whose hands twisted in her apron, still half afraid she would give offense to the elegant Miss Carpenter who was kind to her for no reason she could fathom.

"Oh, yes, please, Annie. Bring them to me as soon as they finish eating. And tell Emma to bring a book and we'll read it together." Joanna's heart twisted at the thought of the children alone today. Of course they were anxious. People they loved disappeared for no apparent reason. They had a great deal to be anxious about.

Annie gave Joanna a bob and a quick smile, then left the room. Joanna fell to her lovely hot tea, pleased to see there was toast and porridge as well. Not what she'd usually fancy for a nice breakfast, but then she wasn't sure she could eat that much. She was strangely excited. Her insides kept doing loops and twists, and if everything hadn't ached so badly she would have loved to leap from the bed and dance around the room. Even the pain didn't seem to bother her the way it should have. All she could seem to think about was the way Giles had held her last night, the endearments he had whispered, the gentleness of his touch. And what they had done together—she blushed again, remembering the heat of his hands—there had been such love in it. How could anything so loving be wrong? Perhaps she was a fallen woman, polite society would so dictate, even if they had stopped short of the unthinkable, but there was only goodness in Giles, and she could find no regrets in her heart.

There was a brief scampering outside her door, then the door flew open. Tom and Emma stood on the threshold, peering anxiously into the room, Annie behind them.

"Come here, my darlings! I am so happy to see you!" Joanna called.

Creeping, tiptoeing softly, the two children made their way into the darkened room.

"Annie, could you take my tray and then open the draperies so we can have some light?" Joanna asked, smiling at the little faces that stared so earnestly into her own. "Now, children," she went on, "Annie must have told you I took a nasty fall on the stairs. I've hurt my face and I believe I look rather awful, but you mustn't be frightened, because it will get well again in no time."

As the curtains parted, light flooded into the room. Joanna could see by the shocked looks on the little faces that her bruises and cuts had not improved overnight. Very gently, as if he were afraid she might break, Tom put out his hand to touch her swollen cheek.

"Missy hurt?" he asked simply, his baby's touch soft on her face.

For a long moment, she stared into his rounded eyes. Lifting her hand to his, she held it tight against her cheek, willing the tears not to come. "I am not very hurt, my darling. It looks much worse than it is. Come, sit up here with me. Emma, did you bring a book we can read?" she finished brightly.

He talked! Tom could talk! There was so much she could teach him.

The children climbed happily onto the bed, settling themselves around Joanna. Annie took the tray and, with a thoughtful look at Tom, left the room. Joanna had no doubt that the entire household staff would know before long that Tom could talk. Good! Idiot, indeed!

They were thus arranged when Giles came upon them a short while later, interrupting a particularly good part where the princess was about to escape the goblin by means of a magic cloak.

"Don't let me disturb you, Miss Carpenter," he said warmly. God, she was so beautiful with the sunlight dancing in her hair, children's heads resting on her shoulders.

"Come here. Missy hurt."

Giles stared. The boy had said that! Without a

204

word, Giles walked over to the bed, not taking his eyes from Tom. When he got to the bed, Tom reached for his hand and guided it to Joanna's cheek. "Missy hurt," the child repeated. His eyes were questioning and a little worried.

Very gently, Giles let his hand trace over the bruised and swollen cheek. He should have killed both of those men. Turning to Tom, he put his other hand on the boy's shoulder. "Yes, Miss Carpenter is hurt a little, Tom," he said quietly. "She fell down. But she'll be well again soon, and in the meanwhile we'll have to take good care of her, won't we?" He ruffled Tom's hair and gave Joanna a wondering look. She answered him with a smile, her heart in her eyes.

Lily helped Joanna dress with the greatest of care. After Annie had collected the children for their baths, Lily had come to her, to ask if she felt up to joining Sir Giles at supper.

It felt good to get up and move around. Lily had filled the tub in the bathing room down the hall, and Joanna had soaked in the hot water, the aches fading into the warmth. She had not let Lily see her unclothed. There were too many injuries to be explained by a simple fall on the stairs. Fortunately, Lily had left her with a dressing gown and clean shift, and instructions to soak as long as the water stayed warm, and this Joanna was pleased to do.

She would have supper with him. Her heart gave a leap at the thought of spending the evening with Giles. And then what? Would he want to kiss her again? She would not say no. At the very thought, the fire leaped again in her belly. And if he touched her again like that, would there be anything left of her will, any thought at all in her head except how good it felt?

But what if Lady Eleanor or any of her guests were taking supper with them? Joanna could hardly bear the thought. The woman poisoned the very atmosphere they breathed. Everything about her was tainted and frightening. Well, Joanna would sup with the devil himself if it meant she could be with Giles, so if Eleanor and her friends were to be there, then so be it.

The cooling of the water finally drove her from the bath. She stood carefully and toweled herself dry. The long cut on her leg didn't look so very bad. At least it did not look as if it would leave a scar. There was a cheval mirror in the bathing room and she looked at herself, wincing at the ghastly purple that spread across her side. Well, that too would heal, she thought, carefully rebandaging herself, then stepping into the shift and tying the dressing gown around her.

Lily was waiting for her in her room and helped her to get the serviceable gray silk dress on.

"Let me do your hair up real nicely, miss," Lily said gaily. "Then no one will even notice your face."

"Oh, I'm sure everyone will notice, Lily," said Joanna, grimacing at her reflection. The swelling had gone down slightly but the discoloration seemed more violent than before.

"We could paint you up a bit," Lily said, her tone dubious.

"Never! I prefer the blues and purples to leaded whites," Joanna replied, giggling.

Laughing, Lily again worked her magic with Joanna's long tresses, brushing them out with long, careful strokes. In no time at all, her hair was pinned lightly, leaving soft tendrils to curl about and shadow her bruised face.

"Now, you look beautiful!" Lily said, stepping back and surveying her work with enthusiasm.

"Well, as good as I suppose I can look for a while, anyway. Thank you very much, Lily."

Lily gave a curtsey accompanied by a little giggle. "My lord awaits my lady," she said, her eyes alight with the hint of a secret.

Oh, Lord, did they all know he had spent the night in her room? Joanna thought in alarm. The trouble with falling from grace was that the fall was often public knowledge before one even landed. Her face crimsoning, Joanna gave Lily a nervous smile and made her way from the room.

She was surprised to find the hallways alight with the glow of the candles in sconces on the walls. Proceeding to the small supper parlor, she noted that the entire house, everywhere she looked, was bathed in light. Suddenly it seemed like a very pleasant house indeed, walls painted in fresh, light colors, clean, beautifully furnished. As long as one's eye did not linger too long on the artwork . . .

The door to the supper parlor stood open. Stepping in, Joanna breathed a sigh of relief to see that only two places were set. She gave a start as arms came around her from behind.

"Oh, you startled me. I didn't hear you," she said, giggling. Gently Giles turned her around and she found herself staring into warm brown eyes.

His lips came down softly on hers, teasing lightly. His hands roamed her back, coming to rest possessively on her hips, pulling her to him. The kiss deepened and she found herself responding, opening her lips to his, her arms going around him, pushing herself tightly to his strong, wide chest. His tongue teased at her lips. She could feel her heart start its staccato rhythm as the need inside her began to burn.

With a sigh he withdrew his lips from hers, catching his hand up in her hair, his eyes roaming her face, eyebrows drawing together in a frown as he studied the swollen and purple cheek.

"Did I hurt you, my sweet?" he asked gruffly, the concern on his face belying his tone.

"No, you never hurt me," she answered a little breathless, and staring mesmerized into the brown depths of his eyes. It was shocking what happened to her body when he touched her, shocking because of the intense exhilaration and because she could put no name to the feeling.

"Come and sit down," he said, leading her carefully to a chair, as if she might break. "I don't think you should be standing or moving about much, but I did not think I should be seen having supper in your room with you in bed, and I couldn't bear not to see you."

Joanna's heart leaped at his words. He must care about her. He must! All the dire moral mutterings she had ever heard were chasing around in her head. She was as near to a fallen woman as anyone could be. She had happily allowed him to take indecent liberties with her. She was not fit for decent company. He would use her and discard her like the rubbish she had become.

But he was looking at her with such caring in his eyes. There was no disgust, no shadow, no aversion.

"I dismissed the servants. I did not wish us to be interrupted," he said, a glint of amusement in his eyes. "I was not certain I could keep from kiss-

Thrill to the most sensual, adventure-filled Historical Romances on the market today...

FROM  LEISURE BOOKS

As a home subscriber to Leisure Romance Book Club, you'll enjoy the best in today's BRAND-NEW Historical Romance fiction. For over twenty-five years, Leisure Books has brought you the award-winning, high-quality authors you know and love to read. Each Leisure Historical Romance will sweep you away to a world of high adventure...and intimate romance. Discover for yourself all the passion and excitement millions of readers thrill to each and every month.

Save $5.⁰⁰ Each Time You Buy!

Each month, the Leisure Romance Book Club brings you four brand-new titles from Leisure Books, America's foremost publisher of Historical Romances. EACH PACKAGE WILL SAVE YOU $5.00 FROM THE BOOKSTORE PRICE! And you'll never miss a new title with our convenient home delivery service.

Here's how we do it. Each package will carry a FREE 10-DAY EXAMINATION privilege. At the end of that time, if you decide to keep your books, simply pay the low invoice price of $16.96, no shipping or handling charges added. HOME DELIVERY IS ALWAYS FREE. With today's top Historical Romance novels selling for $5.99 and higher, our price SAVES YOU $5.00 with each shipment.

AND YOUR FIRST FOUR-BOOK SHIPMENT IS TOTALLY FREE!

IT'S A BARGAIN YOU CAN'T BEAT! A Super $21.96 Value!

LEISURE BOOKS A Division of Dorchester Publishing Co., Inc.

GET YOUR 4 FREE BOOKS NOW—A $21.96 Value!

Mail the Free Book Certificate Today!

4 FREE BOOKS

A $21.96 VALUE

Free Books Certificate

YES! I want to subscribe to the Leisure Romance Book Club. Please send me my 4 FREE BOOKS. Then, each month I'll receive the four newest Leisure Historical Romance selections to Preview FREE for 10 days. If I decide to keep them, I will pay the Special Member's Only discounted price of just $4.24 each, a total of $16.96. This is a SAVINGS OF $5.00 off the bookstore price. There are no shipping, handling, or other charges. There is no minimum number of books I must buy and I may cancel the program at any time. In any case, the 4 FREE BOOKS are mine to keep—A BIG $21.96 Value!

Offer valid only in the U.S.A.

Name _____

Address _____

City _____

State _____ *Zip* _____

Telephone _____

Signature _____

A $21.96 VALUE

If under 18, Parent or Guardian must sign. Terms, prices and conditions subject to change. Subscription subject to acceptance. Leisure Books reserves the right to reject any order or cancel any subscription.

4 FREE BOOKS

Get Four Books Totally FREE – A $21.96 Value!

ing you for so long a period as it takes to eat, and you can see I was right." While he talked he took the covers off of the steaming silver serving dishes on the sideboard. "How is your prodigious appetite this evening?" he asked.

"Prodigious, sir," Joanna laughed. "I've had nothing to eat but toast and porridge and I'm famished."

"You are always famished," he replied, serving a plate for her with heaping portions and then one for himself.

He sat next to her and poured wine into crystal goblets. Joanna picked up her fork, relieved to see a delicious-looking cut of beef with sauce and nothing strange on her plate. They ate for a moment, the silence lengthening between them. What did one talk about with a man one had slept in the same bed with? she wondered, feeling a bit embarrassed.

Suddenly he put down his fork and stared at her. Startled, she swallowed and put her fork down as well, her nerves on edge.

"I had meant to take you into the drawing room and ply you with sherry and kneel at your feet, but I find I simply cannot wait, Joanna," he said. "Would you do me the honor of marrying me? As soon as possible?"

Joanna found herself just staring at him while his words sank in. He wanted to marry her? Then she wasn't just a dalliance? Could it be that he really cared about her? Or was he offering to marry her because he felt he had gone too far and was trapped? She could feel her chest tighten at the thought. She would never marry a man who asked her merely out of a sense of duty!

Giles watched the play of emotions on her face.

His heart sank as he saw the shadow cross her eyes. If she said no, what would he do? Thinking all day of making Joanna his wife, of turning his blighted existence into one of joy and light, he had not stopped to consider that she might turn him down, might send him back down alone into the dark regions he had inhabited for so long.

"I—I don't know what to say, Giles," she began haltingly.

"Say yes," he said simply, his heart twisting at the uncertainty in her eyes.

"I would not wish you to feel that you must do this because of what has happened between us, sir," she went on, miserable, turning red. "I could not bear to marry you knowing that you felt forced to do the honorable thing after I allowed such . . . well, we would have such a dreary time together . . ."

"I love you."

There was silence while she just stared at him. What had he said?

"You love me?" she finally asked in a whisper.

In answer he took her hand and brought it to his lips. "I don't wish to make it seem like a chore, but if you don't marry me I will never draw a happy breath again as long as I live."

It was as if he watched the sun break through dark clouds. She smiled into his eyes.

"I love you, too, you know," she said, somewhat breathlessly. "I've loved you since the minute I first laid eyes on you. Well, no, actually. Not quite. When I first laid eyes on you, I was quite terrified. I would have turned tail and run, but it would have set such a bad example for the children."

"Say you'll marry me."

Her eyes danced in merriment. "I believe that I

am supposed to faint into your waiting arms, or perhaps I am supposed to snatch my hand away and blush and say that this is all so sudden, but it really isn't too sudden, under the circumstances, is it?"

"Say it." He was in earnest now. His hand was gripping hers tightly.

"I will marry you."

With a great laugh he stood and pulled her up, catching her close but careful not to crush her too tightly.

"How long does it take to read the banns?" he asked, kissing her hair.

"Three weeks, usually. Do you wish to marry right away?" His kisses were having their usual effect, making her dizzy and unable to concentrate.

"As soon as possible. I am too old to wait, and we needn't satisfy any family with a big elaborate wedding. That is"—he pulled back and gazed at her thoughtfully—"if you have always dreamed of a big wedding, I wouldn't deprive you of it, but—"

"Heavens, no! I've never dreamed of a wedding at all. And I should be embarrassed to death to have all that fussing about. The only weddings I've ever been to were small, country affairs, and that's just how a wedding should be."

"Three weeks then, my darling. It seems like an awfully long time . . ." He broke off, his lips seizing hers again. And there was no further discussion.

Eleanor paced the floor like a tigress in a sultan's menagerie. She had sent word to Hawton that she would see him tonight under the usual arrangements. He'd been out all day. Her seemingly casual inquiry of Mrs. Davies had elicited the information that Hawton was out somewhere on the property, doing whatever it was that stewards do. So she had seethed inwardly all evening, entertaining those houseguests left over from last night's debauch, who jabbered and tittered and maddened her with their inanities till she thought she would scream. Would the man never come?

At last there was a small tap on the door. In an instant she was across the room, flinging the door open, barely concerned now with keeping things quiet. Unless she was much mistaken, her sanctimonious stepbrother was locked away in the library, no doubt having at the governess, and those few houseguests who were still here had arranged themselves in the usual, or unusual, couplings.

"Where the hell have you been all day?" she snarled, closing the door behind him with almost a slam.

"Checking the horse trails in the fells for scree, my lady," he replied evenly. "Sir Giles asked—"

"Bugger Sir Giles, Hawton!" she shrieked, mindless of the noise. She crossed back to her divan and threw herself down, picking up a nearly empty brandy glass. He could smell the fumes all the way across the room. God, he'd be glad to make some quick money and be quit of this wicked witch.

"Did you know that he is intending to marry the bitch?" she spat out.

There was no doubt in his mind that she referred to Sir Giles and the governess, though he was, indeed, surprised. He had thought the man impervious to female charms.

"Who is marrying whom?" he asked, deliberately leaving off the "my lady." Eleanor was rattled; he could see it, and he was still smarting under the dusting off she had given him last night, panting after that padded-up false count. Not that Hawton hadn't managed all right himself. One of Eleanor's overpainted gorgon friends had been delighted to oblige, and what she had lacked in youth she had made up for in experienced variety.

"Giles says he is marrying the chit, the governess!" she fairly screamed. Her eyes were wild and her face was mottled red under the cracking white paint. The veins stood out on her neck. He wondered idly whether she might drop down with apoplexy on the spot.

"Are you certain?" he asked mildly, planting a look of surprise and concern on his face. So much the better, really. There was nothing much to complain of in having Miss Carpenter as the mistress of Queen's Hall, and it would be amusing to watch the high and mighty Lady Eleanor deal with her displacement.

"Of course I am certain, you cretin! He told me so himself, this afternoon!" She had swilled down the last of her brandy and held out the glass with imperious fury. "What's more, he is moving me out, into some cottage somewhere, away from here. He won't even set me up in London!"

Hawton weighed this bit of information as he filled her glass. Facing away from her, he allowed himself a small smile. So the old harridan would be carted out of here, would she? Then he and Lord Beeson could carry on without her. No share for Lady Eleanor, and no interference from her. He carefully replaced the crystal stopper, schooling his face into an expression of distress.

"I am horrified to hear that, my dear," he said,

handing her the glass. "How soon must you leave?"

He would let her go! The bastard didn't give a damn where she was! He was probably already planning to cut her out of the operation.

"I wonder if you realize, Hawton," she said, sipping daintily at her brandy, "that if I go, so goes all our plans. I spoke with Lord Beeson about it before he left this afternoon, and he was much provoked. Said he'd have to move his operation elsewhere if I weren't going to be here to oversee matters." She was bluffing. Lord Beeson had long since departed by the time Eleanor had made herself presentable enough to appear before her guests. And she doubted seriously whether he'd care who was here to run things as long it was someone he could rely on. He was quite anxious, in fact, to use this stretch of coastline because of its very isolation. It was working. She could see the confusion crossing Hawton's face. Oh, he'd been planning to doublecross her all right.

"What would you propose we do about it, my lady?" Hawton asked, absently giving her title. Indeed, he was nonplused. He'd begun to count on this extra avenue of income. The risks, objectively assessed, seemed slight in relation to the money that could be made. He was making plans. He would not be able to bear being thwarted now, not when it was so close.

"It's perfectly simple," she answered with a mean smile. He'd swallowed it. Now for the hard part. "We'll have to stop Giles from doing this to me, Hawton."

"What on earth is simple about that?" he asked peevishly. He poured himself a brandy, not waiting to be asked, and sat down next to Eleanor on the divan. She twined her legs around his hips and began rubbing against him with her bare feet. He wanted to tell her to bugger off, but sensed this was not the time to burn his bridges.

"I've lived like a poor relation since my mother married into this blighted family, Hawton," she began, sipping at her drink. "I am tired of being at the mercy of fate and Giles Chapman. I had thought we could seize a little for ourselves with Lord Beeson's proposal, and I'm not about to be cheated of it now." She paused. He was nodding. Good, because she needed him to feel it the way she did now. Hungry. Desperate.

"As long as I am financially dependent on Giles, I am at his mercy. For that matter, so are you. Do you want to be a steward all your life? Working on salary. Skimming little bits of leavings from other men's good fortune. Being a nobody. A 'yes, sir, no, sir' sort of life. Aren't you tired of that, Hawton? Wouldn't you rather be rich, really rich?" Her feet were rubbing him where it counted. She could feel him growing hard, and it was an angry hardness. Good. "Buy a house just for yourself," she went on, almost crooning, her feet pressing harder against him, rubbing. . . . "A big house, bigger than this one. A manor house. Have a fleet of servants who say 'yes, sir' to you. Never have to spend your day again slaving for your betters. Wouldn't you like that, Hawton?" She sat up suddenly and put her arms around his neck. "Lots of money," she whispered, biting the lobe of his ear hard.

With a moan he sank over her, grinding his crotch against hers. He fumbled at her neckline, seizing a nipple between his thumb and forefinger, rolling it, pinching it hard.

"Don't you want it, Hawton?" she whispered, insistent.

"Yes!" he gasped, pulling her skirts up beneath him.

"Will you help me get it for you?" she prodded as his hands found her wet and ready.

"Yes, yes!" he moaned, slipping his fingers in and out.

She reached for the fastenings of his breeches, expertly freeing the buttons. His shaft leaped out and she seized it in her hand, rubbing it hard, pushing against her wetness, slipping him inside. With a cry, he arched into her, pumping hard, gasping in his need.

"It won't be easy, Hawton," she went on, now breathless herself with the feel of him pounding inside her. "You'll need to be hard and strong, my love. Hard," she gasped. "Can you do that for me? For us?"

"What do you want me to do?" He could barely talk as his hands squeezed her breasts, almost hurting.

"We have to kill him," she whispered in his ear, as he shuddered on top of her, emptying himself into her waiting wetness. Then she herself cried out as the waves overtook her, and she could not remember when she had had such a climax.

Chapter Eleven

"There, you see, your fears of the carriage ride were all in your mind, my darling," whispered Giles, nuzzling against Joanna's neck. "We've been traveling over two hours, and we're almost half way to Carlisle, and you haven't felt at all ill, have you?"

Joanna giggled as his teeth nipped her ear lightly. "I suppose you are right, Giles, but it may also be that you haven't given me a chance to think about feeling ill." She gave a shudder as his warm breath tickled her ear, sending delicious shivers down her spine. She was still amazed at the magic he wrought with his hands when he touched her, the fire and ice, so shocking and yet so right. He had wooed her gently, aware that she had only the barest schoolgirl knowledge of this sort of thing. But she found she was in this, as in all things academic, an apt pupil.

"That proves it's all in your mind, as I said. And besides, those public coaches you endured are notoriously foul." His lips found her neck as his errant hands slipped around her waist and pulled her to him. For a moment there was no sound at all in the comfortable, well-sprung carriage except for their ragged breathing and the clip clop of the horses' hoofbeats.

At last Giles raised his head and sat back, a lascivious smile curving his face. Joanna was blushing as she tried to control her breathing, but it was all too obvious that she was as out of breath as he was.

"I think if you continue to keep me from your bed for two more weeks until we are married, you will find yourself wed to a gibbering idiot," he said. His hands had not stopped their errant wandering.

"If you continue to importune me, I will yield, and then you will find yourself wed to a wanton," Joanna said, laughing and gently disengaging the hand which had crept to her breast. She broke off, startled by the hard look that crossed his face, then cursed herself as she recalled her long-ago conversation with Mrs. Davies about Giles's first wife, Violet. Joanna had spared little thought for this first marriage, and had asked him nothing about it.

Giles turned away from her, withdrawing his hands and looking out the window. Joanna felt a chill race through her. It was as if he had suddenly built a wall between them.

"What have I said?" she asked softly, not daring to touch him as she so longed to do.

For a moment there was silence, then he turned to face her. Joanna drew in her breath sharply at the pain she saw in his eyes.

"It is not really anything you said, Joanna," he said, his voice raw. "I must lay my own demons to rest." He turned back away from her, his face toward the window.

They said nothing more for a moment. Joanna felt the sadness between them as if it were a tangible thing. What could she say to bring back his laughter? How could she fight off the malicious ghosts of the past? She looked out of her window and tried to fight back the tears welling up in her eyes. She saw nothing of the spectacular purple fells that stretched away in the distance.

She felt a warm hand on her own, and caught her breath in a short sob. She kept her face turned away, embarrassed at her weakness.

"I have made you cry," she heard him say softly. "I am a fool." She felt his arms go about her, his chin resting on her shoulder. His hand reached around and, cupping her chin, turned her face gently to his own. He leaned forward and kissed away the tear or two that had slipped down her cheeks, then he gently pressed her to him, ever mindful of her sore ribs.

"Do you know anything at all of my first marriage, Joanna?" he asked softly, his voice in her hair.

"A bit," she said, hesitating. "You and Violet were not well suited. She was—rather like Eleanor, I understand," she broke off, unsure how much to say and feeling awkward that it would be obvious she had gleaned her knowledge through household gossip.

"That is a charitable understatement, my darling. Someday I'll tell you about it, but not now." His hand stroked her cheek, and once again she felt the comfort of the warmth between them. "But I do promise never to let the dark memories intrude between us again. Never were there two women less alike than you and she, and I bless you for it."

His lips were nibbling at her throat. Joanna felt her contentment nudged aside by the quickening of her heartbeat. It was amazing what his touch could do to her, scattering all rational thoughts like chickens in a windstorm. She felt his arms tighten about her, and her hands crept up his chest. She loved the hot strength of him under her fingers.

"Joanna?" she heard him whisper at her neck.

"Mmm?" she answered, mesmerized by the feel of his fingers in her hair.

"I promise I won't think you a wanton if you let me . . ."

"Oh, you are such a devil!" she laughed, pulling away from him, but secretly pleased that he seemed to have recovered his sense of humor. "I'm not going to let you 'anything,' you cad. I don't trust you at all!"

"You wound me, beloved," he said, attempting to look hurt and failing miserably. "You can trust me. Besides, we're in a moving carriage. I haven't done it in a moving carriage for years. I'm too old to do it in a carriage, for heaven's sake."

"Well, I'm not too old," she answered, trying to pout. "Does this mean I cannot look forward to performing my wifely duties in a carriage?"

"Well, I could make an exception this once," he murmured, slipping his hand under her skirt.

"Oh, no you don't, laddie," she said, firmly removing his hand and placing it neatly in his own lap. "Someone around here has to remember the decencies, and I suppose that will be me." She tried to sit primly, her hands folded in her lap.

Out of the corner of her eye she watched as his hand slowly crept out. She felt it snaking around her waist, then suddenly she was pulled to him.

"Just a taste," he whispered. "There's nothing else to do on these long trips." He seized her lips with his own.

"Mmm," she murmured as the now familiar heat rushed through her. She thought she would never get enough of his kisses, and somewhere in the back of her mind wondered if, perhaps this time, he wouldn't make himself stop. . . .

"When will it be done, Hawton?" asked Eleanor, pacing on the library carpet. He was about to jump out of his skin watching her.

"Tonight, as I've told you," he said, trying to keep his impatience from sounding in his voice. "I heard Will mention that Sir Giles will be taking Joanna to see *The Winter's Tale* in the theater in Carlisle. It is arranged that the carriage will be held up on the way home from the theater. It will look like a robbery; indeed, it will be a robbery, since I promised my man he could take Sir Giles's fat purse."

"But how will your highwayman know what carriage it is, or what route they will take? Damn it, Hawton! Why didn't you just arrange a carriage accident on the highway as I suggested?" Her voice was shrewish. He watched as she knocked back yet another brandy. The woman drank more than any man he knew.

"As I have told you, my lady," he said, "a carriage accident is too uncertain. Will is an excellent coachman, and I had no way of assuring that Sir

Giles would actually die. Nothing would be worse than if he came out of it with no more than a bump on the head." Hawton crossed over to the decanter and poured himself a tot. He needed it to steady his own nerves. These arrangements had been tricky, all the more so as he had had to smuggle messages back and forth over the last few days to Carlisle with Sir Giles underfoot here until yesterday.

"And what about the route, Hawton?" she asked again.

"My man will follow the carriage, my lady. I know Carlisle well. It is not a large city, after all. There are few routes to take from the theater to the inn where they'll be staying, and the carriage must pass through some dark streets."

"Where did you come up with this fine fellow, Hawton?" asked Eleanor. "And what makes you think he can be trusted?"

"I have known him for a long time, my lady. He owes me a favor. A large one. I provided him with an alibi once when he was charged with a hanging offense. I can trust him, most certainly."

He watched as she digested this information. He had tried to keep these details from her, not wanting her interference. He should have known she would gnaw at him till she knew everything.

A slow smile curved her face. "And he will kill only Giles, is that correct, Hawton? I prefer that the little tart have the rest of her impecunious life to mourn what she almost grabbed from me. I may even let her stay on and take care of the children—on my terms, of course."

"Aye, my lady. Only Sir Giles will be shot."

There was a silence while she poured herself another snifter full. She turned to the steward. "To tonight then, and freedom," she said, raising her glass to him. He raised his glass as well and took a long sip.

She finished her brandy and set the glass down on a small table next to her. "Why don't you come to my room tonight, Hawton?" she asked, almost purring. "About midnight. We can celebrate." Without waiting for an answer, she turned and left the room, leaving Hawton staring at her retreating back.

He drained his glass, hoping it would quiet his queasy stomach. He hated this business of murder, messy and risky as it was. But Eleanor was right that it was the only permanent solution. And perhaps he could console the delectable Miss Carpenter in her terrible grief. . . .

"Oh, Giles, it was so wonderful. I've never seen anything like it in my whole life. Why, in Little Haver we were lucky to get an occasional traveling troupe playing on a haywagon in front of a hanging painted canvas."

"I'm glad you enjoyed it, but I still say it's one of Shakespeare's stranger plays," Giles answered, steering her through the small crowd to where Will waited down the street with the carriage. Away from the theater, the street became dark, but he spotted Will only a few yards away.

He handed Joanna into the carriage, noting with approval the good fit of the deep blue silk gown he had purchased for her today, quickly taken in by the modiste so that she could wear it tonight.

It had been fun dressing Joanna, watching her face as the dressmaker brought out bolt after bolt of the finest silks and satins that could be found this far from London. Indeed, the woman, styling herself a couturiere, had assured him in her ridiculously inaccurate French accent that her materials and her styles were straight from the very fashion plates of London, au courant, up to the very minute. Joanna and Madame DuPre had had a disagreement over her necklines, Joanna favoring a height that Madame deemed hopelessly prudish and unfashionable. But Giles had broken the deadlock by siding with his bride. As much as he looked forward to the delights so fetchingly covered by her prim, tailored gowns, he had to agree that the entire north of England needn't be intimately acquainted with her bosom.

Indeed, this entire trip was for the purpose of dressing his beautiful Joanna—that and having a new will drawn up for himself. He had also wanted to get her away from Queen's Hall for a bit. Eleanor seemed reluctant to leave for some reason, and was making herself as unpleasant as she knew how to be. He had entrusted the children to the care of Annie and Mrs. Davies, and brought Joanna away, hoping some of the dark poison of Queen's Hall could be washed away by the sights and sounds of Carlisle, a small town to be sure when compared with London, but great indeed compared to Little Haver.

Joanna had been aghast at the prices of things, refusing point blank to make a number of purchases she insisted were unnecessary, forcing him to signal to the shopkeepers over her head to add them to his tab. He had quite assured himself that he was not marrying a fortune hunter, having spent all day arguing her out of trying to purchase the least expensive, most meager selections. In fact, if she kept on this way throughout their married life, he was going to die a very wealthy man.

He settled her into the carriage, then knocked on the front for Will to get started.

"I will take you to London soon, Joanna," he murmured into her ear, his lips tickling her neck. "I like having you all to myself in a carriage."

"I like being in a carriage with you, but I am not at all sure I wish to see London again," she answered, closing her eyes while he laced his fingers through her hair.

"London's not so bad if you've got money enough to enjoy it. Wouldn't you like to see David Garrick at Drury Lane? His Shakespeare is impeccable, and I hear his leading lady, Peg Woffington, is much admired, and he has concealed the stage lighting from the audience, a remarkable dramatic effect, I understand."

The carriage gave a sudden lurch and came to a halt.

"What the devil?" Giles said, sitting up sharply. "Stay inside, Joanna, while I see what's wrong. On no account are you to open the door after I get out, do you understand?" He reached for the door handle and stepped out, not bothering to wait for her agreement.

In truth Joanna was frightened, not so much by the fact that the carriage had stopped as by the hard, apprehensive look in Giles's eyes. She listened, hearing nothing, then quietly raised the window flap. All was blackness outside. She closed the flap and sat for a moment.

It was no good. She could not sit here like a ninny and just hope Giles was all right. Slowly she pushed the carriage door open, then, seeing nothing, stepped out into the darkness. Still there was silence all about her, and she began to grow truly alarmed. Surely if Giles and Will were discussing a problem with the carriage or the horses, she would hear the sounds of their voices.

She stepped carefully forward, her kid slippers making no sound on the rough pavement. As she came to the front of the carriage, she looked up to the box and saw that Will was slumped over, lying half on, half off the seat. Suppressing a gasp, she stepped up, then climbed as quietly as she could onto the box. There was still no sign of Giles. She put her hand to Will's neck, relieved to feel a pulse.

She froze as she heard a harsh, whispering voice on the other side of the carriage. It did not sound like Giles. As carefully as she could, she leaned over Will and peered around the side of the box. The street was in darkness, but she could make out a figure directly below her and in his hand, the glint of a pistol. Giles stood a few feet away to the rear of the carriage. He appeared to be leaning, almost negligently on the side of the carriage. There was a taunting grin on his face. He had not seen her.

"You'll have to take it from me if you want it," she heard Giles say. "Come and try it, why don't you?"

"I could just shoot you now and take it off yer dead body, sir," came the man's voice in his gruff whisper.

"You could, couldn't you?" replied Giles. Joanna marveled that he could sound so bored looking down a gun barrel as he was. "But considering the noise that cannon of yours will make, the horses will bolt with the carriage. And within seconds a crowd will come running. We are only a half block away from an inn, in case you haven't noticed."

"Throw me the purse now or I'll have at yer

woman after yer dead," the man snarled, brandishing the pistol.

"I am alone. What makes you think I have a woman?" Giles replied, but Joanna had seen him stiffen and heard the suppressed rage in his voice. A sudden thought struck her and looking down, she saw the coach whip sitting in its bracket next to her hand. Hoping her movement would not draw attention to her perch, she lifted the whip silently. Her heart was hammering in her throat. She had never used a whip in her life. It looked easy, but suppose there was a trick to it?

"I saw the lady, mate, gettin' into yer carriage. A lovely bride-to-be she is, too. Dark hair, just like I like 'em, and had a blue dress on. I'll enjoy her, won't I?"

Giles started forward, his face feral, just as the man raised his pistol to Giles's chest. Like lightning, Joanna flicked out with the whip, aiming for the pistol in the man's hand. She missed the gun, but the tail of the whip caught the man's arm and jerked it up, just as he squeezed the trigger. Joanna had time to see the shock on Giles's face as his eyes met hers, before the horses, mad with the explosion, bolted forward, throwing Joanna against the back of the box.

Joanna could see that Will had been dislodged and was slipping down off the box. If he fell through the front, he would be hit by the carriage, and likely mauled by the impact. She grabbed at his arm and with all her strength fought his dead weight as it tried to pull her down, too. The horses were running wild through the narrow, cobbled street, and Joanna was bouncing so hard that she thought she, too, would be thrown off. Finally, she managed to drag Will back onto the seat. Looking forward, she could see the reins dangling over the horses' backs, well out of her reach. She clutched at one of the coachman's holds and leaned out, looking behind her, but the darkness had swallowed up all signs of Giles and his attacker.

"Whoa!" she cried, knowing that the horses would not respond to a voiced command.

But the horses, having heard no further loud noises and free to decide for themselves what they wished to do, seemed to agree that they had put enough distance between themselves and whatever menace had threatened a few blocks back, and they slowed sedately, then stopped, as if it were no longer of any concern to them.

Sobbing softly, Joanna climbed down from the box and grabbed the reins, careful not to pull too hard on them as she climbed back onto the box.

"Oh, Will, I wish you'd wake up!" she cried to the inert form beside her. He didn't move.

She held the reins in her hands, wracking her brains to remember anything she had watched a coachman do.

"Come on, let's go!" she said, flicking the reins over the horses' backs and making clucking noises. To her surprise, the horses began to amble forward.

"But I want to turn around!" she said, as much to herself as to the horses. That, she knew, was impossible. She allowed the horses to continue forward, while she looked for a side street on which to turn. If she couldn't turn around, perhaps she could take the carriage on a roundabout and wind up back on the street going in the right direction. She refused to allow herself to wonder what she would find when she returned to the spot where she had left Giles and the assailant. Mumbling prayers for his safety, she spotted a side street, then set herself to convincing the horses that this was where they wanted to go. She pulled lightly on the reins to her left, then when that got no response, she pulled harder.

"Good horse!" she cried when the horses turned and plodded down the side street. With horror she realized that the street ahead seemed to be a dead end. She nearly sobbed in her frustration when she felt a violent tug on the reins, nearly jerking them from her hands and making the horses skittish again.

She grabbed for the whip as she saw hands reach for the box. Then Giles's face appeared as he hoisted himself up.

He grabbed the reins from her and, with no movement at all that she could discern, halted the horses.

"Are you all right?" he rasped out. His chest was heaving as if he could not get enough air into his lungs. He turned to her and put out an arm, drawing her close.

"I'm fine," she whispered, throwing her arms about him. "What happened to that man? Is he after us?"

"Not in this life, he isn't," Giles said, his voice grim. "We scuffled and he hit his head on the cobblestones. The bastard's dead, and more's the pity that I did not get a chance to ask him some questions." He flicked the reins and the horses started forward again.

"What questions, Giles?" Joanna asked. "He was just a bandit, wasn't he?"

"I am not so sure," replied Giles. "Apparently, he watched us get into the coach. It was far enough away from the theater and dark enough there to accomplish his mission. And he got rattled too easily. He let me argue with him when he should have just shot me dead and grabbed what he wanted. It was almost as if he were following a script that didn't go as planned." Not for anything would Giles mention to Joanna that the ruffian had known she was his intended bride.

Joanna said nothing, resting her head on his shoulder as the carriage made its sedate way through the streets. Giles seemed to know where they were going, which was a good thing, for Joanna was utterly lost.

She reached down and felt again at Will's neck. She was relieved to feel the strong pulse. But she was troubled at Giles's words. If the attacker was not a simple bandit, then who was he, and why had he wished to kill Giles? She shuddered and held Giles more tightly, praying that they would reach the inn before any more horrors arose in the dark.

Joanna sat in the warm tub and steamed away the terrors of the evening. Giles had had to move heaven and earth to get this bath for her at such a late hour, but it felt so good. He had pressed a glass of brandy on her before leaving the room, promising to return when she had finished. She used the lilac soap he had purchased for her this afternoon, shunning the soap provided by the inn, which smelled harsh and felt worse.

At last the cooling water drove her from the tub and she dried herself on the large towel provided with the bath. Drawing on her long white cotton nightgown and tying her quilted dressing gown about her, she sat at the dresser and began brushing out her hair.

There was a tap on the door which connected

their two rooms. The door opened and Giles came in. He was wearing a dressing gown over his shirt and breeches and looked uncommonly handsome.

"I was rather hoping to catch you still in the bath," he said, coming up behind her and taking the brush from her hands. He ran the brush gently through her long hair. "I cannot decide whether to thank you for saving my life or to be angry that you disobeyed me and exposed yourself to such danger."

"I think you should settle for just thanking me," she replied. "And I do have a request."

"And that is?" he asked, tangling his hands in her curls.

"I want to learn how to ride a horse and drive a carriage. I don't want to go through life not knowing how to do such simple things."

He laughed softly and bent over to kiss the nape of her neck. "Done, my lady. You'll be the finest whip in Cumberland when I've done with you." His hands slipped to her shoulders, rubbing them hard. She turned abruptly and buried her face against him.

"What is it, Joanna," he asked softly, his arms coming around her. "You're trembling."

"Do you think he was really planning to kill you, Giles?" she asked, looking up at him, the fear back in her eyes. "I saw him raise the gun and he tried to fire it directly at you. I couldn't have borne it if . . ." She broke off and clutched him more tightly.

He bent down and lifted her effortlessly from the chair and carried her to the bed. Laying her down, he lay down beside her and took her in his arms.

"I think I must have been overly upset, Joanna,"

he lied. "He was just a highwayman, that's all, and now that he's dead, we have nothing more to worry about."

"Stay with me," she whispered.

"All night, my love," he answered, drawing the covers up over them both.

He held her tight against him, giving her a chaste good night kiss. After a while he felt her breathing slowly to a steady, sleeping rhythm. But it was long before he slept, turning the incident over and over in his mind. It had not been a random robbery; he was sure of that. But what was it? The only thing he knew for certain was that he would have to protect Joanna with his life. And have a new will drawn up tomorrow, making Joanna his heir, and guardian of the children.

Chapter Twelve

If a simple country wedding required this much effort, Joanna shuddered to think what an elegant city affair would entail. And three weeks was not much time, no matter how eager the bride and groom. Giles had been ridiculously generous about providing Joanna with a new wardrobe, overriding all of her protests that such finery was an unnecessary expense. In fact, the more she had insisted she needed nothing of the sort, the more he had insisted she did. A dressmaker procured on short notice from Carlisle had worked magic, and now on the morning of her wedding, Joanna and Emma were fingering the gossamer wedding gown as if it were enchanted.

"Look how soft it is, Aunt Joanna!" said Emma, her carefully washed hands gentle on the silk and lace.

"I have never, ever seen anything so beautiful,

Emma. I'm almost afraid to wear it. Suppose I spill something?"

"Big people never spill anything," giggled Emma. "But we'd better be careful around Tom."

There was a light tap at the door and Lily walked in, carrying another box.

"Another one? What on earth can this be? I've more gowns now than I can wear in a lifetime, Lily!" laughed Joanna. For all she thought it was a dreadful extravagance, there was something in her that did enjoy opening the tissue paper and finding something lovely, just for her, underneath.

Opening the package, she picked up a folded bit of nothing, mere wispiness as far as she could see, with feather-like stitches. The lace trim seemed the most substantial part. Shaking it out, Joanna blushed to see that it was a nightgown. Why, if she wore a cobweb, it would cover more!

"Oh, how beautiful, Miss Carpenter!" squealed Lily, touching the fine stuff with reverence. "It's for tonight!"

"Oh, Lily!" laughed Joanna, blushing, darting a look at Emma by way of warning to Lily to mind the innuendo.

"You'll be awfully cold in that nightgown, Aunt Joanna," said Emma dubiously. "Why would you want to sleep with almost nothing on?"

Lily snorted and pulled out her hanky, covering her face and blowing her nose with noisy gusto. Joanna schooled her expression to one of bland unconcern and said, "Yes, darling, I'm sure my flannel nightgown would be warmer, wouldn't it? Let's try some of my new slippers again, shall we? There are so many pairs I feel like a princess!"

Thus diverted, the child skipped happily to the armoire where several boxes of tissue-wrapped slippers in fairy-tale colors awaited her inspection.

"Where's Tom?" asked Lily, looking around. "I rarely see one without the other."

"Giles has taken him horseback riding. The boy doesn't seem afraid of horses, and Giles thought perhaps he could be taught to ride."

"I think it is amazing that men have nothing better to do on their wedding days than ride horses. Why, we will spend the whole day, the whole staff, getting things in order for this afternoon," said Lily, picking imaginary specks off the fine wedding gown. "Are you ready for your bath? Mrs. Davies is getting anxious about the hot water."

"Yes, I suppose I'd better bathe now. Giles will want a bath, and I'm sure Lady Eleanor will bathe too." Joanna tried to keep her voice neutral. Living in this house with Eleanor had been difficult, to say the least. Thank heaven, the woman had tired quickly of baiting Giles and snubbing Joanna and had taken herself off to one of her friends. Eleanor had returned several days ago, and while she still acted the mistress of the house, she would raise not a finger to help with the wedding preparation. Indeed, she seemed to be a deliberate hindrance, demanding attention from this or that servant who had been set by Joanna or Mrs. Davies to a wedding-related task. By tacit agreement, neither Mrs. Davies nor Joanna had mentioned the situation to Giles, knowing it would goad him into a battle with his stepsister and turn the household into a battleground. Instead, they allowed Eleanor her pettiness and calmly went about the business of putting together the wedding in spite of her, with the staff in silent agreement as to which side had the right of it.

"I'll go down and order the hot water to be sent up. Then, when you finish, I'll do your hair. Mrs. Davies is in the kitchen with Cook. Everything is ready and looks perfect, but they are both flying around in a stew about all the possible things that could go wrong. I swear if we have an earthquake this afternoon, we are ready with alternative plans." Lily giggled as she left the room.

Joanna glanced over at Emma, who had surrounded herself with new slippers and was carefully trying each one on her little feet. The children had been wonderful about welcoming her into the family, Emma calling her "Aunt Joanna" at every opportunity. Even Tom had taken to calling her "Auntie," though he still said little.

And now in a few hours she would be Giles's wife. It still seemed amazing, even three weeks later, that her life could be so happy, so full of love and light. Papa had been right after all, but then, hadn't Papa always been right?

Giles whistled to himself as he tied his neck-cloth, sorry for the first time in his life that he did not have a fastidious valet to see to it that he looked absolutely perfect. He hadn't paid any attention to his appearance in years, not since Violet and Eleanor had taught him to scorn the upper-class worship of all things sartorial.

A bloodcurdling shriek split his reverie and sent him hurtling from his room. He stopped for a moment in the hallway, trying to determine where the scream had come from, then heard his step-sister's shrieks coming from above. He took the stairs three at a time and had time to note that Joanna's door stood open, before Mrs. Davies came rushing from the room.

"Oh, sir, thank heavens you've come!" panted the woman. "I was just coming to fetch you. Lady Eleanor is . . ." She broke off as Giles ran past her and disappeared into Joanna's room.

Inside, he stopped and took in the scene. Joanna stood, gowned in her beautiful wedding gown, her face as pale as death, clutching at her throat. Lily stood to one side but in front of Joanna, her face set as mutinous and belligerent as Giles had ever seen it.

And Eleanor stood screeching like a mad-woman, her arm extended, pointing at Joanna.

"Giles, she's stolen my jewelry! Look at her neck and her ears. She's stolen my jewels!" Eleanor wailed, turning to Giles and grabbing him by both arms. "It's bad enough you have to marry a slut, but a thief as well?"

"Shut up, Eleanor," growled Giles, shaking her off and walking over to Joanna. He put up his arms and tried to gather her to him, but she pulled back.

"No, thank you, Giles," Joanna said, her voice like shards of ice. "I can handle this myself. Madame," she said, turning to face Eleanor. "These are my mother's garnets. I've had them since she died and my father gave them to me."

"Mother, hah!" spat Eleanor. "Since when did the likes of you have a mother with jewelry like that? And as for a father, if your mother did come by such gems, then she wouldn't be the sort to be sure who your father was, now would she?"

There was a moment of shocked silence, then Giles was the first to recover himself. "Eleanor, it is only mid-afternoon and you are already drunk," he said in a quiet, cool voice. "The garnets are not yours and you know it. You've never owned garnets as long as I've known you, and Joanna wouldn't steal a crust of bread thrown into the garbage if she were starving. You have ruined the past ten years and more of my life. You will not ruin one more minute and you will not spoil our wedding. You are not welcome at the ceremony and you are not welcome at the party afterward. I am more than willing to bind and gag you and throw you in the stable muck until everyone has left. Or you can stay in your room and drink yourself to death, as you please. Which is it to be?"

For one furious moment, Joanna thought the woman would go mad and launch herself at Giles. Then Eleanor drew herself up and with a sneer on her face said, "I wouldn't be caught dead at this pitiful little excuse for a wedding, Giles. I don't believe anyone here will have a title but you, if one can count being a knight as anything much. And as for staying in my room, I shall do so, and be among the best of the company, all by myself. By the way, dear," she threw at Joanna over her shoulder on her way out, "I thought those were my rubies. A trick of the light, you understand. I certainly wouldn't bother myself about garnets. They're such common little stones."

"Joanna, I'm so sorry," Giles said gently, taking her hand in his. "I wouldn't have let her spoil your wedding day for the world."

"Nothing is spoiled, Giles," she replied, smiling up at him. "Except you weren't supposed to see my gown. But since you picked it out, I suppose there's no harm done."

Unnoticed by either of them, Lily slipped from

the room, shutting the door quietly behind her with a smile on her face.

"I imagine your gown is quite lovely, Joanna," Giles said, tracing his finger along her cheek. "I do not seem to see anything but your beautiful face when I'm around you, so I can't be sure." He bent down and kissed her, gathering her in his arms. His lips were warm and hungry and the kiss deepened even as he pulled her more tightly to him.

Joanna could feel the length of him molding against her, and her heart raced as his tongue found hers.

Then he pulled away gently, drawing in a great, shuddering breath. "I've spent these last three weeks holding myself at bay. I suppose it would be self-indulgent, to say the least, to ravish you on the brink of the altar," he said, his voice husky with desire, his hands working their errant way down the length of her body.

Joanna giggled and buried her face in his neck. He smelled so good, like soap and clean cotton. And the struggle for honor had not been one-sided!

"Eleanor will be gone next week, my darling," he murmured, inhaling the scent of her clean hair. "I'm sorry I let her stay this long, but I wanted to make sure I could rent a decent establishment for her to solve the problem once and for all. I did not expect her to be this vicious to you."

"It doesn't matter, Giles, really it doesn't. I can see how sick she is. You can see it, too, can't you? It's not just the brandy and the way she lives. There's really something wrong with her mind. I know I haven't been here that long, but she honestly seems to have grown madder by the day. There is nothing to do but feel sorry for her and not let her have an opportunity to hurt any of us further."

"You are a good soul, my darling. I don't know where you find your wellspring of charity. I confess mine is bone dry where Eleanor is concerned." He planted one more kiss on her forehead. "I'll go and finish dressing. And in case you are worrying, I'm quite sure I haven't so much as glanced at your gown."

Then he was gone, and Joanna turned a smiling face back to her mirror. Lily would have to come back up and fiddle with her hair again. The man was impossible on hairpins!

"The ceremony was beautiful, Lady Chapman, and it was so kind of you to invite us. You know, neighbors are few and far between here. It would give us great pleasure, Bertram and myself, if we could have you and Sir Giles over for a little supper party one evening, nothing like the London Season, you understand. I am afraid we are all rather happily provincial, but you are such a lovely bride, and it is a pleasure to see this house alive again. That is, I mean . . ."

"Oh, thank you, Mrs. Desmond," Joanna picked up the thread as smoothly as she could. She had had any number of such conversations this evening, greeting her guests and her neighbors. It would seem that Lady Eleanor had not endeared herself in the neighborhood, and from the occasional odd remark, it seemed the neighbors had long viewed Queen's Hall with confusion and distaste. It had been hard enough in the first half hour, hearing herself referred to as Lady Chapman. In the last three weeks, with all the lists and the details to see to, it had not actually occurred to her that she would be Mrs., much less Lady anything. She was a bit uncomfortable about it, feeling that any moment now someone would appear and unmask her as a mere vicar's daughter.

"How much longer?" Giles hissed in her ear. His hand had been straying along her back all evening, occasionally venturing a squeeze just a bit too far down for social decency. Joanna had started and blushed at first, but she had not complained. Indeed, if the truth were known, she was eager to go upstairs, to be alone with Giles, to touch him, to kiss him, this man she had come to love above all things.

"Just a few moments, Giles. They are setting up the card tables now, and I don't suppose anyone will expect us to play."

"I don't care what they expect. I'm taking you upstairs in five minutes if I have to throw you over my shoulder," he growled in her ear, giving her rump another hard squeeze.

"You have a lovely bride, Sir Giles," came a pleasant voice. "Where is your stepsister?" The question, a little tentative, had been asked a good many times tonight.

"Eleanor was unable to join us this evening. She had a prior engagement," Giles said smoothly. "Do you play whist, Mrs. Davis? I see the tables are forming."

"Oh, indeed I do," the lady replied with enthusiasm, turning and heading toward the tables.

"Giles, you are dreadful," Joanna giggled, only to be patted on the derriere again. "I do believe we could slip away now, if you wish to," she purred in his ear. "They do all seem to be stampeding for the cards."

He said not a word, taking her arm firmly and

shepherding her through the room, nodding and smiling pleasantly at whoever glanced their way. Joanna's face was flaming by the time they reached the door and disappeared through it.

Once the door was closed behind them, there was a sweet silence in the hallway, bright with candles in the heavy sconces. Giles swept Joanna into his arms and made for the stairs.

"Put me down, Giles," she remonstrated, laughing. "What if someone sees us?"

"They will think I have been patient long enough," he muttered gruffly, nibbling at her neck. "And if I carry you, you cannot run away from me."

In answer, she put her arms around his neck and hugged him tightly. In no time at all they stood before the door of his room. Kicking it open, he carried her in and set her down gently, his eyes roving over her face as if he would memorize it. He turned back to shut the door, and Joanna looked about her with interest.

"You know, I've never even seen your room, Giles," she said. "Very . . . masculine . . ." She trailed off, trying not to laugh. The room was as spartan as an army barracks. Oh, the bed looked soft enough and there was a large dark red comforter spread over it, but nowhere was there a sign that this room was well loved or even much lived in.

"Giles," she said as he pressed a snifter of amber fluid into her hand, "I don't even see a mirror. Surely you have a mirror somewhere?"

"There's one on the back of the door to the armoire, Joanna," he replied, his eyes dancing. "But I can assure you that you look lovely, and if you have any thought of fixing your hair, I can assure you further that you are wasting your time." As if to illustrate his point, he reached over and gently tugged at a few pins, spilling dark, curling tendrils about her face.

For a moment they stood apart, staring at one another, then he stepped toward her, the need plain in his eyes.

In response, she held up her arms to him. In a flash his arms were about her as he crushed her to him, his lips in her hair, on her neck, her cheek.

With gentle, unsure fingers she traced a line down his chest.

He moaned and grabbed her hand, bringing it to his mouth, kissing her fingers, the palm of her hand, her wrist. She could feel the heat building inside her.

His hand strayed to her neck, then down her shoulder. His touch was velvet soft but hot as fire. So lightly she could hardly feel it, his hand brushed across her breast. A moan rose in her throat as the heat rushed through her. She heard his groan as his hand cupped her breast through the silk of her gown. She could feel him pushed against the length of her and she knew she needed to be closer, pressed tightly. He slid his hand down her back to her buttocks and pulled her more tightly to him. She could feel the hardness of his chest, his muscled thighs pushing against hers. He was hard. Some small, faraway part of her registered the wonder of the feeling even as her body responded, driving her hard against him. She heard him gasp as she pressed herself to him.

He kissed her softly on her neck, moving his lips to the base of her throat, leaving a trail of fire on her skin. His hand parted the buttons on the back of her gown and he slipped it down softly, exposing her in her shift to the soft lamplight. He pulled back and gazed at her, his breath coming in jagged gasps. Gently he lifted his hand and found her breast, kneading the soft flesh, circling her nipple, now taut, with his fingers. Joanna felt as if she could hardly breathe. Never had she imagined such a feeling. It grew inside of her with an urgency she could put no name to, yet she knew she would explode if he kept on touching her like this.

Her hand slipped into his shirt and she found herself working open the buttons. She could feel his chest now, hard and muscled, his skin hot as fire to the touch. He moaned as she moved her hand over him, pulling his shirt open, flesh against flesh.

His lips slipped still lower, still gentle, still hot. She cried out as his tongue found her nipple, circling, sucking. And his hand moved down, down over her hip, her thigh. She could feel her gown sliding slowly down her legs, and she heard his moan as his hand met her soft flesh. He stroked her gently, running his hand up and down her leg, then, suddenly, sweeping her into his arms and walking over to the bed. Gently he laid her down, working the dress off where it had caught about her legs. She lay now with her shift half on and half off, her breasts gleaming in the lamplight, heaving with each breath she took.

"You are so beautiful, Joanna," he whispered, his finger tracing around her peaked nipple.

He slipped next to her in the bed, pulling the bedclothes out from under them both. He pulled her tightly to him, half tearing her shift out from between them, and Joanna gasped when she felt the heat of him, felt the evidence of his passion hard between them. His hands began their roving again as his lips seized hers, his tongue plundering her mouth. Cupping her buttocks, he again pulled her tightly to him.

She gasped when his hand slipped between her legs, and she pulled back.

"Do you want me to stop, Joanna?" he whispered raggedly in her ear. "Am I going too fast for you?" But even as she tried to say yes, that she was frightened, that she wanted to slow down, she could feel herself pushing toward him, craving his touch, needing that pressure, there, there where he touched her.

"No," she whispered brokenly, driving herself hard against him. Fire was shooting in waves through her belly and she could not stop. She could feel him hard through his breeches, pushing against her leg. Almost without thinking, she slid her hand to the front of his breeches and rubbed the hard bulge she found there.

"Ahhh," he groaned. "Joanna, if you do that I won't be able to stop." He spoke in gasps, at the same time holding her hand against himself. "I need you so much."

"Don't stop," she whispered, rubbing him hard now. "I don't want you to stop." It was maddening to touch him so. She wanted desperately to tear away the cloth that separated them. She felt that if she could not feel him against her, flesh against flesh, she would go mad. The tiny bells of fear in her brain were silent now, drowned out by the rushing pulse of her desire.

She could feel him fumbling with the fastenings that held his breeches shut. Then he was free, thrusting forward, large and hard—and daunting.

"You're frightened," he whispered softly, seeing the fear suddenly in her passion-filled eyes. He pulled her gently toward him. "I will be as gentle as I know how to be, my love. I wouldn't hurt you for the world." He nibbled at her ear as he spoke, sending little shivers down her neck.

In answer, she reached down and took him in her hand, hearing him groan as she did so, squeezing him tight. It was amazing that something could be so hard, and yet so soft as well. He thrust against her hand harder and faster, pulling back abruptly.

"Wait, stop. I will lose control," he rasped. He reached down again between her legs, probing at her secret place, hot and moist. She started as his fingers touched her, sliding between her nether lips, then she moaned and rocked against him, building her rhythm, faster and faster. He drew back his hand and she moaned her protest. Quickly he straddled her, holding himself up, taking care not to lean any of his weight against her chest.

"This will hurt you, my love," he whispered. "I'm sorry I won't be able to keep from hurting you."

"It's all right," she answered through a haze of passion, wanting him to touch her again.

With one quick thrust he was inside and she cried out in pain.

"I'm sorry," he said softly, holding himself still while she grew used to the feeling.

She smiled up at him and reached a hand to his cheek. He groaned and began to move, slowly at first, then building his rhythm. An answering rhythm grew inside her as the pain receded, and she found herself thrusting forward to meet his thrusts, both of them breathing in gasps, reaching toward something she knew she must find. Suddenly she cried out as wave upon wave of pleasure washed through her. Above her, Giles, too, cried out as his seed burst forth with a shattering intensity.

For a moment there was no sound except their ragged breathing. Carefully he lowered himself to her side, pulling her close within his arms and pulling the blankets up around them both.

"Are you all right?" he murmured into her ear. "Did I hurt you?"

"Only at first," she answered softly.

"It will not hurt again, my love," he whispered, kissing her on the side of the neck, his hands beginning again to move slowly, wonderingly, over her flesh.

As Joanna felt the heat rising again within her, she turned and pushed herself tight against the length of him, laughing softly at the shudder that ran through his body, and wondering at the powerful magic of it all.

Chapter Thirteen

"I must go, sweetheart, I hope you understand. I would never leave you if it weren't urgent." He held her hand tightly and brought it to his lips.

"Of course you must go, Giles. There's been a death. And please do not worry about us. We'll be fine, although we'll miss you." Joanna's eyes strayed down to the beach where the children, barefoot, were trying to outrun the surf, but not trying very hard. Their squeals could be heard at quite a distance.

They lay on a blanket, spread out on the grass of the bluff overlooking the beach. It was a windy day, but with just enough spring in the breeze to make the day bracing instead of cold. She had been so pleased when she'd seen him coming to join the picnic, then so alarmed as she'd taken note of the stricken look on his face.

"Do you know how it happened, Giles?" she

asked gently. It was clear he was distressed about the accidental death of Jimmy Bigod, one of his foremen in Dufton.

"Not yet. The messenger just arrived a little while ago with a short note. A cart accident of some sort. My God, Joanna, his wife has just finished her lying-in with her third babe. Why is the world so cruel?"

"It's not cruel, really, Giles," she said gently. She had listened to her father take part in this sort of discussion so many times over the years. "The world just plays according to its set laws. And it doesn't change them to suit any of us. But there's no cruelty in it." It wasn't much comfort, she knew, but he sounded so bleak and it was hard to explain away the senseless death of a fine young man.

"I had not planned to leave you here alone with Eleanor, darling. I'd take you with me, but the mines are no place for a woman." He toyed with her fingers, as if he drew strength from her mere touch. "Of course, I could take Eleanor," he went on, his eyes growing more playful, "but I'm quite sure I'd murder her before the week was out and I'd hate to have to go through all the bother of an inquest."

Joanna giggled. She loved the way he touched her. It seemed that whenever they were together he was always touching her, gently, not pawing. And when they were completely alone . . . she blushed at the thought of what his hands could do to her, and other things as well. . . .

And his eyes never left her, as though he were hungry and the sight of her gave him sustenance. It still seemed like a dream to her. They had been married only three days and it seemed hard to believe even now.

"In all seriousness, Joanna," he said, sitting up, "I know you like to see the good in all people, but can you, at least for my peace of mind, agree to keep clear of my stepsister until I return? I'll be gone only a few days. You don't know her like I do, and she is not to be trusted."

"Please don't worry. Lady Eleanor has given us a wide berth for the past few days, Giles, so I do not suppose we'll be running into her. Honestly, I don't think she and I are even awake many of the same hours a day."

"That's true. But she is not happy about our marriage and is unhappier still that I'm moving her away from here, and I do not want her venting her considerable spleen in your direction."

Joanna was greatly relieved that the details on renting the house for Lady Eleanor were nearly complete. She felt a bit cruel about it—after all, Queen's Hall had been the woman's home for a good number of years—but she contented her conscience by telling herself that Giles had rented a commodious, well-seated house near St. Bees, far enough south of Queen's Hall that they could expect little but financial correspondence between the two households. And the artwork would be going with her ladyship, so she would feel right at home!

"And if she tries to fire me, I am not to go?" Joanna asked, teasing the light back into his brown eyes.

"Not unless I fire you, Lady Chapman. But so far, you have given satisfaction, so you needn't fear your departure is imminent." He reached for her and pulled her close for a quick kiss.

"How soon must you go, Giles?" asked Joanna, breaking away with a giggle. He had a very short fuse and it would not do to let him get started in full view of the children and the household!

"I must leave right away, my love. Are you certain you'll be all right?" His eyes roamed her face as if he were memorizing it.

"Of course I will. I've so much to keep me busy. Tom is like a difficult puzzle. I keep finding one piece at a time and the picture grows clearer and clearer." Indeed, the boy had opened up like a flower over the past few days. His speech was rudimentary—perhaps it would always be so—but he made himself understood. He had even gone so far as to hail Annie by name, which had brought a smile to the girl's face and been the talk of the kitchen.

"I'll send word to you. Tell Mrs. Davies or Hawton if you need anything. And remember, I am only a few hours away by horse. You can get word to me if you find yourself uneasy for any reason." He pulled her to him, holding her tightly.

"Please take care of yourself, Giles," she whispered into his neck. "I couldn't bear it if anything happened to you."

"Nothing will happen to me, goose. It's you I'm worried about." His lips seized hers for a hard kiss. Then with another quick kiss dropped on her nose, he was gone, disappearing up the hill.

"Children, it's time to go in now," called Joanna. Unaccountably, the wind had picked up, bringing with it the hint of a chill rain. The sun vanished into a deep cloud she had not noticed before, and suddenly everything looked gray again. . . .

* * *

"It's hard to fathom, Sir Giles." Robbie MacAran's eyes were troubled. "It was so much like your accident that I mislike the coincidence. Particularly as we was bein' careful-like, because of what happened to you. It just doesn't make sense." MacAran was glad to see Sir Giles, to turn the reins of control over to a man he deemed truly his better, intelligent beyond all other men.

"Was the ground wet?" asked Sir Giles. They stood at the rim of the pit and looked down at the scarred track where the cart had borne down on Jimmy Bigod, deadly in its silence.

"Yes, sir. Wetter than it should have been. We haven't had all that much rain for the past few days. But it weren't any mudslide that caused this one. What's troublin' is that the bricks were gone, the ones we use to anchor the cart in place. The men who brought it up last clearly remember placin' the bricks, and when we looked after the accident they weren't nowhere to be found."

"Couldn't the men be lying to cover up their own negligence?" Giles asked. He could sooner believe that than deliberate subversion.

"Aye, sir, they could. But they're a senior crew. Very sturdy and reliable, they are. And they was all so shocked by it. Nobody looked guilty-like, and Johnny even said he'd checked the bricks special because of what happened to you, and anyway, they was all sure the cart was much further from the rim than the tracks look like now."

Indeed, the culprit had been easily determined after the cart had come crashing down on Giles, and drunken John Duffy had been let go for his negligent anchoring of the heavy cart, angry and belligerent as always.

Giles clapped MacAran on the shoulder and

turned away. He had arrived after the body had been hauled up from the pit. Jimmy Bigod had been cleaned up as well as could be and taken home to his wife for burial. It had been grim, and now Giles had to go and see the woman, to assure her that she and the babes would have enough to live on. He'd never had a death of an employee before, but as of right now he was creating a death payment. Mrs. Bigod would at least have a living if she could not have her husband.

"It's arranged, my dear. I have a man inside the works. There's nothing to fret about. It will be taken care of tomorrow night." Hawton had his feet up on his desk. He had nearly sprung to attention when Lady Eleanor had come barging into his office but had checked the impulse.

He'd been doing some thinking and some snooping. He'd pried open the drawer in Sir Giles's office where the man kept his personal papers. Hawton had found a will, dated just before Sir Giles's marriage to Joanna, leaving everything to her, including guardianship of the children. There was a small trust fund set up for Lady Eleanor, to be administered by the solicitors in Carlisle. The children, of course, had a good bit of money from their father's estate, and this was to be administered by Joanna. In the event that Joanna and Giles both died, childless, the children stood to inherit Giles's entire estate, except for Eleanor's small portion. Only in the event that no relations by blood or marriage survived Giles or Joanna did Eleanor inherit the entire estate, and that would be administered by the solicitors, or by a husband if she married.

But Joanna, as bride and widow, would not be

enjoying her newfound wealth. The poor thing would be so distraught at his death that she would be taking her own life in a few days. Her clothes would be found on the beach, but not her body.

Hawton felt fairly certain there would be no other claimants on the estate. Miss Carpenter, as she was then, had informed him on her arrival that she had no one, so it seemed unlikely that anyone would step forward and make a claim based on a blood kinship with Joanna.

So now the real question was that of the guardianship of the children. As far as Hawton knew, Giles had no heirs other than his brother's children. They were minors. One would be a legal incompetent all his life. With Joanna dead, the guardianship could very well then go to Eleanor. Along with control of the estate until Emma came of age. And so many things could happen. There were fevers, bolting horses, stomach complaints. So many things that could stand between a little girl and her twenty-first birthday.

And now Hawton had control over Eleanor. She had grown more and more dependent on him, more shrill with her demands, but less haughty in her demeanor. It was no longer "my lady and her steward." No, now she needed him, relied on him to do all the thinking and planning and the execution. Now she would not be able to cut him loose. Not after tomorrow.

"But that's what you said when you hired that bumbling fool in Carlisle. And the shipment is tomorrow night!" Eleanor wailed at him.

"Be quiet! Do you want the entire household to hear you?" Hawton snapped before he could control the impulse. Seeing the light of hauteur kindling in her eye, he softened his tone. "You must remember, my dear, that this is the servants' wing. They pass back and forth in front of my door all day long. We are not nearly so private here as you are used to in your part of the house."

"Very well," she said peevishly, but he was relieved to note that she had lowered her voice. "But we cannot have anything go wrong tomorrow night, Hawton. Everything will collapse around our heads if we are discovered. Oh, why couldn't it have been managed before the wedding? I hate having to leave everything until the last minute, and now we have the problem of his wife to deal with." She actually wrung her hands.

"You know perfectly well we could not move any sooner than we did after what happened in Carlisle. The man has the devil's own luck. It took a great deal of time to set this up, and it was all the more difficult with Sir Giles here all the time. As it is, we are moving more quickly than I'd like. You must trust me to see to it, Lady Eleanor," he said, taking her hands in his and chafing them. He had not yet been able to bring himself to drop the "Lady," and he was not sure when he could presume to do so. Perhaps after they had committed this murder. "Lord Beeson assures me that the boat will not arrive until very late, after midnight. Everyone will have been long asleep by then. The servants retire very early, as do Lady Chapman and the children. There will simply not be anyone awake who can hear us, and in any case, there is a new moon, which casts no light at all."

"I wish it were over with. I wish we had the money in our hands," she said, sinking into one of two hard-looking chairs in his office. "Did Lord Beeson tell you how soon he would get the money to us?" she asked eagerly.

"As originally agreed, my dear," he said, trying to keep the impatience out of his voice. "Half of the money when the girls arrive here and the other half after they have been deposited in London. It'll take about four days after that for the money to reach us."

"So within the week we'll have it all?"

"My lady, I believe you are being short-sighted in this," he said. The financial possibilities had been rocketing about in his brain all morning and he needed to share it with her, to test his theories. "Have you given any thought to where Sir Giles's estate will go?"

"Of course I have," she snapped. "If his upstart of a wife disappears, then it will go to those horrible brats. Every penny, as far as I can tell. The only benefit I will get out of his demise is that we will be able to stay here and run our end of the operation."

"And who will be the guardian of the brats, Lady Eleanor?" he asked smoothly. The woman was a blithering fool. She could see no farther than her own painted nose.

He watched while there was a gradual dawning of light in her eyes. "I—I really hadn't given that any thought, Hawton," she said slowly.

"Then I take it he has said nothing of the matter to you?" Hawton could feel himself growing excited. Eleanor would be the logical legal choice for guardianship. She was of age, after all, long since, and there would be no other interested parties to complain that she was unfit.

"No, of course not," she said, as though he were the dimwitted one. "Giles would never share that sort of information with me."

"Well, I found his will today and looked it over.

There appears to be no provision made for guardianship in the event of Joanna's death. I don't see any reason why you could not act as the legal guardian."

"Do they let women do that sort of thing?" she asked, her tone dubious.

"Not as a rule, but they do when there are no suitable male relatives. Imagine the fun we could have as guardians of the entire estate. And if we continue to be an important part of Beeson's operation, we could be very rich indeed, my dear." There. He had deliberately used the word *we*. Now he waited to see if she had caught it and if she would balk.

Instead, to his surprise and great glee, she launched herself into his arms.

"Oh, Hawton, you are so clever! Whatever would I do without you?" she said, laughing and placing wet kisses on his cheek. "We can have all of it. Every cent! If no one is overseeing our estate bookkeeping, we can do anything we like! I can even take a house in London and go when I please!" She nuzzled his neck and placed her leg suggestively high around his hip.

He chuckled softly and seized her lips with his own. If she got guardianship of the brats, then perhaps he would stick around. He might marry her. There would be a great deal of money in it for him. Indeed, it would set him up for life. He could go to London with her and hobnob with the swells. They wouldn't be able to cut him then, not if he were married to an earl's daughter and had plenty of scratch to throw around. And when he needed something younger on the end of his pole, he was sure there'd be any number of willing ladies. . . .

Chapter Fourteen

Giles found it impossible to sleep. Twisting and turning in the sheets, he had them all bunched up uncomfortably around his legs. They were scratchy as well, something he did not recall noticing before. He had had this room set aside for himself at the inn at Dufton for at least five years. He had spent more nights here since then than he had at home, by far. Why did it now seem so strange, so much more like a room at an inn than it had before? A few nights in a wide, comfortable bed with the love of his life curled into his arms had made this little room seem dreary indeed.

But it was not really the room that kept him awake. Over and over he had puzzled it out, his precise, analytical mind trying to make logic where he could find none. What had made the heavy cart tear down into the pit? Why had it happened at just that moment when Bigod was below? The man had been working after the shift on the cart tracks, great iron rails that allowed the cart to roll smoothly up and down regardless of the weight it bore. One of the tracks had a loose bolt and Bigod was repairing it, a brief task that would have been finished moments later. And who knew he was down there? The work site had been closed down for the night and no one was supposed to be about at that time. The site had no wall around it, of course, but then, there was nothing to steal except raw lead, not valuable in small quantities in a black market. What perversity of fate had loosed the cart at that exact moment, still full with the last load it had carried up that evening, to crush the man beneath its deadly weight?

Or was it fate at all?

MacAran was dissatisfied. So were a number of the senior men. Giles could see it in their faces and hear it in the occasional muttering. They had no quarrel with Giles's management. To the contrary, they seemed to admire and respect him. He had been known to stand an entire shift to a pint after a particularly good day, and it was widely understood that if a man had a legitimate complaint he would find a willing ear in Sir Giles Chapman, an unusual thing in an owner. Even his foremen were chosen not only for their knowledge, but for their sense of fairness. There was little favoritism on site. What little there was, was earned through diligence, competence, and seniority. Although there was the occasional dust-up, too much to drink here or a smart mouth there, on the whole it was as successful a work site as could be found in these parts, and a man who could get hired on by the Dufton Mining Works was considered lucky indeed.

Until yesterday.

Giles's interview with Mrs. Bigod had been painful, as he had known it would be. She had three babes, ages two, twelve months, and one at the breast, newborn. He had looked into her careworn face and seen such yawning grief as had made him look away. The pain was raw and so deep he felt as if it might swallow him up. She had cried when he offered her the pension settlement. He would pay her a yearly stipend and she could stay in the cottage for her lifetime. It was a generous offer, outrageous really by prevailing standards, but Giles had heard too much about the poorhouses filled to overflowing with young widows, orphaned children and men too old, sick, or injured to hold a job. Jimmy Bigod had been a decent man, a good husband, and a good worker. Giles could do no less for his widow. He had offered her a job at Queen's Hall as an alternative, when she was well enough to travel, and had promised to find work for the children as they grew. Her sad eyes had widened and she had spilled forth with such tears of gratitude that he had felt like a fool for offering her such a pittance from his bountiful portion in life, when she had so little.

The funeral would take place tomorrow morning and then he would return to Queen's Hall. At the thought he smiled to himself in the dark. Joanna in his bed, Joanna at his table, Joanna in the schoolroom, anywhere, she was balm to his long-troubled heart. No longer did he awaken in the dark, sweating with the nightmare that Violet had returned to torment him anew.

And Joanna had fit herself so seamlessly into the household. When he had announced the news of their engagement to the staff, he and Joanna had been met by great smiles of goodwill and best wishes. It was apparent that no one was harboring the dark thoughts about the governess getting above herself that Eleanor had so meanly predicted. Indeed, it seemed as if the staff would have no trouble transferring allegiance from one mistress of the household to another. Eleanor had been, if anything, a lazy chatelaine, leaving all the management to Mrs. Davies and Hawton, bestirring herself to issue orders only when she was entertaining, or when something did not suit her.

Of Eleanor herself, he had seen little since the day of the wedding. She had kept to her own rooms as far as he knew, and if the stock of brandy was being depleted at an alarming rate, he neither knew nor cared. Oddly enough, she had not disappeared on one of her usual visits. She had never before spent so much as a week at home alone with none of her raucous friends to keep her entertained. Giles could not understand why, and assumed she was nursing her grievance against him, staying close by so that she could keep an eye on his plans for her. Well, the lease agreement for the St. Bees house was signed and sitting on his desk at home. The agent assured him that a few days more of paint and cleaning should make it utterly charming. The wagons would arrive in three days to load up her ladyship's belongings, cupids and odalisques and all, and then she would be nothing to Giles but an obligation on monthly drafts.

The thought of packing Eleanor off brought another smile to his lips. She had been a blight on his life for so long. She had had a hand in ruining everything for him, corrupting his wife. Not, he supposed, that Violet had needed to be led into her corruption. No, the taint had been bred in the bone with Violet, the angelic beauty of her face hiding the darkness in her heart.

Contrary to Eleanor's vituperative accusations, he had no intention of being stingy with her. He had promised to look after her and he would honor that promise to the best of his ability. She would have a generous allowance, and perhaps it would do her good to learn a little discipline in living within it. She could continue with her parties; he had seen to it that the St. Bees house was large enough to accommodate a slew of her friends in style, and there was no reason why she couldn't go on just as she had always done—at a distance from him and his bride.

There was a noise outside the door, a faint scratching sound. Had he been asleep, as usual at this time of night, he would have heard nothing at all. He had the last room at the end of a long corridor on the top floor. He had selected this room based on its distance from the common room below and the relative lack of hallway traffic. Well, he thought, turning over on the scratchy sheets yet again, someone is abroad in the night, but it does not concern me.

There was another scratching sound. Already annoyed that he was unable to sleep, Giles sat up. It was no good. He could see nothing. The room was nearly pitch dark. He had let the fire die down and now he could make out only a few bare embers glowing. There was no moon out tonight, and he had shut the curtains against the early morning sun.

Then he saw the door begin to open slowly. His mind raced. He had no pistols and no knife—he had no reason to go armed about Dufton. But he had his fists, and many a man could attest to his talents in that regard, a weekly boxing match being part of the immutable culture of Dufton.

Here, perhaps, was another piece of the puzzle that had bedeviled him over the past two weeks. Under normal circumstances, no one would attack him in Dufton, of that he was certain. He had no conceivable enemies here, and anyway, in Dufton, disputes between men were settled like men, by fisticuffs, not an assassin's knife in the dark. He was sure it was not Sally, the tavern serving girl. While he had occasionally availed himself of her willing services, it was a business relationship only, and she had gladly accepted the little sack of gold sovereigns that he had pressed on her as a parting gift.

Watching the bulk appear against the faint light of the hallway as the door swung silently open, he hoped it was a knife and not a gun he would have to deal with. The intruder could not see him, he was certain. The man came from the hallway where a single candle burned on every level, faint, but spoiling his night vision.

He waited. The shape came closer to the bed, then stood over him.

As fast as an adder's strike, the intruder's arm came up. Giles saw a faint glint. Good! A knife, he thought as his arm came out to grasp the other man's arm, his fingers like steel around his wrist.

"Drop it!" Giles growled, twisting the man's hand down to his side. Leaping from the bed, Giles grabbed his would-be assassin and spun him around, catching his arms up behind his back and ramming his knee at the back of the man's legs. His adversary buckled to the floor, a howl of pain coming from him as the knife clattered from his hand. Giles could see little, but from the stench he judged the man was none too clean and had been drinking. Now he knew who it had to be. He kicked the knife away.

"Good evening, Mr. Duffy," he said cordially, digging his knee sharply into the man's back as he knelt on top of him. "To what do I owe the pleasure of your visit, sir?" Giles reached for his neckcloth on the chair by the bed, and tied Duffy's hands together tightly behind his back. Tying his stockings together with a tight knot, he wrapped them around the man's feet and bound them tightly. Judging Duffy to be secure for the moment, Giles rose and took his candle over to the fireplace, blowing up the embers enough to kindle a flame at the wick.

"Much better," he said genially as the light sprang up around the room. "Now," he said, seating himself on the bed. "Start at the beginning and tell me what this is all about. When the cart came down on me a few weeks ago—were you trying to kill me then? It was you who neglected to fix the bricks in place. We are certain of that, Mr. Duffy."

"I told ye before," Duffy spat, his face down on the dusty floor. " 'Twere an accident. Ye had no cause to go firin' me fer an accident!"

"It wasn't the first bit of willful negligence on your part, Duffy, and you well know it. There were several other instances, and you had fair warning." Giles eyed the form on the floor. He knew the flimsy bonds would not hold long, but so far Duffy did not seem inclined to test them. He was a big, strapping man, but even from here Giles could smell the whiskey about him, that habitual alcohol smell that persisted day and night. The man was beyond redemption, Giles thought. He was a mean drunk. It was rumored that his wife had died from one of the numerous beatings he had inflicted on her, but there had been no new marks on the corpse and no way to prove the widely held belief. He had a daughter, but she'd run off after her mother died, doubtless to escape the abuse that would then have been directed solely at her. Of all the Dufton inhabitants, good and bad, he was the worst, his existence tolerated because he was one of them, but liked by none.

There was something incongruous about the appearance of the shape sprawled on the floor. Beneath the large man protruded a bit of red material, some kind of purple and lilac pattern apparent in the dim light. Where had he seen that material before? thought Giles. Recently, but where? Reaching down, he pushed Duffy's bulk up slightly and grasped the end of the cloth, pulling it away from the man's body. It seemed to be stuck down the front of his pants. Giles held it up and could see that it was a woman's shawl.

Maggie Bigod's shawl. She had had it wrapped around her and the babe yesterday when he had visited her. He had told her it was pretty, hoping a compliment would coax a smile from her. She had smiled, and told him that her Jimmy had spent a great deal to buy it for her when the first of the babes was born. It was her prized possession, she had told him, the prettiest thing she would ever own. And her face had crumpled again in front of him.

"Where did you get this?" Giles asked, his voice harsh. There was no response from the form on the floor.

A swift kick brought a grunt from Duffy and an unseen grimace from Giles. He should put his boots on before he started kicking information out of the man!

"I asked you a simple question, Mr. Duffy," Giles spat out. He seized the man's hands and pushed them again, hard, up his back. "I know this shawl belongs to Mrs. Bigod. She would never have given it to the likes of you. Why did you steal it?" Giles leaned over and picked Duffy up, turning him over on his back so he could see his face. The man's eyes were mutinous, and he held his tongue.

"I can summon the magistrate now, Duffy, if you'd like. You will be hanged in a matter of days for trying to kill me. Or I can ask for mercy and get you some gaol time instead. It's your choice, Duffy. Now, let's see if you can remember. How did you come by this shawl?"

"I took it tonight when they was all asleep," was Duffy's muttered response.

"Good. That's a start," Giles said coolly. "Hanging is not pleasant, you know. It often takes a good while before you die. Now, why did you steal Mrs. Bigod's shawl?"

There was another angry silence.

"I really don't care if you hang or not, Duffy. And most in the community would agree with me. Shall I roust the magistrate now?"

"I was told to leave it here. Make it look like 'twere she that knifed ye. Fer killin' her man. It's her knife, too."

It was not surprising to hear that the shawl was to be planted, to make Mrs. Bigod appear to be the guilty party. It didn't bear thinking of that this man would have let the widow hang for his crime, leaving three babies orphaned and penniless. But what surprised Giles was the implication that someone else had a hand in planning this crime. Up until this moment he had assumed Duffy was retaliating for his firing.

"Did you kill Bigod, Mr. Duffy?"

"No! 'Twere an accident, I swear it! I went on site that night to do some mischief, to get ye to come back here. That was the plan. I saw the cart and Bigod below and I thought 'twould just nick him, like it did ye. I never meant fer him to die!"

"Do you know anything about an attack on me a few weeks ago in Carlisle?"

"Nought but that it failed."

"Who planned this for you, Duffy?" Giles asked, his tone deceptively mild.

Silence.

"I asked you who told you, Duffy," Giles snarled, aiming another kick at the man's ribs. "You know, I don't really have to call the magistrate at all. I can slit your miserable throat right now. I believe the mayor would give me a medal for it." Another kick brought a moan from the bulk on the floor.

"One more time, Duffy. I am not a patient man." He leaned over and picked up the knife, allowing Duffy to watch him run a hand carefully over the blade. "She's a good housewife, Mrs. Bigod is," Giles said mildly. "It's as sharp as a razor. You won't suffer long."

"It was yer man. Yer Mr. Hawton. He tried to cover his face up in the dark and put a hat over his hair, but I recognized him anyway from the way he walks, and he was ridin' one of yer stallions!" Duffy's eyes were wide, fixed on the knife blade that Giles was turning in his hand, letting it glint in the light.

"What?" Giles's hands were at the man's throat

and he was lifting him off the floor by his shirt collar.

"It's true, sir! I swear it! He gave me five sovereigns. Ye can look in my pocket if ye like. He told me ye've stolen all yer stepsister's money. He promised me a permanent job at Queen's Hall." Duffy's eyes were popping and he gasped out his words.

With a snarl, Giles threw him to the floor. Hawton. Hawton and Eleanor. And Joanna was at Queen's Hall with the two of them!

He threw his clothes on, not bothering to fasten his shirt over his chest. He jammed his stockingless feet into his boots and, grabbing his coat, made for the door, taking the candle with him.

He paused downstairs just long enough to rouse the innkeeper and tell him to summon the magistrate to take the prisoner away and hold him. Then he was off to the stables, saddling Red Devil in the dark. It was five hours to Queen's Hall. Four, the way he would ride it tonight. God grant that he would not be too late. . . .

Chapter Fifteen

It was just past midnight and the house was quiet. Eleanor had slipped downstairs in the dark and waited now in Hawton's office with him. Her nerves were jangled to the point of madness, and she had brought in a decanter from the dining room.

"How much longer now?" she asked in a brittle, near hysterical tone.

The woman would drive him mad. She was worse than a child on a long carriage trip. She must have asked him a half dozen times, as if he knew precisely where on Solway Firth the ship lay at this moment.

"Anytime now, my dear, as I've told you," he answered as patiently as he could. Fortunately, she could not see his face in the dark. They stood in his window which overlooked the sea. It was calm tonight with only a mild breeze to ruffle the black waters. Their eyes had been skimming the darkness for half an hour now, and he had to admit that his nerves were frayed, too.

"And when will your man take care of Giles, Hawton?" she asked peevishly. "When can we be sure he has done it?"

"It will be happening even as we speak, Eleanor. I told you, he has instructions to wait until the inn has quieted down for the night. He will make his way up the back stairs and take care of it. But we'll have to be very patient about finding out about it. We must wait until we are notified by the Dufton authorities. There is no reason to show our hand by acting anxious, as if we anticipate something. We probably will hear nothing until tomorrow afternoon." He sipped at his own brandy, a concession to his nerves. "And don't forget, you are going to be horrified and prostrate with grief. Can you do that?"

It was Eleanor's turn to be impatient. "Of course I can do that!" she snapped. "I've told you that a thousand times." She missed the rolling of his eyes in the dark. "What I do not understand is why you couldn't have arranged to take care of that little upstart of a governess at the same time."

"I've explained it to you, my dear," he said, the impatience now clear in his voice. "It was too risky to try to arrange some sort of accident to them both here at Queen's Hall. If one were only injured instead of killed, it would do us no good. As it is, she will die in a few days, and everyone will be certain she committed suicide because of her overwhelming grief. Just trust my judgment on this, Eleanor." He had left off the "Lady" several times tonight and had heard nothing from her about it.

There was a slight winking of a light out at sea, so brief he wasn't sure he had seen it at all. But the moon was dark and any light had to come from a ship.

"There! Look out and see if you see a light!" he whispered excitedly.

Again the light flashed, then disappeared. The ship must be riding swells.

"Yes, I see it!" Eleanor exclaimed. "Oh, Hawton! It's going to happen! We're going to be so rich!" She threw her arms around his neck and kissed him full on the lips. He suffered her embrace for a moment, then disengaged her arms.

"All right! Are you ready?" he asked, his voice urgent. "Please do not forget. No talking unless you absolutely must, and then only in a whisper. The girls have been drugged—just a bit, mind, because we need for them to be able to walk by themselves, but you'll need to keep a sharp eye. Remember, they think they are coming to be legitimate servants, so do not say anything to set them straight. Can you do this?" he asked, grasping her shoulders so hard she flinched. "If you are uncertain, go back up to bed now. I can take care of it without you."

"Of course I can do it!" she spat out, twisting out of his grasp. "Do you take me for an idiot? We have gone over all this a hundred times. Let's just go!" She made for the door, her haughty anger apparent in the set of her shoulders.

Well, let her prance around all she wants, he thought, picking up the shielded lantern from his desk and following her silently into the hall. As long as she doesn't mess things up. And now he knew how to keep her arrogance in check. After all, they were in this together—murderers both.

They made their way on the carpeted floor of the hallway, disappearing down the wooden back stairs. Thank God the stairs did not creak. He had deliberately gone up and down these stairs several times in the last few days to make sure their tread would not give them away. Not that he was so terribly worried about noise. The servants slept on the top floor. All their rooms faced the fells, the other side of the large attic being devoted to storage. And the only others in the house were Joanna in Sir Giles's room and the brats up on the third floor. Joanna's bedroom on the second floor faced the fells as well, so she would hear nothing, and he had long since dismissed the children from consideration. Children as a rule were heavy sleepers, and he had never heard any household complaint about Emma and Tom being up in the night.

They left through the garden door. The hinges, oiled this morning, were silent. They made their way down to the beach, where they waited in the dark. The light on the water had disappeared, as planned. The ship was to show a light only for a few minutes, which was why he and Eleanor had waited so long, watching upstairs so as not to miss it. They stood in silence on the beach, straining for a sight of the boat. The ship itself would moor out in the water, guided by a lantern placed earlier by Hawton up under the bluff, visible to the sea but not to the house. A skiff would bring the cargo onto the beach.

At last there was the flash of an oar in the water, then the rhythmic sound of rowing. Something loomed in the black water. Hawton and Eleanor made their way to the water's edge as the shape of the skiff appeared from the dark. Hawton ran forward, and in silence the boat was beached.

Hawton motioned Eleanor forward. As she approached, she could see a number of small forms huddled in the boat. They appeared to be covered by some sort of tarpaulin. Two large men, heavily swathed so nothing showed but their eyes, jumped over the sides of the boat. Speaking not a word, they began to pull the girls out, one by one, dumping them on the beach like the cargo they were. The girls appeared dazed and sleepy. They sat up, blinking, but it was clear they were confused. The lantern Hawton had set down gave only a seam of light from its shutters.

Five bundles now sat on the ground. Eleanor watched as something passed from the hand of one of the men to that of Hawton. A few words were exchanged in whispers, then the men pushed the boat back into the water and disappeared into the dark.

"Get them up carefully, Eleanor," Hawton hissed in the blackness.

With hands she forced to be gentle, Eleanor began helping the huddled forms to stand. Several swayed on their feet but managed to stay upright, blinking in confusion. Eleanor could make out little of their faces but she could see tangled, dirty hair and smell unwashed clothing and bodies.

"We'll walk a little ways down the beach," Hawton whispered when the girls were all standing. "I want everyone to be silent. It wouldn't do to wake up the neighborhood." He bent down and picked up the lantern, lifting the shutter that faced toward his cottage, angling it away from the house. There was little of the stretch between here and the house that could be seen from the windows, but he was taking as few risks as he could get away with.

"I want me da!" came a shriek in the dark. "Me da said I could come home if I wanted to. I want to go home!" the little voice ended in a long wail.

"Shut her up!" hissed Hawton furiously as Eleanor bolted toward the sound. But the girl saw her coming. Sick to her stomach during most of the voyage, the child had kept little down and had not drunk the tea laced with laudanum. She had slept all day and had awakened full of the energy of fear and despair. With a scream, the little form turned and ran, shrieking down the beach.

Emma was restless. One of her back teeth was trying to come in, a large one that ached a bit as it pushed its way through the tender gum. Her curtains were drawn back the way she liked them. Her bed lay near the window, and she often contented herself with counting stars as she fell asleep. There were two that were particularly bright tonight, and she knew they were Mama and Papa, looking after her and Tom.

Things would be all right now. This house which had been so cold and dark when they had first come was now bright with love and laughter. Emma had walked beside Joanna in the wedding and Tom had carried the ring. And while there would never be Mama and Papa again, at least they would be a family now, where they would be loved and looked after. Aunt Joanna was the very next best thing to Mama, and even Uncle Giles, whom Emma had thought to be cold and distant when they first came, spent a great deal of time now playing with them. And Aunt Joanna had said they would not need to hire a governess. She said she enjoyed their company too much to turn over their teaching to anyone else.

Emma wiggled her toes against the sheets and smiled to herself in the dark. Aunt Joanna. It sounded so nice.

And that other aunt, the one who hated her and Tom so, Aunt Eleanor. She was going away, a long way away, and they wouldn't have to see her anymore.

Suddenly she heard a scream, faint but unmistakable. It seemed to come from the beach. Emma froze. She was not a timid child, but she knew about the banshees that cried in the dark and lured small children to their dooms. There it was again!

In an instant, Emma's feet hit the floor and she dashed to the door. Fumbling with the handle in the dark, she managed to get the door open. Aunt Joanna had moved downstairs to Uncle Giles's room after the wedding, but with little feet pounding on the carpet and down the stairs, Emma made it to her door in no time. She did not bother to knock, throwing Joanna's door open.

Joanna came awake at the commotion at her door. "What is it?" she called softly.

"Aunt Joanna," came a sobbing whisper. "I heard banshees down on the beach."

"Come here, darling," Joanna called. She reached over and turned up the wick which she had trimmed on her lamp before going to bed. The lamp put out a faint glow and revealed Emma, white-faced, standing in the doorway in a nightgown and bare feet. Joanna sat up and patted the bed next to her. With a bound, Emma was beside her.

"Now, Emma, tell me what you heard," said

Joanna gently, pulling the covers up around them both. The house had taken on a chill in the middle of the night with the fires long-since banked. "You know there are no such things as banshees, don't you, darling? It's a tale made up to frighten children and keep them in their beds after dark."

"But I heard two screams down on the beach, I really did," Emma stated with absolute conviction. She was not going to allow herself to be lumped in with silly, frightened children, and she knew what she had heard.

"Shall we go up to your room and listen, sweetheart? Perhaps it was just the gulls fighting over some bit of food." Joanna pulled the covers back and stepped from the bed. Actually, she was fairly certain that gulls did not forage at night, but then she hadn't made much of a study of the creatures' nocturnal habits. She quickly wrapped her dressing gown about her and stepped into her slippers. "Come on, sweetheart, I don't want you to catch cold with no slippers on." Joanna put her arm around the little shoulders and shepherded the child from the room. She must have had a bad dream, and if Joanna could show her there was nothing to be frightened of, she would likely go right back to sleep.

Once in Emma's room, Joanna found the child's dressing gown and slippers and helped her put them on. Then they went to stand in front of the window. Joanna opened it a bit so any sounds would be more easily heard. She wanted Emma to hear the silence of the night, broken only by the dull sound of the sea.

"Let's be very quiet, Emma," said Joanna in a whisper. "We mustn't wake up Tom." She had glanced at the open door that connected the children's rooms, but had decided against shutting it. She knew from experience it had a dreadful squeak.

For a moment all was silence. The night was pitch dark, all the better to see a million stars winking bright.

"There, Emma," said Joanna, pointing. "Do you see the Pleiades, that small group nearly over-head? That means it's just after midnight. They are called the Seven Sisters, although you can only see six of them. That's because one is so little she must go to bed when it gets dark, like all good little girls."

Emma giggled and buried her face in the soft cotton of Joanna's dressing gown. "Let's go back to bed, shall we? Everything is quiet and there is nothing to be frightened of, darling." Joanna turned to lead Emma gently back to her bed.

Suddenly a shriek rent the dark. Clutching Emma to her, Joanna turned back to the window and peered out in confusion, but could see noth-ing in the blackness. She could feel Emma trem-bling beneath her grasp.

"You see, Aunt Joanna, I did hear a scream," Emma could not resist saying. "It does sound like a banshee, doesn't it?"

"No, precious, it sounds like someone is hurt or frightened. You get in bed and I'll go outside and check, all right? Then I'll come back and tell you what it was, as soon as I've solved the mystery."

"Can't I go with you?" came the anxious little voice.

"Heavens, no, child. The beach is no place for you to be at this hour of the night. I'll come back in a few minutes, I promise." Joanna lifted the girl into the bed, aware that she would not get in of

277

her own accord. She was troubled by the scream. Queen's Hall was too remote to attract any local traffic. Perhaps one of the servants had gone out in the night, but if that were so, she had found something that terrified her, from the sound of that scream.

Joanna dropped a quick kiss on Emma's brow, then hurried back to her own room where she donned shoes and threw a cape over her dressing gown.

She made her way as quickly as she could down the hallway and to the kitchen, where she took an outdoor lamp from the sideboard and lit it from the embers of the fire that still smoldered in the large kitchen hearth. She let herself out the kitchen door and stood staring into the dark.

"Emma!" a fierce little voice whispered in the dark of the girl's bedroom. "Emma!" it insisted.

"I'm here, Tom. Is that you?" came another voice from the direction of the bed.

"Tom," answered the voice from the door.

"Come here, Tom!" called Emma, glad of an ally. "Look out the window with me and see if you can see Aunt Joanna." Emma crept again from her bed and ushered her brother over to the window which Joanna, in her haste, had left cracked open.

"Auntie outside?" asked Tom.

"Yes. Did you hear those screams? Aunt Joanna went to see who was screaming."

As they watched they saw Joanna's form, lit by the lantern she carried, cross the bluff and disappear down the path to the beach. Still they stood in the window, each child remembering what fate could do to those they loved.

* * *

All was quiet. Joanna walked down the path that would take her to the beach, stopping once when she thought she heard a scrabbling sound near her. But when she searched with the lamp in the tall grass around her she could see nothing. She reached the foot of the path, well below the house. Ahead of her stretched the white of the beach, barely glimmering in the faint light of the distant stars. The sea was black. The earth could have ended right there, for all she could see. Lifting the lamp high, she peered left and right down the beach. There was nothing.

Then she heard a noise and looked up. A figure was trudging toward her, carrying a heavy burden from the looks of it. As he came closer, her eyes found his in the white blur of his face. Hawton! They held for a second, eyes locked. Then she looked at what he carried. It was a girl, a child it seemed, bleeding from a great gash on her forehead. He continued toward her, breathing heavily with his burden. He smiled, then bent over to put the child down, and Joanna relaxed, starting forward to see if she could help. A split second later a shriek tore from her throat as his powerful arms wrapped about her. A large hand clapped itself over her mouth. She struggled, but to no avail. As the hand was lifted, a cloth was pulled across her mouth. Within seconds, something dark and woolen had been thrown over her head and she could feel herself being bound tightly. Her legs were left free, but she was pushed to the ground where she lay stunned, barely able to breathe through the heavy cloth that covered her face.

Emma and Tom turned stricken eyes on each other as they heard the high, bitten-off cry. It had to be Aunt Joanna, coming as it did from a place close to where they had seen her descend to the beach.

"Get shoes on and a coat!" hissed Emma. Tom nodded and ran for his room. In seconds he was back, his little feet stuffed into sturdy boots, his coat on but not buttoned. Emma, too, had donned her boots and had put her small cloak about her.

"Let's go out the kitchen door, Tom. Don't make any noise and stay with me. We won't take a light, so it'll be dark. Are you all right?"

"Help Auntie. Let's go!" whispered Tom urgently. He grabbed Emma's hand and they ran for the door.

Once outside, Emma pulled him close and held his hand as they ran for the path that led away from the house. Crouching low, making hardly a sound, the children crept down through the long grass to the beach. They could see nothing in the dark. When they got to the bottom, Emma put out her hand and halted Tom, listening. When she was sure she could hear nothing, she motioned him forward again.

They had not gone far when Emma stumbled over something large in the dark, emitting a slight cry as she fell. A low moan came from the object, and both children started up in horror, scrambling away. The object was all blackness, just a large bulk, but Emma could see legs at one end and as her eyes peered in the darkness, she could see shoes. Shoes she recognized.

"Aunt Joanna!" Emma said in not much more than a whisper. Scrambling to the figure, Emma shook what she hoped was Aunt Joanna's shoulder. Tom was right behind her, bending over with fear in his eyes.

"I'm here, Aunt Joanna! It's Emma!" the child said.

The body moved as if agitated and made grunting noises. Emma could see white bands around the dark figure. Feeling carefully, she could tell that there were ropes binding her beloved aunt.

"You're all tied up, Aunt Joanna," Emma whispered as she tugged ineffectively at the bonds. "I can't get any of the knots loose. We'll have to go for help." With that, the figure stopped its struggling, as if its point had been made. Emma stood, about to grab Tom's hand, when hands seized them both from behind.

"I've got you now, you little brats!" hissed a voice close in the child's ear. "Be quiet or I'll kill you and your idiot brother. Your former governess too."

Emma twisted her head around as much as she could. She stared into ice cold eyes, mad eyes. Her Aunt Eleanor was going to kill them all. It was too much for her ten-year-old mind. With the barest of sighs, the child sank to the beach in a dead faint.

"What in hell's name are you doing, Eleanor?" a voice growled from the darkness.

"I found the girl and the half-wit down here next to the governess, Hawton. I heard her say they were going for help. You didn't expect me to just let them go, did you?"

"Oh, God, what are we going to do now? This is disastrous," Hawton snarled. He was furious. The runaway Irish girl had given him the fright of his life. She had cried out one last time as he came upon her. A crack on the head had silenced the girl, and now she, too, lay bound and unconscious down the beach. Eleanor had run the other girls back to his cottage, before they had a chance to realize that the pursuit of their friend was deadly serious. And just when he thought his obstacles were behind him, he had seen Joanna, her eyes wide with horror, staring first at him, then at the limp bundle he had carried in his arms.

Now he drew a length of cloth from his pocket, thankful that he had had the foresight to bring gags in case something went wrong, and wrapped it tightly around the unconscious Emma's mouth. Tom just stared at them both as Hawton gagged him too.

Plans this far awry had a way of twisting up badly. And while the children would have presented a problem in the long run, it was a problem Hawton was prepared to address at some later date. Not now, on the beach in the middle of the night, with a murder being committed in Dufton and Irish girls being held for prostitution in his cottage.

"Well, it's plain we cannot let them go now, Hawton," came Eleanor's furious voice in the dark. "You'll have to kill them."

Hawton froze at her words. He considered himself as brave as the next man but he'd never bargained for the slaughter of children. And even if he could steel himself to do it, how could he do it to make it look like an accident? Or at least something that had nothing to do with himself or Eleanor? It was too dangerous to leave bodies lying around. Blood could splatter in the most unpredictable way, and he didn't fancy getting caught because of an overlooked blood stain somewhere on his clothes. No, they would have to disappear entirely, but how was he to manage that?

With the clarity of a lightning bolt in the dark, the solution hit him. In a few hours, maybe less, an unmarked carriage would be at the door of his cottage, ready to set out without stopping for London. In it he would put the Irish girls, drugged and lethargic. Why not send Joanna and the children along? He could come up with some story, couldn't he, about how Joanna herself had kidnapped the children? After all, the only person in the world likely to put up much of a fuss was Sir Giles, and he, in all likelihood, was breathing his last about now.

There was only one serious hitch he could think of as his brain worked feverishly on salvaging this debacle. He would have to go to London with them. He was quite sure the minions sent by Lord Beeson to drive the carriage would take no responsibility for what would be an obvious kidnapping, however he explained the circumstances. Moreover, he had no wish to tell them of Sir Giles's murder—the fewer people who knew about it, the less likely they were to be caught or blackmailed. Lord Beeson would need soothing. He was a careful, fastidious man who planned his operations with precision, and who had impressed upon Hawton, in no uncertain terms, his intolerance for foul-ups.

"I have a better idea, Eleanor," Hawton said finally, after making sure Joanna was securely tied. "We cannot kill them here. It is too risky, and the last thing we want is more risk. Instead, I will take them to London, along with the shipment of Irish girls. I'll present them to Lord Beeson, explaining that the foul-up was caused by one of the girls not being drugged properly. He should pay us more, as well. We can accuse Joanna of kidnapping the children."

In the darkness, Hawton could barely make out the gleam of Eleanor's teeth as she smiled slowly, and he breathed a sigh of relief. Let Beeson and his whorehouse deal with them, he thought to himself. It was, after all, not his fault that one of the Irish girls had been awake enough to scream the length of the county.

"I like it, Hawton," came Eleanor's voice, purring with obvious satisfaction. "I like what they'll do to our ex-governess. Just what the little tart really deserves, isn't it? And since Giles is dead, no one will be very concerned, will they?"

"Precisely, my dear," said Hawton, his relief short-lived as the twists and turns of the problem began to reassert themselves in his consciousness. "I don't know how we'll all fit into one carriage, now that I have to go, too. Let's get them back to my cottage," he said, irritation in his voice. "You carry the girl and march the boy alongside. I'll bring the governess. And for God's sake, let's try not to make any more noise. We might as well have hired bagpipes to accompany us this evening!" He shouldered his burden and strode off into the dark, leaving Eleanor to struggle along behind.

He cut along the small path that led slightly up and away from the beach, toward his cottage, breathing more easily now that he knew he could not be seen from the house. He could hear Eleanor grunting under her burden behind him. He could have left her to stand guard and come back and fetched the children himself, but enough things had gone wrong tonight that he would brook no further delays.

He opened the door to the cottage quietly,

schooling his face into an expression of bland composure. Good. The Irish girls were lying on the floor, wrapped in their threadbare capes near the fire he had left burning low. They appeared to be sleeping soundly; not one so much as flickered an eyelid. He carried the lump that was Joanna into the small room to the rear and dropped her onto his bed. Even in his angry state, he felt a stirring as he noted her trim ankles peeping beneath the blanket she was wrapped in. It was too bad Eleanor was in the next room. He had no doubt that in the cramped coach over the next few days he would have no opportunity to avail himself of Joanna's delights, and when they arrived in London she would belong to someone else before he got a chance at her.

He left her on the bed without a word, ignoring the grunts and the twisting beneath the rough blanket, and walked back into the main room. Eleanor had entered and had sat Emma in a chair. Tom sat by the hearth where he had fallen. The boy stared at Emma's white face as if the sight of her were his last touch with life itself. Emma was stirring, her eyes rolling in her head.

"I am going back for the girl who ran from us, Eleanor," Hawton said in clipped tones. Only his fingering of the heavy purse in his pocket was keeping him steady. "She's lying a ways down the beach. Keep Emma as quiet as you can. The coach could arrive at any time, and I want everything ready."

When he returned a few minutes later bearing the unconscious girl, Eleanor had thought of a troublesome consequence to Hawton's plan. "But what will happen to the guardianship if there are no children, Hawton?" she wailed. "With Giles dead and the children as well, what happens to me?"

"Think, Eleanor!" he snarled, grabbing her shoulders and giving her a shake. "Giles has no close blood heirs with the children gone. Remember what I told you about his will? If everyone else is dead, you are the final heir, you get it all! It's something we would have managed eventually. We're just taking care of it all at once, that's all!" He softened his grip to a caress as he watched comprehension dawning in her frightened eyes. She would be the heiress, he reminded himself. And as of this minute he resolved that he would, indeed, marry her. His hands slipped away from her shoulders, trailing gently down her sides. He pulled her closely to him and nuzzled her hair. It smelled of goose grease.

"I need you to be strong now, my beautiful one," he whispered, his voice all tenderness. "I will be gone at least a week. There will be extra profit in this for us all, but there is extra risk as well, and Lord Beeson will need soothing. But he will also need to improve the delivery of these girls. It was an unforgivable slip-up to have the one child awake and screaming. That is no doubt the direct cause of all of these added complications." He gently disengaged himself from Eleanor's tight embrace. It would not be so awful, being married to Lady Eleanor. She would bring him money and social standing. And if he allowed her her dalliances, she would have to allow him his. And if she did not, he would find a way, anyway.

"It will be a difficult week for me, darling," she sniffed. "I hope I'll be hearing that your man in Dufton has succeeded, and I'll be dealing with the flight of the governess and the children. How do I explain that she and the children are nowhere to be found?"

"I have thought that through, Eleanor. The easiest way to keep a story straight is to say very little in the first place. I will leave a note to say that, unable to sleep, I heard the noise of a carriage in the night. I checked the house and found that Sir Giles's office had been rifled and it appeared there was money missing. When I went to awaken Lady Chapman to report the theft, I found her gone and the children, too. My note will say that I suspect they have gone north to Carlisle and that I am in hot pursuit. You need know nothing about any of this, except, when confronted with the idea that Joanna has kidnapped the children you must say that you overheard Giles and Joanna having a dreadful fight before he left. You heard him say he had discovered she was really just a tart before she came here. He yelled at her that he would not tolerate another slut for a wife and he would have the marriage annulled. It will appear that she seized the opportunity presented by Sir Giles's absence to kidnap the children and take the money and disappear. I'll try to post a ransom note from one of our stops on the road. Anyway, with Sir Giles dead, the authorities will not be pressured to exert themselves in the matter."

Eleanor was thoughtful for a moment. He could see that she was working it through in her head. Just as well. If there was a flaw in this thin story, he wanted to catch it now, before it caught them.

"I guess so," she said slowly. "No one needs to have heard the quarrel except me. And the fact that the servants knew nothing of this quarrel will make even more sense when it is found that she has fled. She would never have wanted anyone to be suspicious of her plans." She paused again, her brow furrowed.

"Sit down, Eleanor, and I'll make some tea," he finally said, willing his voice to sound calm. "You are right that we should talk all of this through, since our plans have been turned upside down. But you must be quiet and let me puzzle it out. Everything will be all right if we don't get too upset to think."

He had set up the tea things, swinging the kettle off the hob. He worked in silence, his mind running in furious, frantic circles. It was all well and good to tell her to be calm, but he needed badly to calm himself. There were too many variables now, too many things that had gone wrong.

"But, Giles, they all love her," Eleanor said, breaking the silence. "No one will ever think ill of her. She has bewitched everyone."

"They love her now. But they'll be quick enough to believe ill of her when Sir Giles is found dead under mysterious circumstances and she has fled in the night with the children. It almost makes me sorry I set up Sir Giles's murder to cast the blame on someone else, but there will be those who link Joanna to his death, regardless."

Hawton ran his hands through his hair. He was sweating in spite of the chill in the air. He blew on his hot tea while Eleanor did the same, her eyes never leaving his face. He took a few sips of tea.

"See," he went on. "Emma has her cloak over her nightdress and Tom has his coat on. They are both wearing their regular shoes, not night slippers. And Joanna is wearing the same. You must get into their rooms tonight and remove an outfit for Tom and a dress each for Joanna and Emma. Hide them in your room until you can smuggle them away from the house. It will look as though she planned to take them away and hold them for ransom or some kind of settlement with Sir Giles. You must also leave my note in the hallway and make a bit of a mess in Sir Giles's office. No one but me knows how much money is supposed to be in there, me and Sir Giles, and at least he won't be around to argue the point. Do you think you can do this? Everyone will still be asleep when we finish here, so you'll have time."

Eleanor was quiet for a moment, sipping her tea. "I'm sure I could manage that. It would only take a few moments," she finally answered. "But what happens afterwards?"

"When I return in a week's time, I will have a sad tale to tell of having traced them as far as Carlisle and then scouring the country for the week." He sat back, rather pleased with himself.

"But Hawton, what if the authorities try to trace them?"

"Then they won't find anything, will they? Joanna will have vanished. Abroad in the night as she is, she will be assumed to have fallen afoul of some highway villains, and the children as well. Who can prove otherwise, my dear? It will be highly regrettable. We will have been badly misled as to her character. You will be prostrate for at least a week. There will be evidence from only you and me, and everything we say will fit into this scenario." He finished with a flourish. He would almost be enjoying himself if the stakes weren't so high. He wished he could feel secure that Eleanor could get this right. If she forgot any part of it in her brandy-befogged state . . .

"Eleanor, you must promise me—talk to no one if you have been drinking. The brandy will make it harder for you to keep the story in your head. Stay to your room and plead hysteria. Can you do this?" Now he was rattling himself, cursing his luck that his partner in crime was a lush.

"Of course I can do it, Hawton," she retorted, a touch of the old hauteur back in her voice. "I am perfectly capable of sticking to a simple story about a quarrel. And what little I drink has no effect on my ability to remember things."

He let it pass while he got out his writing things and bent over in the dim light to craft his note. Her part was simple. If worse came to worst, he would try to blame her for everything and set himself up as the innocent dupe. But, God, let her get it right!

They both started as they heard a sound outside the door. Hawton leaped to his feet and pulled back the curtain a crack, peering out. For a moment he could make out nothing in the dark, then he heard the unmistakable sound of a horse stamping its hooves.

"It's the carriage!" he stated, the tension back in his voice. "I did not expect them quite so soon." He raced to the door and opened it to admit two burly, dark shapes. The men wore caps pulled down low and black cloaks. They had city faces, mean and white and pinched.

"Is the cargo ready?" asked one, not bothering with a greeting.

"Here they are." Hawton gestured to the girls on the floor. The men's eyes narrowed as they took in the whole scene.

"Whut'r these doin'?" asked the other. "Ye've two 'ere 'oo are gagged, and one's a boy at that. An idiot, by the looks of 'im." Anger was plain in the man's tone. He was not going to stand for complications.

"One of the Irish girls was not properly sedated.

She got out of the boat and screamed and ran down the beach. We managed to catch her, but not before she had awakened these two children and their governess from the house. We'll have to take them with us," Hawton finished defiantly. None of this was his fault, damn it! Nor would he tell them that Joanna was actually the wife of a knight.

"Oh, no, we won't," growled the first man, his tone surly. "There's nowt in our instructions about takin' extra passengers, unwillin' ones at that. It's dangerous enough, whut we're doin' without addin' kidnappin' to it." He set his legs and glared at Hawton, his expression angry and mulish.

"Well, naturally we did not expect you to run extra risk without extra pay, man. You'll be amply compensated when we arrive in London," Hawton said, trying to keep the desperation from his voice. If they refused to transport Joanna and the children, he would be forced to dispose of them himself, a thought he could not stomach.

"We'll be paid, now, and 'andsomely, too, sir, or we take the girls and leave ye to yer own mess." The two men now stood side by side, glaring at Hawton.

"One sovereign to split between the two of you," stated Hawton with as much arrogance as he could muster. He had no idea what these men were being paid to take these Irish girls, and at least they had been sold willingly by their parents.

A look passed between the two men. Hawton felt some relief that now they were haggling over price. That meant they would eventually agree to take the extra passengers, however dearly he must pay them to do it.

"We'll take ten sovereigns, gov, not tuppence

less. If not, we'll take the Irish girls like we was paid for, and be on our way."

"Ten sovereigns! That's outrageous! Why, that's nearly all we're being paid for this whole operation!" Hawton sputtered. It wasn't true, of course, but he was counting on Lord Beeson having kept the financial arrangements confidential.

The men shrugged and moved over to where the Irish girls lay huddled and sleeping soundly on the floor. Each man lifted one up, none too gently, and hefted her to his shoulders. Without another word they turned and left by the open door.

"Do something!" hissed Eleanor. "Unless you have a foolproof plan for getting rid of three extra bodies tonight!"

Hawton shot her a venomous look. "I am trying to preserve some of your profits, Eleanor. Give me some credit. We are not through negotiating. Hsst!" he gestured for her to be quiet as the men approached the door again.

"I'll give you six sovereigns, total. That's more than fair. You'll be running no more risk than you are already, and neither of you will be inconvenienced in the slightest." Hawton was speaking to their backs as each had crossed without so much as a look in his direction and picked up another girl.

"Ten it is, no less, guv'nor" said one matter-of-factly. "These girls is all bought and paid for. There'll be no hue and cry after the likes of them. But unless I miss my guess, this girl is gentry." He gestured in Emma's direction. "And we don't fancy riskin' the stretchin' of our necks for less'n ten sovereigns." Out they went again, each burdened with an Irish girl. Only the smallest one now remained, the one who had run away. She had not stirred, and Hawton hoped she would not regain consciousness until they were well away in the carriage.

Eleanor was glaring at him in the firelight. It was just as well she was holding her tongue or perhaps he'd decide to get rid of four corpses tonight.

"All right," he said, not bothering to mask the rage in his voice, when the men returned. "I'll give you the ten sovereigns, but don't think I won't mention to Lord Beeson how you've cheated us on this."

Without so much as a flicker of an eye to acknowledge victory, the larger of the two men stopped and held out his hand silently.

"I'll have to get the money in the next room," muttered Hawton angrily, unwilling to allow the men to see how heavy his purse was. He went into his bedroom while the other man hefted the last Irish girl and strode with her through the front door.

Once in the bedroom, Hawton cast a glance in Joanna's direction. She did not appear to have stirred, but he made sure her chest was still moving up and down. He fumbled in the purse and pulled out ten sovereigns, trying to soothe himself with the knowledge that he would have paid more if he'd had to and that he was likely to be paid further for Joanna and Emma. Emma, in fact, would be a plum. A gentried, innocent schoolgirl was likely to fetch a pretty penny. And Joanna, for all that she was no longer a virgin, was sweet and succulent, with an innocent air about her. Surely Lord Beeson could find a brothel that would be glad of her charms. Mollified by that thought and by the weight of the purse he shoved deep into his pocket, he passed back into the main room. The men stood by the door mutely. He noted they had made no move to lift Emma or Tom. Eleanor said nothing, her face white and strained in the dim firelight.

Hawton counted out ten sovereigns into the open palm of the larger man. Pocketing the lot and nodding to the other, the man moved over to Emma while his confederate walked over to Tom. Emma lay limp in the man's arms, her eyes wide with terror. Tom struggled and grunted, and did not quiet down until his captor slapped him hard in the face. Then both men left with their burdens.

"I must go now, my dear. There's the note for you to leave," said Hawton smoothly. He needed to get away with no fussing from Eleanor. He also did not want her to remember that he was holding the purse. While he wasn't sure there was much point in cheating her, he knew he would need some money while on the journey and once they arrived in London. And he felt he was entitled to withhold a few sovereigns from her share because it was he who'd be taking all the risk from this point on.

"When will I hear from you, Hawton? I tell you, it will be maddening to know nothing while you are gone." Eleanor's eyes looked confused and uncertain, and Hawton hoped fervently she wasn't going to go to pieces on him now.

"We will drive nearly straight through, Eleanor," Hawton said, crossing to her and taking her in his arms, anxious to calm her. "We cannot risk stopping for the night anywhere, and Lord Beeson has mapped out which inns can provide us with food and fresh horses with a minimum of questions asked. Nevertheless, it will be a very long ride. More than two days, at least. The drivers have an address for the delivery of the girls, and I shall find out there how to get in touch with Lord Beeson."

"He lives in Hanover Square, number 34, as I recall," she said thoughtfully. "But he won't be pleased to see you. You'd better think of how best to approach him without him feeling that you are putting him to any risk. I imagine he is considered a good customer of the house you are taking the girls to. Perhaps you could arrange to meet him there as if he were merely looking for entertainment. More than that I cannot suggest."

"That's enough," Hawton said, dropping a kiss on her forehead. Bless her at least for coming up with an address. He would not have relished inquiring after Lord Beeson in the House of Lords. "I'll get word to you as soon as I can, but I will likely turn around and come back the very instant I resolve everything. I'll be most anxious to aid you with matters here. Remember what you are supposed to do tonight, and to stay prostrate and hysterical while I'm gone. I hope to see you in a week."

Putting Eleanor aside, he strode into the bedroom and lifted Joanna's form from the bed. She was nearly limp in his arms but she had been breathing a moment ago so he was sure she had not smothered. It was likely she had fainted from the stress and lack of air. Just as well. He walked back through the main room carrying her in his arms.

"I'll put her in the carriage and come back and lock up here, Eleanor," he said, striding out.

Outside, he noted with approval that the coach bore no lanterns. Even the four horses were black as night. The coach itself was unmarked and plain, not the sort of vehicle to attract attention. It was built to hold six in relative comfort. Well, for the next few nights and days it would seem like a prison with the nine of them crammed in. If he kept the boy and one of the girls on the floor for the whole trip, they would have some minimum degree of comfort.

"I'll be just another five minutes," he said in hushed tones to the man who stood guard by the open coach door. "Do you have the medicine the girls are supposed to take to keep them from getting sick from the rocking of the coach?" A look passed between them. Hawton knew the man had a good-sized bottle of laudanum packed away, enough to keep all the girls sedated throughout most of the trip. Although their stops would be brief, it would not do to risk any repeat of tonight's outburst.

The man gave a short nod and stepped to the rear of the coach where he fumbled among the baggage tied there. He returned seconds later and handed Hawton a dark brown bottle which appeared to be full.

"One sip fer each o'them every few hours, no more. I was told too much would disagree with their stomachs, if you take my meaning, sir."

"Indeed I do, sir. I'll be very careful." As Hawton shut the carriage door he caught a glint from within. It was the boy's eyes, murderous with impotent rage. Dismissing Tom instantly from his mind, he turned and strode back into his cabin.

Eleanor had not moved since he had left. "Be a dear and put away the teacups, Eleanor," he said with as much nonchalance as he could muster, striding back into his bedroom. He threw a few things into a bag—it would not do to take too much, since according to their story, he would not have expected to be gone long. Still, if all went well, no one would see him return, and they needn't know he had taken anything at all with him. Nevertheless, he'd be gone at least a week, most of it in cramped quarters and he was fastidious enough to require a few changes of clothing.

"Well, that's it then," he said coming back into the main room, trying to sound more confident than he was feeling. "I'm sure I don't need to remind you to be as quiet as you can possibly be when you return to the house. It's still a good number of hours until the servants awaken, so I do not think you'll run into anyone. If you do, just make it seem that you've heard a noise or come down for a drink or a book or something. Are you all right?"

He waited while she gave him a slow nod. She seemed uncertain, an unusual trait for her, and he wished he could put aside the nagging fear that she would foul everything up with ill-thought-out remarks and reactions. He noted with some surprise that the tea things had been washed up and put away. He had half expected her to refuse to perform such a menial task, and his lips curved in his first grin for many hours. It boded well for the future of their marriage if she would fetch and carry for him without argument. Indeed, if he could just get them through the next week without getting them all hanged, he could look forward to a far more comfortable future than he had ever dared contemplate before.

"Come here and give me a kiss, my girl," he said, smiling broadly at her and opening his arms. She smiled back, still looking like a frightened doe, and came to him. He wrapped her in his arms and gave her a hard, swift embrace, then set her away from him.

"Off you go, my dear. I'll take care of everything. Don't worry at all. Go back up to Queen's Hall, leave the note, rifle the office, get the clothing, go to bed, and I think you'll hear the tragic news about your stepbrother sometime tomorrow." He watched as her eyes lit up, then he turned her around and pushed her toward the door with a pat on the rear end. Amazing how far he had come with her over the last few days. He rarely saw the haughty Lady Eleanor anymore. Yes indeed, things could be looking up. Once they were both outside, he shut and locked the door behind him and stepped into the waiting dark.

Chapter Sixteen

Joanna's head ached with a dull thud but she was barely aware of the physical pain. Giles dead. She had heard those words as Eleanor had spoken them on the beach, and they had been driven like lead shot into her heart.

There was so little air inside the blanket, and the gag further hampered her ability to breathe. As she had digested the muffled words of Lady Eleanor and Hawton, she had almost wished she would just suffocate—slip away to Papa—and Giles. But the children were prisoners as well, held by these vicious people, and Joanna knew that as long as she could force some small breath of stale air into her starved lungs, she would fight to stay alive for their sake.

She felt the bouncing along of the carriage. She had been shoved over to the side and lay as she had fallen. Her arm was twisted up unnaturally behind her, and she could feel nothing in that hand. She had lain as quietly as she could, hoping to hear more of the plans. While lying in Hawton's bed, she had heard nothing but a low, indistinguishable murmur from the next room, and there had been only silence since she had been thrown into the coach. All she knew was what she had heard on the beach—that Giles was dead, or soon to be, and she was to be accused of kidnapping the children.

Would they believe her capable of such madness? Of course they would, with Giles not there to defend her. She was a stranger here, and there was no one to attest to her good character. It would be an easy solution for the authorities to accept the evidence of Lady Eleanor and the steward that the ex-governess had run off with the children.

But where were they being taken? She could not bring herself to believe that Hawton meant to kill her and the children. He had had ample opportunity to do so on the beach. Of course, that would have meant disposing of their bodies locally, so perhaps he did mean to take them away somewhere and murder them in some godforsaken spot. But then, who was the child he had carried bleeding in his arms on the beach? And who were these men she knew only by their muffled voices who had pulled up a carriage in the middle of the night to Hawton's door, surely by prearrangement?

"I'll take the blanket off now, Joanna, but if you struggle, it will go right back on, do you understand?" a low voice hissed in her ear.

She nodded, uncertain if he could see the gesture beneath the heavy wool. She felt hands fumbling at the ties that bound her, and it was some time before she felt the bindings loosen and the heavy wool being lifted away.

She fairly gasped as the cold, fresh air hit her face, and she took deep breaths through her nose. The gag still bit into her mouth and she hoped he would remove that also. The coach was nearly pitch-black, but as she looked around her she could just make out dark shapes. She tried to move the arm she could not feel, and was frightened to find that it would not respond at all. She flexed the other arm and was relieved that she could move it.

"Don't try anything or I'll bind your arms, Joanna," Hawton hissed again. She glared at him, able to speak only with her eyes.

"I could take the gag away. I would if I thought you'd be quiet. We're a million miles from anyone here, so it won't do you any good to scream. In fact, I rather expect one of those two gentlemen driving up front would silence you fast enough if they heard a scream. Will you be quiet?" he asked. He was too close, whispering near her ear. His tone made her skin crawl. She pulled back away from him but gave him a short nod.

He pushed himself even closer and reached around the back of her head, fumbling with the knot. As the gag dropped, he moved his face toward hers and she found herself staring into his dark, mean eyes, inches from her own.

"Don't touch me or I will scream, Mr. Hawton," she said in a cold, quiet voice, pulling away from him. "I'd rather be dead at the hands of those two up on the box than have you touch me." She watched as his eyes narrowed. She thought he would come at her anyway, but with a foul oath he pulled away and sat back against the seat.

"Where are the children?" she asked, pressing the advantage for the moment. Perhaps he really didn't want her to raise a fuss. Perhaps he was none too keen on dealing with those men either.

"At your feet, my dear, safe and sound. See for yourself."

Joanna sat forward quickly and peered into the darkness at her feet. She could just make out the light color of Emma's hair. She reached down with her good arm and placed her hand gently on the child's head. Tears sprang to her eyes as the child looked up at her. She could see little but the shine of Emma's frightened eyes, but it appeared the girl had a gag across her face.

"Take that gag off the child at once!" Joanna spat at Hawton, her rage outstripping her fear.

"I'm not sure I want to do that just yet, Joanna. Just be patient. I don't want any more difficulty just now. I've had a troubled night."

"You've had a troubled night?" Joanna said, her tone incredulous. "You've kidnapped us all and probably done murder as well, and you dare to tell me that you've had a troubled night?" Too angry to care what he would do, she reached down and put her one good arm around the slight form of the child, hauling her up into her lap.

"Where is Tom?" she asked, trying to settle Emma comfortably. The child was shivering uncontrollably.

"I don't know, damn it. He's somewhere in this pile on the floor," Hawton spat back at her, his tone surly. He was feeling thwarted at the moment. He had badly wanted to kiss her, to reach into her neckline and squeeze her lovely little tits, and now she had one brat covering her lap and was threatening to scream the carriage apart. And he had had a rotten night, damn it, no matter how nasty she sounded about it. She should be down on her knees thanking him for saving their miserable lives so far, not challenging him as if she were the lady out for the evening air.

Joanna's dead arm was coming back to life. It was on fire, tingling and burning till she thought she would scream anyway. Well, at least it probably wouldn't turn black and fall off. Holding Emma to her, she leaned forward and looked about in the blackness of the carriage. She gasped as her eyes told her there were a number of bodies, at least three on the floor and, unless the darkness was playing tricks on her, three more on the seat across from her.

Her eyes finally found what she sought, the tousled, brown curls of Tom's head on the floor against the far door. She shifted Emma to the seat next to her and leaned forward. The nerves of her arm danced with fire as she forced it to work, but she ignored the pain and gently lifted the boy to her lap, wrapping her arms around him and kissing his cheek. He did not stir, and she knew a moment's terror as she felt his chest to be sure he was breathing. His eyes were closed and his breath was warm on her cheek. Incredible as it seemed, he was asleep. She carefully disengaged one arm and pulled Emma tight to her, holding her close.

The children safe for the moment, Joanna turned her attention to her captor. "Who are these others?" she demanded, taking courage from the warmth of the little bodies next to hers. "They look like children. And what has happened to the child who screamed on the beach?"

Hawton turned angry eyes on her. He was still

smarting from her rebuff and mentally berating himself for allowing her to get the upper hand. But now that he was safe for the moment and the progress of the plan was in other hands for the time being, he found his courage and his energy flagging badly. He had not had the spirit to force Joanna to kiss him, and keeping himself from trembling convulsively in front of her was taking all the strength he had left.

"Who they are is none of your business," he snarled in the dark.

"The children and I have been bound, gagged, thrown into this coach, and kidnapped by you, Mr. Hawton. That makes it my business."

He said nothing, staring at the blackness in front of him. Joanna drew a deep breath. Fear clawed at her heart, but she must ask about Giles, however much she dreaded Hawton's response.

"What have you done to Sir Giles, Mr. Hawton?" she made herself say, forcing her voice to be steady. She held her breath, hoping that he would answer and fearing that he would, as he turned his face slowly toward her. Even in the dark, she could see the malicious smile that curved his lips.

"Sir Giles will not be able to help you, Joanna," he said smoothly, his courage growing with his words. "I regret to inform you that Sir Giles met with an accident this evening in Dufton. I believe he fell against a knife."

Joanna drew in her breath sharply and sat back against the seat, clutching the children to her. Madly her mind scrambled away from what he had said. It could not be true! It could not! What would there be left for her if Giles were gone?

What kind of fate would snatch him away from her now, when she had just dared to dream of love again? She could feel the children's strong little hearts beating against her hands. Their hearts beating. They were alive. She could save them yet from whatever evil Hawton and Lady Eleanor had planned. She would get these babies to safety somehow, and then she would face the loneliness that would stretch on and on, forever. . . .

Giles cursed himself for the hundredth time as he finally stumbled into the stables at Queen's Hall, leading his badly lamed horse. It was late morning and he had walked most of the night after his sure-footed Red Devil had done the un-thinkable, stepping into a deep rut on the dark road and laming himself. Giles was enraged with himself for the accident. He had known it was too dark to ride at that punishing speed, but he would not allow his or Red Devil's common sense to set the pace. And now he had paid a price for his folly in the worst imaginable way, plodding along in the blackness at a snail's pace, his imagination racing with the horrors he could conjure out of the dark. If they planned to kill him, what could they have planned for his beloved Joanna?

At first he had held some hope that he could get a ride from someone traveling along the same road, but that hope had faded over time. He had seen only one conveyance, a dark coach-and-four, just after Red Devil had gone down, and that had been headed in the wrong direction. At least Red Devil was quiet now. He was sure the leg was not broken, but there was no doubt the horse was in pain.

"Jims!" he shouted into the stables. Odd, he

thought, that there was no one about. Albeit he was not expected to return at this time, the stables were usually bustling with activity from dawn till dark.

His heart clenched in his chest as he threw Red Devil's reins over a post and ran for the house. Someone should have been in the stables—Jims came into the house only to eat and it was not yet dinner time. Were his worst fears coming true?

He burst through the rear door and ran through the back hall to the kitchen where he could be sure to find someone. He stopped open-mouthed at the door as he viewed virtually the entire staff seated or standing, some openly crying into their pocket handkerchiefs. Swiftly searching the room, he knew Joanna was not among them.

"Where's Joanna?" he fairly shouted, his heart hammering in his chest. Oh, God, let him not be too late!

"How on earth did you know, Sir Giles?" asked Mrs. Davies gently, wiping her eyes. "Allow me to say on behalf of the entire staff that we are so dreadfully sorry. Had we known what sort she was, what she was planning, of course we would have stopped her. But we never dreamed—"

"What in the name of hell are you blathering about, madame?" he shouted, advancing into the room. "Jims," he said, turning abruptly to the head groom, "Where is Lady Chapman?"

"We do not know, Sir Giles," answered the man uncomfortably. "Mr. Hawton's note says she kidnapped the children and ran off in the night, but I dunno—"

"What?" Giles thundered. "That's absurd and you all know it! Where is Hawton and where is Lady Eleanor?" His face was murderous.

Only Jims dared to speak. "The note told us that Mr. Hawton has gone to try to fetch them back. He left early this morning, apparently, before dawn," he said. "I'm not sure where Lady Eleanor is," he finished, looking inquiringly at Mrs. Davies.

"I believe her ladyship is in her room, Sir Giles," answered Mrs. Davies, her voice quivering. "Her ladyship was prostrate with the news. She said she overheard the quarrel that you had with Lady Chapman before. . . . "

"What quarrel?" came Giles's voice, dangerously low.

"Er, the words you had with Lady Chapman before you left. About her being a . . . that is, apparently she was a . . ." The woman broke off, her face crimson.

"A what? Mrs. Davies," asked Giles, biting back his frustration. "It's important that you tell me what my step sister said."

"Lady Eleanor reported to us that you had discovered your wife was a tart, Sir Giles, before she came here, and that you planned to have the marriage annulled," Mrs. Davies stated in a rush.

There was a moment's silence, deadly in its intensity.

"There was no quarrel, Mrs. Davies. I want that understood by everyone here," said Giles, raising his voice to a near shout. "My wife is innocent of all such charges. Is that clear?"

They found themselves staring at an empty doorway as Sir Giles, not waiting for an answer, had turned abruptly on his heel and strode away. For a moment there was silence in the room, then they all began speaking at once, a hubbub of accusation and denial, each claiming to have been the only one to have steadfastly believed in the innocence of poor Lady Chapman.

Giles took the back stairs three at a time. He did not bother to knock at Eleanor's door, slamming it against the wall as he threw it open.

She was lying on her chaise longue in a dressing gown, a wet cloth thrown across her forehead.

"I thought I told you I did not wish to be disturbed," she screeched, sitting up and tearing the cloth from her eyes. She froze at the sight of him, her face draining of color. He stood in the doorway staring at her, deliberately saying nothing, drinking in her reaction to seeing him.

"You!" she whispered. "I thought. . . . " She broke off, her chest heaving.

"You thought what, Eleanor?" he asked, his voice deceptively mild. "You are surprised to see me?"

"Yes—I mean, no! I mean, you are supposed to be at some funeral in Dufton, aren't you?" She spoke raggedly, her hands working convulsively at the wet cloth in her lap.

"Whose funeral would that be, Eleanor? Mine, perhaps?" He smiled a slow, twisted smile, aware how his lip pulled into a grimace from the scar she had put across his face.

"I don't know what you are talking about, Giles!" she cried. "You come barging in here, making absurd remarks, when you can see how upset I am. Don't you know what has happened? Your precious little tart has stolen your money and kidnapped the children. What do you think of that?" she finished in a wail, burying her face in the cloth.

Giles came into the room and shut the door quietly behind him. He stared at her for a moment, willing himself not to walk forward, not to take her in his hands and shake her like a rag doll, not to wrap his hands around her throat and choke the life out of her. How could he have been so blind as to assume she would go quietly, that she would allow herself to be displaced, pushed out of her cozy nest?

"Where is Hawton?" he asked, forcing himself to be calm. He badly needed this information out of her.

"He's gone to try to fetch them back, Giles! Everyone is doing everything possible to see that the children come to no harm, that she is brought to justice for her evil, scheming—"

"Enough!" he roared, taking several long strides to bring himself directly over her. "Hawton tried to have me killed last night in Dufton, and you well know it, you slut! Now, where has he taken them? So help me God, woman, if either of you has harmed so much as a hair on one of their heads, I shall strangle you with my bare hands!"

"I know nothing, I tell you! Nothing!" she shrieked, trying to slip off of the seat, only to find his hands clapped around her arms like steel bands.

"I will let you hang, you know," he said, his voice deadly cold.

Eleanor stared into his furious eyes, gasping, silent, weighing her options. He knew too much already. Hawton had fouled up everything. After repeatedly berating her and nagging her about making sure she could handle her part, he had failed at the most important part of the plan. Not only was Giles alive, he knew Hawton had set up the attempt on his life. But Giles couldn't be certain of her part, could he? He thought perhaps she knew of it, true, but he had not quite accused her of the act. And threatening her with hanging! Since when did a peeress ever hang? He would never have the nerve to drag the family through the seamy criminal courts!

She took a deep breath and steadied herself. "Take your hands off me. I know nothing, I tell you," she said, her voice surprisingly calm.

He stared into her eyes, then slowly released her, letting her drop back onto the chaise longue. "You told the household preposterous lies about Joanna. There was no quarrel between myself and my wife, therefore you are lying. And you must have some reason to lie." His voice was deceptively soft. His body cast a hulking shadow over her from the light of the lamp that burned behind him. He stepped slightly to one side so that he could watch her face while she spoke.

Calmly, taking her time, Eleanor arranged the folds of her dressing gown, smoothing the material over her legs. She hoped she appeared relaxed while her mind chased in circles, creating stories, discarding them, creating another, anything to buy time, to get herself off the hook. She must deny any knowledge of the attempted murder, but perhaps if she implicated herself in a more minor way, he would believe her.

"I really know nothing of any plot to kill you, Giles," she began, watching his face carefully to see his reaction to her words. "I do not doubt your word," she continued hurriedly as she saw his eyes narrow at her denial, "but I would never have agreed to anything so stupid. I am guilty of envy, nothing more. I made the remarks about the quarrel to make sure the staff understood what we are dealing with here. After all, the woman has fled with the children. There must be some reason—"

She stopped as he took a menacing step toward her.

She allowed herself a plaintive look in his direction. "Don't you see? That woman has taken everything from me! You are besotted by the conniving little witch. For God's sake, for the governess to scheme to marry the master of the house is the oldest trick known to servants!"

"You disgust me, Eleanor," he spat out through clenched teeth. "You care for no one but yourself. You'd see the whole world go to hell if it meant more for you. Where has he taken them?"

"I—I know nothing about it. Only what I read in his note. Carlisle, wasn't it?" She plucked distractedly at her gown, unaware that her eyes rested covetously on the brandy decanter across the room.

"If you weren't so evil, you'd be pathetic, Eleanor. Go on, have yourself a swill," he said. "And so help me God, you'd better hope I find my wife and the children safe in Carlisle." With that he turned and strode from the room, slamming the door behind him.

Eleanor waited, listening to his footsteps retreating down the hall. When she could hear them no more, she rose and went to the decanter, pouring herself a liberal tot in the oversized snifter she kept on the tray. Her hands shook as she brought the snifter to her lips, downing the entire contents in one practiced gulp.

She poured herself another and went over to the door, locking it. She dropped heavily onto the chaise and sat staring at nothing. He would get to Carlisle tonight. He would spend the better part of tomorrow chasing a wild goose. Then he would be back, late tomorrow night at the earliest. And he might surmise that she had lied to him.

Well, she would be gone by the time he returned. She'd get herself to Philippa's where, at last report, a rather raucous gathering was scandalizing the provincials. She'd need to get word to Hawton as soon as possible, to head him off from returning here. And she would need to work out a plan to kill Giles. Something foolproof. Something that looked like an accident perhaps—none of this messy murder business with inquiries being made. Indeed, he would be distraught at his failure to find his little tart. Yes. Perhaps Sir Giles Chapman was soon to be a suicide. . . .

Carlisle. North of here, a few hours' hard run. He could make it before nightfall if he went like the wind. Again he damned himself for laming Red Devil, his best horse.

"How does he travel?" Giles asked Jims in the stables. "Did he take our coach or horses?"

"That's a mystery, sir," replied Jims. "There's no horse nor conveyance missing."

"Then he must have a confederate. The man seems to have quite a network of cutthroats at his beck and call."

Issuing orders in clipped tones, leaving his groom scurrying faster than he had in years, Giles returned to the kitchen, where he found Mrs. Davies, then left her scrambling to produce a substantial packet of food fit for a journey. Upstairs again, he read the note from Hawton, then, stuffing it in his pocket, threw some clothing into his travel bag. He was back in the stables within minutes, where Jims had two horses saddled and ready and was himself standing by with a small bag packed and a well-wrapped package from the kitchen. Without so much as a word to each other, they mounted and rode out into the early afternoon sun, heading north for Carlisle.

Joanna stared with unseeing eyes out of the window flap that she had dared to unhook when Hawton had drifted off to sleep. He had finally told her they were going to London, but would not say for what purpose. She had to force herself to care for the sake of the children. It barely seemed to matter now what he had planned for her.

The air coming in was fresh and cool and she breathed it in great gulps. Everyone was sleeping now except her. It was unnatural the way the girls slept and Joanna suspected they were drugged. Hawton had insisted that the girls each take a spoonful of some foul-smelling liquid, claiming it was medicine to keep them from getting sick inside the carriage, but Joanna had refused to allow him to give it to Emma or Tom and had taken none herself. She noted that Hawton did not avail himself of the "medicine" either.

They had stopped just before dawn, having pulled way off the road, behind a large stand of trees. All had been ordered out to relieve themselves, with the dire warning from one of the drivers that this would be the last stop for many hours. Back in the fetid carriage a few minutes later, they were given chunks of bread and cheese to eat, washed down with cold tea. Joanna's stomach was rebelling now, and she fought to keep the foul stuff down.

In the light of early afternoon she studied her fellow captives. She had ascertained that they were Irish from their muted speech, but so far none had been awake long enough to offer to converse with her. Indeed, she was not sure Hawton would allow her to talk directly to these girls, and she was under the impression from their docile demeanor and the lack of any sort of restraints that they were willing, if perhaps ignorant, passengers. The littlest one, the one who had run away on the beach, had been barely roused to take care of her needs and had fallen back into a deep sleep without eating anything. Joanna noticed that the deep cut on her forehead had been cleaned up, but she wondered whether the child's sleeping had more to do with the blow to the head than with Hawton's dosing.

She studied the passing scene, aware that Hawton would insist that the flap be closed when he awoke. It was no use—she recognized nothing. She had been so ill on the way up from London, and crammed into the middle of the seat by the other passengers, that she was unlikely to recognize any landmark. They had traveled through a small town a few minutes ago, and Joanna had briefly cherished a mad plan to scream for help. But she had seen no one, and the carriage was traveling too fast for her to think of hurling herself from it. Penniless and attired as she was in a cloak over a dressing gown, she rather feared she would be going from bad to worse, and she bit her lip in frustration.

Hawton had told her that she would be bound and gagged again whenever they stopped to change the horses. And there would be no stops other than brief convenience stops in wooded areas. If only she knew what to expect. If only she had some hope that Giles was on his way to rescue them. . . .

Chapter Seventeen

Giles sagged in the saddle as he saw Queen's Hall looming in the rainy dark. Beside him rode Jims, a silent, loyal, wet presence.

Between the two of them they had scoured Carlisle. No matter how high a bribe was offered, no sign was found of Joanna, the children, or Hawton.

Eleanor had lied to him. It was that simple. She must know more than she had told him. He had been fooled once again by her tears and protestations. God help her if she was home. God help him if she was not.

They finally reached the stables, the rains running in cold rivulets from their greatcloaks. Without a word he slid from the back of his horse and handed the reins to Jims who had just dismounted himself. They had not slept at all, and the old man's eyes were rimmed red with fatigue.

"Get one of the boys to take care of the horses, Jims. You need to get some sleep. I'll call you when I'm ready to ride again." He turned away into the dark toward the house, missing the look of pity on Jims's face as he watched his young master trudge dispiritedly through the mud of the yard.

Giles let himself in, noting with relief that the kitchen staff had retired for the night. He would need to rouse Mrs. Davies and get a report from her in case there was any news, but for now he would tackle Eleanor.

Removing his streaming greatcloak and dropping it on a chair, he made for the rear stairs. He paused in front of Eleanor's door but did not bother to knock. He had never in his life done violence to a woman, but was not at all sure he'd be able to say the same an hour from now. He opened the door and blinked in the darkness.

"Eleanor?" he growled, sensing that the room was unoccupied. With an oath he took a candle from the sconce across the hall and held it high in the room. Empty. The bed not slept in. Damn. Had the bitch flown?

Carrying the candle, he made his way to the servants' floor, pausing at the door he knew to be Mrs. Davies's. This time he did knock, softly so as not to awaken the entire staff. In less than a minute, Mrs. Davies opened the door, blinking the sleep from her eyes and knotting the dressing gown about her ample form.

"Sir Giles!" she began, confusion and distress plain in her face. "If I had known—"

"It's all right, Mrs. Davies, I'm sure we were not expected. Any news of Lady Chapman and the children?" The desperate longing in his voice made the woman want to weep.

"No, sir, I'm sorry. Come down to the kitchen with me and let me brew you some tea. You look cold and wet, sir." Indeed, the man looked like a bedraggled dog. Mrs. Davies had fallen asleep listening to the relentless rain, and it looked as if the poor man had not so much as bothered to pull the hood up over his head.

In silence they made their way down to the kitchen, Giles lighting the way with his candle.

"Where is Lady Eleanor?" he finally asked when he had seated himself at the great kitchen table. Mrs. Davies bustled about, pulling the kettle off the hob and pouring steaming cups of tea.

"She went off yesterday evening to one of her friends. She did not say where she was going or when she would return." Mrs. Davies was too tired and upset to mask the contempt in her voice. There was no doubt how she felt about Lady Eleanor's pastimes.

"Has anything turned up that would give us any further information, Mrs. Davies?" he asked. Again the edge of desperation in his voice made her want to sit down and cry.

"We had the grounds searched as you asked, sir. Charles and Will checked around the outside as you suggested, them being familiar with horses and all. It seems there was a carriage at Hawton's door sometime recently. There were wheel marks there, which is unusual, given how far it is from the main road. There was nothing odd about the cottage itself. I searched it thoroughly myself and found nothing of interest. A cautious man, that Mr. Hawton. I confess myself completely taken in by him."

"As were we all, Mrs. Davies. No point in fretting

about that now. Any idea which way the carriage went?"

"Well, as to that, yes, sir. With all the rain we've had recently we traced the wheel ruts out to the main road and then could make out that the carriage turned down the road toward Penrith and Dufton. It seemed from the depth of the ruts to be a large, rather heavy thing, according to Charles and Will. It's a wonder you didn't pass them that night yourself, you walking Red Devil home on the same road."

"Damnation!" he roared, causing her to slosh her tea down the front of her gown. "I did pass the bloody thing! How can I have been such an imbecile? I passed a dark carriage soon after Red Devil was lamed. I paid it no mind because it was nondescript, no markings, nothing about it to attract interest. It was drawn by four horses, two men on the box. Oh, God, what a fool I have been! And how much time have I lost?" He stood abruptly. "Would you be so kind as to pack me a few changes of clean clothing, Mrs. Davies, and a bit of food as well? I plan to leave within the hour. I'll not take Jims with me—the man is exhausted—but I'll take Will, so we can trade off sleeping and only stop to change horses. I'll speak to him now, and then I intend to search my stepsister's room. I've been fool enough to overlook clues in front of my very nose and I hope I won't be so stupid again."

"But, Sir Giles, you're exhausted as well," the woman remonstrated. "When was the last time you slept, sir?"

"I don't really remember," he said wearily, passing his hand through his damp hair. "But I cannot take the time to sleep now. God knows where the

villain has taken them. I must go. It won't be the
first time I've snatched sleep in a moving carriage."

He turned and left the room, his back disappearing into the dark of the hall. And now the
good woman did sit down and weep. . . .

It was three hours before he climbed wearily
into the carriage, allowing Will, at Jims's insistence, to take the first turn driving. Giles was furious with himself for falling asleep in Eleanor's
desk chair. He'd been skimming her vapid corre-
spondence—the insipidity of the woman's existence would drive him mad. There had been only
one bit of interest tucked in among the innuendo
and drivel, and he pondered it as the dark carriage
made its way along the road to Penrith. It was a
letter from a Lord Beeson in London—a rather
large, mean-looking man, as he recalled—an enigmatic sort of letter which contained no sexual
allusion, no nasty bits of gossip, and no reference
to gambling debts. Indeed, the letter had been
short to the point of rudeness, reminding Eleanor
to hold her tongue and exercise the utmost caution, and wishing her good luck in their "mutual
endeavor for a successful arrival in London." But
one part caught Giles's attention, reading simply:
"I have the utmost faith in your man, Eleanor. He
seems to be steady and have good judgment."

It had to be a reference to Hawton. For the life
of him, Giles could think of no one of Eleanor's
male friends of whom it could fairly be said he
was steady or had good judgment.

London. It might as well be the moon. It would
take him days to reach London, even traveling
without stopping for sleep. The horses would have

to be changed, and he knew enough about the quality of posting-house horses to know that the best speed they could expect to make would be with his own team, before they were forced to change. And by his calculation, Hawton now had a full 48-hour start on him.

He settled against the squabs, cursing the ruts in the road which he knew would slow them down, and blessing the same ruts which would even further slow a larger, heavier carriage such as the one Joanna must be in. He could feel his eyes closing, but he knew that sleep would not bring him a merciful oblivion. He was trapped inside a nightmare and he was not sure he would ever awaken again. . . .

Joanna could hear angry, muffled voices outside. Something had gone wrong with the carriage—she knew that much when it had given a drunken lurch a half hour ago and come to rest on the side of the road. Hawton had refused to enlighten her, but she rather supposed they had broken the rim of a wheel, or an axle, something difficult to fix.

The door to the carriage was pulled open and Hawton climbed in, his face taut with anger. "We'll bide here awhile," he said to her. "Help me wake the girls. We might as well eat while we wait."

Joanna held her questions, figuring she would be able to see well enough what was wrong when she got out of the carriage. Gently she shook the girls, who took an inordinately long time to rouse themselves. It was close to dawn now and they had been traveling nearly straight through since night before last. Joanna had yet to see any of the girls any more than semiconscious enough to tend to their most basic needs. Emma and Tom had slept until late morning and had each taken long naps in the afternoon. When they were awake they were silent with fear, holding Joanna's hands as if her grip alone kept them alive. Hawton had removed their gags after more threats from Joanna, but had managed to impress upon the children the fear that if they so much as whispered, the consequences would be unspeakably dire.

One by one, in the daze that Joanna was now convinced was induced by some sort of opiate such as laudanum, the Irish girls stumbled from the carriage into the deep, muddy ruts. Hawton led them away from the road over the hedgerows and left them to their sleepy business. Joanna followed with Emma and Tom, taking her time as she surveyed the carriage.

As she had thought, one of the carriage wheels was broken clean through, its spokes gaping drunkenly, the iron rim bent beyond use. The two drivers, with whom Joanna had shared not so much as a word, had unhitched one of the four horses. It appeared that one of the men was set to ride bareback, no doubt to fetch help. With a flame of hope leaping within her, Joanna shepherded the children over the hedgerows. Perhaps there would be some possibility of help now— someone might pass along the road and she could call for help, or she could appeal to whomever came to make the repairs. There had to be some way to break free. If not, she was surer and surer that evil awaited them. . . .

Giles did not know whether to laugh or cry. He had finally yielded to Will's insistence that they stop and change horses at one of the scarce posting houses along the road. They had stopped very briefly at each inn along the way to seek word of their quarry. At two ostleries, they had found stablehands who seemed to remember a carriage fitting the description, after a liberal dose of memory restorer in the form of silver coin. The descriptions given by each lad were identical, so Giles was hopeful that they had been accurate, but no one had seen hide nor hair of any passengers. Indeed, both lads had assumed that the coach, driven by two unremarkable sort of taciturn men, was carrying baggage only, since no one had dismounted to make use of the inn's facilities.

Now, at a rather run-down ostlery between two larger towns, they stopped to inquire about renting a team of horses. The ostler informed them, quite sorrowfully at the loss of the potential income, that he had rented out a team late last night by prearrangement and he had no more horses to rent. Giles questioned him closely, and, indeed, it seemed that it must have been Hawton's coach that had taken the horses. Giles asked if he could rent out the horses that the other coach had left and was told, with all the more sorrow, that after the requisite rest, those mounts, too, had been pressed into service, it being market day locally. The man suggested another establishment further down the road, and Giles could all but see the bile rising in his throat at having to pass good business along to his competition.

He and Will had traveled as fast as they had dared, fearing most a horse's broken leg or axle on the rutted, muddy roads. It appeared they had made up a great deal of time, gaining a number of hours on the heavier, bulkier coach. But it was nowhere near enough, and the coach was still better than a half a day ahead. And they drew nearer to London. Giles had nothing more than an address for a Lord Beeson in Hanover Square. God help them all if this was but another wild goose chase.

Having wrung all the useful information he could from the unhappy ostler, Giles climbed up onto the box. It was Will's turn to sleep, though neither was getting much rest, jostled about inside the carriage. The horses had slowed considerably, he noticed as he made his way down the road to the next inn. They would have to be changed, and he would lose even more time.

Joanna thought it must be just past dawn when she felt the carriage slowing. They had been traveling about three days, she figured, having nothing more to tell time by than the light and dark of day and night showing through the cracks in the closed window flaps. Meals and stops were erratic, and certainly their sleeping habits were much disrupted. The Irish girls remained comatose—Hawton had continued to dose them, Joanna had noted. Emma and Tom had retreated more and more into sleep, a depressed, heavy unconsciousness that a child seems capable of in times of great trouble. Even in sleep, neither lost a fierce grip on her hand, and she tried to be as still as possible so as not to awaken them.

The carriage stopped altogether and Hawton sat up, alert. He had been tense and irritable for the past 24 hours. They had lost a good half day in repairing the wheel, and Joanna was downhearted about her inability to turn that mishap to her advantage. No one had happened by at that hour of the morning, and to her great disappointment, the driver had returned alone, a large carriage wheel lashed to the horse's rear. The repairs had been swift from that point and they had been on their way again, Joanna's spirits sinking as her chance at flight or rescue receded into the distance.

The door of the carriage opened suddenly and Joanna could make out in the dim light the two hulking figures of the drivers standing outside. "We're here," she heard one of them hiss. "We're going inside to get help. You wait here and keep everyone quiet."

Hawton nodded curtly as the carriage door was shut again. Joanna could hear that his breathing had quickened. The man was nearly more agitated than she was, but as yet she had no answer to the mystery.

Moments later the door opened again. Now Joanna could see several burly figures outside, muffled up. With a studied precision, each grabbed two of the Irish girls, none of whom did more than stir sleepily as they were hauled from the carriage.

One man was left now at the door to the carriage. He peered in intently at Joanna. "The mistress wants to see ye, sir, right away," he said gruffly to Hawton. "These be the three ye've brought us unexpected?" He gestured at Joanna and the children. Hawton nodded. Joanna could see that his lips were thin and white and his hands were clenched at his sides. She watched his Adam's apple bob up and down as he swallowed convulsively.

"Will they come quiet-like? We don't fancy scenes in the street 'ere." The man's voice was cold in the gray dawn.

"Of course they'll be quiet," Hawton answered,

nudging Joanna and glaring threats at her.

"I'll take the children, then," said the man, reaching in with large hands.

Joanna's grip tightened around each child as she shrank back into the carriage. "The children will stay with me, sir," she said, summoning courage from where she knew not. "We'll come quietly if you'll keep your hands to yourself."

"Ah, the girl's got spirit, 'as she?" the man said, his grin showing a mouth with blackened stumps where the teeth should be. "The men'll like that, they will. They'll take pleasure in beating that out o' 'er. Bring the brats as ye please, my fine lady, but if there's a noise from any o' ye, I'll be 'appy to split yer pretty skull fer ye." He withdrew his head from the carriage and stood to one side as Joanna gathered the children to her and rose. Hawton waited while she stepped down, then he disembarked, following closely.

In the dim light of dawn, Joanna could just make out that they stood in an enclosed mews with high walls all around. She looked around quickly and could see that the coach had come through a narrow alleyway that seemed to be the only way out. They began walking toward a rear door, and her heart sank as she felt the heavy gray stone close in around her.

The door opened without a sound, and Hawton gave Joanna an ungentle push. Once inside, Joanna could make out little in a darkened hallway. She held a sleepy Tom in her arms. He was heavy but she did not dare put him down, afraid that if he stumbled in his fatigue he would be beaten or snatched away. The man leading them had said not another word during their short trip to the house.

"Come this way, Mr. Hawton," said a cold voice from the dark. "And bring your excess baggage so that I can get a good look at the proffered merchandise."

A tall, dark figure preceded them down the hallway, opening a door and entering. Light from a lamp spilled into the hall. The man who had escorted them in had vanished. Joanna had not noticed him leaving. Hawton put his hand under Joanna's arm, pushing her through the door. Through her sleeve she could feel that his fingers were trembling.

"Set the children down," came the imperious voice. Keeping her head down, Joanna raised her eyes just enough to see the speaker. It was a woman, older than Joanna but not elderly, rail thin, with a tight, high-boned, gray face. There was no warmth in her icy eyes and no softness about her tight, thin mouth.

Joanna could feel the woman's eyes on her, a disquieting sensation, as if she were being stripped bare and examined for defects.

"She's too old for my establishment, Mr. Hawton, even if she were a virgin, which is doubtful at her age. Are you a virgin, girl?"

Joanna gasped, her hand clenching on Emma's shoulder. For this child to hear such a thing, let alone Joanna herself being asked such a question! Joanna suffused a bright red as she struggled to regain control. Not for anything would she answer this horrible old harridan.

"She is not a virgin, of that I am certain, ma'am, but she was an innocent until recently," came Hawton's oily voice next to her.

A malicious smile curved the woman's thin lips but there was no sign of mirth in her eyes. "Are you bringing me your castoffs, Mr. Hawton? This is not an admirable way to dispose of an unwanted mistress."

"How dare you? How dare either of you discuss such matters in front of these children!" Joanna found her voice, no longer caring what the penalty might be for speaking her mind.

To her surprise, the woman began to laugh, but the amusement that lit her eyes was unholy. "Mr. Hawton, I take it the young lady has no idea where she is or what she is doing here?" she asked.

"No, madame," was his awkward reply. He had not quite dared to share the moment's amusement with her.

"The little girl will do nicely, Mr. Hawton, once I have satisfied myself that you will not bring the authorities down around my ears, and the young woman can be of use in a more routine sort of establishment. But what on earth do you expect me to do with an idiot boy? I have no clients who would amuse themselves that way." The woman's voice had turned icy again, as if she had never laughed in her life.

"We could take him down to the docks and turn him loose, madame. It doesn't matter to me as long as he disappears. But he can fetch and carry and could be sold, I imagine, for a small price."

Joanna stood, paralyzed by what she was hearing. A brothel. It had to be. And they would actually force Emma to submit to such a thing. Selling Tom or turning him loose on the docks in London was no better. They would all be better off dead than forced to submit to such a fate. She could feel panic welling up in her chest, and with all the strength she could muster she forced herself to breathe calmly, fighting down the terror. Their only hope of salvation lay in her ability to stay calm, to think it through. There had to be some way out of this nightmare. There had to be!

Both Emma and Tom were standing quietly beside her. She blessed providence that they seemed too sleepy and befuddled to be taking in what was being said, perhaps lulled cruelly into a sense of safety by her soft, warm grip on each shoulder.

"Well, I'll send him to the scullery for now, but if he cannot perform simple tasks or if he frightens the staff I'll get rid of him," the woman said, as coldly as if she were talking of throwing out some fish that had gone off.

She apparently had signaled in some way because the door opened softly and a large, burly man stepped in. He said nothing, but stood respectfully waiting to be told what to do.

"Take these two upstairs." She gestured toward Joanna and Emma. "Give them over to Isobelle to clean up. Tell her I'll come up later. Then come back and get the boy some clothes and take him to the scullery. That will be all."

Without a word, the man moved forward and laid a heavy hand on Joanna's arm.

"No!" Joanna shrieked, bending down and grabbing Tom. "Let him stay with me! He won't understand if you separate us! Please! I'll do anything!" She choked on the last words as the tears of terror and despair fell. She buried her face in the boy's neck and clung to him.

"Shut up this instant, you slut!" snapped the woman, standing, her icy rage apparent. "We have no scenes here, is that understood? Now, if you do not leave that drooling idiot and go upstairs quietly, I'll summon Teddy. Teddy will be glad to take the boy out into the streets and leave him wherever I tell him to. It matters not to me one way or the other. It's your choice."

For the briefest moment Joanna stared into the adderlike eyes, then she took a deep breath and put her face next to Tom's.

"Go with this man, my darling," she whispered, swallowing her sobs. "Listen carefully to whatever they ask you to do and try to do it. Emma and I will try to find you when we can."

Tom looked into her eyes for a moment, then gave a brief nod. As Joanna leaned in to plant a kiss on his cheek, the man behind her jerked her to her feet. He steadied her none too gently, then with a viselike grip on Joanna and on Emma he propelled them roughly from the room. Joanna twisted her head back around and gave Tom the biggest smile she could plaster on her face, but she felt it twist as she was racked again by sobs. She did not hear the door close behind them.

Alone with Hawton and Tom now, the woman took her seat calmly, as if she had just fussed at a parlor maid for missing a speck of dust. "You may sit, Mr. Hawton," she said coolly, gesturing peremptorily at a high-backed, uncomfortable-looking seat. Tom was forgotten and he stood unmoving in the shadows. "I said nothing in front of the girl, because it was apparent that you have kept her in ignorance, probably the one sound thing you have done with regard to this venture," she continued. "But you must know that our patron is likely to be extremely annoyed that you have managed to kidnap two children of the gentry and their governess as well. You will start at the beginning, please, and tell me precisely what occurred. We have no trouble with the London constabulary for obvious reasons, but I have no wish to become embroiled in a kidnapping charge from Cumberland."

"You need have no fear of that, ma'am," said Hawton. She had not even bothered to give him her name, and it was surprising how something so slight as that kept him off-stride. "It is the governess herself who will be accused of the kidnapping, and there will be no one else to refute the charge. Indeed, Lady—er, my partner is the only one there who will be giving any relevant evidence, and she knows what to say." Hawton took a deep breath, willing his words to be true. If Eleanor had fouled everything up, all was lost anyway. He had been too unnerved to correct the coachmen's tale that Joanna was merely the governess. What did it matter anyway, with Sir Giles dead and no possible connection to be made between this brothel and Queen's Hall?

"And how did all this come about, Mr. Hawton? It is apparent something has gone badly wrong. Our patron favors very clean, neat operations, and he would never have allowed something so sloppy as a kidnapping to jeopardize the success of his venture."

"Well, he didn't plan this one carefully enough," snarled Hawton. He was tired of being made to feel like a schoolboy who had pinched his little brother. "One of the Irish girls damn near brought the whole county awake screaming. She was supposed to be sedated but she was not." He went on, briefly describing the aftermath and why he and Eleanor had decided on the course of action that had brought him here with Joanna and the children.

"I see," was the woman's enigmatic comment as he finished, but he noticed that she did not seem quite so austere, leading him to hope that their next topic of conversation, fair compensation for Joanna and Emma, would not go too badly for him.

"I shall have to contact our patron, Mr. Hawton, and that is something that is not done directly, as I am sure you will appreciate. No doubt you will want to haggle with him over payment, but I must warn you, he'll be terribly upset at this turn of events. He is a careful man, a pillar of society, and he does not sully his hands with risky ventures. You may stay here if you wish until he can speak with you, but you are to touch none of the merchandise, none. Do I make myself clear?"

Another arrogant bitch. By damn, he'd like to take this one down a notch or two. Unfortunately, it was he who was in the weaker position at the moment, but when Beeson realized that he had two prize beauties on his hands and no possible ugly repercussions, they'd see who had the upper hand.

"I do not find myself in the mood for anything except a bath and a clean bed at the moment, madame," Hawton answered, allowing his voice to drip with the same haughtiness that she employed on him.

"Excellent. I imagine we can expect to hear something shortly, at least by this evening. I do expect our patron to be in attendance tonight. We are having a little private gathering for our best clients who've been avidly awaiting this latest shipment."

The door opened again, silently. Hawton only knew it by the rush of air against his neck and the fact that the woman raised her eyes and looked behind him.

"Did she cut up rough, Bobby?" she asked.

"No, ma'am. I 'eard nothin' from neither of 'em," came his brash voice in response. "Quiet as mice they both was, but the older one cried all the way and was still 'angin' on to the little 'un when I turned them over to Isobelle."

"Fine. You may take the boy to the scullery now. Tell Martine to set him to washing up. He may also be able to help with the laundry. Tell her if he is a hindrance in any way, or if he lacks the wit to do the job to her satisfaction to let me know."

Nodding his head, the man clapped his large hand around Tom's arm and pushed him from the room.

"I'll show you to your room, Mr. Hawton, and order you a bath and some breakfast. You may nap, if you wish, but if our patron arrives and wishes to see you, I expect you to present yourself at once."

"Certainly, madame," Hawton said, his teeth grinding. This woman was the madame of a whorehouse and she gave herself enough airs to take on the queen. He would like to throw her and Lady Eleanor in a room together and lock the door on them for a while. He wasn't at all sure which one would be left standing when the door was opened again.

Upstairs, Joanna felt as if her nightmare was just beginning. Emma and she had been separated. Joanna had deemed it best not to protest, noting carefully which door in the long corridor Emma had been taken through. Joanna herself had been stripped bare and examined by the woman, Isobelle, and it had been the most embarrassing moment of her life. Isobelle had pronounced that she "would do," clucking over her lack of virginity as if it were a seam that had come loose on her gown.

Otherwise there had been no conversation. Joanna's attempts to ask about Emma or about this establishment had been met with thin-lipped silence.

Joanna had been dunked into a tub of barely tepid water and scrubbed within an inch of her life. Under any other circumstances, she would have enjoyed being fussed over—hair washed and brushed, perfumed, powdered—but these were ungentle hands, and when the two surly young maids came at her with pots of white leaded paint for her face, she balked, pulling away, and throwing up her hands.

"Leave it anyway, Alice," said Isobelle, her first words in a good hour. "I do not yet know what the plans are for this one. She will likely be sent elsewhere, and there is no point in painting her up yet."

Alice backed away, glaring malevolently at Joanna. Isobelle gestured imperiously at a dressing gown which lay across the back of a chair. "Put it on," she said coldly.

Joanna was only too glad to cover herself, but her heart sank as she put the wispy gossamer fabric around her. It hid nothing. Indeed, she could see herself reflected in any one of a number of mirrors that stood about the room, and the gown revealed more than it hid, in a most provocative way.

Isobelle took Joanna's arm, holding her with tight fingers, and propelled her from the room. They walked through the hallway, and Joanna's heart lifted as they paused in front of the door she was sure she had seen Emma taken into. Indeed, as Isobelle unlocked the door and pushed Joanna through, Emma's bright little curls were visible on the elaborate bed.

With a cry she could not help, Joanna stumbled toward the bed. Emma seemed to be sound asleep.

"You will wait here until you are sent for. Do not awaken the girl. She will need her sleep. Food will be sent up eventually. If you make any trouble you'll be sold to Madame Fanny on the docks. It is said her girls don't survive longer than a week. Understood?"

Joanna nodded miserably and waited while the door closed behind Isobelle. She heard the key grate in the lock and the sound of the woman's footsteps receding down the hallway. Then she turned to examine her surroundings.

The room was sumptuously, ostentatiously furnished. It reminded Joanna of Lady Eleanor's taste, without the money to lend it true elegance. Everywhere she looked were hangings and swirls, bows and flowers. But it was not the decoration that held Joanna's attention. Her eye was drawn immediately to the window, and in several short strides she was across the room, pulling back the heavy draperies that shut out all light.

There were bars on the window, thick iron bars, closely spaced. Not even Tom could squeeze through such a small space. Still daring to hope, Joanna tried the window, pushing up as hard as she could on the sash. It would not budge. She dragged a small chair over to the window, but when she climbed up on it she could see that heavy nails had been driven into the top of the sash, securing it to the window frame. There would be no escape through the window, and from what little she could see, they were some four flights up.

"Aunt Joanna?" came a tiny voice.

"I'm here, darling," Joanna answered quickly, hurrying over to the bed. Emma was sitting up, her gray eyes troubled. The child's face was painted garishly, Joanna noted, with kohl on her beautiful little-girl's eyes and rouge and paint on her cheeks and lips. With a snarl to herself, Joanna sat on the bed and, dampening a towel from the washbasin, she wiped away at the offensive paint, singing a pretty lullaby, as much to calm herself as Emma. She wondered how much time they had, and where Tom was. There was no way out. No hope. Nothing but this small warm body hugging her. And a fate for both of them worse than death itself.

Chapter Eighteen

Lord Beeson's face was as black as a thunder-cloud. His footman stood at what he hoped was enough of a distance to avoid the blow that seemed so imminent. The boy would have retreated if he could, but he had not been dismissed and he knew better than to quit the room without leave. It was obvious there was bad news in the note his master had received. The missive had arrived early this morning, not long after dawn, but it had lain in the hallway on a silver salver until this afternoon when Lord Beeson had made his usual first appearance of the day. There had been nothing about the note itself to indicate that the matter was urgent, and even if there had been, no one could have been found on the staff brave enough to awaken the master for a bit of corre-spondence.

"Have my carriage brought round at once,"

Lord Beeson snarled at his retainer. "See that there is no delay." The man stormed from the room, leaving the boy sighing with relief and scrambling out to the stables.

In the small breakfast parlor, Lord Beeson slathered marmalade on his toast with a viciousness that nearly broke the bread. He should have known that nothing involving Eleanor would go right. But he had trusted her man, Hawton, had thought him sharp enough and hungry enough to do the job well. And now it was a disaster. Mrs. Boyd's note was short and to the point—one of the reasons Beeson did business with her was there was no nonsense about her—but she had conveyed enough information for him to recognize the potential for disaster. He would have to go over there this afternoon, breaking his ironclad rule never to be seen in the establishment in a guise other than that of satisfied patron. He was under no illusions that a society which tolerated the existence of such places would equally tolerate his ownership of one.

He would have someone's head for this, and if this man Hawton was still on the premises, his would be the head to roll.

Giles drove the coach slowly down Hanover Square, looking for number 34, the address elegantly engraved on the back of the envelope of Eleanor's letter. He was weary to the bone. He had wanted to drive the last leg of the journey into London, because Will was not familiar with the lie of the streets, even though it had meant cutting short his rest time in the carriage. Not that either of them had gotten much rest along the way. Stopping at every inn and asking questions made for sleeping in short snatches, particularly as they had neared the city. But he was sure they were on the right track. There had been the occasional stablehand who had recalled seeing the coach they sought, and Giles was certain he was only a half day behind. He shut his weary mind from the thought of all the evil that could be accomplished in half a day. Hawton had no reason to know he was under pursuit. Eleanor fancied that she had thrown Giles completely off the scent by sending him to Carlisle, and, in any event, it was not likely that she could have sent a message to Hawton while he was on the road.

He stopped at number 34, a large townhouse with a great stone facade. A carriage stood in front, a driver on the box. Giles climbed down from the box and walked back to the door of his own carriage. He could see Will stirring through the window flap. As he reached for the handle, he heard a commotion behind him and turned to see a large, florid man descending rapidly down the front steps of number 34. A hapless footman hurried to stay ahead of him, and a man who was obviously the butler struggled to keep up.

"Cancel it, damn you," the man shouted over his shoulder at his butler. "I do not know when I'll return. Tell them I was called away on urgent business. I've no time to write a note now."

The footman had reached the door of the standing carriage mere seconds before his master, struggling with the catch on the door to get it open quickly enough so as not to keep the man waiting. He barely made it, but the relief on his face was obvious as he closed the door behind the man and took his own place at the rear of the coach. The butler turned and made his way up the stairs, shaking his head as if in some distress. The carriage started off abruptly, the footman having to grab on to keep from falling.

Not one of them had spared so much as a glance at Giles or his coach.

Like a flash of lightning, Giles was back on the box, flicking the reins over his mismatched, weary team of rented horses. He was quite sure he had recognized Lord Beeson, the sardonic twist to his mouth, the dark, mean eyes. Wherever the man was bound for, he was angry and in a hurry. It was unlikely that Hawton would have dared to deliver his kidnap victims directly to Lord Beeson. Better to follow along at a discreet distance and see where the man was going.

They drove along at a fast clip for some quarter of an hour. Giles's fears that the footman would look back and note that they were being followed proved groundless. The young man rode with his head down, showing no interest in his surroundings. Nevertheless, Giles kept his coach back as far as he dared, particularly since they appeared to be rapidly leaving the fashionable district and making for an older, commercial part of the city.

Finally the coach slowed to a stop in front of a large townhouse on Lombard Street. Giles stopped his own coach well down the block and, keeping his hood over his face, leaped down. He watched as Beeson's footman jumped down as well and made his way to the door of the carriage. Lord Beeson stepped out and brushed past the boy, taking the steps of the townhouse two at a time, his great cape swirling black around him.

"Let's go, Will," Giles said softly as he opened the door to his carriage. Will stepped out quickly.

The fast drive through city streets had put him on the alert.

"I saw our man, Beeson, coming out of his house and I followed him here," explained Giles tersely. "He went into that establishment. I recall this general area from my younger days, and there were a number of brothels around here then. I do not know if that is one of them, but we shall find out." His mouth set in a grim line, Giles made his way down the street, Will following closely behind.

At the door, Giles lifted the large brass knocker and set up a din. The door was opened almost immediately. Giles felt his guts grind as he took in the appearance of the man at the door. Here was no butler from a well-positioned, merchant-class family. This man was a thug, beefy and scarred. While his clothing was neat and clean, he wore none of the trappings of a well-placed servant. He looked like what he had to be—a tough doorman for a rough brothel.

"We don't open until ten this evening, sir," said the man, taking in Giles and his servant in one look and starting to close the door in their faces.

"I'm here to see Lord Beeson," said Giles, stepping swiftly in and putting his hand on the door so that Will could enter behind him.

" 'Ere, there's no one 'ere by that name, sir, and I've told you we was closed. Come back at ten if you want what we 'ave." The man looked annoyed but it was clear he was not inclined to offend potential clientele.

"I saw Lord Beeson enter this establishment not three minutes ago. It's a matter involving kidnapping, so unless you want the law down on you, you'll tell him I'm here at once."

The man's eyes narrowed and his jaw set. Without a word he closed the door behind Giles and Will. Giles could hear a heavy bolt sliding.

"Wait 'ere. I know now 'oo you mean and I'll fetch 'im for you. Don't move a step, sir," the man said, his voice quiet and cold. With no further word, he turned and disappeared into a door down the hall. Seconds later the door opened and he re-emerged with three men, even larger than he, right behind him. Too late, Giles turned behind him, seeing that a heavy bolt held the door fast. It would take too much time to get it open, and these thugs were nearly upon them. Two closed upon Will, one smashing his fist against his face as he struggled against them.

"Beeson! I know you're here, Beeson!" Giles shouted as loudly as he could, before the two others converged on him. One shoved a fist as hard as a brick against his jaw, the other came up behind him and grabbed his arms. Knowing he was beaten, but unwilling to go down without a fight, Giles kicked hard against the shin of the man in front of him, then aimed another kick at his groin. The man doubled over, groaning, but threw his arms around Giles's legs, preventing further attack.

"Beeson! Kidnapping is a hanging offense, Beeson!" Giles shouted, his words cut off as a large square of cotton closed around his mouth. Now he was trussed tightly, ropes cutting mercilessly into his flesh. He twisted his head around and saw that Will was writhing on the floor, blood gushing from his nose. He, too, was being bound.

He cursed himself a thousand times for being fool enough to walk into such a trap.

Just then another door off the hallway opened.

Beeson stepped out, followed by a tall, thin woman, hands clawed at her sides, her mouth tight with rage.

"Bring them in here," Beeson said, gesturing imperiously. Giles was half carried, half dragged into the room and was thrown to the floor. Will was carried in and thrown beside him. Giles could see that the bleeding from Will's nose had slowed to a trickle, but he was covered with blood and showed no signs of being conscious.

Beeson and the woman followed, Beeson seating himself behind a large desk and leaving the woman to stand next to him.

"Fetch the man who brought the shipment here," Beeson snarled. There was silence while one of the men left the room. Beeson stared down at Giles, his eyes dark with anger.

"I want something to drink, Mrs. Boyd. Make it brandy, and not that swill you serve your customers," Beeson said.

Mrs. Boyd nodded at one of the three men and he left the room immediately.

"You can go," Beeson said, nodding to the two men who remained. "Check outside and make sure they arrived alone." As they left, the other walked back in carrying a silver tray with a brandy decanter and snifter on it. Beeson poured himself a generous amount and knocked it back. As he poured himself another, the first man walked back into the room, followed by Hawton.

Giles lay as he had fallen with his face to the floor but he twisted his head to the side to observe the newcomer. Their eyes met, and Hawton gave a start of pure terror as he saw who it was. Giles could see his steward's hands start to shake as he stood in front of the desk. Beeson's face was purple with rage.

"You told Mrs. Boyd the man was dead, Mr. Hawton," said Beeson, his voice barely controlled. "Well, he doesn't look very dead to me. What else have you fouled up?"

"I—I thought he was dead, sir. Now we'll just have to make certain it's done properly this time." Hawton shifted his eyes away from Beeson.

"You are a bleeding imbecile, Mr. Hawton. You'll be very lucky if it isn't you who winds up dead. You've made a mess of this operation from start to finish. You and Eleanor. I should have known better than to have involved that drunken madwoman in my business. You also neglected to mention to Mrs. Boyd that Sir Giles had married the wench a few days ago. Did you think Eleanor had not spewed her venom to me in a letter? Not that it matters any longer. Now you have stuck me with an ex-governess, two children, one an idiot, *and* Sir Giles Chapman."

"But Joanna and Emma can serve in this or another establishment, my lord," stammered Hawton. "Mrs. Boyd told me the girl would fetch a pretty penny among your clientele and that the governess could be sold off to a brothel that does not specialize in virgins." He broke off and skipped aside as Giles began to thrash on the floor, too close to his own feet for comfort.

At the barest of nods from Lord Beeson, one of the thugs approached Giles and landed a swift, hard kick in his belly.

"You'll have your turn to speak, Sir Giles," sneered Lord Beeson. "For now, I expect silence from you while I get to the bottom of this mess."

343

He took his time sipping the brandy, giving it a long, approving sniff.

"As a rule, we do not use girls or women kidnapped from the gentry, Mr. Hawton," Lord Beeson went on. "You can appreciate that we would not last long in this business if such a thing were to become known. But I can see that in this case the choice has been made for me. Take the gag off of Sir Giles, Teddy," said Lord Beeson. "Now, Sir Giles," he continued, while Teddy pulled at the knot holding the cloth around Giles's mouth, "I trust you understand you are not holding a particularly good hand here. I want some information from you. If I get the truth, and if I like what I hear, I just may find myself able to spare your wife and your niece. You, of course, will not be spared under any circumstances. This fool of a steward and your sot of a stepsister have seen to that. Nevertheless, you may make a noble gesture and spare these two you seem to be so fond of. Do we have an agreement, sir?"

"You can rot in hell for eternity, Beeson," snarled Giles as the gag fell from his face. "I trust nothing you say."

"Whom did you tell of this little escapade before you hared off so precipitously for London?" Lord Beeson asked, his tone mild, as if he had heard no insult.

"My entire household staff knows where I was bound for, Lord Beeson," countered Giles, matching the man's even tones. "You can kill me, you can kill the lot of us, but my whole household knows the name of Lord Beeson and your Hanover Square address. Moreover, my housekeeper had arranged to meet with our local constabulary the day after I left to report the entire matter. No doubt word is on its way to the London authorities even as we speak." None of this was true, of course. Giles had mentioned nothing of Lord Beeson's letter to Mrs. Davies, but the pinched, gray look about Beeson's mouth made the lie worthwhile.

"Gag him, Teddy," snarled Lord Beeson, taking an angry gulp from his brandy. Teddy made short work of it, landing several more well-aimed kicks at Giles's gut before the procedure was completed.

"No one in my household can trace me to this establishment, except as an evening visitor, and they all know enough to hold their tongues anyway," Beeson seemed to be musing to himself.

"Bobby," he said, turning to one of the men who stood at respectful attention, "Sir Giles and his man arrived in his own carriage, did they not?"

"Yes, sir, the carriage 'as already been brought round back," was Bobby's response.

"Good man. See to it that the horses are fed and watered, then harness them again. I'll want to move that carriage to a place where no one will think to look. In the meanwhile, offer Sir Giles and his man our hospitality." Beeson set his snifter down and stood.

"As for you, Mr. Hawton, I am seriously displeased with how this affair has been handled. I can understand that the girl screaming on the beach put you in an awkward position, but it is obvious that you and Eleanor were running your own nefarious enterprise on the side, and that has now involved me as well. I'll pay you for the Irish shipment as we agreed, but I'll give you no further money for the two females because you are putting me to the trouble of two murders and the risk of being caught up in a kidnapping charge. And you may tell Eleanor that she will be hearing from me regarding the future of our partnership. I suggest you get yourself back to Queen's Hall as soon as you can. No doubt you left a mess there for Eleanor to wallow in." Beeson flung a small purse in Hawton's direction, not bothering to aim. Hawton had to bend down and pick it up from the floor where it lay next to Giles.

"I will return this evening, Mrs. Boyd, as originally planned. I'll send word to you regarding these men," said Beeson as he disappeared through the door.

"Get them out of here," Mrs. Boyd spat at her henchmen. The four men converged on Giles and Will, lifting them roughly and carrying them through the door into the hallway. Giles hung between his two captors, face down. He lifted his head and looked over at Will, and was relieved to see that the man's eyes were open now and focused. Will met his glance with angry, determined eyes. Giles wondered how much he had heard.

They bumped roughly up four flights of stairs, Giles making a mental note of the twists and turns along the way.

"Watch out for the idiot," growled one of the men, and the procession came to an abrupt halt. Giles could see a small pair of feet in the hallway and he heard the faint intake of breath. Lifting his head up, Giles met the startled, frightened eyes of Tom, peeping at him over a tall stack of what appeared to be clean bed linens.

"What do we 'ave 'im for?" asked one of the men over Giles's head. Giles and Tom held one another's glance, Giles willing the boy with his eyes to be silent. The boy looked stricken, as if all hope in him had been drained away. Giles tried to smile at him but it was hopeless, his face twisting into a bloody grimace.

" 'E's 'armless," answered one of the other men. "Fetches and carries like a dog with a stick. Doesn't talk. Needs to learn about 'is betters, though. 'Ere, you, boy, when you see any of us comin' you get out of the way, is that understood, idiot?" The man emphasized his words with a clout to Tom's head that sent the boy reeling and spilled the linens to the floor.

Giles ground his teeth at his own helplessness, watching as Tom bent over slowly and began picking up the sheets. The boy straightened and again met Giles's eye. Giles read anger in him now, and Tom watched them from the rear until the men turned with their burdens into a room several doors down.

Once inside, Giles and Will were dumped onto the floor. Their bonds and gags were checked, the man who had suffered Giles's kick to his groin taking great pleasure in tightening the ropes around Giles's arms and legs to the point of cutting off circulation. Giles hoped they would go away and leave him lying as he had been dropped. He had every intention of crawling over to Will and working the man free as best he could. But apparently the thugs were thinking along the same lines, because Giles and Will were each tied to the bed legs, too far apart to reach each other and too tightly to twist loose. With not another word, the men left the room, closing the door behind them.

For a few moments all was silence except for the sound of Will's breathing, rasping as he struggled for air around a gag that was apparently too tight. Giles struggled for a few minutes, but the ropes were bound too tightly for him to work any slack into them, and he could feel that he was fast losing sensation in his hands. At least his legs were protected by his boots.

His every thought was on Joanna. She was somewhere in this hell house, a prisoner like himself, but her fate, and Emma's, would be so much worse than his own death. Giles struggled anew, the veins standing out on his forehead, only to find that the fiend who had tied his ropes knew how to do it in such a fashion that pulling on them made them tighten even further.

And then, incredibly, there were small feet standing in front of him. Looking up, Giles saw Tom, the boy's eyes now burning with the light of determination. Speaking not a word, Tom stepped around Giles and began working the gag free. Giles looked over and saw that Tom had had the presence of mind to close the door behind him, and marveled that the thugs had felt so confident of their own ropes that they had not bothered to lock it.

It took a long time, but finally Giles felt the knots slip and the gag loose itself from his mouth.

"Good work, Tom," whispered Giles. "Did anyone see you come in here, son?"

"No," replied Tom. "I waited." He spoke slowly, as if searching for the words, but his tone was deliberate and he knew exactly what was being asked and what his answer should be.

"We must be very quiet now, Tom. Do you know where Aunt Joanna and Emma are?" Giles all but held his breath, watching Tom look for his words.

"Downstairs. A room. I took them sheets," he finally said.

"Have you seen them? Are they together? Are they all right?" he asked, fear and impatience making him ask too many questions at once of the child.

"Yes. Together. But Auntie cries," was the boy's measured response.

Giles could feel himself breathe again. "Do you think you could find their room again, Tom, if I can get free and go with you?" Again he waited.

"Yes," was all the boy replied.

"Good, son. Do you think you can go and untie Will's gag, like you did mine?"

The boy nodded and made his way to Will, where he worked carefully on the knot until Will, too, could speak.

"Sir Giles!" the man whispered, as soon as he could. "What manner of place is this?"

"A worse hell than you've ever dreamed of, Will, and we've got to get Joanna and the children out as soon as we can."

Tom had returned to Giles and squatted behind him, working at the ropes that bound his hands. It took a long time, but Giles finally felt them loosen, then slip away altogether. His hands fell motionless at his side and he cursed to find he had no feeling in them. They were useless until the nerves came back.

"Go and work on Will's hands next, Tom," said Giles. "You're doing a fine job. I'm very proud of you." Tom gave Giles a wide smile, then went over and worked on Will's bonds.

Gradually, Giles could feel the sensation return to his hands and he almost wished he couldn't. They were on fire, as if he had shoved them into flames.

Tom worked in silence freeing Will's hands, then his feet. He returned to Giles and loosed the knots around his legs, just as feeling and movement were returning to his hands.

"Tom, is there a back stairs? Is there more than one way to get up and down stairs here?" he asked, hoping the boy would understand.

Tom nodded. "Two stairs," he said slowly.

"Do you think you can show us the back stairs and then take us to Aunt Joanna's room?"

Tom's eyes looked troubled as he thought about the question. "Yes," he finally said, but he sounded uncertain.

"What is wrong, Tom?" asked Giles carefully. It was clear there was plenty enough knowledge in the child's head. He'd have the skin off the next person who called the boy an idiot. If he got the chance.

"They will see us," Tom said, picking his way through his words. "The bad people."

Giles sat back, kneading his legs where the ropes had cut into his flesh above his boots. He was thoughtful. He looked over at Will who was rubbing his hands and arms and wincing.

"We have to be very careful and quiet, Tom," Giles finally said. "Not everyone in the house knows who we are, only Mrs. Boyd and the four men who brought us here. Other people might have heard about us, though, so we don't want to see anyone if we don't have to. But things seem pretty quiet now, and I know the house does not open for business until ten tonight, which is a long time from now, so maybe we could sneak downstairs without anyone seeing us."

Tom stared at Giles, then slowly nodded.

"Your mama and papa would be very proud of you, too, son," Giles said, reaching up and hugging the boy to him.

Giles stood slowly, testing his legs. "How are

you, Will?" he asked in a low voice. "Do you think you can move about now?"

"I can go anywhere, Sir Giles. Let's go and get the ladies and turn our backs on this godforsaken place."

"Amen to that, Will, but we have a long way to go before we are safe."

Giles stared about him for a moment. Apparently they were in someone's actual bedroom. In his youth he had been in a brothel once or twice and knew that the rooms set aside in which the girls entertained the clientele were elaborate to the point of decadence. This room was well furnished, but it looked a bit down-at-heels, as if everything in here were a castoff that had seen better days. Perhaps several of the girls slept here in their off hours or perhaps it was a servant's bedroom. In fact, now that he thought of it, the girls would be here if it was set aside for their daytime use, so it seemed likely it was a servants' room. He crossed over to a small chest of drawers that doubled as a washstand. Pulling open the drawers, he found what he had hoped to find, several maids' uniforms carefully folded. These he pulled out and threw on the bed.

"Will, I have an idea," he said, excitement in his whisper. "If we can get to Joanna and Emma, we can get them into these maids' uniforms. I'm willing to bet they haven't been here long enough for most of the staff to know them on sight. You and I can attempt to look like workmen. We can carry this chest down the steps, as if we've been ordered to move some furniture. If we run into any of our friends we'll have to stand and fight, but if we don't see anyone who recognizes us, perhaps we can bluff our way through. If anyone stops us, we can say we've been ordered to move the chest down temporarily because the one downstairs is broken. Then we can take it into Joanna's room. If we're lucky, we can use the same ploy to get us out the back of the house, to the mews. Did you hear the man—Bobby, I think it was—say that my carriage is out back? We'll need a great deal of the devil's own luck, but failure is out of the question. What do you think?"

Will had been following along, nodding and smiling as Giles had explained his plan, but it was Tom who spoke.

"We can leave? Emma and Auntie, too?"

"Yes, Tom, if we are lucky and careful. You must walk along ahead of us as if we weren't there. Don't pay any attention to us. Can you carry that big pile of linens you had when I first saw you?"

Tom nodded and gestured over to the door where the linens stood where he had deposited the pile on the floor.

"Good. Will, see if there's any water in that basin and wipe the blood off your face, then toss the cloth over to me," said Giles, stripping off his coat and neckcloth. He stuffed the neckcloth in his pocket, mindful that as a potential gag it might come in handy. His coat he rolled up with the uniforms and placed in one of the drawers. The ropes, too, went into the drawers.

"I think we are ready," he announced after looking at Will's face, now wiped clean of all traces of blood. "Tom, pick up your load, and Will, come and get one end of this chest. We'll listen at the door before we open it. If we hear nothing, we can go. I rather think we are on the servants' floor, so we may be lucky enough not to meet anyone, at least on this level. Tom, walk straight to Auntie's room, if you can. Don't speak to us again until we are inside. Do you understand, son?"

"Yes," said Tom, the simplicity of his answer belying the depth of his comprehension. He crossed to the door and picked up the load of linens.

Giles and Will hoisted the chest between them and walked to the door. They paused for a moment, listening, and heard nothing. Giles nodded at Tom and the boy opened the door and stepped through. He proceeded down the hallway, opposite from the way they had come, Giles noted. He prayed the boy knew where he was going.

They reached what had to be the rear stairs without meeting anyone. Giles looked at Will. After several nights sleeping in a moving coach, Will looked just like the laborer he was pretending to be. Giles hoped he looked no better. Neither had shaved since they had left home, and Giles was sure the effect was disreputable, to say the least.

On the second floor at last, Giles looked down the hall. His heart froze at the sight of a maid coming toward them. As she approached, she spotted Tom.

" 'Ere, you, there, the idiot. Where have you been? Them sheets should have been on the beds a quarter of an hour ago, and Mrs. Andrew'll 'ave my 'ide for it if they're not. Why'd she 'ave to go an' 'ire an idiot, that's what I'd like to know." The girl grabbed Tom by the ear and hauled him down the hall, not sparing a glance for Giles and Will. Tom cast a desperate glance back at them.

Giles took a deep breath. "'Ere, girl, where's this chest supposed to go?" he asked, murdering his speech and hoping it sounded authentic enough to pass muster. "The boy was sent to show us." He

prayed she would find nothing amiss in this remark. He did not want to have to start binding and
gagging people this early on.

"Where're they supposed to go, you little 'alfwit?"
she asked Tom, giving a cruel twist to his ear for
good measure. "Although it beats me why we'd 'ave
the likes of you be showin' anybody anythin'."

Tom, relief plain in his eyes, pointed to a door
three doors down on the left. The girl, grabbing
his arm, began to march him down the hall again.

" "Wait a minute, my girl," whined Giles, exasperation plain in his voice. " 'E's supposed to tell
us where to put the old chest, too, and it's one floor
up. Don't take 'im away now, or we'll never find it.
This place's wors'n a rabbit warren." His heart was
hammering in his throat. If the girl bought this
crock of nonsense, he was going on the stage.

"Oh, all right, then. Give me them sheets, boy,
and get along with you. But mind, when you've
finished with these ever-so-fine gentlemen"—she
gave a withering emphasis—"you come and find
me down 'ere. I'll need plenty of 'elp just catchin'
up." She grabbed the sheets from Tom and
flounced down the hall in a huff.

Tom walked slowly to the door he had indi-
cated, watching the retreating back of his erst-
while captor. Giles picked the large key off the
hook next to the door and turned it in the lock.

It was dark inside. Apparently there were no
lamps or candles burning and the draperies were
shut. Giles and Will stepped in right after Tom,
Will shutting the door behind them with his foot.

As they set the chest down, Giles looked around,
but it was too dark to make out much. He could
see the dark shape of a bed and just make out that
it was occupied, but nothing more.

"Are you sure this is the right room, Tom?" he asked in a whisper.

A small sound gave him the answer he needed. Like a juggernaut, a small shape launched itself from the dark of the bed at Tom, wrapping itself around his little body.

"Tom?" came a ragged whisper, Emma's little voice. "Oh, we didn't know when we'd see you again."

"Emma, who is it?" came a sleepy voice from the bed. In two long strides, Giles was across the room, dropping himself on the bed.

"Joanna," he murmured, gathering the sleepy figure to him. For a few seconds there was silence, then he heard a whisper at his neck.

"Giles, oh, my God, please don't let me wake up, ever again. And if I'm dead, that's wonderful," she said, burying her face against this warm specter of a dream.

"I'm here, my darling. I'm really here. And we're going to get you and the children out of this place, I promise you." He kissed her throat, her neck, moving his lips across her hair.

"Is it really you, Giles?" came her tearful whisper. "Hawton said he'd had you killed. Knifed at Dufton. Am I dreaming?" Her hands worked spasmodically at his back.

"He tried, but his assassin wasn't quite up to it. When I came home and found you and the children gone, I pieced together what had happened, but it is just good luck that I was able to find you." He stopped talking to kiss her again, all over her face and hair.

"Did they hurt you and Emma?" he made himself ask. He had so wanted to get here in time to save them from the worst of it.

"Not yet, my love," she answered, "But they plan to do unspeakable things to Emma, and to me also. I honestly thought of taking both our lives . . ." She shuddered in his arms and he tightened his grip on her.

"Hush, love, don't think anymore about it. I have a plan to get us all out of here. It is risky but it will just have to work. It's worked so far, at any rate. Do you know how much longer we'll be alone here?"

"No, I know nothing. But we are supposed to be sleeping. Emma, at least, is supposed to be brought out tonight. Oh, Giles, do you know what this place is?" she sobbed, clutching convulsively at him.

"Yes, darling, I know. And once we're away from here you need never think of it again. Will," he hissed. "Bring me the two maids' uniforms."

Will reached into the drawer and took out the two uniforms. Giles disengaged one hand from Joanna's tresses long enough to turn up the wick on the lamp that burned low by the bed. The room brightened enough that he could see her face.

"Oh, my darling, I thought I'd never see you again," he moaned, crushing her to him. His lips seized hers in a ravenous kiss, broken only when he felt a tug at his pants leg.

"You're right, Tom," he said smiling when he looked down and saw Tom's reproachful eyes on him. "This is no time for such silliness, is it?" He took the uniforms from the boy and handed them to Joanna.

"Can you take Emma behind a screen and get yourselves into these outfits? If you can pass for servants long enough to get downstairs to the back entrance, we may be able to get out."

Joanna took the uniforms and with a great sigh disengaged herself from Giles's arms. She and Emma disappeared behind the screen, but were out in no time.

"Let me see you," said Giles, still keeping his voice low. Indeed, they looked almost like maids, but their hair needed to be put up. He cursed himself for forgetting to bring mobcaps, then smiled as he remembered they had likely brought the servants' wardrobe with them.

In a few seconds he had unearthed mobcaps, frilly white affairs, from the drawer, as well as a few bent hairpins. He tucked and pinned Joanna's hair up into her mobcap while she worked on Emma's.

"Now," Giles said, holding Joanna out at arm's length. "Yes, you look perfect. Oh, no . . ."

"What is it?" Joanna asked, her face draining of color.

"Shoes!" he whispered. "I never thought about shoes and you are barefoot!" He was furious with himself. How could this whole plan unravel for the lack of two pair of shoes?

But Joanna just smiled and walked over to the side of the bed. She bent down and came up with two pair of soft house slippers.

"But, darling, you cannot wear those. They'll give you away."

"Have you seen any of the female servants, Giles?" she asked, putting the slippers on her feet. "They all wear these slippers, at least the ones I've seen upstairs do. I imagine it's because the other—inmates"—she grimaced at the word— "are sleeping during the day when the maids are about their cleaning. We won't look the least bit odd." She bent down and pushed the slippers onto Emma's feet.

Giles smiled his relief, realizing he had given not a thought to the footwear of the maid who had grabbed Tom. He looked down at Tom's feet and was surprised to notice that Tom, too, wore house slippers, just like those Joanna and Emma had on.

"Tom," said Giles, bending down to the boy. "The next part of our escape is going to be much harder, I think. Do you know if there is a back door to the outside that does not go through the kitchen? I want to stay away from the front of the house and I do not want to see many servants."

Tom puzzled it out for a moment. "Back door to outside? I don't know. The hall goes way back past the kitchen."

Giles let out the breath he did not know he had been holding. "I don't suppose you or Emma saw much of the layout of the house, did you, Joanna?" he asked.

"No, we were carried up from the front," was Joanna's discouraging response.

"Then we'll just have to chance being able to find the way out on our own. We still have one big problem to solve, and that is how to get us all out of doors at once. It wouldn't be so hard to explain taking the broken chest out to be repaired, but why would Joanna and Emma be going out, too?" He paused, considering, while Joanna finished tucking up Emma's hair.

"I have an idea," he said slowly, still piecing it together. "There is a small Oriental rug on the floor by the door. Let's roll that up and you and the children can carry it down. If anyone stops you, you can say that one of the girls got sick on it and it needs to be aired. Will it work?" he asked

Joanna, desperate that she should find no flaw in the plan.

"It's as good a plan as we can possibly come up with, Giles," she said, considering it. "I noticed that the windows are heavily barred and the bedroom doors are locked from the outside. I am quite sure the girls here do not have free run of the house, but the maids seem to. I think we have a very good chance, indeed."

He knew she was being deliberately optimistic but he blessed her for it.

"Emma, the rug will be heavy, but I think you and Tom can manage one end of it. Can you do that, darling?" he asked gently, taking her hand.

"Yes, Uncle Giles," she said, looking up at him. "Can you really get us out of here? Everyone is so mean to us."

"We're going to try our best, sweetheart. Stick with Aunt Joanna and if anyone asks you anything, let her answer." He gave her a kiss on the cheek.

"When we go out, I want you to lock the door behind us and put this key back on the hook so that nothing looks amiss," Giles said, handing the key to Joanna. "This is the part I don't want anyone to see, because I don't want anyone to think to check on you two if they see us all leaving from one room. We'll just have to pray that we can all get out and away from this door before anyone comes down the hall."

"It has been fairly quiet in the hall until now, Giles. I've heard very little noise," Joanna said.

"Good, we'll listen at the door and hope for the best." He tried not to sound as grim as he felt. If he had to, he would fight to the death to save them all, but he had few illusions about what would happen if a general alarm was sounded. This was their only hope.

They rolled up the small rug and Joanna and the children lifted it between them. Giles was relieved to see that Emma seemed able to manage her end with Tom.

"Let Tom take the lead, and Will and I will be right behind you. Tom, take us down the back stairs and back hall. We will pray for a door to the mews."

Giles and Will hoisted the chest between them. They stood at the door, listening, but heard nothing. Carefully, quietly, Giles eased the door open with one hand and put his head out. The hallway was empty. He stepped out with Will and they waited while Joanna and the children brought the carpet out. Joanna put down her end and fumbled with the lock on the door. When she finally heard the tumblers fall, she placed the key on the hook outside the door and picked up her end of the rug. Giles nodded at her to go forward, and she and the children started silently down the hall, Tom in the lead.

By Giles's mental calculations, they were now on the third floor, but he did not know whether this house, like many in London, had a rear entrance that was one floor down from the one at the front. In all likelihood it was so, because he remembered coming up a flight of steps to get to the front door. Praying that Tom could lead them to the right place, he followed behind, his eyes burning into Joanna's back.

The back stairs were dark, lit only at intervals with lamps mounted on the landings. They plodded slowly down, looking, he hoped, like put-upon servants and workmen. Between the first and second floors, a young maid passed them, carrying a tray with a cloth over it, a meal of some sort. Noting how they were burdened, she stepped aside and let them all pass. Looking back over his shoulder, Giles was relieved to see that she continued on her way without so much as a shrug of acknowledgment in their direction.

Tom reached the first-floor landing and kept going. Now they would be heading into the servants' regions, the area of the house populated only by those they were impersonating. Giles had no way of knowing where Teddy and Bobby and the other henchmen were, but if his experience upstairs was any example, they stayed close to the front door and the mistress of this establishment, to be at her beck and call. Of course, there was always the grim possibility that one or more of them was having a meal now, and that would likely be down here in the servants' dining hall or the kitchen. Giles tried to reckon what time it might be. In a normal household it would be past luncheon, but who could say what sort of schedule was kept in this palace of evil? He could smell food cooking or cooked, but large kitchens smelled of food at all times, the odors lingering many hours after the meal had been eaten and cleaned away.

They passed two more maids, scullery by the looks of them, who paid no mind to the procession other than to step to one side as it passed, not breaking so much as a word in their conversation to look up.

Now they were on the bottom floor and the hallway stretched on into darkness ahead. Doors on either side of the hallway were standing open. On the left they passed what appeared, from the side glance Giles gave, to be the kitchen. There were several women in it, busy at their tasks. No one looked up, as far as he could tell. The scullery area was empty, but piled high with dishes and pans to be washed. Good. Perhaps that meant the midday meal had been taken.

Looking ahead, he could still see no signs of a door that might lead outside. The hallway ended just up ahead, and with a sinking heart, Giles saw that there was no door at the end, merely a brick wall with a bench in front of it.

He was smelling soap now, and boiling laundry. Tom stopped at the last door and looked back at Giles. Confusion and fear were plain on the child's face.

"There you are, you worthless little idiot!" came a voice screeching from inside the room. Tom disappeared abruptly as if he'd been plucked up. Emma staggered under the weight of the front end of the carpet and lost her grip.

"Wot're you doin' with that carpet, may I ask? No one told me nothin' about no carpet." The voice was full of exasperation. Giles saw Joanna swallow. He and Will moved up behind her but he could not see into the room.

"We're takin' it out to be cleaned in the back. One of the girls sicked up all over it and it stinks," Joanna said. Giles marveled at her coolness. He and Will could take care of a few people if they had to, but it appeared this hallway had led them down a blind alley, not a good defensible position.

"Well, take it out then. Don't unroll it in 'ere. I put up with enough smells as it is."

Joanna hesitated. Giles knew what her problem was. Where was "out"?

"Well, wot're you waitin' for? I'm not 'elpin' you none, that's for certain," came the voice.

"Which way is the door?" came Joanna's voice with a tremble in it that Giles hoped would pass unnoticed.

There was a pause from inside. Then the woman's voice came again. "Are you new 'ere? I 'aven't seen you before, 'ave I?" Was there suspicion now in her voice or were Giles's nerves putting it there?

"Started this mornin', ma'am," said Joanna, her voice more steady. "That's why I get stuck with the puke, I suppose."

"Oh, don't think it gets any better than this, my girl," the woman cackled. "Your troubles are just beginnin'. Git on with you now, the door is right through 'ere, so's I can get my wet wash out to 'ang."

Giles could see Joanna's sigh of relief.

"If you please, ma'am," Joanna said, her voice uncertain again. "Can the boy bring out a bucket of suds and a brush?" Bless the resourcefulness of his bride, thought Giles. She would get Tom back for them, a problem that Giles had been dealing with since the woman had grabbed the boy.

"All right, but I need 'im back 'ere in a 'urry. These wet sheets are 'eavy to lift and I need strong young legs to do the carryin.' "

Joanna started forward into the laundry room. Throwing up a quick prayer, Giles stepped after her with Will on the back end of the chest.

"Now wot, for the love of . . . wot'll you be doin', if I may be permitted to ask?" The woman stood over a large steaming washtub. Giles could see that her reddened arms were covered with soap well past her bare elbows.

Joanna cast a nonchalant glance over her shoulder at Giles and Will. "The girl chucked all over the chest, too. I wiped it up but it's marred the finish. We was told to get it out and clean it up better."

"Well, go on then, the lot of you," retorted the woman, bending back down to the large tub. "You, boy, there's a bucket and a brush in the corner. Fill it from the kettle and mind you don't burn yourself." She paused, eyeing him thoughtfully. "One of you should 'elp the tyke," she went on. " 'E's just an idiot, after all, and 'e's no good to me all blistered."

Joanna set down her end of the rug and went over to fill the bucket for Tom, blessing the woman's selfish championship of the boy and cursing the delay. She went as slowly as she could force herself to go, aware that servants rarely hurried unless they were being overseen by their superiors. She found some chips of soap and added a few to the boiling water they had absolutely no use for.

"All right, be careful with this now," Joanna said, hating herself for the cool tone she forced herself to use to the child. Tom took the bucket, his eyes appropriately vacant. Joanna was surprised at what a fine little charlatan he was turning out to be.

Giles and Will had moved forward with their burden to the door in the back wall. Giles slid the bolt back and held the door open while Joanna and Emma struggled through with the carpet, and Tom followed behind with the heavy bucket. Giles had time to note that the one window that looked out the back was filmed over with years of soap grease. Well, at least this woman would not be able to see where they went after the door was shut behind them.

And then they were all through, Will pulling the door closed.

They stood for a moment, Giles looking about. He had not seen the back of the house before, so he had to do some guessing as to the layout. There were the stables across the small yard. There were several sheds and outbuildings against the high wall which ran all around. There was a gate, which stood open, and a driveway leading from the stables into an alleyway.

"Follow me and keep your faces down," Giles said, as low as he could and still be heard.

He and Will moved toward the stables. His heart was hammering in his chest. Their story could plausibly get them as far as the back, but there would be no way to explain them all climbing into a carriage and trotting merrily off.

They made it across the small yard without seeing anyone and disappeared into the dark of the stables. Giles set down the chest, signaling for Joanna and the children to put the carpet down as well. Peering back at the house, he noted that while the draperies on all the upper-story windows were closed, some on the first floor were open. They could have been seen from the house. Giles signaled for Joanna to take the children and step back behind the large stable door.

Casting a quick look about him, his eye fell on his carriage. Thank God it hadn't been moved. He and Will walked toward it slowly.

"Wot do you want 'ere?" came a surly voice from the dark. A figure emerged from the back, a very large man with a scarred face and an ear that looked like a cauliflower. Out of the corner of his eye, Giles could see no sign of Joanna and the children, but who knew how long the man had been standing there watching?

"We've been sent by his lordship to take this coach," said Giles. The man either bought the story or he would regain consciousness sometime this afternoon with a very bad headache and a lump on the head.

The man was silent for a moment, as if weighing these words. "Where're you takin' it?" came his unexpected response.

"We're not allowed to say." Giles was deliberately laconic. It seemed unlikely that Lord Beeson would want this man to know where the carriage was being sent.

"All right." The man stepped back and gestured to the carriage. "Bobby said it was to be kept ready to go, and it is." The man seemed proud that he had followed his orders correctly. Giles began to wonder whether he was simple, but did not waste any time thinking about it.

Giles cast a glance back to the door, behind which he knew Joanna stood with the children. The man had done nothing to indicate he knew there were others in the stable.

Shrugging with feigned indifference, Giles started forward, motioning for Will to follow. As Will moved, apparently the chest and carpet became visible to the man.

"Wot's that stuff doin' there?" he asked, suspicion clear in his voice.

Now it was clear he suspected them of stealing.

"We were told to bring that chest and carpet out here to be picked up by the junk man," said Giles in what he dearly hoped was a reasonably disinterested tone of voice. "We left it inside so it doesn't get rained on, because we don't know when they'll come for it."

Now he had the man's attention. He could almost see the calculations working through the slow brain as the eyes narrowed and the expression became thoughtful. Then a slow smile spread across the man's ugly face.

"Aye, leave 'em 'ere," the man said. "I'll move 'em back if it starts to rain."

Giles shrugged. Unless he missed his guess, Lord Beeson was going to be short one Oriental carpet and one chest of drawers in a matter of hours.

"Let's go," Giles said to Will as they continued on to the carriage. Giles prayed that the man would leave them so that Joanna and the children could come out of hiding, and considered their options in case he did not.

The carriage stood facing the wide door, so it would be a simple matter to drive it from the stables. He and Will climbed to the box. The man showed no signs of moving, staring with a rather vacant, covetous expression at the carpet and chest, too close to where Joanna and the children hid behind the door for Giles's comfort.

Giles made a great show of fiddling with the reins, but the man just stood there. Finally, with a great sigh of exasperation, Giles chucked the horses forward. They ambled pleasantly toward the door, posting-house nags that they were. Just as the carriage came abreast of the door to the stable, Giles brought it to a halt. "Get them in," he hissed under his breath to Will, who gave the slightest of nods.

"One of 'em's pullin' wrong," said Giles, in a loud aggravated tone. He leaped from the box and moved quickly to the front horse away from the side where he hoped Joanna and the children could climb in unnoticed.

He and the man reached the horse's head at the same time.

"Check the bit. It may be her mouth is tender, but we've no time to delay. Of course, it could be her shoe. But if it is, you'll have to get us a different horse, because we can't be hangin' around here all evening," Giles nattered on, the corner of his eye watching the faint crack of light through the window flap as the far carriage door opened.

"There's nothin' wrong with the bit," the man said, inspecting it.

"Well, check the shoe then," said Giles. He bent over, seemingly to adjust the way his breeches cuffed his knee, watching surreptitiously as shadows crossed the crack of light inside the carriage. The carriage rocked slightly, and Giles held his breath, praying that the man, bent as he was over the horse's hoof, would not notice. After a moment, the crack of light closed up, and all was darkness inside the carriage again.

"There's nothin' wrong with the shoe, neither," said the man, who stood and dusted off his hands as if that was the end of it. Just then Will materialized at Giles's elbow.

"Well, let's just go, then," said Will gruffly with a look that spoke of success.

"All right, climb up," responded Giles, pulling himself to the box. Will climbed up beside him and took the reins.

"They're in," Will whispered below his breath, chucking the reins over the horses' backs. They started to move forward and Giles started to breathe again, not certain he had taken a breath since he had first seen Joanna in this place.

Painfully slowly, the horses moved forward. The

sun moved faster, Giles thought. Glaciers were reckless and precipitous. These horses were sluggish. Just as he thought he would go mad, Giles saw the high wall of the property slip past them. They were in the alleyway and so far there was no pursuit.

"Turn to the left as we reach the street," said Giles to Will. "When we get away a few blocks, stop and I'll get in the carriage. Good work in the stables, Will. I'm surprised that fellow didn't notice anything."

"He was too set on filchin' that chest and carpet to care what we did, Sir Giles," replied Will, his mind on the narrow turn. "By the way," he continued as the turn was safely negotiated. "I took the liberty of filchin' the ropes from the chest myself, in case we've got more trouble comin'."

"Good man, because we are not clear yet," responded Giles. "Some of the first-floor windows were undraped and open. Anyone could have looked out and seen us, and some might know this carriage was not supposed to be leaving yet." Giles leaned over the side of the carriage and looked behind him. He could see no one. They were now on the small side street. Not too much further on, the street gave onto the main boulevard that the house fronted. "When we get to the boulevard, turn right, away from the house, so we don't have to pass in front of it. Once we are on the boulevard it will be harder for anyone to assault us in broad daylight on a busy street."

The attack came without warning. Giles only had time to note that it was Teddy coming at him before the man had hoisted himself in one fluid movement onto the box. He carried a riding crop in one hand and a large pistol in the other. A shout from Will caused Giles to look around, in time to see Bobby hurling himself at Will.

Giles swung back around toward Teddy, his fist coming up in reflex. Teddy had lifted the riding crop and was bringing it down at Giles's face. Like lightning, Giles reached out, catching the crop in his fist, but sustaining the crushing weight of the blow against his shoulder. For an instant they hung suspended, then, finding the strength from he knew not where, Giles heaved Teddy back. At that moment, Will, in lifting his hands to ward off a blow from Bobby, jerked wildly on the reins. Both horses reared, whinnying, throwing the still-moving carriage off balance. His purchase slipping, Teddy made a wild grab at Giles's arm, dropping the pistol as he did so. Teddy fell backwards, bringing Giles down on top of him. They landed on the rough cobblestones with Giles's full weight against Teddy's chest. Giles could hear the wind being knocked out of the man, and he knew he had only a matter of seconds to get the upper hand. He jammed his fist into his assailant's stomach, just as the man struggled to draw in a breath. Giles slammed another blow to his jaw, while Teddy brought his knee up hard into Giles's gut. Giles doubled over from the pain, but brought his arm hard against Teddy's throat, throwing his whole weight against it. He could feel the man struggle beneath him, but his struggles became feebler as his face turned purple. At last his eyes dimmed and he went still. Giles sat up, whipping his neckcloth from the pocket where he had stuffed it earlier. Swiftly, he tied Teddy's hands tightly together, noting that the man's chest rose and fell slightly. Good. He didn't want him dead. Not that easily.

Will had dropped the reins and the horses had quieted and halted, the carriage righting itself. Giles could hear shouts from Will, above on the box. At least the man was still alive. As Giles stood, willing his muscles to hold him up, the door to the carriage opened and Joanna all but tumbled out, her face ashen.

"Giles!" she screamed. "What is it?"

Giles reached down and picked up the pistol from the ground where it had fallen. He tossed it to Joanna. "Take this and get back inside," he shouted. "Toss me one of the ropes Will put in because my neckcloth won't hold this one long if he wakes up. There's one more up there fighting Will and I don't know if they alerted anyone else at the house. If anyone but me or Will opens that carriage door, shoot him!"

Joanna nodded, and pulled herself back into the carriage. A second later the door opened and she handed out a rope.

Giles made quick work of securing Teddy, hands and feet, and then he ran around the back of the carriage, noting that no one seemed to have come out into the street to see what the commotion was all about. When he reached Will's side he could see that his man was taking the worst end of a bad beating. Will's head was lolling to one side and his nose was bleeding copiously again. Bobby had drawn back his fist to land one more, killing blow to Will's head. In an instant, Giles was upon him, grabbing at both of his legs from below and twisting sharply. As he had hoped, Bobby was thrown off balance. The last blow never landed. The man fell backwards, and Giles had only enough time to step to one side as the heavyset man hurtled down, smashing on his side against the cobblestones.

As Giles leaned down to pull him up, Bobby's leg shot up, trying to aim a kick at Giles's groin. Giles grabbed the man's foot and twisted it hard, causing him to cry out and turn his body to lessen the pain. Now Bobby lay face down and Giles dropped to sit on his back, still holding the man's foot twisted at an unnatural angle.

A shadow fell over him and Giles looked up, startled, fearing reinforcements from the house. Instead, he looked into the calm eyes of Tom who held the other length of rope in his hand which he proffered silently to Giles.

"Bless you again, boy," said Giles, grabbing the rope and tying the man's arms behind him. "I don't know what I would have done next. I'm about done for, you know."

Tom smiled, and waited while Giles made short work of it.

Giles struggled to his feet, placing his hand on Tom's head. "Get back into the carriage and take care of your Aunt Joanna, please, Tom. I've one more of these miscreants to deal with and I'm sure she's frightened to death." He hobbled a bit when he walked and was quite sure he'd be crippled for days.

"Auntie is watching him," said Tom simply, taking Giles's arm as if he'd help him walk.

"Oh, God!" Giles bolted around the carriage, only to run smack into Joanna who was coming around the other way, the pistol held out before her as if it were a cross in front of a vampire.

"Giles!" she screamed, jerking the pistol to one side as he knocked into her. "I might have shot you!"

"I thought I told you to stay inside the carriage!" he thundered, grabbing her arm and propelling her back toward the carriage door. "That man is still alive and he is not above figuring out how to knock you down, even tied up!"

"No, he couldn't. He was quite unconscious still."

Giles just stared at her, then, recovering himself, walked over to where Teddy lay, breathing shallowly but still unconscious. Giles turned a wry smile on Joanna. "I am grateful that you wanted to help, my darling, but the next time we are attacked by cutthroats, I would appreciate it if you'd just let me handle it." He gave up and threw his arms around her, pulling her close and burying his face in her hair which had come loose from its mobcap.

"I couldn't let them have you again," he murmured against her neck. "Now," he said, pulling away, "back in with you this instant. I'm going to heave these two up onto the box with me. I'll put Will down with you if I can move him. We're headed straight for my solicitors' office. Pray that these lowlifes did not alert anyone else in the house before they ran after us. I think someone would have been here by now if they had. One of them must have seen the carriage leaving from one of the windows." Gently he disengaged the pistol from her grasp and, tucking the weapon into his waistband, he led her to the door of the carriage. Tom was there ahead of them, climbing in and holding the door open for Joanna who climbed in.

"You'll call us if you need help, or if anyone comes, won't you?" she asked, anxiety shading her eyes.

"Well, you'll know if anyone comes, because all hell will break loose again. But, yes, I'll let you know if I need you," he said, touching her cheek softly and slamming the door shut behind her. He would not, of course, but better to get her back in than stand around discussing it.

Climbing up onto the box, Giles found that Will was barely conscious. His nose had stopped bleeding and he had to be helped, half-carried down from the box. Giles's shoulder screamed with the effort, and he was vaguely aware that this was the same shoulder he'd laid open to the bone only a few months ago. Well, he had too far to go this day to worry about it now.

He got Will into the carriage, Joanna pulling as hard as he pushed. She clucked and exclaimed over all the blood and was busy ripping up her cotton petticoat when he closed the door again.

Lifting Teddy and Bobby, dead weights both of them, felt as if it might very nearly be the death of him. Only the thought of what the courts would do to Lord Beeson and his establishment, once these men gave their confessions, got them heaved up onto the box.

Giles took the reins into his hands and clucked the skittish horses forward. The whole attack could not have taken as much as five minutes, yet it seemed a lifetime since they had driven through the gates of hell. It also seemed it would be a long, painful drive to the solicitors' office near Lincoln's Inn. Giles hunched forward, favoring his shoulder as best he could, and prayed that he would not lose consciousness.

Chapter Nineteen

If Messrs. Lynch and Lowe found anything unusual or distasteful about all the blood, or the peculiar attire, or the presence of two semiconscious thugs deposited in one of their smaller offices, by not so much as the lift of an eyebrow between them did they allow such thoughts to be made known.

It had, however, taken Sir Giles Chapman a moment or two to talk his way past the chief clerk to secure the august presence of the two senior solicitors. Now they sat arrayed about the large, deeply polished mahogany table. Water and cloths had been fetched to mop up the blood, but that had only marginally improved the group's appearance as a whole. A surgeon was on the way to see about Will's face, which was purple and swollen, and Giles's shoulder, which now seemed virtually useless and sounded like dice rattling in a cup when he tried to move it.

"Bringing them all to justice is of paramount importance, of course, Mr. Lynch," Giles said, "but I would prefer to leave Lady Chapman and the children out of it completely. Were it known that they were in such a place for even a short period, it would make for social difficulties."

"Indeed, Sir Giles," murmured Mr. Lowe, his soothing, deep tones polished to perfection over the years, "should you wish Miss Emma to have a Season, it would present great awkwardness, even a number of years hence. Society is so terribly unforgiving, and memories are long."

"I do believe we can proceed as you suggest, Sir Giles," said Mr. Lynch in a lighter, mellifluous voice. He seemed the happier of the two, and Giles imagined that, in the partnership, Mr. Lynch passed about the good news while Mr. Lowe was reserved for those more funereal bits of legal result. "We do have those two most dreadful specimens of humanity, or lack thereof, trussed up in the next room. What you have described, kidnapping, attempted murder, and forced—er, yes, well, these are hanging offenses. The courts would lose no time in stretching their necks. But if they will give evidence for the Crown, and implicate those who are the real backers of the scheme"—he gave a shudder of distaste—"perhaps the courts could be persuaded to commute their sentences to some sort of lifetime of penal servitude."

"Mr. Lynch, I must implore you to send the constabulary right away to that—establishment," cried Joanna. "I cannot bear the thought of what will happen to those Irish girls tonight. Why, some were no older than Emma. It is deplorable!" She held Emma on her lap. The child had not loosened her grip on her since they had first gotten into the carriage.

"Indeed, Lady Chapman, we understand," said Mr. Lowe—it seemed to Joanna that when one was addressed the other answered. "We did not wish to distress you further by discussing it, but we have dispatched word to the chief superintendent. You must understand that these things must be done at the proper levels. Otherwise we will run into the very corruption that permits these sorts of places to thrive in the first place, and we do not wish any of these people to be given warning. I must say, Sir Giles," he went on, "there will be quite an uproar over Lord Beeson's involvement. I may tell you that he is not held in the highest esteem by most of society. His, er, proclivities"—he cast an abashed look at Joanna—"are known to some and not overlooked. But to have involved himself as an owner of one of these sorts of places. It will simply ruin him."

"I want him hanged, not ruined, Mr. Lowe," growled Giles. "A man like that slithers across the face of this earth on his belly. He has ruined innocents without qualm and had every intention of doing the same to my wife and my niece. In addition, he was planning to kill Will and myself. I don't give a damn whether the ladies cut him at soirees. I want him hanged."

"It may come to that, Sir Giles, but he will have to be tried in the House of Lords and we have no way of predicting the outcome. Nevertheless, I can assure you that there will be nothing left of his name or his fortune when this is done. If he is not hanged, he will be penniless and no doubt stripped of his title."

There was a soft knock at the door and a rather

timid looking clerk entered when bid to do so.

"If you please, Mr. Lowe, there's a Chief Superintendent Wicker here to see you, and Mrs. Oldham has brought the dresses you asked for."

"Thank you, Carstairs. Show Superintendent Wicker into my office. Lady Chapman, Mrs. Oldham is the proprietress of a small dress shop nearby, catering to the merchant class. She will have brought a few ready made items for you and Miss Emma to wear until more suitable clothing can be obtained. Would you care to remain here and be fitted while we speak to the superintendent?"

"I want to see the superintendent, too," said Joanna, her tone sharp. "I want to assure myself there won't be any of this corruption you've been talking about. I'll not stand for all of this to be hidden tidily because they've paid off the constables, not if I have to go to the papers about it myself!"

"Oh, dear me, that would never do," murmured Mr. Lynch. "You may assure yourself, my dear, that the corruption is at much lower levels and isn't as bad as all that. And we really would prefer that you and the children not meet the superintendent, isn't that right, Sir Giles?" He turned his helpless eyes on Giles. The thoughts of the firm of Lynch and Lowe featured prominently in the next issue of the *Gazette* in connection with a whorehouse for virgins now made him pine for a cup of tea.

"Stay here with the children, my love," whispered Giles, leaning over to speak into her ear. "I will tell everything I need to tell, and it will be enough to bring them all to justice." He squeezed her hand, then winced as the pain of the small movement tore through his shoulder.

"All right, Giles," Joanna said, mutiny in her eyes. "But only because of Emma. If you think I care what a bunch of overdone old harridans think of me . . ."

He chuckled and touched her cheek. He stood with difficulty and walked slowly from the room, followed by a nearly somnambulant Will and Messrs. Lynch and Lowe.

For a moment the room was silent, then a small lady bustled in carrying several boxes. Joanna and the children busied themselves selecting a few things that fit, including shoes. Mrs. Oldham made one or two attempts to inquire as to their singular attire, but Joanna, very nicely, led the conversation elsewhere. It did not appear that the woman even knew their names. So much the better. Scandal could percolate from any source, and the fewer who knew, the better.

It did feel good to be decently gowned again and freshened up. Joanna had sponged off the children and herself with the fresh water that had been brought in. They now looked like a highly respectable middle-class family, and if Joanna's shoes pinched a bit, she was not going to complain about it.

They were no sooner presentable than a knock on the door admitted the gentlemen again. Giles gave her a reassuring smile.

"The house will be raided this evening, Joanna," he said, taking her arm. "Whoever is there, peers on down, will be taken in. The superintendent has taken my evidence, and it will be enough without involving you and the children at all. And Bobby and Teddy are on their miserable way to the station now. I do not think they will be out of leg irons ever again."

Joanna smiled in return. Now that it was done, she was relieved that she and the children would not be dragged through the court system as the ones who had spent hours as prisoners inside a brothel.

"What about Hawton?" Joanna asked, her face clouding again.

"He is likely to still be there tonight. If not, a warrant for his arrest will issue. Don't worry about Hawton, my love. He will not bedevil you again."

She did not ask about Eleanor. She had noted that throughout all of the explanation to the solicitors, Giles had carefully avoided mentioning his stepsister's involvement. She knew something would have to be done about the madwoman, but perhaps Giles was right in keeping that part of it in the family. Eleanor had her own devils to face now, from within and without.

A few hours later, Joanna lay back in a steaming tub, soaking away the perfumes and oils from the brothel. Emma had been bathed, Joanna scrubbing as hard as she dared at the last traces of kohl about the girl's eyes. Tom, too, had been forced into the tub, never one of his better moments. Now the children lay sound asleep, tucked up in the next room, an elegant little bedroom in the small but exquisite townhouse Messrs. Lynch and Lowe had magically procured on such short notice. A rather imperious cook had come with the establishment, and Joanna and Giles had enjoyed a sumptuous meal, just the two of them, staring into one another's eyes so much that it was difficult to remember to eat. They would be here for a few days only, long enough for Giles to wrap up the legal matters and see to a few business matters as well, since he was here.

The door opened softly behind her. Startled, she turned, only to meet the dancing brown eyes of her handsome husband.

"I came to see if Madame wished her back to be scrubbed," said Giles, his tone dripping with haughtiness.

"Oh, Giles wasn't she just awful?" Joanna giggled. "Standing there asking if there'd be anything else and looking at my ready-made gown as if she knew quality when she saw it and this wasn't quality. I thought the way she said 'madame,' she meant to imply 'you offal.' "

"I believe she did, my dear. You haven't met snobbery until you've dealt with London servants. They'll size you up and toss you out on your ear in the space of a heartbeat."

"Well, I've been judged and found wanting, I suppose. Perhaps it's a good thing we changed at the solicitors' office and didn't wait until we got here. She might have had a seizure."

"Oh, never fear that Lynch and Lowe would have allowed any of us out of the front door looking the way we did. As it is, I'm sure they'll have some explaining to do in Lincoln's Inn." He had picked up a soft bath sponge and was rubbing it gently down her back.

"Not that you and Will looked any better, mind you," Joanna mused. She was drowsy with the heat of the water, but his touch felt so soothing. "I wonder whether the woman will come downstairs at all tomorrow. Perhaps she will, if only to give notice."

"Cook jobs are not that easy to come by, and she knows we are here only for a few days. If she annoys you, I'll have someone else come in." The sponge dipped lower.

"Oh, heavens, I don't care how offended she is. It'll give her something to be in a nice snit about. And the food was delicious."

"Madame's back is clean. Shall I wash Madame's front?" Without waiting for Madame's permission, he slipped the sponge around to the front of her. Joanna smiled and leaned back. She could feel the heat of his chest against her hair. The sponge had disappeared. His warm, wet hands rubbed soap gently into her skin, pausing over her slippery, taut breasts. His lips were in her hair, working their way down to her neck. His hands slipped lower, sliding across her belly, then lower still, finding the sweet place that so craved his touch. Joanna arched her back, pushing herself against him. His fingers played below the water and the water felt like fire.

"Madame is as clean as she needs to be just now," he whispered, nibbling her neck. "Shall I dry you off?"

In answer, she stood slowly. He could not take his eyes off of her, her body wet and gleaming pink in the lamplight. He seized the large square towel and wrapped her in it, rubbing her briskly, then propelled her toward the bedroom.

Laying her gently on the bed, he unwrapped the towel. He stared at her while he divested himself of his clothes. Then, naked, he stood before her, and it was she who stared at his hard, sculpted body.

He lowered himself beside her and pulled her to him. The heat flared between them. His hands roamed while his lips sought hers in fierce possession. Joanna felt the fire building as his tongue played gently against hers. Forsaking her mouth, he let his lips slide along her throat, down, down to where he seized her nipple, circling it with his tongue, causing her to gasp out his name and arch herself closer against the length of him, his desire for her plain and hot and hard.

Joanna heard a moan deep in his throat as she put her arms around him, stroking his back softly, then lowering her hands to his taut buttocks, pulling him tightly to her where she badly needed the pressure of his swollen shaft.

Then his hands, too, moved lower, gently trailing along the soft pink and white of her, coming to rest at last against the secret place. She cried out as his fingers found the spot and she arched against him again and again. Then abruptly his fingers were gone as he stretched himself on top of her and she felt the hard bulge of him. With a cry he buried himself deep, then lay still for a moment. Joanna could feel their two hearts pounding, and his breathing was ragged in her ear. Slowly, rhythmically, he began to move. She could feel the slippery hard heat of him and matched his rhythm, thrusting herself up to meet his thrusts.

Again his lips found hers as his tongue plundered her mouth, matching the rhythm below. His hands were around her, hard against her buttocks as he pulled her tightly to him with every thrust. Joanna could hardly breathe as the heat built within her, until with a sobbing cry she shuddered against him. For a moment he let her finish, then he, too, cried out and thrust forward, spilling himself hard within her slippery heat.

They lay quiet for a moment, breathing in jagged gasps. Giles pulled his weight off of her, but holding her tightly, rolled her with him, nestling her in the cradle of his arms.

"I don't think I will ever let you out of my sight again," he whispered in her hair.

"That's good," came her whispered reply, "because I hadn't intended on letting you out of my sight ever again." His lips trailed along the back of her neck, sending a delicious shudder through her.

They made sweet love again before they slept, tangled in each other's arms all night long.

It was a week before Giles and Joanna and the children were able to get away. The coach had needed repair, and Giles had taken the opportunity to purchase a rather splendid team to draw it. Will had knitted up nicely and was judged fit to be the coachman.

In the meanwhile, Giles took Joanna to see Mr. Garrick and Peg Woffington in *The Merry Wives of Windsor* at Drury Lane and insisted on buying her more gowns than she thought she could use in a lifetime, and of such quality that Cook lost her sneer and redoubled her awesome culinary efforts.

But they were both ready to leave at week's end. It was a strain keeping to themselves in the face of the riotous scandal that rocked London in the wake of the raid at what became known as "The Beeson Establishment." It was astonishing how many euphemisms the newspapers could come up with, yet still make it perfectly clear what had been going on. The Irish girls had been freed, apparently unharmed, as well as several other young girls who had been there already. Of Joanna and the children the papers made no mention, and Sir Giles was referred to only as "the Northern knight who had, nobly and at great risk to himself, saved the Irish girls from a fate worse than death." Hawton had been arrested in the raid and languished in prison. Lord Beeson had managed to post bail, but he was in seclusion and public sentiment was running high against him.

Sir Giles and Joanna made a leisurely trip north with the children, in sharp contrast to the trip south, stopping at the better inns and enjoying decent meals and soft beds.

All too soon, it seemed, the dark outlines of Queen's Hall appeared on the horizon. Joanna was annoyed with herself. She had felt a sense of unease building in her since they had started out this morning and now it had settled like a black weight against her chest.

This was her home, for heaven's sake! She should be happy to see it, glad of the smell of the sea and the purpling beauty of the fells to the east. And she was, of course.

Except that Eleanor was still here, this bitter, twisted woman who hated so wildly in her madness.

"She will not be down to greet us, my dear," said Giles softly.

Joanna looked at him, startled and guilty that her thoughts had been so transparent. By tacit agreement, they had not discussed Eleanor, not after Joanna had told him of his stepsister's part in the abduction. Now she could see that his eyes were shadowed. The children napped on the seat across from them.

"I sent word to the house last week that Eleanor

should be detained in her room. I have not been able to bring myself to report her to the authorities. I may yet do so. But she is mad, I know that. And I am afraid that her next home must be an asylum. She cannot be permitted to go on the way she is. She is too hungry and unscrupulous."

"It's all right," said Joanna softly. She had taken his hand and held it now tightly to her chest, as if she could draw courage from his fingers. "I agree with you. An asylum is a dreadful place, but we have no way of knowing what sort of evil she would get up to if we left her free to do so. There seem to be no depths to her. Papa always said there was good in everyone, but I think Eleanor would have been his one defeat."

"Well, I will see her and make all the arrangements. I want you to promise me that you and the children will stay as far away from her as you can get. Don't even take them to the side of the house that her windows face, until I can have her removed. I wouldn't put it past her to hurl something heavy down on you, if she had the chance."

Joanna gave a shudder at his words. They had driven up to the great front entrance of Queen's Hall. Why did it look so unwelcoming?

The carriage slowed to a stop and the door was opened. Charles stood outside. "Welcome home, sir, Lady Chapman," he said, but his smile was weak, and disappeared without a trace at the end of his words.

Joanna alighted with Giles and the children right behind her. Charles's eyes were everywhere but on her own. Without another word he closed the carriage door behind them and turned his attention to the baggage. Emma and Tom ran happily up the front steps. Well, let's hope there are no dark memories for them, Joanna thought, following behind them. Somehow, even the sound of their laughter did nothing to alleviate the feeling of gloom that hung over this place. Something was not right.

The front door swung open. Joanna peered up the steps but could see no one behind the door. The hallway was dark, and she made a mental note to remind Mrs. Davies that the new rules of the house allowed for a great deal of light. She glanced at Giles and saw that his jaw was tight, his mouth a grim line. He had closed his fingers about her arm, his hold almost too tight, a protective grip that did nothing to soothe her nerves.

As they stepped into the house, they could see Annie ushering the children rather hurriedly upstairs. Emma's lively chatter, telling Annie all about the wonderful sights of London, struck a discordant note in the grim silence.

Joanna looked about and saw Mrs. Davies standing by the door. The woman's face was positively gray.

"So happy to see you home safely, Lady Chapman," Mrs. Davies murmured. "And you too, Sir Giles. Thank heaven you're home." The woman's voice faltered.

"What the devil is going on around here?" Giles's voice thundered in the cavernous dark.

Seemingly from nowhere, Jims materialized. "Sir Giles, we must speak to you right away," he said. "It's about Lady Eleanor."

Joanna could not help the sharp intake of breath that gave her away. Giles's hand tightened around her arm.

"Where is my stepsister?" he asked in cold, measured tones.

"Perhaps if we could step into the library, Sir Giles," said Mrs. Davies, sounding tentative. "I've some brandy waiting to warm you."

"Yes, Giles, let's go into the library," Joanna intervened quickly, seeing that he looked about ready to explode. Whatever had happened, she did not want the children to overhear any unpleasantness regarding their Aunt Eleanor. There were too many ugly memories. . . .

Without another word, Giles led her into the library. Joanna seated herself while Mrs. Davies bustled unnecessarily with the brandy. Giles stood by Joanna, hands clasped behind his back as if he were trying to keep from strangling someone. Jims looked as if he'd never been in a library in his entire life, and perhaps that was so.

"Well?" was all Giles said.

"We did as you requested, Sir Giles," Jims said, clearing his throat. "We locked Lady Eleanor's door. We showed her your letter, and we only opened the door to bring in food. The last time we brought her her supper—that would be three nights ago—well, she was hidin' behind the door. She smashed young Bessie on the head with one of them statues of hers. Bessie ain't been quite right since. . . . "

Joanna gasped in frustration. The poor girl could be badly hurt if she'd been hit with one of those heavy figures.

"Go on," said Giles. Joanna could see that his hands were fists behind his back.

"Well, Lady Eleanor, she ran out then, but it was just good luck that I was comin' up the hallway then to have a look at the lock on her door. Mrs.

388

Davies had been concerned that it was not terribly strong and that . . ."

"Yes, yes, man, get on with it," pressed Giles. Joanna could appreciate his impatience. She herself was on pins and needles. If the woman had bolted, they wouldn't know a moment's peace until she was found again.

"Well, I didn't hurt her, I swear I didn't, sir, you must believe me," Jims went on. He looked as if he were about to cry.

"Of course not, man. I know you'd never hurt her deliberately. You were doing as I had bade you to do, after all."

Giles's speech did nothing to ease Jims's anguish. If anything, the man looked worse than before.

"Well, we put Lady Eleanor back in the room, Sir Giles. She was callin' out for brandy, but Mrs. Davies said there had been a full bottle in there in the mornin' and it must just be a ploy. She got real wild-like, but we was afraid to open the door. She's got plenty of that statuary there in the room with her, and young Bessie was in a real bad way, with her head split open and all. We let her scream . . ." He trailed off.

Mrs. Davies looked up from the handkerchief she held to her face and Joanna could see that she was crying softly. "Sir Giles," the woman said, her voice breaking, "please believe me when I say we did not mean for this to happen. We had no idea she would attempt such a thing. No idea . . ." She broke off, too choked up to speak.

"Please tell me what happened then, Jims," said Giles, his voice as gentle as he could make it.

"Well, after a while it grew quiet. We couldn't hear her anymore. We figured she'd got tired and gone to bed. We thought she'd be more—herself in the mornin.' " He stopped. He looked at Mrs. Davies. She nodded to him. Drawing in a deep breath, he said, "We were closin' things up for the night. It was late. Me and Mrs. Davies were havin' our little drop before bed. That's when we heard the scream, bloodcurdlin', it was. Sent me cold all over. It came from outside, from high up-like. I got one of your guns and went outside. That's when I found her, on the stones below her window."

There was a long pause. Joanna could hear her heart thundering in her chest.

"Was she dead?" Giles asked finally, his voice oddly flat.

"Indeed, sir. No one could have survived such a fall. I went upstairs later and found that she had opened up her window. I believe she climbed out on the narrow ledge. Perhaps she was plannin' to get in by another window further down, but she was wearin' those flimsy little slippers and the ledge would be all dusty and hard to walk on."

"She had been terribly upset, Sir Giles," put in Mrs. Davies. "She had torn her room apart."

"And was there any brandy in the room when you went in, Mrs. Davies?" was Giles's unexpected question.

"No, sir," the woman replied. "Now that you mention it, the decanter was over on its side and it was empty."

"Ah, I see," was all that Giles responded.

"We have our resignations ready for you, Sir Giles, Jims and me. We'll leave tomorrow. We know we should have left immediately, but the house was at sixes and sevens, and we did wish to be able to explain to you that no one else is to blame, just us." She nodded to Jims, who took her hand.

"That's right, sir. We gave the orders that the door was not to be opened again until morning. No one else is at fault."

"Nor are you, Jims," said Giles slowly. Joanna had slipped her hand up to grip his behind his back. His hands were like ice, but he held hers tightly. "I do not accept your resignation, either of you. If anyone is at fault, it is I for having set this responsibility on you." He paused, as if searching for words. "You must understand that my step-sister was ill, very ill. You have an inkling, I believe, that she was engaged in some unpleasant events involving Lady Chapman and the children. You do not, however, know anything near the awful truth." He stopped again and took a deep breath. "And while I would not be so crass as to say that you have done me, or the world, a favor, I will tell you that Lady Eleanor's madness would have led to her immediate confinement in an asylum for the insane. I do believe she would be the first to thank you for offering her a way out."

There was no sound in the room but the ticking of the ornate, cupid-laden clock on the mantel. Joanna stood up, still holding Giles's hand.

"Perhaps Mrs. Davies and I could see about the children and our supper, Giles. You and Jims may have a few more things you want to talk about." With a quick squeeze to her fingers and a smile to Mrs. Davies, she whisked herself out of the room, leaving a grateful Giles looking after her. She knew he had to discuss the more gruesome details, such as what they had done with the body, and he had not wished to bring any of that up with her present.

"I believe we should have that brandy now, Jims," Joanna heard Giles say as she followed Mrs. Davies out.

"Yes, sir, if you please, sir," was Jims's grateful reply. She shut the door quietly.

It was late before they climbed into the big, comfortable bed in Giles's room. They had sat long over supper, Giles telling Joanna things about Eleanor, things she had done to him, things he had never told another living soul, and about Violet. It seemed that having broken the seal, the words kept coming. Joanna let him talk, knowing that like the lancing of a bad boil, the putrid ooze could be washed away. It was shocking to her, knowing now what she did, that he had ever considered remarrying, a great leap of faith for him. That he had survived in such a morally bankrupt setting so long spoke of his character and goodness.

It would be long before the demons were excised, long before the defiling presence was washed clean from this house. But as he closed his arms about her in the big, wide bed, Joanna smiled, turning to him in the dark. They were well on the way to healing, all of them, and they would fill this house with such joy that there would be no trace of the darkness.

Epilogue

The gurgle from the baby was followed by a great belch. Little Anna Katherine, named for two grandmothers, was adored and adorable, but there would be manners to learn someday. Tom crowed with delight and held the baby up in the sunlight. Joanna smiled at them both while she gathered up the picnic things and packed them away into the large basket Mrs. Davies had so amply filled.

A year had made such a difference in Tom, so attentive was he now and speaking new words every day with such care for his pronunciation. Joanna felt a personal triumph as she recalled the darkened schoolroom where she had first met the children, and the challenge they had brought to her new life.

"Let's go back now, Tom," she said, dropping a kiss on the top of his dear little head. "Uncle Giles will be back from Dufton in a little while and I want us all to be cleaned up and looking presentable. Emma!" she called down to the beach below where Emma sat on her haunches, peering intently at some bit of flotsam thrown out by the sea. Emma stood and ran, laughing as the wind tried to take her bonnet from her.

The procession moved rather slowly up the hill to the house. Joanna surveyed the outside with great contentment. She had planted just a few things, some flowering shrubbery and some roses, but already the place was transformed. The dark gray of the stone caught the sunlight, and the deep rose of the early blooming flowers gave a contented, cared-for look to the once forbidding edifice.

Inside, Mrs. Davies divested Joanna of the heavy basket and Annie took the baby for her nap.

"Baths for each of you," announced Aunt Joanna. "No nonsense, Tom. I expect you to be wet when you finish, and use the soap."

He grinned sheepishly and ran off after Bessie, who still walked with a bit of a limp and was slower than she used to be. But she was coming along and grew stronger by the day. Perhaps one day this last evidence of Eleanor's madness would be gone.

"I've laid out your tea in the drawing room, Lady Chapman," said Mrs. Davies. "I thought you'd wish to enjoy looking at the new draperies and furnishings. The whole house looks just lovely with all the new things." Mrs. Davies fairly beamed.

Joanna smiled her thanks and made her way to the drawing room where the tea steamed invitingly. Indeed, the room did look nice. Giles had been so indulgent, insisting that she replace most of the furnishings. There had been much that was of excellent quality and taste, and Joanna's frugal upbringing had chafed at tossing it all out. But in the end, Giles had prevailed, saying that he wanted to start clean and fresh, with as few reminders as they could manage. Gone were the naked cupids and the voluptuous, reclining women. The rooms were less cluttered now. There was no need, reasoned Joanna, to have five or six settees in a room that rarely saw more than five or six people at a time, one of those being an infant.

And the windows! There was not a window in the house that knew the darkness of a drapery in the daylight. Wherever one went in this house there was a magnificent sight to meet the eye, the sea and the sunset to the west, the misty, purple fells stretching as far as the eye could see to the east. Giles had laughed when she took the heavy draperies out of the bathing room, but she had explained that she had walked around the house and that one could see nothing of the room from the outside. It was too high up, after all, and what better way to enjoy one's bath than under the magic of the fells?

She had poured herself a steaming cup when she heard the door open behind her. She felt warm hands in her hair and nestled back against the lips that found her neck.

"How did you find the mine, Giles?" she asked when he let her speak.

"Running smoothly in spite of my recent neglect. MacAran is a good man. I will not have to go back again for some time."

"Thank heavens," she said, pouring him tea. "Emma and Tom asked after you on the hour and even the baby was fussy. We don't seem to do very well without you."

"Good. Then you won't mind if I hang around here. I find there are so many things to enjoy about this house that I never paid attention to before. Did I tell you I've worked out a way to lay hot water to the laundry room? No more lugging heavy buckets if it works."

"And if it doesn't we shall have an indoor swimming area. How lovely." She felt his hands again as he reached for her and drew her close.

"I missed you," he said simply, his lips in her hair.

"And I missed you," she answered.

His lips found hers and they held each other. Joanna could feel the peace around her, and thought yet again how Papa had always been right.

DECEPTION AT MIDNIGHT

COREY McFADDEN

When Edward, Earl of Radford, meets a winsome tomboy in a midnight encounter, his only thought is to see the lovely vagabond to safety. But under Maude Romney's dirt-smudged face is an enchanting sprite who ignites his passion like no other woman ever has. Yet once Edward learns of her impoverished nobility and tainted past, unsettling doubts plague him. Is Maude truly in danger—or has she cleverly used her innocence to force him into marriage?

_3520-0 $4.50 US/$5.50 CAN

Notorious Deception

Adrienne Basso

Young, beautiful, and tempestuous, Diana Rutledge is shocked by the unexpected death of her husband. And a trip to London to set her husband's affairs in order brings even more unexpected surprises for the dowager countess—not the least of which is her introduction to Derek, the new Earl of Harrowby. Dark and brooding, Derek is far too handsome for Diana's peace of mind, and against her will, she finds herself growing attracted to the arrogant peer. But his accusations that Diana is a bold impostor force her to risk her reputation, her heart, and her very life to prove that neither she nor her burning desire is part of a notorious deception.

__3687-8 $4.50 US/$5.50 CAN

WHO WROTE THE BOOK OF LOVE?
ELEVEN OF THE TOP-SELLING
ROMANCE AUTHORS OF ALL TIME—
THAT'S WHO!

MADELINE BAKER, MARY BALOGH, ELAINE BARBIERI, LORI COPELAND, CASSIE EDWARDS, HEATHER GRAHAM, CATHERINE HART, VIRGINIA HENLEY, PENELOPE NERI, DIANA PALMER, JANELLE TAYLOR

From the Middle Ages to the present day, these stories follow the men and women whose lives are forever changed by a special book—a cherished volume that teaches the love of learning and the learning of love!

ALL PROFITS WILL BE DONATED TO THE LITERACY PARTNERSHIP!
JOIN US—
AND CELEBRATE THE LEARNING OF LOVE
AND THE LOVE OF LEARNING!

_4000-X $6.99 US/$8.99 CAN

Dorchester Publishing Co., Inc.
65 Commerce Road
Stamford, CT 06902

Please add $1.75 for shipping and handling for the first book and $.50 for each book thereafter. NY, NYC, PA and CT residents, please add appropriate sales tax. No cash, stamps, or C.O.D.s. All orders shipped within 6 weeks via postal service book rate. Canadian orders require $2.00 extra postage and must be paid in U.S. dollars through a U.S. banking facility.

Name _____
Address _____
City _____ State _____ Zip _____
I have enclosed $_____ in payment for the checked book(s).
Payment **must** accompany all orders. ☐ Please send a free catalog.